The Red Lily Crown

Elizabeth Loupas

arrow books

Arrow Books
20 Vauxhall Bridge Road
London SW1V 2SA

Arrow Books is part of the Random House group of companies
whose addresses can be found at global.penguinrandomhouse.com.

Penguin
Random House
UK

Copyright © Elizabeth Loupas 2014

Elizabeth Loupas has asserted her right to be identified as the author of this
Work in accordance with the Copyright, Designs and Patents Act 1988.

First published in paperback by Arrow Books in 2015

www.randomhouse.co.uk

A CIP catalogue record for this book is
available from the British Library.

ISBN 9780099571537

Text designed by Elke Sigal

Printed and bound by CPI Group (UK) Ltd, Croydon, CR0 4YY

MIX
Paper from
responsible sources
FSC® C018179

Penguin Random House is committed to a sustainable future for
our business, our readers and our planet. This book is made from
Forest Stewardship Council® certified paper.

For my sister and brother,
Barbara Ann and Laurence Frederic,
Because family and home are at the heart of this book.

Note to Reader

A list of characters is included with the Author's Note at the back of the book.

Be warned, however—the identifying details included with some of the characters' names might give away parts of the story.

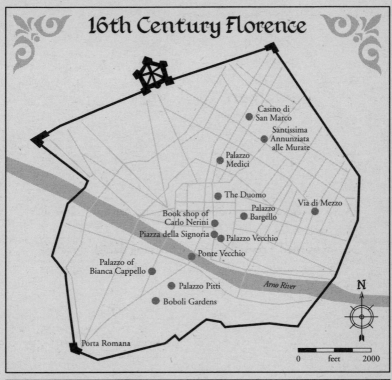

16th Century Florence

Casino di
San Marco

Santissima
Annunziata
alle Murate

Palazzo
Medici

The Duomo

Palazzo
Bargello

Via di Mezzo

Book shop of
Carlo Nerini

Piazza della Signoria

Palazzo Vecchio

Ponte Vecchio

Palazzo of
Bianca Cappello

Palazzo Pitti

Boboli Gardens

Arno River

N

Porta Romana

0   feet   2000

Seravezza

Bottino

Pistoia

Cafaggiolo

Poggio a Caiano

Villa di Pratolino
Villa di Castello

Pisa   Cerreto Guidi

Florence

Arno River

Livorno

Italy

N

Piombino

0   miles   20

Milan

Venice

Ferrara

Florence

Rome

Naples

Sardinia

ITALY

Sicily

Mediterranean Sea

The Red Lily Crown

PART I

Chiara

The Silver Descensory

CHAPTER ONE

The Piazza della Signoria

20 APRIL 1574

The prince was a Medici, richer than Satan, and people said he loved only two things—women and alchemy. To feed her Nonna and her two little sisters, Chiara would have sold herself to him quick as a stray cat, but she wasn't very promising *concubina* material—her chest bones stuck out and her wrists and ankles were knobbly as a colt's fetlocks. True, she was fifteen and a virgin and had a braid of dark hair down to her hips, but on the other hand she had the curved scar on the left side of her head, just above her ear. Her hair covered the mark but she couldn't always hide the headaches and the falling-spells. Sometimes she heard demons' voices.

No, not very promising *concubina* material.

Alchemy, then.

Her father, her Babbo, had been a bookseller, just as his family the Nerini had been for two hundred years. Behind the backs of his guild, though, he'd dabbled in alchemy. After the accident and her brother Gian's death, the alchemy had turned to darker things. Babbo had let the business fall to ruin, and had eventually blown himself up along with half his secret laboratory. Sometimes Chiara heard his voice, too, whispering that he wished she'd died instead of Gian. He'd have beaten her black-and-blue if he'd known she was planning to sell the last few pieces of his alchemical equipment to Prince Francesco—he'd hated the Medici, Babbo had. Damned pawnbrokers, he and Nonna called them, staunch supporters of the old republic that they were. But pride was delicious, now wasn't it, with a little *olio* and a sprinkle of salt?

Oh, it was all so beautiful, Babbo's alchemical paraphernalia, hidden away in the burned-out cellar under the shop where the long-nosed masters of the booksellers' Arte would never find it. It was fantastical, disconnected from hunger, hunger, hunger, worn-out clothes and winter cold, as mysterious as if it had been created by some kind of magic. There was an athanor made of brick and clay from Trebizond—wherever that was—and a green glass alembic in the shape of a crescent moon. There was a gold-and-crystal double pelican and a silver funnel engraved with an intricate circular labyrinth design, supposedly a thousand years old. There were books of alchemy, too, ancient yellowed parchment pages scritch-scratched with Latin incantations she couldn't read. In the back of one book her father had written secret things in his own hand, in Italian, but she couldn't read more than a few words of that, either.

If Prince Francesco de' Medici was half the alchemist people said he was, he'd want it all. He'd pay for it all. Oh, how he'd pay. Chiara could almost taste the yeasty fresh bread, its crust hot and crisp as her teeth tore into it. The salt pork, luscious with fat. The briny olives. Her stomach twisted around itself and made growling noises. Her mouth watered.

She'd been waiting in the Piazza della Signoria for hours in a drizzle of rain, praying it would clear enough for the prince to come out. She was drenched—mantle, gown and camicia, all the way to the skin. Her linen cap was limp and her slippers were sodden. Chopines? She'd shared one last pair with Nonna, until she traded them for a loaf of bread in the marketplace. Now when she walked in the rain, her slippers got wet and that was that.

Devil damn him, couldn't he order that iron gate winched up and ride out for one last visit with his father, dying at the Villa di Castello? The piazza was empty. The streets were deserted. The whole city knew the old grand duke was going to die soon, tonight, tomorrow, the next day. People were creeping around under a black cloud of dread, because if Duke Cosimo had been an iron-fisted tyrant, at least he'd been a familiar tyrant. Prince Francesco, with his alchemy and his women, his favorites and his dark vengefulness, would change everything. Once he put the red lily crown of Tuscany on his head, who knew what he might do?

One thing was certain—once the old grand duke died, the prince would disappear into the ceremonies of funerals and coronations, into crowds of courtiers fawning for favors like packs of wolves. If a bookseller's daughter was going to empty his princely purse for him, it would have to be soon. Today. Now. Please—

Metal chains shrieked and grated. The iron *cancello* set into the palazzo's arched gateway began to inch upward. Chiara could hear horses' hooves on the stones and men's voices calling and laughing; no sorrow or respect for Duke Cosimo, then. Chiara made her way closer, keeping flat against the outer wall of the palazzo so the guardsmen wouldn't notice her. She reached into the pouch tied to her belt and touched the silver funnel, reassuring herself it was there. Her hands were as wet and cold as the metal. No fingernails left—she'd bitten them down to the quick.

The prince rode out first, on a gray horse with a thick arched neck and a tail like a banner of white silk. Its nostrils flared crimson as if it were breathing fire. Chiara hated the huge, terrifying horses of the nobles—it was one of them, after all, that had knocked her down and with one of its iron shoes made the crescent-shaped scar on the side of her head. Two steps later it had trampled her brother Gian to death.

Breathe, breathe—terror—hunger—terror—just do it—

"Serenissimo!" she cried.

She ran up to the horse and caught one of its reins. The leather was decorated with gilding and small colored stones, every single one of them worth enough to pay for a month's bread. She looked up at the prince. He was dark and didn't look any bigger than an ordinary man. He didn't look back at her. She said, just loud enough for him to hear, *"Qui vult secreta scire, secreta secrete sciat custodire."*

Whosoever would know secrets, let him know how to keep secret things secretly.

It was the first line in one of Babbo's books, the one sentence in Latin he had ever taught her, sounding it out, telling her what it meant. The prince would recognize it. Please please, let the prince recognize it, the prince and the prince alone.

The horse threw up its head and stepped sideways, delicate as a dancer for all its size. Sparks scattered where its shoes struck against the stones. At the same time rough hands caught Chiara from behind. The guardsmen,

may they be damned straight to the deepest pits of hell for being so attentive to their duty. The gems on the rein cut into her palms as her grip was
torn away.

The prince never turned his head. He rode on, trailed by his friends and
courtiers, the scarlet feather in his hat blowing gaily in the rain-wet breeze.

"*Qui vult secreta scire!*" Chiara screamed. "Serenissimo! *Secreta secrete—*"

Something crashed into the side of her face. Her vision flashed bright
white and her head jolted around; the inner flesh of her cheek burst open
against her teeth and she tasted blood. The paving stones of the piazza
slammed into her knees. More hooves clattered around her. If she fainted
now she'd be kicked again—she had a vivid sickening flash of Gian's face,
crushed and misshapen.

"Up with you, witch girl." A guardsman dragged her to her feet. "Cast
spells at the prince, will you? The Dominicani will make quick work
of you."

The Dominicans. The Dogs of God they were called, Domini-Cani, a
grim play on San Domenico's name and his symbol, the little dog with a
torch in its mouth.

The Inquisition.

"I'm not a witch." Chiara swung at him with her free arm. Her head
throbbed and the demons clawed at the backs of her eyes. "It wasn't a spell,
bischero. I'm as good a Christian as you are, and probably better. Let go
of me."

The guardsman only laughed and twisted both her arms behind her,
hard enough to make her cry out and arch her back. Another guardsman
stepped up in front of her, jerked her mantle off, and tore the front of her
gown. In the rush of air she could feel the thin wet linen of her camicia
clinging to her breasts. She'd only been angry up to that point but suddenly she realized what they intended and her belly turned liquid with
terror.

"Bit skinny for my taste." The guardsman in front of her drew his poniard and cut the cord at the neckline of her camicia. "Let's have a better
look."

Her slippers were soft and her kicks were useless. Her mouth was so dry
she had nothing to spit. The first man jerked her cap off and began to pull

the thick coiled braid of her hair loose from its pins; the second man laughed and squeezed her breasts with his calloused hands. It hurt. She could see his eyes darken with lust.

"Let's take her to that wine shop over on the Via della Ninna," the first man said. "They have rooms upstairs, and the barkeep won't mind a few screams. We can take our time driving the devil out of her, and then sell her for a few—"

A sharp cracking noise exploded. A scarlet weal appeared on the second guardsman's face, from his cheek across his mouth and down to his chin. He stared at Chiara for the space of a breath, his mouth still open, his fingers still sunk into the flesh of her breasts. Then blood beaded up along the line of the weal and he shrieked, letting go of her and throwing up his hands to cover his face instead.

"Release her."

A foreign voice.

A man on a red-brown horse. Not the prince. Not an aristocrat at all, and Chiara had seen enough of them to know. He was a workman, an outsider in a courtier's clothes. A whip in his hand. As Chiara stared at him he flicked the braided leather back into its coil, neat as a tame snake.

"And who the devil are you," said the first guardsman, "to take your whip to us? Don't you see the Medici colors? We're the prince's own guardsmen, and this girl cast a spell at him as he rode by—she's for the Dominicani, she is, and little they'll care if we have a bit of fun with her first."

"All words in Latin are not spells," said the foreigner. "And I know the Medici colors well enough, as I am also in the prince's service. Now let the girl go and be off with you, both of you. It is the prince's command that I deal with this matter."

"I know you." The guardsman with the whip-cut across his face looked at the foreigner between bloodied fingers, hate in his eyes. "You're the English alchemist, the prince's pet sorcerer. The Dominicani—"

"I am a metallurgist and a scientist, not a sorcerer. If you value your places you will do as I say, and be quick about it."

A metallurgist. That meant something to do with metals and mines. He had the look of a miner, a man who'd worked in the dark depths of the earth and lifted great weights of rock and ore. His Italian was fluent enough but accented, with the careful precision of a person who thought in one language and spoke in another. Educated, then. Like the courtier's fine dark doublet and hose, his manner of speaking didn't fit with his workman's look.

And English? She'd heard Englishmen try to speak proper Italian before, because foreigners from all over the world came to the booksellers' quarter to buy and sell. This one didn't sound the same as the others—there was a peculiar lilting pitch to his voice, and at the same time hard edges in unexpected places. She wasn't at all certain she'd be any safer with him than she was with the prince's guardsmen.

"Take her, then." The fellow behind Chiara let go of her arms and pushed her, hard. She stumbled forward and only barely managed to keep herself from falling on the slippery wet paving stones. She fumbled with the cloth of her mantle, trying to cover herself, wiping the blood from her mouth. Somehow she couldn't seem to breathe all the way down to the bottom of her lungs.

Saints and angels—how had it all gone so wrong, so quickly? But for the foreigner and his whip—

"You, girl," the foreigner said. He looped the whip over his shoulder and swung down from his big red horse. "Are you hurt?"

She caught her breath. He'd saved her from the guardsmen but she was angry with him anyway. Angry with him and the prince and every man in Florence, just for being men. "What do you care?" she said.

"I dislike seeing women mishandled. Where did you learn what you said? Do you know what it means?"

"I learned it from a book." She managed to find the cut ends of her camicia's cord and tie them back together so she was decent again. Her hair was hopeless, the thick braid swinging, heavy with rainwater. "A book that belonged to my father. Yes, I know what it means."

"Do you have this book in your possession?"

"Yes. No. I mean, I have it, but not with me now. It's hidden away."

The foreigner smiled. His face was sharp-boned and sun-weathered, so his teeth looked wolfishly white; the lines at the corners of his mouth were cruel. His head was uncovered and his crest of dark hair had spangles of rain amid the glints of copper. Unexpectedly his eyes were sad, so sad there was no bottom to their sorrow.

"The prince will have the book," he said.

"For the right price." Chiara watched the man's face for any sign of a threat. "And I have other things. I have this."

She took the silver funnel out of her pouch and held it up, taking care to keep it away from his immediate reach.

He said something she didn't understand, an oath by the sound of it, a collection of alien syllables that rolled off his tongue smoothly enough to be his true language. Whatever it was, it wasn't English, and it certainly wasn't Italian. "That is a descensory," he said, when he was finished swearing. "Thracian silver, from the look of it, and the labyrinth engraving— Who are you, and how do you come to have such a thing?"

Arrogant foreigner. Mine-crawler. She might be poor and scrawny and her camicia torn by a pair of stupid guardsmen, but by the Baptist she was a Florentine citizen born and bred and that was more than he could say.

"My name," she said, "is Chiara Ne—"

She stopped. If she told him her whole name he'd be able to find her father's shop, and if he found the shop he might be able to find the rest of her father's equipment and books and take it all for himself without ever telling the prince or paying her so much as a *picciolo*.

"My name is Chiara." She left it at that. "I'm an alchemist's daughter, and I have more things hidden away. This silver funnel is the smallest of the lot. If the prince doesn't want it, I'll find another buyer."

Something sparked in his expression, like a drop of aqua regia sizzling on black iron. It burned. "No," he said. "You will sell it to no one else."

"Try to stop me." Chiara thrust out her chin at him. *Your chin looks sharp as a kitchen-knife when you do that*, Nonna always said. *Your face will stick that way.* "I know alchemical equipment, and I know its true value. If the prince wants it, he'll pay."

"We will ask the prince himself. Come along."

Chiara stepped back. "I'll walk."

"Or run away to find your other buyer? You will ride with me."

"I don't ride horses."

He took hold of her arm, so quickly she never even saw him move. One moment he didn't have hold of her, the next moment he did. So he could've taken the funnel from the beginning if he'd wanted to. His grasp wasn't quite hard enough to hurt, but hard enough so she knew he could hurt her if he wanted to.

"You will ride this one."

Her stomach lurched as he swung her upward. Up and up and up—it was wrong for any creature to be so big, its back so far away from the street. The scent of the horse made her head pound with pain. Its sleek red hide shifted as it stepped from one side to the other. She clutched the funnel with one hand and the back of the saddle with the other. One of her shoes fell off.

"Steady," the foreigner said. "Lowarn, stand."

The horse stopped moving as if by magic. Chiara felt her shoe being slipped back onto her foot.

"Curl your toes so it does not fall off again. You should have stockings."

"I must've forgotten," she said, through gritted teeth, "to choose a fine silken pair from the dozens and dozens in my gold-painted wardrobe chest."

The foreigner laughed and swung up on the horse himself, throwing his leg over its neck like an acrobat. "When the prince sees what you have, he will give you money enough to buy a hundred pairs of stockings, and all the wardrobe chests you want," he said. "Hold on to my jacket and do not drop that descensory."

His arms moved, his heels. The horse turned, swished its long tail in a terrifying way, and stepped forward, first a walk and then a brisk trot. Chiara managed to thrust the funnel back into her pouch, then gave up any pretense of pride and wrapped her arms around the foreigner's waist, pressing her face between his shoulder blades. He smelled of ambergris and metal and stone. If she was going to be sick—not that she'd be able to do much of a job of it, hollow-empty as she was—she'd do it on his fine dark doublet and be damned to him.

They crossed a bridge. She wasn't sure which one because she didn't dare look up, but she knew the hollow sound of hooves on a bridge, and she could smell the Arno, offal and fish and rain.

At last they stopped. She heard other voices and smelled other horses.

"I have the girl, Serenissimo." The foreigner pried her arms from around his waist and swung her down from the horse's back as if she were a sack of artichokes. She staggered and fell back against the horse's muscled hind-quarter. As if she'd stumbled into fire she jerked herself away with a cry and tripped over her skirt. The worn cloth tore. And so she came face to face with Francesco de' Medici, Prince of Florence, the man who loved women and alchemy, with her bodice-strings knotted awry, her hair uncovered, and her skirt hanging torn at the hem.

And a thousand-year-old silver funnel engraved with a labyrinth in her pouch.

"I cannot say I am impressed, Magister Ruanno."

The prince had dismounted from his monstrous gray horse and stood in the street as if he owned the very paving stones. Behind him was a flat-fronted edifice of three stories, ordinary-looking but for the fanciful figures in black and white plaster, only partly completed, that covered it. The *palle*, the Medici balls, yes, they were there too, frescoed in red and gold in the center on the second level, surmounted by the red fleur-de-lis of the grand dukes of Tuscany. Set over the doorway was a carving of a traveling hat with its strings, a *cappello*. That was the name of the prince's Venetian mistress, Bianca Cappello, everyone knew that. This must be her house, then. His father was dying, the whole city was holding its breath, and the prince was visiting his mistress.

He had a narrow, swarthy face with a high forehead, so high he had his cropped dark hair brushed forward—he was losing his hair, then. His eyes slanted downward, sensual, melancholic and secretive. Saints in the churches, painted on panels and murals, had halos of light around their heads and bodies; the prince seemed to have a tracing of darkness, as if he was standing in front of a prince-shaped hole that led into something terrible, and you could just catch glimpses of it when he moved.

"You will be impressed, Serenissimo," the foreigner said. He dismounted from his horse as well and bowed, rather stiffly, as if he didn't like bowing. "Girl, show the prince your silver descensory."

When he said the words *silver descensory* the prince's expression changed. Disdain became interest—more than interest, avidity. Lust, almost. So people were right about his obsession with alchemy.

Chiara held up her head and put out her kitchen-knife chin. Her hands were shaking and she could feel the eyes of the prince and all his courtiers on her. Aristocrats. She hated aristocrats, even more than she hated horses. *Bloodsuckers*, Babbo's voice whispered. *Tyrants. Don't give it to him. Starve instead, until you're dead, like I am.*

With every ounce of strength she had, she took the silver funnel out of her pouch and held it up.

"I will take it." The prince held out his hand.

"I'll give it to you," Chiara said, "when you give me a gold scudo."

She had no idea how much a scudo was actually worth, because her father had never had more than one or two at a time pass through his hands. But from the reactions of Magister Ruanno-whatever-kind-of-name-that-was and of the prince himself, clearly the silver funnel was valuable.

"Are you mad?" The prince was not angry, though. She watched his eyes. He was amused and if anything, more lustful than ever. He wore his darkness like a cloak of fur, the pelts of some sensuous, dangerous animal. "Have you ever even seen a gold scudo?"

Chiara didn't flinch. "I have."

"Serenissimo," the foreigner said. "This girl claims to be an alchemist's daughter, and to have books as well. She quoted from *De Magia Veterum* and her Latin was without a flaw. Consider her—she is barely more than a child, and could well be untouched."

The prince and the foreigner looked at each other as if Chiara wasn't there. Something passed between them, some question, some answer, some understanding. It felt cold, like iron fetters.

The prince said, "What is your name, girl?"

"Chiara."

"And your father's name?"

The foreigner had stepped closer, behind her. The prince's courtiers and friends had spread out on either side, cutting off any way to escape. Had the prince made a gesture to order this? Or did they just know?

"If I tell you my father's name," Chiara said, trying to keep her voice even, "you'll go to his shop and take everything for yourself, and pay me nothing. I'm hungry, and my Nonna and my little sisters are hungry."

"Chiara," the foreigner said. He pronounced it oddly—a liquid *keer-ah* instead of *kee-ah-rah*, the way it should be pronounced. "Do not be afraid. Answer the prince's questions, do as he tells you, and neither you nor your family will ever be hungry again."

He talked to her as if she were a child, and a witless one at that. Chiara scowled at him and said, "I'm a Florentine citizen born, and I believe no foreigners' promises."

The prince laughed. "Well spoken," he said. "Believe my promises, then—I am as Florentine as you are, back to Lorenzo il Magnifico and beyond. Come, let us go to the Palazzo Vecchio where we can speak of this matter in peace and privacy."

Privacy? Did he want her as his mistress after all, bony chest notwithstanding?

"Privacy will cost more," she said. "Five scudi."

All the men laughed. Her face burned like fire.

"Messer Alessandro," the prince said to one of his gentlemen. "Wait upon Madonna Bianca, if you please, and explain to her that I have been interrupted with a matter of importance. I will see her tonight if I can, although if my father dies today everything will change."

The man bowed, with a great deal more grace and panache than Magister Ruanno, although his mouth pursed up as if he'd taken a bite of wormy cheese. Clearly he wasn't pleased with the task of explaining to Madonna Bianca that she'd been put aside for an alchemist's daughter. "Yes, Serenissimo," he said.

"We return to the Palazzo Vecchio." The prince mounted his gray stallion again. "Magister Ruanno, bring *la nostra piccola* Chiara and her silver descensory and her amusing ideas of how much she is worth."

"No," Chiara said. "I don't want to come with you. You can't—"

The foreigner took hold of her arm, just as he'd done before. It didn't hurt, but it could if he wanted it to. Oh, yes, it could.

"Come with me," he said. "You wished to speak of alchemy with the prince? Now you will have your chance."

CHAPTER TWO

"Tonight, perhaps, or tomorrow, or the next day, my father will be dead." The prince's voice was cold, as if he didn't care if his father died or not. He probably didn't. "I will be Grand Duke of Tuscany, and I will have absolute power in Florence. If you are wise, you will wish to please me."

They had clattered back through the *cancello* into the courtyard of the Palazzo Vecchio, renewed rain showers spattering around them. Once again Chiara rode pillion behind Magister Ruanno—she'd survived one ride, so why wouldn't she survive another? In fact, she'd overcome her fear to the point that she could actually feel her poor bruised backside when the ride was over. Horses! Dangerous, smelly playthings of aristocrats. On the other hand, she had to admit they'd arrived back at the palazzo much more quickly than she could have done if she'd walked in the rain.

Another thing about aristocrats—they had so many servants they never did anything for themselves. Servants had run to lead the horses away, run to open every door, run for gilded chairs and embroidered cushions and hot spiced wine, a thing Chiara had never tasted before, not once in her whole life. Just the scent of it made her head swim, and the taste—it was like Nonna's wild-currant cordial mixed with the angelica pasticci she made for stomachaches, like liquid wildflowers and honeybees, sweet and stinging and velvety. It was enough—well, almost enough—to make her think the Medici might not be so bad after all.

"I will please you if I can, Serenissimo," she said.

"Good. Then I will tell you that my true life's work is the creation of the *Lapis Philosophorum*, the Stone of the Philosophers. In this, Magister Ruanno assists me."

He gestured briefly to the other man in the elaborate little studiolo, the English alchemist. In his precise foreigner's Italian, Magister Ruanno said, "We have completed the third stage, the stage of calcination. For the fourth stage, the stage of exuberation, we have decided we require a *soror mystica*."

The prince said, "Do you know what that means, Mona Chiara?"

Chiara looked from one man to the other, the prince who took wealth and luxuries and absolute obedience as his everyday due, and the foreigner in his dark doublet and hose, his shoulders thick with workman's musculature, his mouth so cruel and his eyes sadder than sad. How could two men be so different and at the same time be—well, what were they? Master and servant? The prince clearly thought everyone was his servant, and the foreigner, for whatever reason, was willing to play the part.

"*Soror mystica,*" she repeated. "Something mystical?"

Magister Ruanno smiled his unsettling wolflike smile. "So you do not know as much Latin as you claim."

"I never claimed to know it to speak it every day. I know bits that my father taught me, that's all."

"It means a sister in the art," the prince said. "A female alchemist."

"Surely you have heard of Magister Nicolas Flamel of Paris." Magister Ruanno picked up a flask of wine and refilled her cup for her. His hands were long-fingered and finely shaped, but the palms were badly scarred, as if by hard labor. "You, an alchemist's daughter."

Chiara drank more of the wine. It made her feel as if she was alone inside her head for the first time since the horse had kicked her and cracked her skull. She hadn't heard of Magister Nicolas whoever-he-was but she'd die before she'd admit it.

"Magister Nicolas Flamel," she repeated, parrotlike. "What about him?"

"He is said to have achieved the *Lapis Philosophorum*, and with it the elixir of life, almost two hundred years ago. He and his wife Perenelle."

"His wife assisted him?"

"She did." The prince rose to his feet, assuming command of the little room. "The female principle is necessary to create the *Lapis Philosophorum*, just as it is necessary to create life in the flesh. The woman who supplies that principle is called the alchemist's *soror mystica*."

"And you want me to be that—that woman," Chiara said. Babbo had never told her that a woman could be an alchemist in her own right. "You don't want to buy my father's equipment, you want to buy me."

"Oh, I do want to buy your father's equipment." The prince reached out and pulled on the frame of one of the paintings. She thought he was going to pull it off the wall entirely, but to her surprise it swung open and revealed a secret niche. Something glinted inside, but she couldn't see what it was. "I will pay you generously for it, and put it here—I keep my particular curiosities hidden from any eyes but my own."

"You can't hide me away in a niche behind a painting."

He looked at her rather as if he wished he could. "No," he said in his cold voice. "I cannot. As for you becoming my *soror*, it is not quite as simple as buying you."

"So what is it?"

"First it must be proven that you are a virgin."

"That I'm a *what*?"

The prince laughed. It always seemed wrong when he smiled or laughed—unnatural. It didn't fit his face. He spoke over her shoulder, as if she wasn't even in the room. "There, Magister Ruanno, see? I told you a street girl would not be pure."

"I'm as pure as any lady of the court," Chiara said. "Purer, probably."

"Well said, Monella Chiara." The foreigner smiled at her. "And probably true. Nevertheless, to be the prince's *soror mystica*, you must prove your virginity."

Whatever pit he had originally climbed out of, his Italian was good enough to play with words—*mona* was a perfectly polite form of address for a guildswoman of Florence, but *monella*, however much it might sound like a diminutive for a young woman, actually just meant a street urchin.

She'd show him street urchin. She thrust out her chin at him. "Prove it how?"

"There is an initiation," the prince said. Magister Ruanno frowned and seemed about to speak but the prince silenced him with a single sharp gesture. "Incorporated within the ritual there are four tests of virginity—

the black water, the blood-red ribbon, the silver sieve and the golden fire. If you complete the ritual and pass through the tests successfully, you will be initiated as my *soror* and allowed to vow yourself to my service."

Black water? Blood? Fire?

"That sounds like something out of a dream or an old story, not something real."

Magister Ruanno said, "It is—"

"Oh, it is real." The prince overrode him. "It is a ritual I myself have created, unique in the history of the world. If you pass through it successfully, you will gain more than just a place in my household. You will earn a great deal of gold for yourself and your family. You will be taught the alchemist's art. And you will have a chance, a true chance, to join in the creation of the *Lapis Philosophorum*."

Chiara stared at him.

The Philosopher's Stone.

It could heal anything, even death itself. It would heal the headaches. It would drive out the voices in her head. She would be one person again, whole and right.

She would learn the art of alchemy. Become a female alchemist. How many of those had there been, since the world was created?

And gold. Nonna and Lucia and Mattea, well-fed, warm, dry, safe. The shop restored, busy again with Nonna to manage it and the girls to help. A fine alchemical laboratory where she could practice her art, clean and well-lighted, not at all like Babbo's dark, secret cellar. All of them with clean feather beds and beautiful dresses and all the shoes and stockings and chopines they wanted and gold rings on their fingers. Fresh hot bread and juicy meat and flaky fruit pastries, piles of angelica pasticci and bottles and bottles of wild-currant cordial.

"And what if I agree to do this— this initiation, and don't pass all the tests?"

"Are you not a virgin after all?"

"I am a virgin! But the tests—they sound like magic, and there's no such thing as magic. What can a silver sieve possibly have to do with being a virgin?"

"You will find out in due time." The prince took another step toward her. She stepped backward.

"What if I don't pass the tests?"

The prince took hold of her arm. Unlike the foreigner, he didn't seem to care if he hurt her or not. "You will have to try and find out."

"I won't do it unless you tell me what happens if I fail the tests."

The prince and Magister Ruanno exchanged looks.

"You cannot let her go now," Magister Ruanno said. He shifted his position, stepping behind her. "You would not allow me to stop you, Serenissimo, and you should have. Now she will spread it all over the city that you sacrifice young virgins with blood and fire. They dislike you enough as it is, and with your father so close to death, a story like this could start a revolution."

The prince shrugged. He said, "Take her to the Casino di San Marco, then. Use the secret door. Lock her up there, and allow her to speak to no one."

"I won't say anything," Chiara whispered. The fear she'd felt when the guardsmen took hold of her was nothing compared to this fear. "Not to anyone, I swear it. Here, I'll give you the silver funnel."

She fumbled at her pouch with her free hand, and took out the funnel. *A thousand years old*, she thought. *Thracian silver, from the look of it.* She held it out to the prince.

A free gift.

Please . . .

Magister Ruanno, behind her, put his left arm around her neck. She felt his forearm against her throat, right up under her chin, pressing. Not too hard.

The silver funnel struck the floor with a ringing sound and rolled.

His right hand cupped the back of her head with terrifying gentleness and pressed forward.

Blackness.

CHAPTER THREE

The Casino di San Marco

LATER THAT SAME NIGHT

The first thing she felt was the softness of the bed. The way it smelled—clean, linen and feathers and soap. There was silence inside her head, too, delicious, drowsy silence. Chiara stretched out her arms over her head and—

The headache crashed back, pulsing pain and a sense her eyes were about to burst from their sockets. The demons screamed and screamed. At the same time she remembered it all—the rain, the guardsmen, the horse, the prince, the golden studiolo in the Palazzo Vecchio, the spiced wine, the silver funnel, and the foreigner, may he be damned to hell for all eternity, his arm around her neck just so, and his hand pressing her head forward.

Where was she?

She squinted her eyes and opened them just a slit. No bright light. She opened them a bit more and gingerly pushed herself up on her elbows.

The room was small, five or six paces square. The walls and floor were plain dressed stone. There was a single tiny window with an iron grating, high over her head; the sliver of sky she could see was black. One stoneware lamp, burning steadily, on a lamp stand. That was the only furniture other than the pallet she lay on. There was a wooden door, with an arched shape. It was closed, and there was no handle.

Barred from the outside?

She stood up slowly. The headache snarled and clawed and whispered inside her head, then little by little began to curl in upon itself and go quiet. She went over to the door and pushed on it.

Yes. Barred from the outside.

So where was she? *Take her to the Casino di San Marco*, the prince had said. *Use the secret door. Lock her up there, and allow her to speak to no one.* She knew the Casino di San Marco, of course—everybody in Florence knew it, the grand duke's villa up by the Piazza San Marco. So if she was there, she was still in the city.

What did they intend to do with her? Starve her to death? Babbo and Nonna had told tales of oubliettes under the Medici palaces, cells where inconvenient prisoners were thrust to be forgotten forever. But if they meant her to die, why leave a lamp burning? And why provide a soft mattress and a clean coverlet?

She went back to the pallet and sat down. There was nothing else to do. She was thirsty, so thirsty, and hungry, and she needed a necessary-pot. Her hair had dried. She untied the black woolen cord at the end of the braid and combed it out with her fingers. It was crimped from drying in its braid, but the rainwater had made it unexpectedly soft. Sometimes loosening her hair helped keep the headaches away.

The lamp burned, and burned, and began to flicker.

Just before it went out completely, hinges creaked and the door opened. Chiara wedged herself back in the corner of the pallet, pulled her feet up off the floor and wrapped her arms around her knees. She'd been afraid of a lot of things in her life but she'd never felt sinking, breathless fear like this.

Magister Ruanno stepped into the room. He was alone.

Chiara tried to speak—*Where am I? What do you want?*—but her mouth and throat were too dry to form words.

"Do not be afraid," he said. "I have come to help you."

His voice was grave and impersonal, and he sounded like he was soothing a wild animal. Well, in a way maybe he was. He was holding a pitcher of water and a cup. He put the cup down on the table beside the lamp and filled it with water.

"Drink."

She reached over and snatched up the cup and gulped the water down. It was clean and cool, the best water she had ever tasted.

She held out the cup. "More."

"Wait a moment. Let the first cup settle." He put the pitcher on the table and went back outside the room, then returned with a jug of oil for the lamp, a loaf of bread, and a ceramic basin with a cover. The basin was white porcelain decorated with blue flowers. It was imperfect—she could see small cracks and bubbles in the glaze. He put the basin on the floor and the rest of the things on the table.

"You may pour more water for yourself," he said. "Eat a little, refill the lamp, and use this basin as you may need to. I will return shortly."

He went out. Chiara heard a bar creak down and settle into place on the outside of the door.

For a moment she sat frozen—was she dreaming? Dream or not, whatever he wanted from her, she'd be better prepared to fight him off if her thirst was slaked and her belly was full and she didn't have to piss so badly her legs were shaking. She clambered down and took the cover off the basin—oh, saints and angels, the relief. She replaced the cover and pushed the basin back against the wall. Then she refilled the lamp, drank another cup of water, and ate the top half of the loaf of bread as slowly as she could. It was spread with butter, rich and unctuous and savory with salt. She'd eaten butter only three or four times in her life but she knew what it was.

She was just swallowing the last bite when the bar was lifted again, the door opened, and the foreigner came back into the room.

"Better?" he said.

"Where am I? What do you want?"

She didn't really expect him to answer, but he did. "You are in the cellar of the Casino di San Marco. The prince has a laboratory here, and other secret rooms."

"What day is it? What time is it?"

"You have been here for six or seven hours and it is past midnight, so it is the day after you were first brought here."

Six or seven hours! After midnight! Nonna would be beside herself. The water and bread and butter made her feel strong enough to thrust out her chin at him. "I want to go home."

Magister Ruanno smiled. It wasn't his wolf smile, but a weary smile, and it softened the cruel line of his mouth. A little bit, not entirely. "It no longer matters what you want, Monella Chiara. You should be grateful the prince has chosen you. Your life will be changed forever, and the lives of your family."

"Chosen me!" Chiara unfolded her legs and put her feet on the floor. She wondered if she could jump up, slip by him, and run out the door. Probably not. And she wouldn't know where to go once she got out of the room anyway. "He didn't choose me—he said things he shouldn't have said, magical tests for virgins with blood and fire, and I was unlucky enough to be in the room to hear them. You said it yourself."

"I did." His expression changed. He wasn't looking at her as if she were a fractious nanny goat to be gentled, not anymore. Had he thought she was too stupid to understand?

"I won't tell anybody, but of course you don't believe me." She considered snatching up the water pitcher and throwing it at him. But what good would that do? He would only squeeze her neck again and send her down into the blackness. "It won't do you any good to keep me here. I won't submit to the tests."

"One does not say, 'I won't,' to Francesco de' Medici. He will compel you to submit. That is why I am here."

"So you can threaten me? Half-strangle me again?"

"No. So I can help you. You will be much more likely to pass through the tests successfully if you are willing."

"I'm not willing. I don't know what—"

"Listen to me." He took a step forward. She pulled her feet up off the floor again. As if that would help. "I am going to tell you," he said, "what the tests are."

"Why not just call in a midwife to examine me?"

"Such examinations are far from conclusive."

"And magic isn't?"

He laughed at that. Not a *laugh* laugh, but a half-smile with a single wry exhalation. Maybe he was human after all. "You know, Monella Chiara, from an alchemical standpoint, it makes no difference anyway. Do you think Mistress Perenelle Flamel was a virgin?"

"Of course not. She was that Magister Nicolas's wife."

"Exactly. The prince wishes you to be vowed as a virgin, with all the rituals of magic he loves so dearly, to satisfy his wife and his mistress. They are jealous enough of each other as it is, and when they find out he has taken a *soror mystica* to help him in his experiments, they will immediately conclude he has taken you to his bed as well as his laboratory. Only if you are proclaimed to be a virgin and vowed to remain a virgin will they accept you."

"What about all his other women? People say he's had hundreds of women."

"None of his other women have been made part of his household."

Chiara thought about that for a moment. The prince's household! The prince's wife was an Imperial archduchess, everyone knew that. And his mistress was a beautiful, ambitious and much-hated Venetian noble-woman. Would they really be jealous of her, Chiara Nerini, a bookseller's daughter whose feet got wet in the rain because she had no chopines? Would being the prince's *soror mystica* really vault her up to such unimaginable heights?

But the tests. Blood and fire . . .

"You'll tell me what the tests are, and how to do them safely?"

"I will tell you some things. Passing through the tests safely will be up to you."

"You say I'll have to remain a virgin—does that mean forever?"

His eyes narrowed. "Why? Do you have a lover? A *promesso*?"

"No. But—forever. That's a big promise. That's all my life."

"You will be required to vow yourself to virginity for the length of time you remain in the prince's service as his *soror*. When the experiments are complete and the *Lapis Philosophorum* is ours, you will be released from your vow."

Or I can release myself by running away, Chiara thought. If I act meek and obedient, I can get gold for Nonna and the little ones, and yes, for myself too, and I can convince the prince to trust me. And who knows, maybe we really will find the Philosopher's Stone, and it will put my poor head back the way it was before that aristocrat's horse kicked me, and I'll become the most famous female alchemist since Perenelle Flamel.

She could tell from the downward twist at one side of Magister Ruanno's mouth that he knew exactly what she was thinking. The running-away part, at least.

"I agree," she said. "Tell me about the tests."

"Very well." Something about the way he stood, the way he balanced his weight on the floor—he was relieved. He was glad. It was important to him, then, that she agreed to become this *soror mystica*. Why?

He said, "As the prince told you, there are four tests— the black water, the blood-red ribbon, the silver sieve and the golden fire. Only the sieve is in any way difficult."

"Begin at the beginning. What is the black water?"

"It is a common test for virginity in courts of law, handed down by the Roman historian Pliny and also by Saint Albertus Magnus. The girl is given a potion to drink, and if she can hold her water for a suitable length of time afterward, she is deemed to be a virgin."

"That's ridiculous. What does pissing have to do with being a virgin?"

"Presumably," he said with a perfectly straight face, "it is a test of the tightness of the girl's— Well, you understand."

"What's in the potion? What's the trick?"

"I will tell you this, and no more. If you eat something and use that basin"—he gestured to the covered blue-and-white vessel—"thoroughly just before the initiation begins, you should have no difficulty."

If all the tests were that stupid, she'd pass them easily. "What's the one called the blood-red ribbon?"

"The blood," he said, "is metaphorical. It is performed with a red ribbon, that is all. Certain measurements of your head and neck are made and compared. It is said that expansion of a woman's neck is a sign that—other parts of her body—have been expanded as well."

"That's as ridiculous as the black water. The prince is a fool to believe such things."

He smiled. "Perhaps," he said. "But if I were you I would not say such a thing to his face. Now—the silver sieve and the golden fire. The sieve is really the only one of the tests that will require some care and concentration from you."

"What do I have to do?"

"Carry water in the sieve, and use the water to put out a fire."

"Carry *water* in a *sieve*? That's impossible."

"I take it you have not read any old tales of the Vestal Virgins of Rome?"

"The what virgins?"

"Never mind. Suffice it to say that carrying water in a sieve is an old, old test of virginity. And it is not as impossible as it sounds. If you hold the sieve level and steady, and take care that the underside remains absolutely dry, then you will be able to pour water into it slowly, and the water will be held."

"Are you sure?"

"I am sure—I will see that the sieve is treated with lanolin, which will be invisible but will help create surface tension under the water. Once you have filled the sieve, you must step down the room to a golden grating, under which a fire will be burning. Hold the sieve over the grating and shake it slightly. The water will pour out, and put out the fire. You will then step over the grating in perfect safety."

"Can you bring me the sieve? Let me practice?"

"No. You will have one chance, and you must make the most of it. Just remember—when the prince's guards come for you, eat the food you have and use the basin. And do not show fear."

She leaned forward and looked at him, really looked at him for the first time. They were allies now, the two of them, secretly in league together against the prince. It was dangerous, but it was exciting, too. She saw details, the severely plain richness of his black velvet jacket and the edge of white linen showing above the collar. His skin, smooth-shaven over his jaw line, was youthful despite the effects of sun and wind. He's young, she thought, surprised. Younger than the prince. Younger than he wants people to think.

"Magister Ruanno." It was the first time she had spoken his name. It felt strange to shape her mouth to it. "Why are you doing this? Helping me?"

If there was any sort of ordinary feeling inside him, it was buried very deep. He didn't seem to be helping her because he liked her, or felt any emotion about her at all. Well, maybe some kind of peculiar protectiveness. What had he said in the street? *I dislike seeing women mishandled.*

"I am helping you," he said at last, "because the prince has decided he needs a *soror mystica*. I wish to make sure he gets one."

Chiara took a deep breath. "I'll do my best," she said. "I want the Philosopher's Stone—I want to help my family and I want to heal myself, cure my headaches and—" She stopped there. No need to tell him about the cracked skull and the voices inside her head. No need to tell him about becoming an alchemist in her own right, so she wouldn't need him or the prince.

"The search for the *Lapis Philosophorum* is different for each of us," he said. His expression was hard to read, almost as if he didn't think there really was any such thing as the Philosopher's Stone. But that couldn't be true. Why would he call himself an alchemist if he didn't think there was a Philosopher's Stone?

"What do you mean, it's different for each of us?" she demanded. What he said was wrong. It made her angry and frightened. "There are stages. They're written down in old books. You have to do them right, each step, or the work fails and you have to start over."

"Admirably straightforward." He went to the door and opened it. In his black jacket and breeches he seemed to fade into the darkness on the other side. "Remember what you have just said, when you are taken for your initiation—do each step correctly, or the work will fail."

"And if it fails?" The pain burst back into her head. "If the work fails, I will have to start over?"

From the darkness he said, "Do not fail, for there will be no starting over."

CHAPTER FOUR

R uan kept only two servants, a groom to look after Lowarn in the grand ducal stables and a body-servant to look after his own few clothes and books. He had no personal possessions beyond that—the simple furnishings of his rooms in the Casino di San Marco were provided from the grand duke's storerooms, and to the grand duke's storerooms they would return one day. He treated his servants fairly but did not encourage intimacy. He lived as a stranger in a foreign country, keeping to himself but for his dealings with the prince and the laboratory, the grand duchy's mines and metal-smelting operations, because one day—

One day he would go home to Cornwall.

That skinny, sharp-chinned alchemist's daughter with her questions and her helplessness, her deep-set changeable eyes—she had brought it back, the misery of a six-year-old boy in a Cornish mine, his hands already torn and scarred from carrying rocks, watching his mother die slowly and terribly and helpless to save her. Ruan Pencarrow, the boy's name had been, son of Mark Pencarrow, rightful owner of Milhyntall House and its lands and the mine itself, Wheal Loer—all but for the rebellion, the rising of the old religion against the new English prayer book, which had scorched Cornwall with fire from Launceston to Land's End, and changed Ruan Pencarrow's life forever.

Like malachite, he had gone into the fire one thing and come out of it something else. He was now Ruan the Englishman, Ruanno dell' Inghilterra—the Florentines saw little difference between England and Cornwall and it served his purposes well enough to keep his true birthplace hidden. In Latin he styled himself Roannes Pencarianus, alchemist, metallurgist, scientist, the one man in Florence who was truly a close confidant of Prince Francesco de' Medici. He thought in an amalgamation of Cornish, English, German, Latin and Italian, bits and pieces of voices he had loved and hated and feared and admired in the twenty-four years of his life.

There was a letter in the breast of his doublet, two lines on a strip of paper cut from the edge of another letter. It was unsigned, but he knew the handwriting. She knew he would know it, and she knew he would come. She was afraid, as everyone else in Florence was afraid. She had more reason to be afraid than most.

The secret entrance to the Palazzo Medici was not locked. As he walked in a footman stepped forward and took his cloak without a word. He nodded briefly and made his way up a flight of polished marble stairs. He went straight into an apartment of rooms on the second floor without so much as scratching at the door.

The woman at the dressing table froze. She was wearing only a loose gown, pale rose-colored silk embroidered with gold thread. The mother-of-pearl powder on her skin glimmered in the light from two branches of three candles each. Six candles, no more.

Once, she had surrounded herself with dozens of candles, hundreds of them, welcoming their light. Once, she had studied the cosmos, sponsored readings by poets, judged debates between fine young gentlemen over fine shades of meaning in words. Once, she had sung and danced like an angel, patronized composers and singers, surrounded herself with books so beautiful and expensive, she herself was the only one who dared open them to read. Once he had loved her—more than loved her, worshipped her, as any headstrong sixteen-year-old boy who thought he was a man would have worshipped Isabella de' Medici, princess and duchess, first lady of Florence.

But in the eight years he had known her, she had borne two children, eaten too much rich food, drunk too much wine, intrigued her way through too many passionate affairs. She had been older from the beginning—he had made it his business to find out her birth date in order to cast her horoscope, and the difference in their ages was seven years, eight months, and six days. She had not aged as well as she might have.

Behind her a lady-in-waiting was brushing her hair with a jeweled brush, the masses of rich russet-gold curls unpinned and loose over her shoulders. If she owed some of its color to bleaches and dyes, she was certainly not unique in Florence. In front of her another lady adjusted the angle of a round mirror in a silver stand, set with aquamarines.

In the mirror her eyes met Ruan's.

"I would speak privately with the Duchess of Bracciano," Ruan said.

The two ladies curtsied and left the room without a word. Isabella said nothing. She did not turn her head, but continued to watch Ruan in the mirror. He walked up behind her and put his hands on her shoulders. She shrugged very slightly, skillful as a courtesan, and her gown slipped down over her arms like the falling petals of a flower, leaving her half-naked in the candlelight. The line of her throat was still exquisite, and her nipples were like amber-colored citrines against the lush white velvet of her breasts. Did she intend to seduce him again, after all these years? Did she think it was necessary? The scarred and sun-darkened skin of his hands made a barbaric contrast to her softness and paleness.

"You sent me a message," he said softly. "I am here, Isabella."

"Thank you."

"You know I will always come."

She reached out and turned the mirror away. "Most men would hate me," she said. "I took you into my bed when it pleased me, then put you aside when it pleased me to take another. Most men would be gratified to see me grow old, and sick, and afraid."

"You are neither old nor sick."

If she wanted further compliments, she would be disappointed. He waited.

After a moment she said, "Ruanno. My father is dying. For all I know, he is already dead."

It was like her to state such a truth without flinching. She was hot-blooded, yes, and self-indulgent, avaricious and extravagant, but she had courage and she was nobody's fool. Her father had protected her, supported her excuses to avoid her husband's bleak castle at Bracciano, encouraged her to remain in Florence amid the golden pleasures of her childhood home, her own palaces and country villas. Her father had given her unprecedented freedoms. When he was gone, her freedoms would be gone as well.

"I know," he said. "I am sorry."

"Francesco hates me. You know he does. He will change everything when he becomes grand duke."

"He does not hate you." Ruan ran his hands gently over her shoulders, her arms. Her skin was warm and very soft. She would always be lovely in his eyes, because she was the woman who had taught him the ways of women. More than that, the ways of the court. "You must make more of an effort to please him."

"I do make an effort. I have befriended his insolent slut of a mistress, have I not? You do not know, Ruanno, how much I loathe her and her ambitions."

Ruan smiled. "I do know," he said. "Your brother knows as well, because you talk behind Donna Bianca's back and what you say is reported to him. It makes me afraid for you, *cara*. Do you not remember the first lesson you taught me about court politics? Everything is overheard, everything is repeated."

Isabella frowned. She caught hold of the silk of her gown and drew it back up over her breasts. "Such lessons were for you, not for me. I am a princess of the Medici by blood, and I say what I please."

Ruan lifted his hands from her shoulders, allowing her the freedom to rearrange her gown. "So you do," he said. His voice was lightly mocking. "What do you want from me, then, *altissima principessa*?"

"Do not make fun of me, Ruanno." Her voice was sharp. The tightness of her mouth suddenly showed her age. "You have my brother's ear, more than anyone else but Donna Bianca herself. Speak for me."

"What would you have me say?"

"I wish to continue as I am, here in Florence, living my own life. I wish to have my properties and my children's inheritances confirmed to my own possession."

"Is it not the Duke of Bracciano who should take care for your children? He is their father, after all."

"He does not have a quattrino the Medici have not given him, and you know it. Even if he had riches of his own, I do not wish to be in his debt."

"You are his wife."

"I will not be his possession. My father allowed me to live as I please, and I want Francesco to do the same."

Ruan walked around the dressing table so he could face her. She looked back at him with dread and defiance, and it gave him a pang of apprehension. "It will never be the same," he said. "And it is dangerous for you to try to make it so. Isabella, listen to me. When your father is dead, you must surrender yourself to your brother's authority. Openly, for everyone to see. There is no other way."

"I will not."

"There is another thing you taught me about the court. Do what the powerful require, for the powerful to see. Do what you like in private."

She turned her face away. He could see her thinking about what he had said, and remembering the days when she had taught it to him. After a moment she looked at him from the corners of her eyes, and he saw a glint of guile. It was hard to tell if she thought to deceive him, or deceive her brother, or both. Perhaps she herself was not certain. "Tell me then," she said. "What do you think I must do to please Francesco?"

"You know the answer to that already. Show him sweet submission and respect."

"And truckle to his mistress."

"Not necessarily. If there is any truckling to be done, it should be done to Prince Francesco alone."

She smiled, for the first time. "That I understand. Very well, Ruanno. Do you have any other advice? I suppose you think I should bury myself at Bracciano."

"Not at all. Use your patronage and entertainments to support your brother, and he will be perfectly well pleased to have you in Florence."

Her smile hardened, like hot iron quenched in water. She said nothing.

"Also," Ruan went on inexorably, "rein in Donna Dianora. You are her elder, her sister-in-law, her cousin by blood. She patterns herself upon you, as you well know. Prince Francesco blames you, that she is not a faithful wife to Don Pietro. That she dabbles in treason as well as poetry and music."

Isabella stood up suddenly, grasped the silver mirror, and threw it hard across the room. It crashed into the wall like a harquebus-shot, and the glass shattered into glittering slivers. Aquamarines rolled in every direction. "She patterns herself on me, for faithlessness and treason? Take care what you say, Ruanno. At least I do not abduct tradesmen's daughters off the street for my pleasure."

Her movement brought her scent to life, intense and arousing, a combination of musk and ambergris and jasmine. With the perfume, memories—*re Varia hweg, penn an syns*, what memories, her mouth, her skin slicked with sweat, her silken muscles convulsing around him, intoxicating every sense. The urge to touch her became so strong that he closed his hands into fists to control it.

"Who told you I abducted a tradesman's daughter?"

"Who did not? They say you are sharing her with Francesco, and that two of his guardsmen had her first."

"That is not true."

She laughed. Her eyes were like crystals of mica, gold flecked with gray, shining and opaque. "Probably not," she said. "Francesco would never share one of his whores with anyone, and in any case he is obsessed with Donna Bianca. But I can read it in your face—there is some truth in the tales, is there not? There is a real girl."

He hesitated for a moment, and then he said, "There is. She is an alchemist's daughter, not a whore, and Prince Francesco desires to make her his *soror mystica*."

"What is that?"

"Something he has read about in old books—a woman who assists an alchemist, supposedly providing the feminine element to balance his masculinity."

Isabella laughed again. Her anger was forgotten, and she sounded delighted as a child. "Donna Bianca will be furious," she said. "She is jealous enough as it is, being my brother's childless mistress while his Imperial wife produces baby after baby. All girls, but still."

"The girl is a virgin, and she will be compelled to take a holy vow of virginity before she is allowed to assume a place in the prince's household."

"How titillating! I suppose you examined her yourself, to verify the presence of her maidenhead? You really have no business chiding me, Ruanno, for—what was it? Faithlessness and treason, and too many entertainments."

"Isabella." He had recovered his detachment. He took her by her shoulders and shook her, gently but sharply. "Do not be a fool. You must control

Dianora. You must be more discreet about your own affair with Troilo Orsini."

"I am a princess of the Medici. Gossip cannot harm me."

"Gossip can harm anyone."

She pushed him away. "I had hoped you would help me, Ruanno, not berate me."

"I am helping you. I will always help you in any way I can."

"Go away. I do not need your help after all."

There was no reasoning with her when her temper was roused. He went to the door. "I will come again if you call me. And Isabella?"

She would not look at him.

"It would be best," he said gently, "if you say nothing more to anyone about the alchemist's daughter."

CHAPTER FIVE

The Palazzo di Bianca Cappello

THAT SAME NIGHT

"An alchemist's daughter!" Bianca Cappello's bosom quivered in the deep-cut neckline of her gown, dark crimson silk embroidered with pearls and rubies. She had thrust a living rose between her breasts, white barely tinged with pink and gold, almost exactly the color of her abundant flesh. The petals had begun to fall with the heat of her rage. "A mountebank's daughter, more likely. You are one breath away from the crown, my lord, and you spend your time abducting girls from the gutter?"

The prince found it distasteful when his mistress worked herself into such a sordid passion of emotion. He said in his coldest voice, "I spend my time doing what I please."

He meant to warn her, but she was clearly too frenzied to hear him. Galen had written a treatise on just such a frenzy, which he called *hysteria* and associated with a deprivation of fleshly satisfactions in the female. The prince had every intention of dealing with that deprivation in Donna Bianca's case, but in his own way and at his own leisure.

She continued her tirade. "I am a noblewoman of Venice, and I will not be set aside with a few sweet words from one of your gentlemen, while you go off with that sorcerer of yours and a ragamuffin girl."

She stumbled a bit over her description of herself. Understandable. She may have been born a noblewoman of Venice, but she had lost any reputation she might have had when she ran off with a Florentine banker's clerk at fifteen. When she bore her daughter only six months after her hasty marriage.

When she became his mistress, in the very midst of the celebrations marking his marriage to Giovanna of Austria.

"You will be set aside when I say you are to be set aside, Madonna. I do not care for great ladies, as you well know, or for raised voices."

She stood panting, her curling red-gold hair beginning to tumble down from its jeweled combs. She knew perfectly well that Bianca Cappello, the notorious runaway noblewoman of Venice, would never have been more than a moment's amusement for him, conquered and abandoned like all the others. It was another woman who had held his heart and mind and body in her hands for nine years now, another woman who brought light to the dark, melancholy curiosity-cabinet of his soul.

Bia. His Bia.

Bia, who was Bianca, and at the same time was not.

"I do not want to be *her*," Bianca said. She was clearly struggling to make her voice more temperate. "For one evening with you, my lord prince, I beg you, let me be myself."

The prince smiled. "Yourself?" he said. "Have you not told me, over and over, that Bia is your true self, and that it is your joy and her joy to please the humble workman Franco?"

It was his own elaborate and deeply satisfying conceit, that he was a simple laborer named Franco. Franco worked every day with his hands, with minerals and acids, noble metals and glassworks and fine porcelains, and when the day was finished and he had no more work to do, he needed only to come home to his adoring and compliant little wife Bia, and she would tend to his every desire. Francesco, the prince—he had been the eldest, the heir, but even so he had never been the favorite, never been clever and charming and affable as his brothers and sisters had been. From the day of his mother's death and his father's descent into self-indulgence, his responsibilities had never ended. His wife, the emperor's sister—she was pious and proud and never forgot who she was, not even when they came together in their interminable quest to beget an heir. It was all too much. It was so much easier to be Franco, even if it was only for a few hours.

And as for Bia, well—Bianca had been happy enough to play the game at first. Anything to become the prince's mistress. She had tired of it quickly, he knew that, but he did not care. For him, for Franco, his nights with Bia were like air and water, dreamless sleep and good plain food. They were the only things that kept him sane.

"Fetch my clothes," he said. "And change into your own proper clothes at once."

She refused to obey him for a moment longer, her full glossy brows slanting in a scowl, her eyes stormy. He stepped closer to her and cuffed her across the mouth, not really hard enough to hurt her. Not yet. She sucked in her breath and closed her eyes for a moment.

He picked up the kitchen-knife that lay on the table. "Turn around," he said.

She did not open her eyes. Like a woman in a dream, she turned. He cut the stitches of her embroidered bodice and the corset beneath it, revealing her fine silk camicia clinging damply to her skin. Through it he could see red marks on her back, imprinted by the corset's steel stays. The marks were beautiful.

"Fetch my clothes," he said again. His voice was calm and pleasant. "Bia."

"Yes, Franco," she whispered.

She went into the other room. The prince began to undress himself. His opulent clothing was like a monk's habit to him, penitential: a fine black silk doublet, a padded pearl-embroidered jerkin blazoned with the red lilies of Florence, slashed trunk hose and tight stockings, a gold ring in his ear and a dark sapphire the size of a moscatello grape in his hat. He took it all off, even his underdrawers. They were embroidered with black work, thousands of tiny stitches made by a dozen Benedictine nuns. He preferred plain coarse linen, sewn by his Bia's own hands.

She came back into the room, wearing a simple camicia and overgown, her jewels stripped away, her hair tied up in a white coif. She kept her eyes lowered and said nothing as she offered him the folded clothes that were always prepared and waiting for him, a plain linen shirt and drawers, leather breeches and a jerkin of russet cloth. He put them on. When he did, he felt taller, stronger, freer. He felt as if he could breathe.

"That is much better," he said. "Now, I will have my supper and a cup of wine before we go to bed. I am tired from a long day's work."

He took his seat at the plain wooden table, Franco did, and smiled fondly as his Bia served him. The faint red mark across her mouth where he had struck her only made her lips softer, slightly swollen and more alluring than ever. The doors were locked; outside six Medici guardsmen stood watch to prevent any interruption or disturbance. If a messenger came from the Villa di Castello with news of his father's death, well, the messenger would have to wait.

"I have baked bread for you, my Franco," Bia said. Her voice had become high and childlike. The bread, of course, had come from a shop in the bakers' quarter. They both knew that.

"Tut, my Bia, it is a little burned, here on one side," Franco said. He began to cut slices of the bread with the same knife he had used to cut the stitches of her fine jeweled gown and the laces of her corset. "You must be more careful. Flour is expensive this year."

The bread was not really burned, but Franco liked to find some small fault and inflict some suitable punishment. It was part of the rich, rich pleasure of being Franco. She did not contradict him. She was sinking into the intense trancelike state he loved, compounded of fear and submission and anticipation and sensuous arousal.

He ate the bread, and soft *giuncata* cheese from a plaited rush basket, and a handful of apricots. He drank a cup of cheap wine, well-watered. A good supper. Bia stood beside the table, her hands clasped under her apron like a nun's.

"The alchemist's daughter you speak of," Franco said. "She is to be the prince's *soror mystica*, and assist with the great work of creating the Philosopher's Stone." Franco, of course, would not use the proper Latin name. "She will be—"

"What is a *soror mystica*?"

"Do not interrupt me, my Bia."

She lowered her eyes again. "I am sorry, Franco."

"A *soror mystica* is an alchemist's feminine counterpart, his sister in the mysteries. This girl will be put to the tests of virginity before she is initiated, and she will be strangled if she fails. She will never be the prince's mistress, my Bia, only his *soror*. Virgin she will be in the beginning, and virgin she will remain, under holy vows."

He could see her struggling with herself. After a moment she burst out, "If the prince wanted a feminine counterpart, why did he not choose me?"

"You? You know nothing of alchemy, my Bia. And in any case—you belong to me. I would never share you with the prince."

She folded her lips together and said nothing more. Her golden lashes concealed her eyes. He ate another apricot and drank the rest of the wine.

"I think," he said when he had finished, "that you will have no supper tonight, as part of your penance for burning the bread, and for interrupting me. Go and undress. I would like to enjoy my Bia's flesh, well and thoroughly."

She obeyed him without a word. It pleased him. He left the dishes on the table and followed her to the second room, where there was a plain wooden bedstead, its frame strung with rope and piled with three straw mattresses. The sheets were linen, washed and bleached in the sun, and the pillows were stuffed with sweet dried grass. A length of extra rope lay coiled by the side of the bed. Bia averted her eyes from it, but Franco looked at it with deep satisfaction. He was intimately familiar with the thickness and texture of the rope, and how it looked when it was knotted around Bia's wrists, or her ankles, or her soft white throat.

She took off her clothes quickly, without feigning modesty. Her skin was milky pale; she spent hours, he knew, rubbing it with perfumed oils and lotions so it would be pleasing to him. Her hair was reddish-gold, the color of copper allowed to oxidize for a day or two, falling in silken curls to her hipbones. Not that he could see her hipbones. She was lushly fleshed, magnificently soft, a woman just as he loved women.

Perhaps he would not punish her too harshly for the pretended burned crust on the bread, for interrupting him with questions about the prince's *soror mystica*.

Naked, she helped him undress, taking his jerkin and hanging it from its special hook, accepting his shirt when he pulled it over his head. She knelt before him to unfasten his breeches. It was the moment when he felt more a man than any other, more than when he sat on his father's grand-ducal throne in the Palazzo Vecchio, more, even, than when he condemned a criminal or a revolutionary, man or woman, to torture and death.

But that was Francesco, slipping into his thoughts. He was Franco. Franco.

Bia drew his breeches down over his hips and he stepped out of them. She pressed her face against his belly for a moment, kissing him, adoring him. Then she got to her feet and stood before him. They were of a height, she pale and rounded, he swarthy and sun-burned from hunting. But all the power was his, and none of it hers.

"May I lie in the bed, Franco?" she whispered.

"First," he said, "you will kneel at the prie-dieu. You must do the rest of your penance."

The prie-dieu had been his mother's. He knew its carvings by heart—his mother's impresa, a peahen and her chicks, neatly referencing both his father's splendor and his mother's fertility. The wooden kneeling-bench was worn from Eleonora of Toledo's devout knees, and from the knees of her children—of Francesco, the prince, most of the time—who had been compelled to kneel there for whippings when they failed to fulfill her exacting standards of behavior. Bia walked over to it without a word and knelt, pulling her hair forward over her shoulders, putting her forehead down against the sloping shelf where his mother's praying hands had rested every day, all her life in Florence.

She was trembling, Bia was, and in the flickering candlelight he could see the sheen of sweat on her smooth pale skin. Her hands clutched at the sides of the shelf, her knuckles white with anticipation.

He opened the lid of the chest that always stood beside the prie-dieu and selected a doubled leather strap. He let her wait for a while, breathing in the scent of her fear and arousal and the pleasure of her being so utterly at his mercy. When he saw her relax a little, perhaps thinking he had changed his mind, he drew back his arm and struck her, hard.

She gasped, jumping and pressing forward against the wood. A reddened stripe glowed across her back, from her left shoulder to her right hip. She began to tremble uncontrollably. He struck her again, with calm and perfect control, and she cried out—she knew he liked to hear that he was hurting her. He gave her six blows in all, sufficient to finally force a scream from her, quite sufficient for her transgression. Four stripes from left to right, two criss-crossing them in the opposite direction. They were beautiful, rosy and slightly swollen. She lay over the prie-dieu's shelf, sobbing, quivering helplessly with sensation.

He put the strap away and closed the chest.

"I think," he said calmly, "I will lie down first. I will make myself comfortable, and then you may set yourself to please me."

She said, "Yes, Franco." Her high Bia-voice was husky with tears and, he knew, her own pleasure, the pleasure-in-pain he had taught her. He lay down on the bed, splaying out his arms and legs, breathing deeply. He felt hard and strong. By the gold and copper mines of King Solomon, it was good to be alive.

Bia rose from the prie-dieu and ran her fingers through her hair, letting the rich curls tumble over the sensitized skin of her back. For a moment she simply stood there, allowing him to gaze his fill, as subject to his desires as a *marionetta* on invisible strings. Then she turned and walked to the bed. Without a word she knelt over him, her hair spilling forward over his face, her heavy breasts brushing deliberately against his chest as she mounted him. She knew what he liked. He thrust up with his hips, and reveled in her shudder and whimper of sensation.

"Now," he said. "You do the work, my Bia. Show me you are sorry for your carelessness, and grateful to your Franco for correcting you."

Her thighs flexed sweetly as she sank down upon him. He felt her satiny hide grow warm and moist with her exertion as he ran his hands over her flanks and breasts, over her back, feeling the delicate heat and swelling of the stripes. She made a guttural sound and writhed as he touched her.

"Franco." She groaned, as if in anguish. "More. Harder."

He stiffened all his muscles and drove himself into her. At the same time he sank his fingernails into the welts his leather strap had made on her back. She threw back her head and screamed with her ecstasy.

When she collapsed over his chest, gasping for breath, her flesh twitching, every shred of dignity and rank and birth gone, he wrapped his arms around her and took his own long, slow satisfaction. That moment, when she was his creature, that was what he loved. More, even, than the physical release. This was what bound her to him, and him to her, and damn the conventions of the court and the laws of the church.

He rolled her to one side. She was already deeply asleep. He stretched and closed his eyes. In the contentment of a simple man with a repentant and obedient woman, he had forgotten her questions about the alchemist's daughter.

CHAPTER SIX

The Casino di San Marco

THE FOLLOWING AFTERNOON

Chiara was hungry and thirsty. She'd saved the rest of the bread and hadn't drunk any more of the water—there'd be plenty of time for drinking in the prince's outlandish tests. If the tests ever happened, and they hadn't just forgotten her. Finally the bar scraped and the door opened. Two men in Medici colors came in. One of them gestured to her: *come along now, and no funny business.*

"I have to piss," she said. "Turn your backs."

They just grinned at her. She grinned back and used the basin right in front of them. Then she stuffed the rest of the bread into her mouth and followed them out the door.

All she had to do was obey for now. Pass the prince's tests and lull him into trusting her, and eventually she'd have a chance to run away if she wanted, or choose to become this *soror mystica* if that suited her instead. It might not be such a bad thing, a place at the court with princes and princesses. A chance to hold the Philosopher's Stone in her hands. The headaches and demons' cacklings gone forever. Babbo's voice admiring and respectful, instead of telling her she was a useless daughter and should have died instead of Gian.

The guards stopped in front of a door made from carved black wood, heavy and polished. It looked out of place, as if it belonged in a room like the prince's golden studiolo and not at the end of a stone corridor. One man gestured for her to open the door and go in, then both of them walked away, leaving her alone in the dim light.

There was a line of brightness, like a thread of flame, showing under the door. Chiara closed her eyes, made the sign of the cross—*deliver me from evil, have mercy upon me, forgive me*—Nonna, *I'm sorry if this turns out to be something terrible and you never know what happened to me*—and pushed on the door.

It opened.

Light—dazzling light. Hundreds of candles, all around the enormous room, and behind them cabinets of books, more books than she'd ever seen in one place, even in her father's shop. In between the books there were carvings, glittering crystals, flasks of colored liquids and the hollow-eyed skulls of strange animals. The floor was a pattern in black and white stone chips, a labyrinth like the one engraved around the silver descensory—a circle with paths that twisted and folded to make one way from the outside to the center. The white chips glittered in the light from the fires in two fireplaces, one to the left and one to the right; a third fire licked lazily through a golden grate three steps above the floor, just in front of— She lifted her eyes.

At the far end of the room, a dais and a throne. That was the only word for it—a chair carved and gilded and decorated with colored paint and gems, like something out of an illuminated manuscript. The prince sat in the chair on a purple velvet cushion, looking at her with brooding, narrowed eyes. Behind him, the shadow of the throne falling over his face like a mask, stood Magister Ruanno. Both of them were wearing black cassocks like Minimite friars, with deep cowls and pointed hoods.

There were also three tables in the room, a table draped in black to her left, a table draped in scarlet to her right, and a table draped in what looked like liquid silver in front of her, between her and the fire under the golden grate. That was all she had a chance to register before the prince spoke.

"Chiara Nerini, daughter of Carlo Nerini, bookseller and alchemist."

Saints and angels. How had he found out her full name?

"Strip yourself. You will be naked for your testing."

Her first thought was *try to strip me and see how far you get*. She thrust out her chin and actually opened her mouth to say it. Then she saw Magister Ruanno shake his head very slightly and caught her tongue before it ran away with her. Who cared if they saw her naked? She would prove she was a virgin and they wouldn't dare touch her no matter how she flaunted herself, lest they sully her purity.

She unfastened her mantle and let it drop. Unlaced her bodice and shrugged out of it. Untied the drawstring of her skirt and let it fall. That left her in nothing but her thin patched camicia, long-sleeved and loose, reaching her ankles, the garment she lived in and slept in and never took off, even to wash. Nonna had taught her the proper way for a woman to wash herself, with a basin and a rag, all the while keeping herself decently covered.

She untied the drawstring—the one the guardsman had cut with his poniard, had that been only yesterday? It felt like a lifetime had passed—and loosened the neckline. Let the whole thing slide down over her breasts and hips.

She could feel the heat and light from the candles on her skin. It felt so—so unnatural, to be covered by nothing but her own skin.

"Loose your hair from its braid." It was the prince. He didn't sound particularly lustful, but he did sound intent, almost like the priest when he said the Mass. "You shall have nothing about you that is tied or twisted."

She pulled the long braid over her shoulder and untied the cord. Slowly—now that the first shock was over she was beginning to enjoy herself, to feel the strange power she had just by being young, naked and female—she unplaited the three thick tresses of her hair. When she shook it out, it fell in spirals, like the painting of Mary Magdalene's hair in the mural at the church. She ran her fingers through the dark strands, feeling their weight and crinkly softness, and then instead of pulling them over her breasts and belly and thighs to cover herself, she threw them back over her shoulders. She could feel the ends tickling the backs of her legs.

Let them look at her. She was fifteen and untouched and the only mark on her body was the hidden half-circle over her left ear where the horse had kicked her.

"I'm ready for your testing," she said. No *Serenissimo*. No *my lord*. "What do you want me to do first?"

The prince gestured to the black-draped table. "You will drink the black water," he said. "All of it, in one breath."

She walked to the table—six steps, eight. There was a goblet, carved out of black stone. It looked ancient. It was filled with clear liquid, and at the bottom of the liquid lay several shards of broken black stone, as if another goblet had been smashed and the pieces dropped into the bowl of its mate. Beside the goblet rested an arrangement of two bowls, also black stone, one above the other in a silver frame. Next to the bowls there was a black lacquer pitcher. Behind the table hung a black curtain, embroidered in black and silver thread with symbols she didn't recognize.

Chiara stared at the prince defiantly, picked up the goblet and drank the liquid. Magister Ruanno had been right. It tasted like nothing more than plain water. She was thirsty and so drinking the water all at once was easy.

She tilted the goblet toward the prince so he could see it was empty, then put it down on the black table.

"I have drunk the black water," she said. "What is your next test?"

"Not so fast. You must now wait for the prescribed time. Please pour the water in the pitcher into the bowl at the top of the water clock."

That didn't make a lot of sense, but seemed simple enough. She picked up the pitcher and poured the water into the upper bowl. At once she saw how the so-called water clock functioned: there was a tiny hole in the bottom of the upper bowl, and the water dripped through into the lower bowl.

"You will stand without moving," the prince said, "until all the water has run through."

Magister Ruanno hadn't told her this part. The dripping, trickling sound of the water didn't make much of an impression at first, but as the minutes passed in the silent room, as she stood there naked with the black water inside her and the two men watching her wordlessly, the sound seemed to grow louder and louder. Her belly began to feel taut and full and her thighs quivered. She squeezed her inner muscles together.

"If you wish to go behind the curtain for a moment," the prince said, in a voice full of false gentleness, "you may do so. You will find a clean basin there, fresh towels and more water to wash yourself. Surely you will perform the other tests with more success if you are—comfortable."

If Magister Ruanno hadn't warned her about the purpose of the black water test, she would have gone. Instead she said, "No. I'm perfectly comfortable."

The prince nodded. After more endless minutes, the last of the water dripped through the water clock and the sound ceased. The need to relieve herself lessened.

"What is your next test?" she said.

The prince smiled and nodded. "Next," he said, "is the blood-red ribbon."

He rose from his throne and gestured to Magister Ruanno. The two of them stepped down from the dais and made their way around the edge of the room to the red-draped table, their dark robes making soft rustling sounds. A scarlet velvet ribbon lay coiled on the surface of the table; beside the ribbon lay a dagger, very ancient, its handle set with red and reddish-brown cabochon jewels and its blade glinting bronze in the blaze of candlelight.

But Magister Ruanno had promised her the blood wouldn't be real.

"Come here," the prince said. "Stand before the table, and bow your head."

She hesitated for a moment—courage, courage, what can they do to you? They want you alive to be their *soror mystica*—then stepped over to the table and did as he commanded.

Ceremoniously the prince paced around behind her. She felt his fingers pressing against the curve of her skull, through the loose masses of her hair, then drawing the ribbon up over the top of her head.

"Lift your head."

She lifted her head. Magister Ruanno took hold of the ribbon and placed one finger between her eyebrows, pressing the ribbon against her skin. The prince let go of the end of the ribbon at the back of her head and stepped around in front of her. Magister Ruanno then drew the ribbon from between her eyebrows, down to the tip of her nose and beyond, and held it taut.

The prince stepped in front of her again and picked up the dagger.

Chiara's heart stopped. The black water swelled and trembled within her.

With one perfect, ritualized sweep, the prince brought the dagger up and sliced the ribbon exactly at the end of her nose.

She gasped. She reached up and touched the end of her nose, then looked at her fingertips. No blood.

Magister Ruanno dropped the sliced-off end of the ribbon on the red table, and handed the measured length to the prince. He stepped back. The prince wrapped the ribbon around her neck and brought the ends together in the hollow at the base of her throat.

"It is exactly the right length," he said. "Very well, we shall proceed to the test of the silver sieve."

He put the measured piece of ribbon and the bronze dagger back on the red table and returned to his throne. Magister Ruanno followed him. It was all like some kind of complicated dance, or the way the acolytes assisted the priest in the church.

Chiara fought back a crazy urge to laugh.

"Step forward, Chiara Nerini, to the silver table."

The table was long and narrow, its surface covered with silver cloth. Chiara wondered if it was somehow woven of real silver. On the cloth rested a silver bowl of water—more water, please please don't let this whole business last much longer—a silver ladle and a round silver sieve strung with white horsehair.

"You will fill the sieve with water," the prince said. "You will carry it around the table. Then you will step upon the golden grate, beneath which a fire is burning, and when you have crossed it, on your knees you will offer the sieve to me."

So he only required the sieve to be offered, not the sieve filled with water; he instructed her to step on the grate, not the fire. Again, if Magister Ruanno hadn't explained the trick to her, she never would have guessed she was to shake the water from the sieve upon the fire, to put it out and cool the grate.

First, though, there was the business of carrying water in the sieve in the first place.

She stepped to the table and picked up the sieve. Other than having an engraved silver rim, it looked much like the sieve Nonna used to sift flour, when they could afford to buy flour; its mesh was very fine, tautly and evenly woven, and it appeared to be perfectly dry. She tilted it slightly in the candlelight and caught the faint reflection of oil, not enough to clog the meshes, just enough to give the horsehair the same gleam as the leather of her father's fine old bookbindings.

. . . hold the sieve level and steady, and take care that the underside remains absolutely dry . . .

She transferred the sieve to her left hand and held it level, parallel to the top of the table. She picked up the ladle with her right hand and dipped it into the water, then very slowly, very carefully, with the ladle very close to the meshes but not touching them, she poured a little of the water into the center of the sieve's circle.

To her amazement, the water did not instantly flow through. It formed a flattened circle with a rounded edge, standing up slightly from the mesh of the sieve. *It's like the time Nonna was sick,* she thought, *and I spilled the rose-hip tea on her bedcover. It made round droplets and they stood up on top of the cloth for the longest time, before they sank in. That's what this water is doing. I have time, but not endless time.*

Steady. Steady. Level.

She dipped up another ladleful of water and poured it gently around the edges of the circle of water already in the sieve. It held.

The room seemed to shrink in size. It became round, like the sieve, with a straight line running through it. She added another ladleful of water, and another, keeping the sieve level, willing her hands to be steady.

The shining flat circle of liquid touched the sieve's silver rim.

She put the ladle down and curved her right hand very gently around the frame of the sieve. Steadied it. *Now. Walk. Slow. Easy. One step at a time, keeping the sieve level. Watch the surface of the water inside*—water inside a sieve! She was amazed that it was actually happening—*so it did not tilt or ripple in the slightest. Walk around the silver table—left, forward, right, forward. Three steps up. Careful, so careful.*

She did not dare look down, but she could feel the heat of the fire beneath the golden grate. It licked at her bare toes.

"You must walk over the grate," the prince said. "It is the final test."

Slowly, very slowly, Chiara stretched out her arms, with the sieve in her hands. She looked at Magister Ruanno; he smiled and nodded slightly. Then she shifted her gaze to the prince's face, looked straight into his dark eyes, and deliberately shook the sieve. The water cascaded down and she heard the hiss as it hit the hot metal grate, drenched the coals, drowned the fire. The fumes stung her eyes. Her hands, her whole body, shook with triumph. Without looking down she stepped on the grate—hot, yes, but not enough to burn if she stepped quickly—and crossed over it.

"I walked across your golden grate," she said. Her voice did not sound like her own at all. "And carried water in your silver sieve. I drank your black water and held it inside me and hold it still. Your red ribbon measured my neck perfectly, down to the last hairsbreadth. Never dare doubt that I'm a virgin, pure and untouched, worthy to be your *soror mystica*."

She walked down the three steps and cast the sieve to the floor at the prince's feet. It made a clanging metallic sound on the stones, flipped over and rolled a few feet. She didn't care if it was dented, or what happened to it. She didn't care that she was naked, with her hair loose down her back. She didn't kneel, but stood straight and proud.

For a moment, there was absolute silence.

Then the prince rose from his throne. "You have passed through the tests, Chiara Nerini," he said. "Magister Ruanno, the habit."

The foreigner picked up a bundle of cloth, neatly folded. It was the creamy color of undyed wool. He shook it out to reveal a simple robe, nothing more than a wide, uncut and unsewn length of cloth with an opening in the center for her head to go through.

"Gather up your hair," he said.

She reached back and pulled the heavy length of her hair forward.

He dropped the cloth over her shoulders. It fell straight to the floor, front and back; when she threw her hair back and stretched out her arms, she found it was wide enough to reach her fingertips on either side. Wool, yes, but it wasn't coarse and scratchy like the clothing she was used to. It was smooth and fine and fell in wide, graceful folds.

The prince nodded. He looked pleased.

"Now," he said, "you must vow to remain a virgin while you are in my service, upon pain of death. Magister Ruanno, the relic."

Relic? Pain of death? All Chiara wanted was a chance to slip behind the black curtain, and now there was a relic?

Magister Ruanno stepped over to one of the bookcases on a side wall, then returned with a reliquary made of carved rock crystal in the form of a scallop shell, with a frame of gold and a clasp of gold and pearls and blue jewels—blue, the Holy Virgin's color. Inside the shell, folded over and over upon itself, was a strip of ordinary-looking fabric, dyed green and embroidered with gold thread. The green was much faded but even through the thickness of the rock crystal, the gold glinted in the candlelight. He handed the reliquary to the prince.

"What is it?" Chiara said.

The prince made a scornful sound—*you may be a virgin but you know nothing.* Magister Ruanno said gently, "It is the Sacra Cintola, the sacred girdle of the Holy Virgin Mary, which has been kept in the Cathedral of Santo Stefano at Prato for four hundred years and more. The Princess Giovanna is a faithful devotee of the relic, and so of course the priests and the sindaco of Prato are happy to permit the prince to bring it into Florence for one night."

"It is the greatest relic of the Holy Virgin in Christendom," the prince said. "You will put your hands upon it when you swear."

Chiara pressed her thighs together. The need to pass water was becoming intense. For some reason the holy relic seemed to suck away her triumph at having passed through the prince's tests, and make her humiliatingly aware that she was nothing but a fifteen-year-old bookseller's daughter, helpless in front of these powerful men in their dark robes.

"I will swear," she said.

The prince offered the reliquary. She put her hands on it. The rock crystal was cool and polished, the fluting of the scallop shell perfectly carved.

"Swear, then," the prince said.

"With my hands on the Sacra—the Sacra Cintola of the Holy Virgin," Chiara said, a little desperately. "I swear I will remain a virgin for as long as I am in the service of the prince."

"Upon penalty of death."

"I will remain a virgin, upon penalty of death, for as long as I am in the service of the prince."

The prince made the sign of the cross. "Amen," he said. "You are sworn."

He put the reliquary down and took a silver chain from the table beside his throne. It was hung with a pendant stone with a milky, opalescent sheen, mostly white but with half-transparent tinges of blue and pink and gold. It wasn't a pearl—pearls didn't have that strange transparency. It was big, the size and shape of a dove's egg, and polished, as if it had been worn and re-set and worn again since the creation of the world.

"This is a moonstone from the kingdom of Ruhuna, on an island far to the east, beyond Persia, beyond the Silk Road," the prince said. "The moon, the moonstone itself and the element silver in the setting are symbols of virginity. You will wear this stone as a mark that you are set aside from the world as our *soror mystica*. I have a stone also, a diamond set in gold, symbolizing the sun. Magister Ruanno's stone is hematite set in iron and copper, symbols of the earth."

Chiara stepped forward and he put the chain around her neck. She had never owned a piece of jewelry and never worn a necklace before. It felt heavy and unnatural. The loose folds of the tunic-cape-whatever-it-was felt light and clean, and smelled of herbs.

"From this day forward—" the prince began.

Suddenly the door to the corridor opened. Dark and damp and the outside world flooded in. There were half-a-dozen uniformed guardsmen there. No one said anything, but the prince's expression changed, hardened. Without another word or a backward glance he walked out of the room. Magister Ruanno started to follow him, and then paused.

"You did well," he said. He looked—not surprised, exactly, or at least not surprised by anything she had done. Surprised at himself, perhaps, for being pleased she had succeeded.

"I would have failed if you hadn't told me what you told me," she said.

He touched the hair at her left temple with one finger, almost as if he was pointing at the scar. But no, all he did was untangle a wisp that had caught itself in the silver links of the chain. "Perhaps. Perhaps not. Wait here now, Monella Chiara, and someone will come for you."

He went out.

She waited a moment to be certain he wouldn't return, then went behind the black curtain. There she found a prosaic basin, more blue and white porcelain, and fine clean towels. She half expected her piss to be black, after drinking the black water. But it was reassuringly clear and light. When she emerged from behind the curtain, the crystals on the shelves glittered in the candlelight, and the skulls grinned at her, empty-eyed.

A woman was waiting. She was short and thick-bodied and had plump wrinkled cheeks like last season's apples; her gown and sleeves and head-dress were fine enough but not trimmed with silver or gold or jewels. Beside her stood a little hound, parti-colored black and white and russet, with long silky ears. It was wearing a collar of shiny purple fabric like silk, and although the woman did not have jewels, the dog did, pearls and purple stones sewn to its collar with silver thread.

"I am Donna Jimena Osorio," the woman said. "Related by blood to the late Duchess"—she crossed herself—"Eleonora of Toledo. She invited me to Florence to manage her daughter Donna Isabella's household, and so I have done with all my heart, for thirty years and more. This"—she gestured to the dog, which was looking up at Chiara with dark, intelligent eyes—"is Rina, Donna Isabella's special pet. You are to come with us now."

"I want to go home," Chiara said. She hadn't realized how much she wanted to go home until she said the words. "My Nonna will be afraid for me. My little sisters will miss me. Please, Donna Jimena? I beg you. Just for an hour—no one will ever know."

"The prince has forbidden it."

"*Please.*"

"Your Nonna knows where you are. How do you think the prince knew your name, and your father's name? Magister Ruanno found out for him, as he finds out so many things, and he spoke with Mona Agnesa himself. That is your Nonna's name, is it not?"

Chiara nodded. She didn't know what to say.

"Now come with me."

"Where have the prince and Magister Ruanno gone?"

"To the Villa di Castello," Donna Jimena said. She crossed herself again. "Grand Duke Cosimo is dead. Everything is changed from this night forward, for you and I and everyone in Florence are now subjects of Francesco de' Medici, the first of his name to be Grand Duke of Tuscany."

PART II

Isabella

The Star of the House of Medici

CHAPTER SEVEN

The Villa di Castello

21 APRIL 1574

Breathing hard—grief? fear? simple exertion?—Francesco de' Medici stepped into the room where his father's body lay. It was full dark, and the Villa di Castello blazed with torches and candles. The light wavered and rippled, and there were eyes, eyes everywhere.

Cosimo de' Medici, the first Grand Duke of Tuscany, who had devoted his ambitious, ruthless and vainglorious life to the *precedenza* of his name, his city and himself, had been dead for two or three hours, no more. His body, once so robust, had withered over the past months with sickness and inactivity. He looked like an old man, much older than his fifty-five years, his eyes as hollow as a skull's eyes. The oil of the chrism gleamed on his forehead and lips and the backs of his hands.

Every man in the room, even the priests, bowed to the new grand duke. Some made deeper reverences than others. The new grand duke noticed every detail, measured every inclination of the head and bending of the knee. He would remember.

He began, however, by kneeling beside his father's body and reciting the *De Profundis*. He did not care whether his father's iniquities were forgiven or not, but he wanted his own reign to begin with a public act of filial piety his secretaries could describe in their letters to the pope and to the kings and queens of Europe. He said the Latin words by rote, all the while thinking of alchemy, of his laboratory, of his English alchemist and the girl Chiara Nerini, his *soror mystica* now, initiated and vowed. She would make the difference, and the *Lapis Philosophorum* would be his at last. When he had finished the psalm he stood up and looked about him.

"Where," he demanded, "is Signora Cammilla?"

The priests and physicians and courtiers murmured and looked away. One young fellow, braver than the others, perhaps, or less well-versed in the intricacies of the Medici court, said, "She has retired to her apartments, Serenissimo, to dress herself in the proper mourning garments for a grand duke's widow."

"I have garments in mind for her." The new grand duke gestured to two of his gentlemen. "See to moving my father's body to the Pitti Palace at once. Send for carpenters and upholsterers, so that a proper catafalque may be constructed. Also engage the embalmers, and notify my secretaries and messengers—letters must be sent."

The two gentlemen ran out of the room.

"You, priests," he continued. "I desire that there will be no fewer than six priests attending my father's body at all times, praying for his soul."

The priests looked furtively at each other, counting. There were seven of them. All of them clustered around the bed, knelt, and reached for their beads.

"Physicians, you are needed no longer. You may apply to my major-domo for your fees."

The physicians left. There was a distinct flavor of relief in their flight. Bereaved sons so often held physicians to blame for a father's death.

"You." The grand duke indicated the young man who had spoken. "Lead me to Signora Cammilla's apartments."

"But she—"

"Lead me."

The young man went out, and the grand duke followed him. After him trailed his remaining gentlemen, pushing each other unobtrusively for position. The apartments in question were at the back of the villa, with windows overlooking the garden. The grand duke knew the rooms well—they had been his mother's, in the days of his childhood. He did not remember Eleonora of Toledo fondly, but it enraged him that his father's morganatic wife—little more than a mistress, and four years younger than he himself, by the bleeding severed neck of the Baptist—had dared to occupy them.

"Open the door," he said.

"But Serenissimo, Donna Cammilla asked to be undisturbed in her grief."

"Signora Cammilla," the grand duke said, stressing the lesser title, "will be disturbed if it is my pleasure to disturb her. Open the door."

The young man pushed the door open, and the grand duke walked in. Two waiting-women froze in attitudes of surprise. One held a pair of silver scissors and a red silk skirt-front embroidered with rubies and pearls; she was in the midst of cutting the gems from the decorated fabric and collecting them in a small leather box. The other woman had a glass of golden wine and a plate of cakes on a tray.

At a gesture from the grand duke, two of his gentlemen moved forward to take the women into custody. The woman with the scissors tried to run, slashing at her captor with the pointed blades. The other one dropped her tray—a smash of glass, a spray of wine, a scatter of sticky cakes bouncing and rolling—and screamed a warning. The grand duke walked on serenely through the chaos, past the inner receiving room and into the privy bed-chamber.

Cammilla Martelli was on her feet, with three more waiting-ladies surrounding her—they had all heard the woman in the anteroom scream. Her hair, a bright terra-cotta auburn that clearly had its origin in a dye-pot, was loose over her shoulders; her night-gown was rich but wrinkled and spotted by wear, tied carelessly so her heavy breasts were half-exposed. She thrust a bundle of fabric into the open chest behind her and faced her stepson, her head thrown back like a wild mare's.

"How dare you?" Her voice was high and edged with fear. "I am mourning for your father, and no one, not even you, has the right to interfere with me."

"I have the right to interfere with anyone I choose." The grand duke walked across the room and pushed her aside unceremoniously. She stumbled and would have fallen if one of her ladies had not caught her. "I have the right to decide whether you live or die, *matrigna*. What are you doing with this?"

He picked up the bundle of fabric. It was a camicia in fine white silk, decorated with black work. A silver needle dangled at the end of a piece of thread. He jerked the thread loose and the hem of the camicia unraveled, spilling a glittering necklace of emeralds and pearls onto the floor. The grand duke picked it up. For a moment he was a child again, sulky at being forced to recite a Latin exercise for a group of ambassadors when all he really wanted was to be left alone with his rocks and bird-skulls. The emerald-and-pearl necklace had looped three times around his mother's neck as she pointed out his errors in front of them all.

"My mother's jewels," he said. His pleasant, almost conversational tone was the one Bianca—his Bia—had learned to fear the most. Bia would not defy him as his father's second wife was daring to do. "Sewn into the hem of your camicia. And you ask how I dare?"

"They are my jewels now!" Cammilla snatched for the necklace. The grand duke held it out of her reach. "Your father gave them to me."

"So you say."

"He wrote it in a letter. I have every right to the jewels, and to everything he gave me. I was his wife, however much you and your brothers and your sister hated me, and I stayed with him when he was sick, fed him with my own hands. I earned it all."

"All?" A new voice, a woman's. Everyone turned. There in the doorway stood the grand duke's sister Isabella, the favorite of their father; with his blessing and complicity she had never gone to live at her husband's dreary castle at Bracciano, but had remained in Florence where she lived in luxurious grandeur among the Medici. She was three years older than Cammilla Martelli, but she had a knack of surrounding herself with such a vivid golden glamour that she made her young stepmother look draggletailed and faded. Crowding into the room behind her were Don Pietro, the youngest of the four living Medici children, and his beautiful young cousin-wife Donna Dianora.

"All?" Isabella demanded again. "What exactly did he give you?"

"Sister." The grand duke's voice was cold. "Our father may have encouraged informality from you, but I do not. When you enter my presence you will make the proper obeisance."

Brother and sister stared at each other. Their eyes were the same, brown and gold flecked with gray; everything else about them was different. Isabella's emotions were there on her face for anyone to read, outrage, hatred, frustration, cunning. Her eyes, this night, were swollen and reddened with tears. The grand duke's face was blank. Only his Bia, and to some extent the foreign alchemist Ruanno dell' Inghilterra, could ever discern his thoughts.

Isabella looked away first. She sank into a deep curtsy, allowing herself the luxury of making it too deep, too mocking. She straightened and said, "Your excellency, the highest and most illustrious grand duke my brother, I present you with my deepest condolences on the death of our beloved father, and my most humble compliments on your own accession to his titles and properties."

The grand duke nodded. For the moment, he thought, I will allow her to believe that I accept her extravagant homage as genuine. He looked to Don Pietro and Donna Dianora. After a moment they made their proper reverences as well.

"Now," the grand duke said, "that we have our own positions properly established, perhaps we should make arrangements for Signora Cammilla."

"I agree, Serenissimo," Isabella said. "Signora Cammilla, what do you mean when you say you have a right to everything our father gave you? What things, exactly?"

"I need not make an account to you," Cammilla said. Her voice shook. So many Medici in one room at the same time were enough to make anyone's voice shake. "I have documents, letters—it is all mine and I will keep it, and I will take you to the courts if you try to take it away from me."

"Fishwife," Isabella said. Scorn shot through and through the single word. "Shrieking of courts. That necklace, Serenissimo. I remember it—it belonged to our mother."

"So it did. I came upon Signora Cammilla sewing it into the hem of her camicia."

Isabella's eyes narrowed. "Stealing it, then."

"I was not stealing it!" Cammilla shook off her woman's supporting arms and stepped forward. She was brave enough, one had to grant her that, and not entirely a fool. She could not curtsy properly, dressed in a half-tied night-gown, but she made an awkward bend of her knees and bob of her head. "It is mine, Serenissimo, the gift of your father."

"And the jewels your woman was cutting off a red skirt, in the other room? Those are yours as well?"

"Yes, Serenissimo."

The grand duke walked over to the open chest, dropped the necklace in, and picked up a casket of carved and polished sandalwood. He put back the lid. Again he was back in his childhood, in his mother's apartments, standing stiffly beside her as old Bronzino painted a portrait of the two of them together. Two strings of enormous pearls she had worn, one with a jewel attached, a large square yellow diamond set in a circle of gold, with a pendant pearl shaped like a teardrop. That same jewel, that same smoky yellow diamond—

He took the pendant out of the casket and held it up.

"And this?" His voice was dangerously soft.

"I will make you a gift of that one, Serenissimo," Cammilla said. Fear made her pale, but she was still defiant. "That one, as a memorial of your mother."

Without any warning the grand duke drew back his right hand and struck Cammilla viciously across the mouth, so hard as to knock her off her feet. Her ladies screamed. One of them attempted to run. Don Pietro caught hold of her arm, grasped her hair with his other hand, and jerked her head around like a farmer killing a chicken. There was an audible cracking sound. The woman dropped like a broken poppet, her eyes staring into nothing.

Isabella and Dianora pressed closer together. Isabella put one arm around her young cousin, as if to protect her.

Don Pietro giggled.

"Want me to kill the rest of them, brother?" he said. "I'd not mind breaking Signora Cammilla's neck for her at all."

"Not at the moment." The grand duke held up his hand. He was still able to control his youngest brother. "Go and fetch a priest for that one. And speaking of priests, where is the cardinal? He returned from Rome to be at our father's bedside, and he is not here."

"He is at the Pitti, praying with the Princess Giovanna," Isabella said. The cardinal was their other living brother, Ferdinando de' Medici, who had been a prince of the church since the age of thirteen. "I should say, her highness the Grand Duchess Giovanna. In their piety, they are consoling each other."

"I am sure they are." Ferdinando, of course, was his heir until Giovanna managed to bear a son. One would think they would be bitter enemies, but they were not; Giovanna was so pious that Ferdinando's red hat dazzled her. "Signora Cammilla, dress yourself properly in your plainest dress. Your woman may help you. I have chosen a place for you to be secluded in your mourning."

"I will not be secluded," she said. There was a bright red mark across her face and a smudge of blood at the corner of her mouth, and her eyes showed white all the way around as they slewed from her stepson to the body of her waiting-woman and back. "I do not care what you call yourself, Francesco, prince or grand duke or master of the world. You are not my master and I will not obey you. This is my home and I will stay here for as long as I choose."

"Signora, the Villa di Castello has belonged to the Medici since the days of Lorenzo il Magnifico. You may have made your home here while my father was alive, but you will do so no longer."

"You think not?" Cammilla began to sob in a frenzy of anger and fear. "I have documents. Not only are the jewels mine, but the Villa di Castello as well. Get out! Get out, all of you! Leave me alone."

The grand duke gestured to his guardsmen. They stepped forward and took Cammilla by her arms. The two ladies remaining, goggle-eyed with terror, did nothing.

"Take her to the Convent of the Santissima Annunziata," the grand duke said. "As she does not choose to change, let her wear her night-gown—the nuns will soon strip her and dress her as a lay sister. She is to be locked in a cell and given nothing but bread and water."

"Santissima Annunziata—" Cammilla began. "No! That is Le Murate, where the nuns are walled in and never let out! I will not go! I have documents—they are in the hands of my *avvocato*, and he will show you, prove to you that the villa and the jewels are mine."

"Take her four remaining women as well, these two and the two in the anteroom. We shall see what they will confess, when they have tasted the walls of Le Murate for a few weeks."

The women went quietly, stepping around the body of their dead companion, shocked into compliance. Cammilla Martelli did not go quietly. She shrieked and struggled with the guardsmen, kicking and scratching and biting, until they were compelled to bind her hands and feet and carry her. As her screams and imprecations faded in the distance, the grand duke casually put the yellow diamond back in the casket and closed the lid.

"The Villa di Castello is to be sealed at once," he said. "Tomorrow I will send my secretaries to take an inventory of the jewels and furnishings."

"What of these documents she claims to have?" Isabella's eyes were sharp and acquisitive; she coveted her mother's jewels.

"I will find out the name of her *avvocato* and my own men of law will take up the matter with him."

Don Pietro came back with a priest. At the sight of the waiting-woman's body, the priest knelt and began to gabble through the prayers of conditional absolution.

"Surely he did not do it," Isabella said. "Our father? He would not have given that woman the Villa di Castello, of all places. He would not have given her our mother's jewels."

"He was a fool for her," the grand duke said, "especially in these last few months. It does not matter. A few weeks in an enclosed nun's cell, fasting and with a daily taste of the whip the nuns use to mortify their flesh, and she will happily sign any new papers I choose to give her."

He walked out of the room, forgetting the jewels and the villa and the men at law between one step and the next. Cammilla Martelli naked on her knees, sobbing, her white back striped with whip marks, that remained in his mind a little longer. Then she vanished too. He thought about his laboratory, his English alchemist and his *soror mystica*, and how they would find the *Lapis Philosophorum* together.

He did not look back to see if the others followed him, but he knew they did.

CHAPTER EIGHT

The silver mine at Bottino, northwest of Florence

TEN DAYS LATER

"So the old tyrant is really dead?"

The mine master's lantern flickered and caught sparks of pure silver. Ruan ran his hand over the vein. He could feel the difference in texture between the ore and the rock that surrounded it. It ran deeper into the tunnel, with smaller veins branching away from the primary, what Agricola—the father, the true metallurgical genius, not the mountebank of a nephew—would have called a *vena dilatata*.

"Grand Duke Cosimo is truly dead," Ruan said. The mine master was a Hungarian named Johan Ziegler. His two sons also worked in the mine, and his wife mended the men's shirts, and his daughters were married to miners. It had been the same in Cornwall—the families in the village had lived and breathed the work of the mine. His memories of Cornwall were terrible, and sometimes he wished he could erase them from his brain, like etching on silver erased by a fresh application of acid. At the same time Cornwall was his home, his native earth, and it lived in his nerves and sinews with the metals he loved.

He traced the vein of silver with his hand again and added, "Prince Francesco is the grand duke now."

"One Medici is the same as another. I suppose this one wants more ore, more silver."

The other men murmured. One of them said, "They always want more."

Ruan smiled, although in the black darkness of the mine no one would see it. Perhaps it was just as well. It pleased him that the miners spoke their true thoughts in his presence, despite the fact that he was the grand duke's *praefectus metallorum* for the mine, his prefect. He carefully balanced his authority and his camaraderie because he admired the miners, their hard work, their straightforward honesty. It was a different world from the world of the court.

"You sent me a message that you had found some crystalline silver," he said to Johan Ziegler. "I would like to see it, and collect a sample."

They continued down the tunnel. The original workings of the mine at Bottino were ancient, a thousand years old and more. Men had been taking silver out of the earth in this spot since the days of King Solomon. This tunnel, though, was new. It was on a deeper level, and instead of ladders, Ruan had directed the installation of a machine with a wheel-and-crank windlass, turned by three men. This not only drew up the ore and any accumulated water, but also controlled a wooden basket that lowered the men to the bottom of the shaft more quickly and with less risk of falling.

"This way," Ziegler said. "The new grand duke, this Francesco, has he a mind to make any changes in the management of the mine?"

"No," Ruan said. He heard the miners behind them let out their breaths with relief. "All of you will continue in your positions, and as always I will speak to the grand duke on your behalf if you have difficulties or special requirements."

They went into another branch of the tunnel. Ruan had to crouch to pass through; only Johan Ziegler went with him. The air was warm and stale. The blowing machine, turned by the wind above and by another windlass on still days, was not powerful enough to force fresh air into the side tunnels.

"There is not enough air for the lantern to last," Ruan said. "How much farther?"

"Here."

The mine master held up the light. It glanced off a formation of dark silvery cubes, half-hidden in a pink and gold vein of calcite.

"What is it, Magister Rohannes?" Piero said. "I haven't seen silver like that before."

"It is a sulphide of silver," Ruan said. He took a small pick from his belt and tapped gently around the silver crystals. They fell into his hand like a cluster of hazelnuts from a tree. He put them into the mine master's bag and extracted more samples, taking also some of the shining calcite that surrounded them.

"A neat touch you've got with that pick," Ziegler said. "Not many great men will come down a shaft and into a tunnel, their ownselves."

"I have had experience," Ruan said. He did not specify what kind of experience, or when it had occurred, or what it had cost him. "Let us go back, before the lantern fails in this air. We must sink a ventilation shaft and install another blowing machine—this vein will be rich."

"Just show us where to dig." The mine master led the way as they crept back to the main tunnel. "One thing in this new grand duke's favor—he has the good sense to keep everything the way it was."

"The mine has been producing a fine yield."

"We dig up more," Ziegler said, "when we have a prefect who is willing to listen to what really goes on underground."

Cosimo de' Medici had built the villa at Seravezza so he had a suitable place to stay when he visited the Bottino mine. It had fortresslike towers at the corners—leave it to old Grand Duke Cosimo, always prepared for attack—and at the same time elegant rooms and fine gardens. A small coterie of servants managed the villa, with help from the village as needed, and they knew Ruan liked to be left to his own devices. He laid out his samples of silver sulphide on a writing-table by one of the large windows, and began to write his notes and make his sketches before the light failed.

Francesco was always more interested in curiosities like the crystalline silver than he was in the specifics of ore composition and new veins. Now that Grand Duke Cosimo was dead, the reports would be different. Prince Francesco had been his father's regent for almost ten years, but the old man had always been in the background, cunning, grasping, countermanding his son's edicts when it pleased him to do so. It was hardly surprising that Francesco had retreated to his laboratory when he could, and to his mistress's house. I might have done the same, Ruan thought. Now he will have less time for the things he truly loves.

Ruan drew the mine's new tunnels from memory, and sketched in the location of the veins. *The silver ore is composed of native silver, antimony and arsenic*, he wrote. His letters were tall and angular, a scholar's letters, and he wrote quickly, confident in his knowledge. *There are extensive crystals of what the miners call black quartz, as well as carnelian and jacinth. These crystals are rarely of gem quality but can be useful in alchemical applications.*

Alchemical applications.

There had been no time for alchemy in the strange combination of chaos and ceremony that had surrounded the old grand duke's death. Ruan wondered what the girl Chiara Nerini thought, having been for all practical purposes abducted, put through the prince's fanciful initiation and then abandoned in Isabella's household to twiddle her thumbs as the wardrobe mistress's assistant. He had made it his business to find her grandmother and make sure she knew the girl was safe. The grandmother had not been pleased to learn that her granddaughter was in Medici hands, and she had not hesitated to tell him so.

He smiled to himself, continuing to write with half his attention. The Nerini blood apparently ran true, in both looks and character. The grandmother had the same changeable eyes as the girl, brown and green and gold. Fifteen-year-old virgin or not, Soror Chiara might turn out to be considerably less docile than Francesco expected. The ceremonial silver sieve, flung at the prince's feet—

There was a scratch at the door, and it opened. The majordomo of the villa stepped in and said, "A messenger to see you, Magister Ruanno."

Ruan put down his pen. "Send him in, Piero," he said.

The man who stepped into the room was short and slight as messengers had to be, to spare their horses. His light brown hair, wind-burned skin and blue eyes could have come only from England, as if his English-style mandilion jacket and canions weren't enough to give him away. No identifying badges, but then the messengers Ruan dealt with rarely cared to advertise their affiliations.

How had he found his way to Seravezza?

"I beg your pardon, Master Ruanno, for interrupting you at your work." The fellow bowed. "I called at the Casino di San Marco in Florence, and was informed of your presence here."

"Indeed," Ruan said. "What is so important that you could not wait for me in Florence? I am to be back in the city before the old grand duke's funeral."

The messenger took a packet of papers out of his jacket. "I have a letter from Dr. John Dee in London, which he has charged me with delivering in all possible haste. Dr. Dee told me that there would be a reply, and that I am to return with it to London as quickly as possible."

That meant Dee wanted gold. Being the English queen's advisor on occult and scientific matters was all well and good, but it paid little. And living at the English court was an expensive business.

"I will read the letter," Ruan said. "You may go to the kitchen and refresh yourself. I will send for you when I have prepared my answer."

The messenger placed the packet on the table, bowed again and went away. Ruan broke the seals on the packet and unfolded the letter.

It was, as he had expected, a demand for gold, couched in elaborate terms. It promised the support of Baron Burghley and the Earl of Leicester, as well as the queen's absolute personal favor, in return. Influence at the court of Elizabeth Tudor did not come cheaply. Secrecy was even more expensive.

Ruan prepared a fresh sheet of paper and wrote out a draft on his holding at the bank of the Borromei in Florence in the amount of two hundred gold scudi, which Dr. Dee could present to the branch the Borromei maintained in London. Then he wrote a short letter to accompany it, promising more when there was further news of the queen's support.

Which meant he would have to obtain more. There was never enough gold.

His thoughts circled back to alchemy.

He did not really believe there was such a thing as the *Lapis Philosophorum*, at least not in the magical sense Grand Duke Francesco believed. However, he had seen elements combined, and in the course of the combination become something entirely different. Who would have believed such a metal as bronze to exist, until by accident some man had melted together copper and tin? Who would have known that crystals of silver contained silver and sulphur, until some alchemist had separated them into their component parts with strong acid? While playing at alchemy with the grand duke, who knew what new combinations or separations he might discover, and which ones might result in new, pure gold?

The grand duke believed in the *Lapis Philosophorum*, for its own sake— for the power it would bring him. The girl, Chiara Nerini, believed in it too, for its healing powers. Well, perhaps there was some substance to be discovered that would heal her. He would play his part with the two of them, and the gold that would go into his account at the bank of the Borromei would be gold that already existed, from the grand duke's inexhaustible coffers.

He folded the bank draft and the letter together and sealed the packet with black wax. Into the wax he pressed his personal seal, a design combining a circular labyrinth, a crescent moon and a red-billed sea-crow, the heraldic bird of Cornwall. No one but he himself knew what it really meant.

The messenger could ride for the coast tomorrow, straight from Seravezza, he thought as he went out into the corridor, and then travel down to the port at Livorno. He would finish his reports tonight, and in the morning ride for Florence. There was the old grand duke's funeral to get through first. Then there would be alchemy again.

He needed the gold—that was true as far as it went. But there was another reason, a greater reason, a reason he had never told anyone. He performed his experiments with metals and crystals, stones and acids, alkalis and earths and volatile salts, because he loved them. He loved the fact that they came out of the mysterious depths of the earth. They were ancient and elemental, and yet in his hands they could be changed.

Changed, as he had changed himself, once, twice, three times. And as he meant to change himself one last time, in the end.

CHAPTER NINE

The Palazzo Vecchio, Florence

17 MAY 1574

Babbo would've reveled in Cosimo de' Medici's funeral. Chiara could hear her father's scornful voice. *Drape your coffin in as much black silk as you want, old man, and blazon your Medici balls for the world to see, you're still food for worms like all the rest of us.* Of course, she could also hear him shouting at her. *What are you doing in the Palazzo Vecchio, girl, rubbing shoulders with the likes of grand duchesses and duchesses and princesses? Get home with you, before I give you such a thrashing you won't sit down for a week.*

I'll show you, Babbo, she flung back at him. You won't shout at me anymore when I have the Philosopher's Stone in my hands.

She would've gone home if she'd been allowed to, but she was watched every second. She demanded to speak with the prince—the grand duke now, and never forget it—but he was suddenly so far above her he might as well have been in faraway Trebizond where they made athanors. She demanded to speak with Magister Ruanno. He'd helped her, after all. He'd treated her as if she was special, or at least useful. Donna Jimena told her a thousand—well, maybe ten—more stupid rules of court etiquette and gave her extra sewing to do. The only breath of a hint that she might someday actually act as the grand duke's *soror mystica* was the moonstone around her neck, and the lessons—hard ones, every day, reading and writing, most of it in Italian but some of it in Latin.

No lessons or sewing today, though. Today was the great funeral, a month after Cosimo de' Medici's death, the delay necessary so important people—princes and archdukes and ambassadors and papal envoys and the saints only knew who else—could make their way to Florence from all over Europe. The embalmers had been beside themselves, and rightly so. While carrying messages back and forth between Donna Isabella and Grand Duke Francesco's secretaries, Chiara had seen the black taffeta fly-swatters especially made for the occasion being put to vigorous use.

However many important men there might be following the old grand duke's catafalque to the cathedral, there'd be no women. Women weren't allowed to take part in public funeral ceremonies; Chiara herself and Nonna and her sisters had stayed home from the guild's rites for Babbo. Rich and powerful as they were, the Medici women were bound by the same custom. They could do nothing more than watch the formation of the funeral procession from the second floor of the Palazzo Vecchio.

There were two windows set close together in the fine decorated chamber. At one of them Giovanna of Austria, now the grand duchess and first lady of the court, stood in solitary hauteur, with two of her small parti-colored hounds at her feet. They were the sire and dam to Donna Isabella's Rina, Chiara had learned, and had been sent to the grand duchess some years ago by her sister Barbara, the Duchess of Ferrara. The Duke of Ferrara had hated Duke Cosimo, everyone knew that, and had vied furiously with him for *precedenza* and the title of grand duke, but even so the Ferrarese ambassador would be following in the funeral train, weeping large crocodile tears.

The grand duchess's face was like stone. She was a small, thin woman with a crooked back she disguised with steel corsets and padded dresses; her features were plain but her eyes could be luminously kind if you looked past the piety, the homesickness and that bred-in-the-bone Austrian pride. At the other window, not six steps away but in what might have been a different world, Isabella de' Medici wept with stormy disregard for any such thing as decorum. Her sister-in-law and cousin Donna Dianora— *damned Medici*, Babbo grumbled in Chiara's head, *marrying their own cousins. No wonder they're all mad as foaming dogs*—embraced her and plied her with silk handkerchiefs. Behind them clustered half-a-dozen ladies of honor; Chiara had managed to work her way forward until she stood just behind Donna Isabella.

"What will I do?" Donna Isabella wept. "What will my poor children do? My brother hates me, he lies to me, he has thwarted me at every turn. I cannot bear the thought of living with my husband—this is my home, here, Florence, and I will never, never leave it for that terrible old pile of rock at Bracciano."

Donna Isabella's husband, Chiara had learned, was Don Paolo Giordano Orsini, the Duke of Bracciano. A fine name and a fine title, but not so fine a man. He was hugely fat, too fat for any horse to carry him, and so he rode in litters like a woman. Somehow that didn't keep him from getting into fights over whores and spending Medici gold as if it were water. If I were married to him, Chiara thought, I wouldn't want to live with him either. Poor Donna Isabella.

"You need not leave Florence," Donna Dianora said. "You have the Palazzo Medici, and the villa at Baroncelli. Your father has left you an income of your own, and also provided a rich dowry for your daughter—he promised it, you know that."

"Promised it!" Isabella burst out with fresh tears. "Promised, yes, but did he write it down? Did he put his will into the hands of his notaries and his men of law? No! Nothing is written, so it is all up to Francesco now—will he do as our father wished, or not?"

"Surely he will."

"If he does not give everything to his Venetian mistress. He has already given her our mother's jewels, the ones he took from Signora Cammilla before he locked her up at Le Murate."

"But Donna Bianca is your friend, is she not? After all, you arranged the death of her husband, and sheltered—"

"Shhh." Donna Isabella looked around uneasily. Chiara looked up at the paintings on the ceiling—a beautiful woman kneeling at the feet of a fellow who looked like a king—and pretended she had not been listening. Donna Isabella, with her angel's face—she had arranged a murder?

"Of course I arranged it," Isabella was whispering. "And I have her letters, proving she was part of the plan. She will be my friend in this business of my father's will, or I will make them public."

"It would serve her right if you did. Orazio says—"

"Orazio, Orazio. I am tired of hearing about Orazio. You and your lovers are dabbling in treason, Dianorina, and everyone knows it."

One of the ladies of honor passed cups of wine and a tray of sweet cakes from the sideboard. Chiara wanted a taste of the wine and one of the little cakes, made with fine white flour and spices, baked golden and glittering with grated crystals of sugar. She wanted to see what was happening in the courtyard. If I was free, she thought, I could go to the Piazza della Signoria whenever I wanted to, and see the procession, and maybe even steal a cake from the baker's stall. If I was free—

She edged closer. There was a tiny space at the edge of Donna Isabella's window, and slim as she was, she might fit into it.

If you were free, whispered the demons inside her head, *you'd be dirty and hungry and dressed in your old camicia and gown. How quickly you've forgotten what life was like before you went out in the rain to sell the silver funnel to the prince.*

For once the demons were right. If she was free, she wouldn't have washed herself this morning in warm water scented with lavender oil, or combed her hair with an ivory comb and braided it with black velvet ribbons in the old grand duke's honor. She wouldn't be wearing a new black overgown with crystals sewn on the matching sleeves, and wouldn't have heard Mass in Donna Isabella's private chapel, with a jeweled chalice and paintings of the three Magi on the wall. So no, she didn't really want to be *free* free. She just wanted to see what all the fine ladies were seeing, and pretend to herself she was one of them. Even if they did have awful husbands.

Donna Isabella cried out with fresh anguish; everyone in the room jumped. The lady with the cakes dropped the plate, or had it knocked out of her hands. The other ladies all cried out and clustered around, picking up cakes and trying to soothe their mistress, and Chiara took advantage of the confusion to slip into the space at the side of the window.

In the courtyard below, on the black-draped catafalque, lay the old grand duke's body—but of course it couldn't be his body, not really, not after a month—the grand duke's effigy, then, its face and hands sculpted of wax colored and painted so it was startlingly lifelike. No wonder Donna Isabella had screamed. The grand ducal crown with its jeweled red lily was on his head. Grooms in the Medici colors held the reins of six enormous horses, all caparisoned and plumed in black velvet—yes, Isabella had talked about that as she talked about everything, resenting the expense, the grand duke's six favorite mounts trapped with funereal garb richer than what she herself had received. They would be led, riderless, in the procession. Chiara wondered what would happen to them afterward.

She felt a tug at her skirt, and looked down. One of the grand duchess's little hounds had found a lost cake on the floor, and was about to swallow it. Without thinking Chiara bent down and retrieved the cake—the sugar and the spices might make the dog sick. He looked up at her with woeful dark eyes.

"Rostig."

The dog turned its head, and with a longing look at the half-crumbled cake, reluctantly returned to its mistress.

"I thank you, signorina," the grand duchess said, her Italian serviceable but heavily accented. "Too much *zucker*, sugar, it is not good for them."

Chiara gathered up her skirts and bent her knees in the best curtsy she could manage. Donna Jimena had despaired of her ever learning it properly. Babbo would call it truckling and groveling. "I'm honored to serve you, Serenissima," she said. "I often look after Donna Isabella's little Rina."

The grand duchess lifted her hand and gestured: *Come closer.* No one else was paying any attention—the serving women were fetching more cakes and wine, Donna Isabella was still crying and Donna Dianora was still handing her handkerchiefs. Chiara stepped from the one window to the other.

"This is Rostig," the grand duchess said. Her affection for the little dogs made her plain face more attractive. "Rust-red, in your language, for the color of his head and ears. His mate is Seiden, silky one."

Chiara made a small mock-curtsy to the dogs. "They are very handsome, Serenissima."

"You are the alchemist's daughter, are you not?" the grand duchess said. "The vowed virgin who is to assist my husband in his alchemical experiments?"

Chiara was surprised. "Yes, Serenissima."

"You wonder how I know? The priest at the Cathedral of San Stefano in Prato told me he allowed my husband to have the Sacra Cintola for a night. What better relic upon which to swear a vow of virginity?"

Chiara didn't know what to say, so she said nothing.

"Will you keep it? Your vow?"

"Yes, Serenissima. For as long as I am in the grand duke's service."

The grand duchess did not actually smile, but her eyes crinkled with a trace of humor. She had the protruding Habsburg chin and jaw and she would never be called pretty, but when her eyes warmed like that she looked—pleasant, at least, in a melancholy way. "So you think of running away."

"No, Serenissima," Chiara said. "Of course not."

"If the grand duke wishes to have you in his service, he will not give the opportunity. You are watched?"

"Yes, Serenissima."

"Have you performed any alchemy yet?"

Chiara shifted uneasily. Why was the grand duchess questioning her, showing interest in her? *The prince wishes you to be vowed as a virgin, with all the rituals of magic he loves so dearly, to satisfy his wife and his mistress,* Magister Ruanno had said. Was the grand duchess jealous? How could that possibly be?

"No, Serenissima. So far all I have done is read and study."

"Take care for your immortal soul," the grand duchess said. "There is magic connected with alchemy, evil magic."

"Yes, Serenissima."

The grand duchess gazed out the window again. Chiara looked, too, pleased to have a space where she could see everything. The grand duke had come out into the courtyard, wearing a black robe with a pointed hood. A mourning robe, certainly, or at least that was what people would think—but Chiara recognized it. It was his alchemical cassock. His brother Don Pietro and his brother-in-law, Donna Isabella's husband Don Paolo Giordano Orsini, stepped to his side, wearing similar black habits. Don Paolo's might have made a shop awning all by itself, with plenty left over for kitchen curtains and a few dishrags. The grand duke's second brother, Cardinal Ferdinando, wore his formal scarlet vestments, as did the papal nuncio. The catafalque was lifted, the trumpets sounded and the procession began.

"He was a sinful man," the grand duchess said. "A slave to the flesh, as are all the Medici. But he was kind to me at first. See the frescos in the courtyard, behind the columns? They are scenes from the places where I grew up, in Austria. He had them painted especially for me, when I first came to Florence—he knew how homesick I was."

So, Chiara thought, he did one good thing. One less day in Purgatory.

"Later, though—later he was no longer kind. He allowed—that woman, the Venetian—to flaunt herself at court, pretending that she was not—my husband's mistress. I withdrew, because I could not possibly meet her. People said I was haughty and cold because I was Austrian, but it was just—I could not possibly come face-to-face with her, speak to her."

She sounded deathly sad. And yet she was quiet and self-contained. At the other window, Isabella flung herself against the panes of glass, sobbing wildly with no thought of her place or position. Donna Dianora also pressed close to the window, although she was not crying.

As the procession passed out of the courtyard, through the *cancello*, Grand Duke Francesco did not look up. Don Pietro and Don Paolo did not look up. Cardinal Ferdinando, however, lifted his head and looked at the windows. At them all? No, just at one of them—the grand duchess. He raised his hand and traced a small cross in the air, a blessing. The grand duchess made the sign of the cross over her own breast in return. Chiara felt the connection between them, a connection not of the flesh but of the soul. If Cardinal Ferdinando was truly a devout man, it was not surprising that he admired his sister-in-law.

The moment passed. A few steps behind the princes, Chiara saw another figure in black robes. She could not see the man's face but recognized the height and the shape of the shoulders—it was Magister Ruanno dell' Inghilterra. He also looked up, and for a moment she thought he was looking at her. She felt the heat of a flush in her cheeks, and began to lift her hand in response. Then she realized he was looking at the other window.

And at the other window, Donna Isabella pressed her open palm against the glass.

CHAPTER TEN

The old grand duke had been moldering in his tomb for a month. Grand Duke Francesco had fulfilled some of his father's wishes and put others—many others—aside while he spent half his time closeted in his laboratory with his foreign alchemist and the other half at the palazzo on the Via Maggio with his mistress Donna Bianca. Had he included Chiara in his alchemical works? Oh, no. She'd remained shut up in Donna Isabella's household at the Palazzo Medici, which meant she'd remained Donna Jimena's seam-sewer and errand-runner. Lots of good food and pretty clothes, lots of secrets and whispers and plots, lots of bewilderingly explicit talk about lovers and pleasures, but no alchemy, not unless you counted the endless reading, writing and Latin lessons.

Had they forgotten her, the grand duke and Magister Ruanno, her initiation and her vow? Had they forgotten her father's treasures? Had it all been nothing more than an amusement for them? The comforts and excitements of the court were alluring and seductive, yes, but the headaches remained. The voices remained. Twice Chiara had falling-spells, fortunately when she was alone so no one at the court knew about them yet. Where was her chance to be a *soror mystica*, to learn and practice the art of alchemy in her own right, so she could put her hands on the *Lapis Philosophorum* and cure herself?

Donna Isabella had her own difficulties, which mostly seemed to be about money, her children and her absent lover. He was Don Troilo Orsini, some sort of connection to her horrible husband, a cousin, maybe. Poor Donna Isabella raged and wept and wrote letters, some of them cold and logical, some of them tear-smudged and full of such lust they might have been written by a courtesan. Beautiful, scintillating Donna Isabella, the shining star of the house of Medici, the first lady of Florence—that was what everybody said about her, but in private she ate too much and suffered bilious spells, fretted over feeling ugly and old while her lover disported himself in Naples, and left the covers off her chamber pots. How Nonna would have scolded her for that!

Donna Dianora visited Donna Isabella almost every day. She was the closest to Chiara in age—only a few years older—so beautiful and so unhappy. She had lovers, too. In fact, there was so much talk about lovers that Chiara found herself dreaming of men some nights, faceless men who stroked her face and hair, kissed her breasts, whispered love words to her. In one dream the man wasn't faceless, but looked down at her with the English alchemist's strange, sad dark eyes. The pleasure he gave her made her gasp for breath. Then in the eerie way of dreams he was suddenly behind her, and he put his arm around her throat and squeezed.

Donna Isabella and Donna Dianora sometimes pleasured each other in the long summer afternoons, whispering and moaning together. Chiara wasn't allowed to see what they were doing. The sounds of their delight made her want to try self-pleasuring for herself, but she was afraid to ask how it was done. And if Nonna ever found out, she'd switch her half to death for such sinfulness.

She tried to run away once, and ended up locked in a closet on bread and water for three days as a punishment. She didn't try that again. But today, today, Monday the sunny twenty-first day of June, for the first time since that rainy morning in April, it had been officially arranged and she was going home.

Home—oh, home!

"Donna Jimena," she said, "do we have everything? The new summer mantle for Nonna? The camicias and skirts and sleeves for Lucia and Mattea? Oh, and the chopines? Particularly the chopines, a brand-new pair for each one of them."

"My dear, they have already been sent more new clothes than they can wear in five years. I have seen to it myself."

"What about the money? I had two little bags of silver *lire* for the girls, and a purse of gold *quattrini* for Nonna."

"They have been sent money."

"But I want to give them more, with my own hands. I want to show Nonna that it's not all a bad thing, me being here at the court."

Donna Jimena laughed. "Why would she think it is a bad thing?"

"They were always supporters of the old republic, the Nerini. My father hated the Medici, and Nonna is his mother—he learned it at her knee."

"Best to say as little as possible about that." Donna Jimena collected the two small bags of silver pennies and the fat embroidered purse of gold and put them into the leather trunk where all the other gifts were packed. "There are enough plots against the Medici as it is. And while I am speaking of plots, you have become much too friendly with Donna Dianora. Whispering in corners like children."

"But I like Dianora. She's young, and clever and so beautiful."

"Donna Dianora to you, young lady."

"She and Donna Isabella give pleasure to each other sometimes," Chiara went on. It excited her to know such a passionate secret. "I hear them—"

"*Por Dios*, will you be silent? You cannot say such things in the Palazzo Medici—there are ears everywhere, do you understand?"

"I don't care if they hear."

"You will care if I take my switch to you. Now, let us be off. You carry the trunk. You have younger and stronger legs than I."

The trunk was easy to carry. Chiara danced beside Donna Jimena as they made their way down the stairway and toward the courtyard. She didn't feel like a grown-up *soror mystica* today, and the moonstone was carefully hidden under her neat and snowy-white new camicia. Her head was clear, for once. The voices were silent. She felt like—well, like a fifteen-year-old girl going home for the first time in two and a half months. Going home after becoming rich, successful, friendly with duchesses and great ladies, illustrious beyond anyone in her family's wildest dreams—and in her truest heart half-afraid to own it, because to her family it was the blackest betrayal.

There was a horse in the courtyard, a big red horse—it looked familiar. A long whip was coiled and strapped to the horse's saddle. Chiara stopped midstep and said, "We're not going to ride horses, are we?"

"No." Magister Ruanno's voice, from behind a sedan chair, made her jump. She had learned, among all the other things she had learned, that his full name was Ruanno dell' Inghilterra, which really just meant Ruanno of England, and so probably wasn't his real name. In Latin he wrote it *Roannes Pencarianus*. What the *Pencarianus* meant, she didn't know and no one would say.

"You and Donna Jimena will ride in this sedan chair," he said. "I will ride Lowarn, and carry your trunk of gifts. If you will permit me?"

She handed the trunk over to him and he turned to strap it behind Lowarn's saddle.

"Where have you been all this time?" Chiara put out her kitchen-knife chin at him. He wasn't so mysterious or frightening anymore, not after she'd seen him look up at Donna Isabella, the morning of the old grand duke's funeral. He was a man like other men, with a man's lusts. She had even dreamed—but she wouldn't think about that. "Why haven't you sent for me, you and the grand duke?"

"So many questions." From his expression he might have been reproving a wayward child, not an illustrious young lady. "I have been occupied with my own affairs, Monella Chiara, and my own service to the grand duke. I assure you he will call for you when it pleases him to do so."

"Don't call me that."

He smiled. "But it suits you so well."

"He's set you to guard me, hasn't he?"

"Not at all. I am coming with you to assess your father's alchemical equipment, and determine the prices the grand duke will pay."

"And if I decide I don't want to come back?"

Donna Jimena made a disapproving tsk-tsk sound with her tongue. Magister Ruanno only laughed.

"That is the responsibility of these fine fellows," he said. At his gesture, four stout guardsmen in Medici colors came into the courtyard and took their places beside the poles of the sedan chair, two in the front and two in the back. "You will come back, Monella Chiara, whether you wish to or not. Now in you get."

Donna Jimena stepped into the sedan chair's compartment first, and made room for Chiara to sit beside her. Chiara hesitated, thinking about refusing to go just for the sake of not doing what Magister Ruanno had told her to do. On the other hand, Nonna liked to say *you're stubborn as a goat, girl, and too quick to cut off your nose to spite your face.* Oh, how she longed to see Nonna and Mattea and Lucia.

With poor grace she clambered into the sedan chair. It had the crest of Grand Duke Francesco, with its six Medici balls, painted on its side. Magister Ruanno spoke to the guardsmen. The chair tilted a little as they lifted it, then moved forward. Lowarn's hooves struck the stones of the courtyard as he followed behind.

"Now listen to me, Chiara," Donna Jimena said. "You are to say nothing to your Nonna or your sisters about this *soror mystica* business. You may say that you sold the grand duke the silver descensory, and that he is interested in your father's other equipment, and that out of Christian kindness he offered you a place in Donna Isabella's household. But that is all."

"I wasn't going to say anything."

Donna Jimena nodded briskly, although the glint in her eyes showed she knew Chiara was lying. She was no one's fool, Donna Jimena, at least not on any subject but her beloved Donna Isabella. She and Nonna would either take to each other like long-lost sisters or hate each other like two scorpions.

"See that you don't. Magister Ruanno is here to do more than just assess your father's equipment, you know. He is watching you, and he will report back to the grand duke. Your behavior today will determine whether or not you are allowed to visit your family more often."

Chiara said nothing. The guardsmen were walking briskly and the sedan chair was bouncing up and down. The movement made her feel sick. Or maybe it was the uneasiness of returning home wearing a leaf-green skirt and bodice of *mezzani* silk that had been made just for her and never once re-cut or re-trimmed or turned inside-out for freshening. Compared to anything Donna Isabella wore, or Donna Dianora, or even Donna Jimena, it was all very plain and serviceable; *mezzani* was the cheapest of the silks, but even so it was silk, and the skirt and bodice were new. Her camicia was new as well, her hair was braided with yellow silk ribbons and fastened with silver pins, and her green leather slippers were as soft as peach skins.

The sedan chair stopped. Chiara heard a child's voice shrieking. She looked at Donna Jimena; Donna Jimena nodded and gave her a firm little push. She stepped out of the sedan chair into the street.

"Chichi!" Mattea cried. She was only nine. She had a new smock, rosy pink, with a ruffle around the neckline. "You've come home!"

Lucia, who was twelve and so much like Nonna that she might as well have been fifty-and-twelve, stood to one side with a scowl on her face. She also wore a new dress, although hers was plain, a bright orange color like apricot jam. "You've been away long enough," she said. "I've had to do all your work."

And then Nonna herself came to the door of the shop. She wore the same severe black widow's habit she'd worn for as long as Chiara could remember, with an unbleached linen wimple and a black veil like a nun. Her face was wrinkled as a walnut shell, but her eyes were hard and bright and aware, the eyes of a young woman, a revolutionary. Which she had been, fifty years ago in the days of the third republic. They were changeable eyes, brown to green to gold, set deeply under slanting brows. All her life people had told Chiara she had eyes just like her Nonna's.

Suddenly she felt shoddy and dishonest in her silk gown. Tears—tears? Why tears?—made a swelling in her throat. She swallowed, straightened her back and lifted her chin.

"Hello, Nonna," she said. "I've come home."

"With the balls of the Medici behind you." Nonna glanced over Chiara's shoulder at the crest on the sedan chair, at the guardsmen in the Medici colors, at Magister Ruanno on his big red horse. "They've fattened you up—does the grand duke not like his bedmates with their ribs sticking out and their chins as sharp as a kitchen-knife? *Puttana*—you're no granddaughter of mine."

She turned and went back into the shop and closed the door.

Chiara felt hot blood rush up into her face. Mattea started to cry and Lucia turned to comfort her. Magister Ruanno had swung down from Lowarn and stepped forward, but blindly Chiara put out one arm to stop him. She walked to the door herself, threw it open so hard it banged against the wall, and went inside.

Nonna had gone to the back, where the books for sale and the bookbinding materials were kept. There were more books than there had been. The stock had been replenished then, and how else but with Medici gold?

"I'm not a whore," Chiara said. Anger made her voice hoarse. She kept her eyes narrowed so the tears wouldn't come out. "The grand duke hasn't touched me. The man outside hasn't touched me. No man has touched me."

"There's more than one way to be a whore." Nonna would not look at her.

"Because I took gold from the Medici, for Babbo's silver funnel? You've used the gold I sent you—there are more books to sell, and the girls have new dresses. Look, that window was broken." She gestured. "Now it's mended, with new glass."

Nonna looked up. Her mouth worked. "They were hungry," she said. "They were in rags. You were in rags, Chiara, and now you have a silk dress, like a *concubina*."

"But I'm not a *concubina*. I swear it, Nonna, by the Sacra Cintola of the Holy Virgin."

"What do you know of the Sacra Cintola?"

You are to say nothing to your Nonna or your sisters about this soror mystica *business.*

"I know. I've learned things. I'm even learning to read."

"Decent girls have no need for reading."

"All the ladies of the court read."

Nonna made a disrespectful gesture and spat on the floor. Clearly she didn't think much of the ladies of the court.

"Nonna, I know Babbo hated the Medici." Chiara stepped closer. "I know you hate them. I know you're probably up to your neck in all the republican plots. But the grand duke paid a gold scudo for that old silver funnel—it's called a descensory, did you know that? I knew Lucia and Mattea were hungry, and you were hungry too. I had to sell it to him. I had to try."

Nonna's expression softened. That made it so much harder to keep from crying.

"The grand duke ordered his sister Donna Isabella to make a place for me," Chiara went on, talking fast, "because he wants to buy more of Babbo's equipment, not for any other reason."

"She has lovers. Everyone knows it. She won't go to Bracciano and live with her husband, like a proper wife should."

"I know, Nonna, but that lady in the sedan chair with me? She's Donna Jimena Osorio—she's a cousin or something to the old grand duchess, the grand duke's mother, and she's like a mother, almost, to Donna Isabella. She watches over me. The old grand duchess was strict, and Donna Jimena is strict, too."

"And what about the man riding with you?"

"He thinks I'm just a child. He calls me a street urchin. His name is Magister Ruanno dell' Inghilterra, and he's the grand duke's—well, his friend, his favored alchemist and metallurgist. If he's anybody's lover, he's Donna Isabella's, not mine."

Nonna pursed up her mouth as if she was going to spit again. "Medici," she said. "Whores, the lot of them, women and men. And the court is a cesspool. You can't swim in filth without some of it sticking to you."

"It won't, I swear. The Grand Duchess Giovanna, she's good. She loves her daughters. She has little dogs, and she loves them too. She's devout and proud and so sad—she's homesick and hates that the grand duke has that Venetian mistress—"

Chiara ran out of breath. She held out her hands to Nonna, pleading.

"It was that English alchemist who sent the messenger," Nonna said. She ran her hands over the leather bindings of the new books. She had always loved fine books. She wouldn't have minded being rich, Nonna wouldn't, if it had been in a republican Florence. "I never met him so I didn't know what he looked like, but the messenger said his name, Ruanno dell' Inghilterra. It was the day after you disappeared. Since then there've been messengers half a dozen times, with money and clothes and food. I wanted to throw it all out in the gutters but the little ones cried. Mattea cried, so much."

"It was for the silver descensory, Nonna, nothing more."

"I don't believe that for a minute, *nipotina*. There's something you're not telling me."

Nipotina. Little granddaughter. The pet name Nonna had always called her.

Chiara gave up and started to cry. At the same time Nonna held out her arms, and she ran into them.

"Nonna. Oh, Nonna."

"Shhh. *Mia nipotina*. It's all right, it doesn't matter. If the damned Medici want to give us their gold, we'll take it. We'll use it against them, if we can. I was so afraid for you when you didn't come home—the messenger, I was glad to see him, even in his Medici colors."

"They wouldn't let me come until now. They thought I'd run away. As if I'd ever leave Florence, ever in my life."

Nonna caught hold of her upper arms and pushed her back. She swept her sharp eyes over the green silk dress and yellow ribbons. "You could hide from them, even here in the city. I know ways."

"Nonna— No. It's not the clothes or the fine food or the palaces or the duchesses and princesses, truly it's not." Well, maybe it was, just a little, but she wouldn't tell Nonna that. "There's—there's something the grand duke can do—some way—it might be able to cure my head, Nonna, my headaches and the voices. It might be able to make me *right* again."

"Something to do with his alchemy, I'll wager—the Stone of the Philosophers, perhaps? Don't look at me like that, girl, everyone knows the grand duke's crazy for alchemy, and every alchemist dreams of creating the Stone, and why? Because it turns base metals into gold, yes, but it also cures all illnesses, and makes you live forever, and lets you talk to the dead. That's what your Babbo was trying to do when he blew himself to pieces— make the Stone of the Philosophers, so he could call up the spirits of Gian and your mother and tell them he loved them, one last time."

"Oh, Nonna. I'm so sorry."

"Never mind. They're dead and gone, all of them. And whatever your Babbo thought, whatever the Medici grand duke may think, there's no such thing as the Stone of the Philosophers. It's against the will of God."

"I don't know. Maybe it is." There was no point in arguing, because when Nonna talked about the will of God, she never changed her mind. "Nonna, I've brought some gifts for you and Lucia and Mattea. Let's bring them into the shop, and then Magister Ruanno and I can go down into the cellar and look at what's left of Babbo's equipment."

"We might as well sell it to him, for as much as we can get. If we don't, they'll just take it without giving us the money. So you're going to go back? Live in the palazzo with your fine new friends, and kiss the grand duke's *culo* in hopes his alchemy will cure you of your headaches and demons' voices?"

"I have to, Nonna. I have to try. I'm having falling-spells, too. I'm afraid all the bad things in my head will kill me one day."

Nonna crossed herself. "I'll pray for you. Now invite your foreigner friend in to see your Babbo's things. I'll pour some almond milk and cut up a *schiacciata* for Donna Jimena."

Chiara stared at her. Almond milk and *schiacciata*?

Nonna laughed. "Oh, yes," she said. Her voice was both affectionate and bitter. "Almond milk and *schiacciata*. We've come up in the world, *mia nipotina*, since you've become a plaything of the Medici."

CHAPTER ELEVEN

"Be careful," Chiara said. "The fire damaged the stairway. Step here, along the wall."

Magister Ruanno followed her down the worn wooden steps, walled in with stone on either side. When they reached the bottom, he held the lantern high, then said some words under his breath, in the language he seemed to use only to swear with. "Do you have any idea what you have here?"

"I know my father never told me where it came from." Chiara stepped onto the packed dirt floor. The cellar had originally been a storage space for vegetables, sacks of flour and bottles of wine, pots of ink and bales of paper and leather. Babbo had cleaned and enlarged the space and moved all the stored goods to the kitchen directly above the cellar, much to Nonna's housewifely outrage. He had also constructed a separate, secret entrance, a tunnel that ran under the tiny back courtyard. Chiara was careful not to look at the wooden hatchway under the table. It didn't really look like a hatchway, anyway, just a pile of wood.

Magister Ruanno hung the lantern from a hook and lay one scarred hand lightly upon the double pelican apparatus. Its two crystal necks glimmered in the fitful light, and its gold fittings shone. "This is worth a fortune," he said. "Not so much for its materials, although they are rich enough, but for its design. I cannot imagine how a bookseller obtained such a thing."

"You're not a very good bargainer, to tell me openly it's worth so much."

He smiled. His face did change when he smiled, not the wolf-smile but the rare true smile. Even the dark sadness of his eyes lightened a little. "It is not my money," he said. "The grand duke can afford to pay you a fortune, and so he shall. Do you think your father stole the double pelican? If so, we must find out who originally possessed it."

"Babbo wasn't a thief. The only thing he ever said about his alchemy was that his greatest enemy was his greatest ally. And then he'd laugh. I always thought he meant the devil."

"Perhaps he did. How much was lost in the fire?"

"Most of it. Just the pelican is left, and the alembic—see? It's green glass, in the shape of a crescent moon. There's an athanor, too, that Babbo always said came from Trebizond. Wherever that is."

"It was a Byzantine state on the shore of the Black Sea, the western terminus of the Silk Road." Magister Ruanno examined the athanor closely as he spoke. Of course he'd know. He'd probably been there. "This could indeed be Trapezuntine work. Tell me more about your father, Monella Chiara. I am surprised the grand duke did not know of his work, given the grand duke's own great interest in alchemy."

"I'll tell you whatever you want to know, if you'll stop calling me that."

He glanced over at her. No smile this time. He looked as if he was actually seeing her for the first time since the morning of her initiation. "You are no longer a street urchin, are you?"

"I never was. I may have been poor and ragged, but the Nerini are respectable members of the booksellers' Arte in Florence, and have been for generations."

"Donna Chiara, then." His eyes glinted in the lantern's flickering light.

"Call me that in front of Nonna and she'll knock out a few of your teeth with her broom. The Nerini are for the republic and always have been."

"I am only teasing you. Tell me about your respectable republic-supporting father, Mona Chiara."

She looked down at the green glass of the crescent-moon alembic. It had always been her favorite piece. "The accident, that's where it started. Although it wasn't really an accident. My brother Gian and I were playing in the street outside the shop and two noblemen on horseback rode us down. They didn't try to stop. The children of a shopkeeper—it just didn't matter to them."

"Your brother—" She could see him counting her family in his head, Nonna, Lucia, Mattea. "Your brother was killed, then."

"Yes. His face and head were crushed, and his back broken."

Neither one of them said anything for a moment. Magister Ruanno lifted the top off the athanor and looked inside. Then he put the top in place again and said, "And you were hurt as well."

It didn't seem to be a question. How much did he know? Had he been asking questions about her?

"One of the horses kicked me. Here, on the side of my head."

She put one hand up over the mark. Her hair felt thick and soft. Washing it with Donna Jimena's lotion of vinegar, rosemary water, sweet oil, mint and thyme had made it stronger and more lustrous; the hair growing over the crescent scar was coarser, and had glints of silver she had never seen before. Of course, she had never had a mirror of her own.

"The headaches you mentioned the night before your initiation—are they a result of the injury?"

"Yes. And sometimes I have falling-spells." The demons' voices, that wasn't something she wanted to tell him. Not yet, anyway.

He picked up some broken pieces of glass from the table and idly tried to piece them together. "And you design to heal yourself with the *Lapis Philosophorum*."

"That's one reason."

"So what did your father do, after your brother was killed? Where was your mother?" He brushed the broken pieces from the table; whatever they had been was lost forever.

"My mother—my mother was with child when it happened. She miscarried and died. She loved Gian so much, I don't think she cared about living anymore. He was the heir. The only boy. When she died and her baby died, there was no heir left."

"You and your sisters—surely you could marry, bring sons-in-law into the business."

"That's what Nonna said. Nonna's practical. But my father, he was so angry, so lost—all he cared about was finding Gian and my mother again."

Chiara shivered. Even in the summer, the cellar could be cold.

"Necromancy, then," Magister Ruanno said quietly. It was frightening, a little, how quickly he understood things. "He hoped to create the *Lapis Philosophorum*, and use it for necromancy—raising the dead."

"Yes."

"Did he ever ask you to help him with his spells? Before the fire?"

"Help him? No. I watched, sometimes, when he didn't know. I wanted to learn everything, so I could—be his heir. Not like Gian, of course, but the best I could be. Why do you want to know if he asked me to help him?"

"Some necromancers—" He stopped. He put one hand on her wrist, actually touched her deliberately. His fingers lay against the green silk of her oversleeve, but his thumb touched the back of her hand, with only the thin white ruffled edge of her camicia's sleeve between his skin and hers. She was so surprised she didn't move. He didn't hold on to her or caress her or anything, just let his hand rest on her wrist for a moment. It was as if he wanted to reassure her, or protect her from something, but she couldn't think what.

"Some necromancers what?" she said.

He took his hand away. "It is nothing."

There was something, of course, but whatever it was, apparently he wasn't going to tell her. He went back over to the double pelican and began examining it more closely, looking for ways to take it apart and transport it safely. After a little while he said, "What about his books? The day you offered the silver descensory to the grand duke, you said you had books."

Again, what to tell him? No books? All the books? Some of the books? There was one book, the oldest and most valuable one—Babbo had written his own notes in it, and one day she'd learn enough Latin to read them. That one, she'd keep for herself. Magister Ruanno would be suspicious, though, if she denied what she had said before, and claimed there were no books.

"There are some books. I took them upstairs—I was afraid the cellar might collapse, and I thought the books were the most important things of all."

He looked at her. She had a moment's fear that he'd understood what she hadn't said, as he'd done with the necromancy. That he knew Babbo's book was still here in the cellar, wrapped in waterproof waxed silk, locked in an iron box, and plastered into the wall. Knew the secret of the hatchway and the tunnel. But after a moment he smiled his wolf-smile and said smoothly, "Spoken like a true bookseller's daughter. Let us go up and look at these books, then. I will send some of the grand duke's servants to collect the equipment."

"How much will the grand duke pay?"

"I will speak to him. One large sum might raise suspicion, and be difficult to invest properly. Say, twenty gold scudi a year for twenty years. And dowries, for yourself and your sisters. Whatever your grandmother thinks is suitable. It will not be easy, attracting a husband for a girl with a chin sharp as a kitchen-knife."

Chiara took the lantern down from its hook and started up the steps. She wasn't sure if he was teasing her or not. He'd never teased before. "Who says I want a husband? Come upstairs, then. I'll show you the books, and Nonna will offer you some *schiacciata* and some almond milk for your refreshment."

CHAPTER TWELVE

The Palazzo Medici

16 SEPTEMBER 1574

Chiara slammed the pot of saffron threads down on the table. The unglazed clay cracked and feathery dark red strands floated up into the air. Under her breath she said, *"Che palle!"*

"Chiara." Donna Jimena looked up from her sewing. Her expression was serene but her voice was sharp. "Do not use such language in my presence. It is unsuitable for a young woman, and disrespectful to Donna Isabella, who has been so kind to you."

Chiara collected the saffron threads, one at a time. They were valuable, and even more important, they helped drive out the poisonous vapors of the pox. "Everyone says it."

"That does not mean you may say it." Donna Jimena held out her hand. She was making thin silk bags stuffed with saffron to tie around the children's necks.

"I'm supposed to be the grand duke's *soror mystica*, not a nursemaid." Chiara put the captured saffron into Donna Jimena's hand. "I—"

"Enough." Donna Jimena began to portion out the saffron into her little bags. "A little more humility, if you please, my dear. You should be grateful you are allowed to help, with the grand duchess in mourning."

In August, the grand duke's youngest daughter Lucrezia had died in a wave of the pox that had swept through Florence. She had been not quite two years old and the grand duke had seen her perhaps two or three times in the whole of her short life. The grand duchess, however, had wept over her daughter's sickbed and after her death grew sadder than ever. Five little daughters she had borne in the nine years of her marriage, and now only two remained: eight-year-old Eleonora and four-year-old Anna. No sons. The grand duke took it as a slur upon his manhood, that there had been no sons.

Donna Isabella had fled to the mountains with Donna Dianora, escaping, or so they thought, the heat and the sickness. Both ladies had left their children behind; travel and change were dangerous for little ones. Chiara had dug in her heels and refused to leave the city—in Florence she had been born, and if the pox chose to take her, in Florence she would die. The grand duke had laughed—*I am as Florentine as you are, back to Lorenzo il Magnifico and beyond*—and sent her off to the grand duchess's household with Donna Jimena, to help with the collection of children.

The grand duchess, poor lady, spent most of her time praying, and God only knew that plenty of prayers were needed. Chiara's reading and writing exercises had been put aside in favor of napkins to be changed, lost toys to be recovered, and dogs to be taken out into the gardens. Sad as she was for the little princess's death, she also felt restless and resentful and, well, yes, frightened. What if the grand duke's requirement for a *soror mystica* had been a passing fancy, and he had decided he didn't want her anymore?

"I'm sorry, Donna Jimena," she said. She made her voice meek and soft. It usually worked with Nonna and should work with Donna Jimena as well. "I won't say any more bad words."

"Not till the next time. Do not try your cajolery with me, *ragazzina*."

Chiara looked down at her toes. She was wearing silk stockings and slippers made of velvet, with soft leather soles and red embroidery. For a moment she wondered what had become of the worn, rain-sodden shoes she had been wearing on the day she'd met the grand duke. She'd lost one, when Magister Ruanno swung her up on Lowarn.

Curl your toes so it does not fall off again. You should have stockings.

I must've forgotten to choose a fine silken pair from the dozens and dozens in my gold-painted wardrobe chest.

And now she did have silk stockings. Two pairs, at least. She did have a wardrobe chest of her own, although it wasn't painted with gold. She had so many things she'd never had before.

For the moment, at least.

"I'm not cajole—cajoling—whatever that is," she said. "Well, maybe only a little. I'll try to be humble, Donna Jimena, really I will."

"See that you do."

There was a scratch on the door, and two gentlemen came into the room. They wore the grand duke's colors. Chiara's heart turned over.

"I have a message from il Serenissimo," the first man said.

Donna Jimena rose and held out her hand. "I will take it," she said. "I am Donna Jimena Osorio."

"It's words," the man said. "Not anything written down on paper. We're to take Soror Chiara Nerini back with us, to the Casino di San Marco. She'll have to prepare herself, il Serenissimo says, so we're to wait."

Chiara's knees almost buckled under her. It was as if she'd wished them there with her longings, with her anger, with breaking the jar of saffron. At last, at last, she'd see the grand duke and his foreign alchemist actually practicing alchemy. *We have completed the third stage, the stage of calcination*, Magister Ruanno had said. *For the fourth stage, the stage of exuberation, we have decided we need a third adept.* So perhaps she would actually take part in the exuberation. Whatever that was.

And they called her Soror. Just as they called Magister Ruanno, Magister.

"I'm Soror Chiara," she said. She wanted to dance. To sing. She felt as if she was taller and stronger than she'd ever been before. "I'll go and get ready now—wait here."

She heard Donna Jimena clicking her tongue with disapproval. Not very humble, of course, to give a direct order to the grand duke's men like that, when Donna Jimena, her elder and superior by blood, was in the room. Not very polite, to think Donna Jimena could stay with the children and click her tongue as much as she liked. But she was Soror Chiara and the grand duke wanted her. The grand duke had sent the men to wait upon her.

She ran out of the room.

CHAPTER THIRTEEN

The Casino di San Marco

LATER THAT SAME DAY

Ruan stood with Magister Francesco—in the laboratory there was no nobility, only mastery of the art—in the six-petaled rosette in the center of the black-and-white labyrinth. It was a symbol of the *magnum opus*, the great work itself, darkness and light and the quest for the six elements of creation at the heart of the cosmos; pieced together with chips of quartz and onyx, the labyrinth covered most of the floor. Tables and chests with fine alchemical equipment stood against the walls, outside the circle; everything that had been used in the girl's initiation had been taken away. The room was bright as noontime, with twenty-nine branches of candles, twenty-nine being a prime number divisible only by itself.

Ruan wore his black cassock and his amulet, the unpolished chunk of red hematite drawing power from the iron and copper in which it was set. Francesco was garbed the same, and his double rose-cut diamond on its gold chain cast quivering sparks of light, tiny spectra of color that danced over the labyrinth's path.

The girl Chiara Nerini stood outside the labyrinth in her habit of un-dyed wool, her hair loose down her back to her hips, the egg-sized cabochon moonstone quivering between her breasts. The hard angles of her chin and cheekbones had softened after a few months of good food and easy work in Donna Isabella's household, and the hollows around her remarkable eyes had filled in. Her grandmother and her two little sisters were well, and her father's shop was recovering its business. A word from the grand duke, and the booksellers' Arte had been happy to allow Mona Agnesa to run the shop herself. No, Chiara Nerini had nothing to be afraid of, not anymore. Ruan had made certain of that.

"Follow the path to the center of the labyrinth, Soror Chiara," Francesco said. "We will bring together the powers of the sun, the earth and the moon."

Ruan knew him well enough to hear the excitement in his voice—he genuinely thought the girl's presence was going to make a difference. So be it. Too much of his time and money had been spent wielding his new grand ducal powers against his enemies, playacting with his indolent mistress, and visiting whores behind her back, in the lowest parts of the city. Ruan wanted to move forward with the great work. He had made promises to John Dee in London, and he needed gold to fulfill the promises.

The girl started along the path of the labyrinth, walking left, then right, then left again through the cusps and arcs, turning at the double folds that were symbolic of female power. Ruan closed his eyes and focused his thoughts on the exuberation, the transformation of the heavy, dark red *caput mortuum*, left at the end of the calcination, into purified mercury, triumphant and gleaming. It was not magic, as the grand duke believed, but metallurgy. It required steady hands, exact measurements, perfect timing. From what he had seen of Chiara Nerini so far, she was steady enough, careful enough, but the first task of grinding the red stone into powder was dangerous. What would make a difference was not her femininity, but her skill. Would she be equal to what the grand duke was asking?

The girl reached the center of the labyrinth. "I am here," she said. She had a clear, pure voice, like a novice nun's. In a way she was a novice nun. "Serenissimo. Magister Ruanno."

"Here," Francesco said, "and only here, you will address me as 'Magister Francesco.' In the laboratory I am a master of the great art, nothing more."

"Magister Francesco," the girl said. Ruan could hear awe in her voice. Good. It would keep her intent on doing every task carefully and completely.

"We will now walk the labyrinth again, to the outside," Francesco said. "Soror Chiara, your first task will be to pulverize the *caput mortuum* until it is a very fine powder, so fine your breath will lift it from the stone."

The girl at least had the sense to keep quiet until they were outside the labyrinth. Then she said, "What's *caput mortuum*?"

"It is the result of the step of calcination," Francesco said. "A heavy, red stonelike substance containing, among other things, the essence of Venus. Here, see? In this mortar. Because it contains Venus, I believe it will respond to the female element."

Chiara looked at it. She frowned. "I recognize it," she said.

She sounds like I must have sounded, Ruan thought, fifteen years ago in Vienna, when Konrad Pawer began to teach me scientific metallurgy—essentially ignorant but proud and impatient to show off what little knowledge she had. "It's calcined mercury, isn't it?" she went on. "I'd better cover my mouth and nose when I grind it, because if I breathe in the powder it'll make me sick, even kill me."

Francesco stared at her. Ruan laughed. He said, "You are indeed an alchemist's daughter, Soror Chiara. That is exactly what it is, and it can indeed be poisonous. Look in that small chest, and you will find silk masks to wrap around your face."

She scowled at him and pushed out her chin. The gesture was not quite as pugnacious with the new soft flesh covering her bones. "Was this a test?" she demanded. "Would you have let me grind it without anything protecting me, if I hadn't known what it was?"

"It was a test, of sorts." Francesco had recovered his self-possession. "You have passed it fairly."

"And no," Ruan added. "We would not have allowed you to pulverize it unprotected."

She looked at him as if she did not entirely believe him.

"Mask yourself, Soror Chiara," Francesco said. "We must begin."

She fumbled with the mask, getting it straight and tying the ties properly. Ruan remembered that she had spied on her father—*I watched, sometimes, when he didn't know*—but she had probably never actually put a mask on herself. Once she was prepared she clasped the moonstone in her hand for a moment, then set to work with a will. She had used a mortar and pestle before, that was certain, although not necessarily in a laboratory.

"What . . . is the next . . . step?" she asked after a while, breathless with effort.

"The powder of the *caput mortuum* is placed in an athanor," Francesco said. "We will use your father's Trapezuntine athanor, to redouble your influence, the influence of Venus. Then Magister Ruanno will add the dephlegmated oil of vitriol, and you will add the white spirit, the spirit of Luna, the virgin moon. When that is done, I myself will close the athanor and turn it—circulate the elements upon the earth until they are perfectly united."

"Sounds like Nonna making turnip soup," Chiara said, under her breath. "The powder is finished, I think. Look."

Through the silk mask she breathed out gently upon the fine red powder she had ground, and a little of it lifted and swirled delicately in the air before settling back into the mortar. Ruan felt a chill. It was death, that red powder, a terrible death with one's lungs falling to pieces inside one's chest. Chiara knew it, too. Even masked, she turned her face away before taking a breath again.

"Well done," Francesco said. "The breath of a virgin—perhaps that will make the difference. Use that silver cochlear, Soror Chiara, and transfer the powder into the athanor."

She was careful with the spoonlike instrument, taking up each small amount and depositing it lightly so the powder remained still. When she was finished, she put the cochlear down and stepped back from the athanor.

"It is ready, Magister Ruanno," she said.

Ruan stepped forward and measured out the oil of vitriol. It was clear as water but thick, the consistency of honey. Very gently he poured it over the powdered calcinate of mercury. It was important to do it slowly, to contain the reaction. Little by little, crystalline white granules formed and precipitated to the bottom of the athanor.

"The white spirit is in that flask," he said to the girl, when he was finished.

Chiara picked up the flask and removed the stopper. "What will it do when I pour it in?"

"It should create no visible reaction at first. But take care—one can never be certain."

She closed her eyes for a moment—praying?—and then with steady hands poured the white spirit into the athanor.

The white powder swirled in the spirit. Ruan could see it begin to dissolve. Good.

"Now," Francesco said. "I shall close the athanor and circulate the liquors. Step back, both of you."

There was no danger at this point, but Francesco did like his mysteries and miracles. Ruan stepped back and gestured to Chiara. She withdrew as well. She was still wearing the mask.

The athanor rested on a mechanism that could be turned with a foot pedal. Francesco placed the cover and turned it, slowly at first, then more vigorously, then slowly again. His lips were moving; he was reciting some Latin incantation to himself to time the process.

"Now," he said, when he was finished. "Magister Ruanno, you and I will seal the athanor and transfer it to the fire, then connect the alembic and the retort. The entire dissolved substance must be sublimed three times. The product of the first sublimation will be the exuberate water."

"How long will it take?" Chiara asked.

"In all, several days," Francesco said. "Each step of the great work requires time, and the greatest care."

"Several *days?*"

Ruan smiled. "All three of us," he said, "need not be here for every moment of the process. Now that the stage of exuberation has begun, we will observe it by turns. You will have plenty of time, Soror Chiara, to sleep and eat and perform your tasks for Donna Jimena."

"And you, Magister Ruanno," said Francesco, "will have time to meet secretly with your messengers, who run back and forth to London at your direction. Is that not so?"

He sounded petulant. Ruan was surprised he would say such a thing in front of the girl, and wondered if he himself had made a misstep in the delicate balance between his allegiance to the Medici on the one hand, and his affairs in England on the other. Affairs—that was putting a fine point upon it. What he actually intended to do, when he had bought the English queen's support, was to kill Andrew Lovell as Andrew Lovell had killed his father, and drive the usurping Lovells out of Milhyntall House and Wheal Loer and into the same poverty and misery his mother had known, alone and widowed and heavy with child.

"Perhaps," he said calmly. "I have never kept my dealings with the English a secret from you."

"Now that we have begun this new step of the *magnum opus*, I would have you focus all your mind and thoughts upon it. Leave everything else. No plots, no vengeance, no women."

Ruan bowed his head, as much to conceal his expression as to indicate his acquiescence. "So be it, Magister Francesco."

It was a lie, of course. And Francesco knew it was a lie. The silence was dangerous.

"Let us arrange an horarium," the girl Chiara said suddenly. She had taken off her silken mask. She looked different—older. An adult, not a child. Impossible. Although perhaps the successful conclusion of her first foray into genuine alchemy had given her confidence, enough confidence to speak as if she were on an equal footing. "Magister Francesco, what is the most convenient time of the day for you to observe?"

The sense of danger evaporated. Francesco said, "I will observe from None until the middle of the second watch."

"I will watch from the second watch until, say, an hour after Prime," Ruan said. This was not an inconvenience. He loved the laboratory at night, dark and solitary and full of secrets. "That leaves the hour after Prime until None for you, Soror Chiara."

She nodded. "So be it," she said. "I'm familiar enough with sublimation that I can send a message if it appears to be complete. You will have messengers on duty as well, Magister Francesco?"

"I will," Francesco said.

"The second watch has already begun," Ruan said. "I will remain to tend the sublimation tonight. Soror Chiara, I will see you in the morning, then."

"Come with me, Soror Chiara." The grand duke began to take off his black cassock. The *magnum opus* had ended for the night, and Ruan automatically began thinking of him as the grand duke again. "Magister Ruanno, we leave the great work in your hands."

"It will be safe," Ruan said. "This time, we will succeed."

CHAPTER FOURTEEN

The Palazzo Medici

20 JULY 1575

The necklace was made of square, table-cut rubies and emeralds set in stylized flowers of gold, separated by pairs of matched pearls. A single large pendant pearl swung from the ruby flower at the center.

"Saints and angels, Isabella," Chiara said. In private she and the grand duke's sister now called each other by their Christian names. At first it had been strange but now that almost a year had passed it had come to seem fitting. She was, after all, the grand duke's own *soror mystica*, his sister in the art, just as Isabella was his sister in the flesh. "This is worth a fortune."

"Two hundred scudi, perhaps," Isabella said. She didn't seem to think of it as a lot of money, but of course she'd been immeasurably rich all her life. "You must take it to a certain gentleman. I am watched every moment, and Francesco's guardsmen would follow me."

"Why? What's happened?"

Isabella turned away for a moment, rearranging the pots and flasks on her dressing table, picking up a mirror and putting it down again. She did that, played with things, when she didn't want to tell the truth, but in the end she always told. That would be her undoing one day—that she needed to talk, loved to talk, and couldn't keep herself from telling secret things.

"You cannot tell Francesco." Isabella swung around abruptly. "Swear to me, Chiara, that you will not tell Francesco."

"I have not spoken so much as a greeting to him for weeks."

The exuberation had succeeded, but the stage after it, the fixation, had failed. She and the grand duke and Magister Ruanno had started over, achieved six of the stages over a period of four months—with an interruption for the court's Christmas and Epiphany festivals, *befanini* cakes and wine and fireworks and pageants such as she had never seen before—and then failed on the seventh, the separation. The grand duke had been frenzied with anger and frustration. Madonna Bianca had gone into seclusion for a few weeks, and everyone said the grand duke had beaten her until she couldn't walk or wear proper clothes.

Then in March, before they could start over again with the first stage, the grand duchess had taken to her bed for another childbirth, her sixth. Of course that meant that the grand duke had taken his pleasures in her bed at least once, which might have been another reason why Madonna Bianca refused to show her face for a while.

Sometimes, when the headaches were bad and the voices started their endless whispering, Chiara could stand outside herself and wonder at how her life had changed since she'd become part of the Medici court. She'd grown out of all her clothing, for one thing—she needed longer skirts and sleeves, and camicias cut fuller because her breasts were suddenly the breasts of a woman, not a girl. She ate fine food every day and slept in a tiny cell of her own, like a nun. The other ladies of the household thought she was a witch and refused to share their dormitories with the grand duke's sworn *soror mystica*. She didn't care. She didn't like the other ladies anyway—all they talked about was men and clothes and jewels and being part of the *nobilità*.

The furnishings of the cell were nothing like a nun's, though. The narrow bed had a pillowy feather mattress and clean, soft linens and coverlets. There was a cabinet with a porcelain basin where she washed her face and hands every day, and rubbed her body with a scented lotion. She had a mirror-shard of her own, a piece of a mirror Isabella had broken. She cleaned her teeth with an embroidered cloth every time she ate. Every three months she washed and dried her hair with vervain, licorice root and vinegar—a task that took hours, considering its length and thickness—and when she combed and braided it she used a powder of rose petals and cloves to give it a sweet scent. She reveled in it all. A stranger, meeting her, would never know she wasn't a fine lady herself.

"I swear I won't tell the grand duke," she said to Isabella. "By all the saints, I swear." Even as she said it, she remembered Donna Jimena saying, *There are ears everywhere.*

Isabella must have been thinking the same thing, because she came close and whispered, "Dianora is in trouble. We are both in trouble. Francesco has arrested a man named Orazio Pucci—surely you've heard Dianora speak of him? He has been at the heart of a conspiracy against the Medici, and Dianora has been stupid enough to help him."

"Help him?" Chiara was too surprised to keep her voice to a whisper. "But why? She herself is a Medici, married to your brother."

"Hush! I know. Pietro is the worst possible husband—he beats her, I know that, and leaves her alone in her bed while he cavorts with whores. He's worse than Francesco. Even so, she is mad to have done what she has done, abet assassination and revolution."

"Assassination! Whose assassination?"

"Better you do not know. Listen, Chiara. Orazio Pucci will talk—Francesco will have him tortured and he will talk in the end, however brave he may be. He will tell Francesco the names of the men who have conspired with him, and one of those men is now Dianora's lover. If he is arrested, if he talks—I do not know what Francesco will do."

"But what—?"

"We must get Dianora's lover out of Florence. She cannot do it herself—she dare not do anything to draw Francesco's attention, and in any case she is too terrified to do more than huddle in her bed and weep. I must protect her, because if her lover is arrested, she will be arrested, and if she is arrested, she will babble out everything she knows. Things I do not want Francesco to know."

Like your own long-ago love affair with Magister Ruanno, Chiara thought. Like your present lover, your husband's own cousin, Don Troilo Orsini.

Medici, Nonna had said. *Whores, the lot of them, women and men.*

"What do you want me to do?" Chiara said.

"You must take this necklace to Dianora's lover—his name is Pierino Ridolfi. It is Dianora's own—he will recognize it, and believe you when you tell him he must leave Florence at once."

"Where is he? How am I to get to him with the necklace?"

"I will send a horse as well. You must disguise yourself in a plain messenger's clothes, breeches and hose and a dark cloak like a man, and ride to the house where he is staying. Then you can give him the necklace and the horse, and walk back."

Chiara's stomach lurched. "Isabella, you know I'll do anything I can for you. But ride a horse through Florence at night? By myself? In men's clothes? That's madness. I've never ridden by myself, and you know how much I hate horses."

"I have chosen a very gentle one. You know the city better than anyone, Chiara. You love every cobblestone, I've heard you say it. You can find hidden ways."

"Hidden ways to where?"

"Pierino Ridolfi is hiding at a place you know very well."

Chiara stared at her. "Please don't tell me he's at Babbo's shop. I know my Nonna hates the Medici, but she wouldn't—"

"She would. She has. He's hiding there, in the cellar. You can do it, Chiara. I'll bring you the clothes. The horse is in the mews, saddled and ready. Please, I beg you. I would do it myself if I thought Francesco's guards would not follow me."

"Isn't there someone else in your household, someone you trust to—"

"No! They spy on me, all of them. They report what I do to Francesco. Chiara, I thought you were my friend. If you do not do this, what can I believe but that you are spying on me as well, for Francesco? Are you a spy? Are you?"

She began to cry. Were her tears real or were they artful? Chiara couldn't tell, and real tears or not, her accusations stung. It was so much a part of her new life, being Isabella's special friend, being part of her glamorous, opulent circle. What would she do if Isabella repudiated her?

"I'm not a spy for anybody," Chiara said. "Isabella, I'm your true friend, I swear it. I'll go. Get the clothes."

Sant' Ippolito, she thought, let the horse be a gentle one.

CHAPTER FIFTEEN

If not exactly gentle, the horse was at least well-trained, and well-trapped with a fine leather saddle. A single small lantern burned just outside the stall, casting wild shadows, and yet the horse stood like a rock while Chiara clambered up into the saddle. It blew out its breath with a whickering sound and responded predictably to what she did—a touch with her heels, it walked forward, pull on the right rein and it turned right, pull on the left rein and it turned left. She felt awkward and a little sick. If horses could laugh, she thought, it had to be laughing at her clumsiness.

After more than a year at the Palazzo Medici, she'd been around enough horses that her fear was no longer a paralyzing terror. She'd ridden pillion a good many times, on Magister Ruanno's Lowarn in particular. Still, the smell of the horse, the sound of its hooves against the stones of the street, made her head ache viciously, as if her brain and her eyes were too big for her skull. The scar over her left ear prickled. Babbo's voice whispered, *You should have been the one to die, not Gian. If Gian had lived, your mother would have lived, and I would be alive as well.*

Grimly she clung to the saddle and guided the horse through the dark streets from the Palazzo Medici to the booksellers' quarter near the Palazzo Vecchio. The moon was a couple of days from full and gave just enough light for her to pick her way. Fortunately she wasn't stopped by the watch. She had a story ready—*I'm carrying a message from Donna Isabella to the grand duchess at the Palazzo Pitti*—but she didn't have to use it. She kept to the narrow side streets, streets where she and Gian had played as children, letting the horse walk slowly and quietly. When she reached the shop, she guided the patient horse down the alleyway and into the tiny walled yard at the back.

I'll say a novena to you, Sant' Ippolito, she thought. I really will.

She slipped down from the horse's back, tied it, and in the moonlight crept up to the back door. Before she could even scratch on the wood, the door swung open and a dark figure jumped out at her, and grabbed her by the throat. She flailed at him in panic as he squeezed. Then a broom came down on the man's head, he swore and let go of her, and Nonna jammed the broomstick into his belly. He doubled over with a grunt of pain.

"Blessed Virgin Mary. *Nipotina*. What are you doing here? And why are you dressed like that?"

Chiara put her hands to her throat, gasping. She would have bruises. She whispered, "Donna Isabella sent me. There was no one else she could send in secret, no one else she trusted." Bruises and all, it made her feel important and special that she was the one Isabella trusted. "She gave me these clothes so I could pretend to be an ordinary messenger. She wants to give this horse and a valuable necklace to a man named Pierino Ridolfi. He's hiding here, she said."

The man who had tried to strangle her straightened up. His face was flushed. In a hoarse whisper he said, "I am Pierino Ridolfi. Forgive me. I heard the horse—I was afraid."

"You're a fool, Pierino," Nonna said brusquely. "Why is one of the damned Medici risking my granddaughter's life by sending her with a horse and a necklace for you? It's the grand duke who's out for your hide. And come inside, both of you, before the watch stops to ask questions."

"Donna Dianora supports us," Ridolfi said. "She paid me to—"
He stopped.

"To what?" Nonna closed the door behind them and opened a lantern. The light picked out every wrinkle in her face. Pierino Ridolfi was a good-looking young fellow in a swarthy way, although badly pockmarked. His clothes were the clothes of a courtier.

"To kill them all," he said. He was sweating and sour-smelling with tension and fear. "Her husband abuses her, and she is not a Medici by blood—she is the daughter of Garzia Alvarez di Toledo. She longs to be free of Don Pietro and his brothers, and everything to do with him."

Chiara stared at him. So that was what Isabella had meant by assassination and revolution. Dianora, beautiful, sensuous Dianora, foolish Dianora, desperate Dianora—she had paid this man to assassinate her husband and the grand duke and the cardinal. And everything to do with her husband—what did that mean? Surely not—

"Well, clearly she didn't get her money's worth." Nonna rubbed her fingers against her thumb scornfully. "Who knows about this plot?"

"Only a few—Orazio Pucci, Cammillo Martelli, Piero Capponi."

"Orazio Pucci has been arrested," Chiara said. "That's why Isabella sent me—if they torture him, he may say whatever they want, even if it's not true."

"You'd better take the damned horse and be off, Ridolfi, so you don't bring the guardsmen down on me." Nonna was nothing if not practical. "I'm all for assassinating the Medici, but I don't want to hang for a failed plot. *Nipotina*, let's see that necklace."

Chiara took it out of her doublet. It was wrapped in a silk scarf, scented with Dianora's favorite perfume, a combination of rose oil, chypre, marjoram and cloves. She unfolded the silk and let the necklace spill down from her fingers, the rubies and emeralds glinting in the candlelight, the worked gold and the pearls glowing.

"Blessed Virgin," Nonna said. "That will keep you in style, Ridolfi. Do you recognize it?"

"Yes. It is Dianora's."

"Break it up quickly so it can't be identified, and get rid of that scarf."

Pierino Ridolfi took the necklace and the scarf, and tucked them both into his own doublet. Chiara wondered if he was truly in love with Dianora, and if he'd keep the scarf as a favor. Dangerous lovesickness, if it was true. "I thank you, signorina," he said. "You have taken a great risk for me. Tell Donna Isabella I will never betray her, or Donna Dianora."

Nonna made a scornful sound and closed the lantern. "Off with you," she said. "Keep quiet until you're well out of the booksellers' quarter. Here, take these silver *quattrini*—don't try to bribe your way out of one of the gates with a jewel, or they'll know you're up to no good. Ride fast and ride far, and don't come back."

Pierino Ridolfi took the coins and slipped out the door in the darkness.

Leather creaked as he mounted the horse; its hooves clopped gently as he rode away. Then silence.

Ride fast and ride far, and don't come back.

What would it be like, a life of exile?

"And how do you plan to get back to the Palazzo Medici?" Nonna asked in the darkness. "Surely your fine lady's feet are too soft now for so much walking."

"They're not as soft as you might think. I'd rather walk than ride a horse, any day."

Nonna laughed. There was bitterness in it, and sadness, and fear, and love. "Take care with your Donna Isabella, *nipotina*. Even if Ridolfi escapes, someone else may point a finger at her, and a finger pointed at her points at you also."

"I'll be all right. No one suspects me. The grand duke doesn't think of me as one of Donna Isabella's women—he only placed me in her household for his own convenience."

"Stay close to the grand duchess, if you can. She's a good woman, despite the Medici devil she's married to."

"I'll try, Nonna."

"Good. You'd better go. It sounds quiet out there."

Chiara reached out and took Nonna's hands in hers. They felt like bundles of sticks wrapped in very old, well-worked leather, but they were strong, strong enough to half-stun a grown man with a broom. Strong enough to meddle in conspiracies too dangerous for an old woman. "Nonna," she said. "You be careful, too. I know you've always supported the old republic, but I didn't know you were actually mixed up in plots against the Medici. What would happen to Lucia and Mattea if you were arrested?"

"You will take care of them," Nonna said. "You, the grand duke's own *soror mystica*."

Chiara pulled her hands away. She felt cold, then hot. A headache exploded behind her eyes like a blood-red, poisonous flower. "How do you know that?"

"Not many things are truly secret in Florence, *nipotina*, particularly if they're goings-on at the court. Now run away back to your friend Donna Isabella, and come back in the daylight like a decent woman."

She hugged Chiara once, hard, then without another word pushed her out the door into the moonlit night.

CHAPTER SIXTEEN

The Palazzo Bargello, used as a prison

10 AUGUST 1575

The stone chamber in the Palazzo Bargello, under the Volognana Tower, was lighted by torches in iron brackets. Four men were there, among the chains and hooks and stained wooden implements: a priest with a pen and paper; an executioner in his leather tunic and apron; the prisoner Orazio Pucci, his wrists chained behind him, naked but for a filthy and ragged shirt; and Grand Duke Francesco de' Medici, wearing clothes he might have worn for a court entertainment, a doublet, breeches and hose in rich raisin-colored velvet, sewn with rubies, pearls and jet. A brooch with a Florentine lily in rubies and diamonds was pinned to his hat. His eyes were glittering and his mouth was hard as forged iron.

"You know the question of the four elements, I am sure," the grand duke said. His voice was cool and pleasant. "For air, the strappado—you will be winched high by your wrists, then dropped and swung in the air, until your shoulders crack and come apart from your own weight. For water, the water itself—forced down your throat as you are stretched upon the wheel, until your traitorous belly bursts inside you."

"Torture me with a hundred elements," Pucci said. He was ghastly white in the torchlight. "I will tell you nothing."

"The fire," the grand duke went on, as if his prisoner had not spoken at all. "Irons heated in braziers until they are white-hot, and then applied"—he paused and smiled—"applied judiciously, to such parts of your body as you value most. And in the end, the earth. Great stones to press the breath out of you, and break your bones, one at a time."

"I will tell you nothing," Pucci said again.

The grand duke gestured to the executioner. The man pushed Pucci roughly to one side of the room where a hook hung on a chain from a system of pulleys and winches reaching high up into the ancient vaulted ceiling. He fastened the hook to the fetters that held Pucci's hands behind his back.

"I give you one final opportunity to speak," the grand duke said. "Tell me everything, who was involved in your plot, what you intended to do, how you intended to do it. I will give you a priest for absolution and a clean death, and your body returned to your family in such a state that they can mourn over it and entomb it properly."

"Go fuck yourself."

The grand duke's eyes narrowed. He gestured.

The executioner began to turn the crank of the winch. The chain tightened, and slowly lifted Pucci's arms behind him. He bent forward involuntarily, but that gave him only a moment's respite. The muscles of his arms and shoulders bulged and strained under the rags of his shirt as his whole weight was lifted, and his feet swung free.

"Higher," the grand duke said. "Slowly."

As the winch wound up the chain, Pucci's body began to swing a little. He made a guttural sound, more a grunt of effort than a cry of pain, as his unnaturally twisted shoulders strained against the weight of his body. The grand duke leaned forward, watching closely. Pucci's feet were now a man's height from the floor. There were thick rider's muscles in his thighs and calves.

"Higher. As high as it will go."

The winch creaked. Pucci labored for breath as the strain on his shoulders compressed his chest.

"Now," the grand duke said, when the chain had been wound as far as it would go. "I can leave you to hang there and let your shoulders dislocate themselves slowly as you wear out your strength. I can have you dropped to within a foot of the floor, so your shoulders are torn out of their sockets all at once. Or I can let you down gently. Which would you prefer?"

There was an eerie friendly quality to his voice. He might have been offering a choice of wines to a friend. *Brunello? Trebbiano? Moscato?*

"Drop me," Pucci managed to wrench out. "Medici bastard."

The grand duke waited a moment, as if considering. Then he lifted his finger to the executioner.

Pucci dropped. The chain went taut, with a ringing sound. The wet tearing of ruptured muscles and tendons, the popping sound of joints coming apart—then the only sound was Pucci screaming. His body swung. His shoulders did not look like the shoulders of a man.

"Again," the grand duke said. "Five drops, for the element of air. Then we will begin the water."

By the fourth drop, Pucci was shrieking incoherently, begging for mercy. The grand duke directed the fifth drop anyway. He was visualizing Bia with her wrists bound behind her, her arms dragged up, her body bent over, her hair tied back, wholly naked with her rich breasts swinging free as she sobbed and pleaded. He would never actually lift her, of course, let alone drop her. But a modified version of the strappado, oh, yes. It would be beautiful. And he would tell her carefully, all the details of the real strappado. Her fear would be a fine spice to her pain, and together they would increase his pleasure.

Fear and pain and pleasure. They could not be separated, not really. His mother had taught him that, his father, his tutors. Or had he always known it, been born knowing it?

"He has fainted, Serenissimo," the executioner said. "Another drop might tear his arms from his body—the bones are entirely pulled apart."

"Lower him. Wake him. We shall see if he chooses to confess, because if he does not, we will proceed to the water."

Pucci was lowered to the stones of the floor and unchained. His arms were loose and mottled as stuffed sausages hung in a butcher's shop. His shoulders were swollen to twice their normal size, purpled as the bruising came out. The executioner dumped a bucket of water over him and he whimpered.

"No more." He sounded like a child. "No more, please, please."

The grand duke gestured to the priest, who came forward with his book of paper, his pen and ink.

"Name your conspirators," the grand duke said. "Confess every plan and every person who aided you."

"Capponi," Pucci gasped. Every trace of his defiance was gone. His manhood, his adulthood, were gone. There were tears streaking down from the corners of his eyes. "Alamanni. Cammillo Martelli. Pierino Ridolfi."

"What was your plan?"

"Assassination. The grand duke, the cardinal. Don Pietro. The boy, Cosimino, Don Pietro's seed. Wipe out all the males of the Medici, root and branch, and make Florence a republic again."

He did not seem to be aware, anymore, that it was the grand duke he was confessing to. The priest scratched at his paper, writing it all down.

The grand duke said, "Don Cosimino is two years old."

"He is a Medici."

"And his mother Donna Dianora supported you. You need not tell me that, because I already know."

Pucci's eyes opened. He seemed to come back to himself, to understand, for a moment at least, what he had done.

"No," he said. "Not Donna Dianora. She did not know."

The grand duke gestured with one finger. The executioner picked up a wooden mallet with a three-foot handle, swung it in a great arc, and struck Pucci's ruined left shoulder with casual accuracy. Pucci convulsed, making a high whistling sound of agony.

After a while the grand duke said again, "Donna Dianora supported you."

"Yes. Money. Meeting-places. The assassinations, she knew."

The priest wrote it down.

"And Donna Isabella? My charming sister, my father's favorite, who imagines herself to be the first lady of Florence. Was she part of your conspiracy as well?"

"I do not know. She had lovers, Troilo Orsini, and she was great friends with Donna Dianora, but I do not know more than that."

He fainted again.

"That is quite enough." The grand duke smiled. His sister and his brother's wife could not exactly be dragged into the Bargello, put to the question, and executed, satisfying as that would be. But there were ways. Oh yes, there were ways. "Executioner, take him away. Call the physician. I do not want him executed immediately—I may have more questions later."

"Yes, Serenissimo."

"It is a pity," the grand duke said, "that he broke so quickly. I expected him to hold his silence through the water at least, and even the fire."

The executioner shrugged. "Some men can stand pain, Serenissimo, and some can't. I've seen all kinds."

"You will be seeing more, in the next few weeks." The grand duke gave the executioner a small bag of silver *grossi*. "Yes, it is a great pity he was not stronger. I was looking forward to all four elements of the question."

CHAPTER SEVENTEEN

The Palazzo Medici

22 FEBRUARY 1576

Chiara held the basin as Dianora gasped and choked. She'd been vomiting all day, ever since dinner. In fact, she'd been sick more often than not, ever since Orazio Pucci had been executed last summer. The grand duke was obsessed, whisperers said, with hunting down everyone connected to Pucci's conspiracy. Even the Christmas and Epiphany festivals had been flat and cheerless, full of fear. Pierino Ridolfi had escaped Florence and no one knew where he was, but others were in prison, awaiting the headsman's ax. Lesser conspirators were still being arrested.

Nonna?

So far, there was no indication she was suspected. But the grand duke was cunning and relentless and liked to strike when it was least expected. Chiara herself was very careful about what she ate and drank, and avoided the delicacies that were being served at Donna Isabella's table now that it was Carnival-tide.

"Oh, Chiara." Dianora wiped her mouth with a clean napkin. Her eyes were swollen with tears and her fine complexion was mottled with red. "I am so ill, I think I am going to die."

"Shall I call the physician?"

"*Dio mio*, no. I dare not take any medicament. Who knows what may be in it?"

"You're invited to Donna Bianca's entertainment next week. Everyone's going. If you're not there, it'll cause more talk."

"I do not care. I will not creep and crawl to Francesco's mistress. How dare she act as if she is the queen of the Carnival?"

"You would be better off," said Donna Isabella, who was reclining on a cushioned bench by the window, "if you made an effort to cultivate the Venetian. I do. It is the only way to gain Francesco's favor."

"I do not want his favor."

"You might be sick less often if you appeased him."

Donna Isabella had recently been in a great decline as well. Her lover, Don Troilo Orsini, had fled Florence in the fall, two steps ahead of an arrest warrant. There were whispers—but of course, there were always whispers—that both ladies were being poisoned at the command of the grand duke. There'd certainly been no work in the laboratory, or at least no work on the quest for the *Lapis Philosophorum*. Chiara had been allowed afternoons in the laboratory three times a week, grudgingly, mostly because Donna Isabella wanted her to make love potions. Donna Isabella had never quite grasped the difference between alchemy and witchcraft.

"The grand duchess never goes anywhere Bianca Cappello goes," Dianora said pettishly, "so I do not see why I should have to."

The laboratory was so different from Donna Isabella's apartments, cool, full of space and shadows, smelling of clean pungent minerals instead of heated flesh and perfumes and half-eaten pastries. Chiara loved it there, and loved the simple tasks of distillation, extraction, sublimation and calcination that Magister Ruanno set for her—not because he needed the products she created, but because he wanted her to learn. He was a good teacher, clear and concise, and he told her plainly that one day she might be as skilled as he was. No one had ever told her that before. She had wished Babbo could be there to hear it.

Once, in fact, she had wished for it so hard that Babbo's voice had screamed in her ears and her vision had turned black. She'd come to herself on the floor among shatters of broken retorts, feeling dizzy and light. Magister Ruanno hadn't made her feel as if she was stupid for having a falling-spell. He gave her a tiny cup of some clear liquid—it tasted like Nonna's cordials but without the sweetness or herbs, just aqua vitae all by itself, sharp and burning—and helped her to her feet. His touch was gentle and straightforward. She wondered what his touch would be like if she wasn't a sworn virgin, and she thought of her dreams.

Dreams or no dreams, she liked being alone with Magister Ruanno, wearing her simple habit with the moonstone exposed on her breast. He talked to her about alchemy and metallurgy, not only the processes themselves but the history. He showed her maps of the stars, and two or three times he had taken her outside in the dark to point out the North Star and the planets and the way the stars made patterns, with names. She began to realize that he didn't really believe a lot of the things the grand duke believed, the magical things. While she performed her beginner's exercises, he worked by himself on something. He wouldn't say what it was.

"Chiara, quick, the basin—"

Chiara jumped. Dianora began vomiting again.

"The grand duchess is the emperor's sister," Isabella said, when Dianora had exhausted herself and lay back in her chair. "No one expects her to acknowledge her husband's mistress, not even Francesco, and in any case she does not care for entertainments. You are a different matter entirely. You must be seen, and make some attempt to regain your reputation."

"*Un fico secco* for my reputation." Dianora made a rude gesture.

Chiara put the basin outside the door for the *domestica* to collect, and went to the cabinet for a clean basin and fresh towels. "I have an idea," she said. "Carnival's all very well, but it's followed by Lent. What if on Ash Wednesday we all go out into the city after Mass, with the ashes on our foreheads, and collect alms for the poor? Everyone would see, and talk, and admire the virtue of it. And the alms are always needed."

Isabella sat up straighter, her eyes brightening. "And think of what a slap in the face it would be to Bianca Cappello and her ostentatious entertainments. Everyone would talk about the goodness and charity of the grand duke's sister and sister-in-law, and the greedy vulgarity of his mistress."

Dianora laughed, for the first time in days. "That is a wonderful idea," she said. "We could wear our plainest dresses. No, wait—we could have dresses made, like nuns' habits. Everyone has fantastical costumes for Carnival, masks and jewels. We can put it about that we ourselves have given money to charity instead of making Carnival costumes."

"We could take the dogs." Isabella reached down and stroked Rina's sleek russet head. There was a second little hound beside her, another gift from the grand duchess, this time to Dianora. The new dog had been given a long complicated name, supposedly some forest nymph connected to the goddess Diana. Dianora called her Leia for short. "Have special leashes made."

They began to talk together, making plans, each one more elaborate than the one before. Chiara waited for them to acknowledge her, include her, but they had forgotten her.

It was no longer quite so exciting to be part of the court. Isabella and Dianora, the grand duke himself, even the grand duchess, for all her kindness and piety—like statues of the saints in the church, they all had unattractive places where the bright colors and gold leaf had rubbed off. Isabella was beautiful, yes, or at least she had been in her shining youth. She was kind enough, in her careless way, and she collected artists and musicians as if they were *marionetti*. But she was troubled and sensual and only too willing to involve herself in secret matters that were better left alone.

I'd be her friend, Chiara thought, if she'd let me. But she's my friend only when the humor strikes her. When there's no one else. No one— Well, say it. No one of her own rank.

Magister Ruanno cares enough about her to want to take care of her and protect her. He isn't her lover, I know that now. He was, once, when he was younger, when he first arrived in Florence in the grand duchess's household. What was he doing in Austria? He doesn't say much about his past. But he still cares about Donna Isabella. Does he know that both Donna Dianora and Donna Isabella have been sick, off and on, since Christmas? Does he suspect—

"Chiara!"

Again Chiara jumped. Dianora was staring at her, her eyebrows lifted. Isabella was smiling, pleasantly enough but without real warmth. In her secret thoughts Chiara called it her center-of-the-cosmos look. She thought everything and everyone, the earth and sun and the stars themselves, rose and set around her. Well, it wasn't her fault. She'd been brought up to think that. They all had, the Medici, the aristocrats.

"Chiara," Dianora said again. Her voice was remote, a little fretful, the voice she used when she talked to the servant girls. "I think we would like something to eat. Run down to the kitchen, if you please, and fetch some bread and fruit and cheese, and some of that sweet red wine."

"Should you be drinking wine from the kitchen?" Chiara said. "I'll go and buy a fresh bottle, if you—"

"Just do as you are told," Dianora said. She picked Leia up and hugged her. "We do not want to wait."

Chiara went hot and cold all at once—her face hot as fire with humiliation, her hands cold as ice with fury. She waited for Isabella to say something, to exclaim that Dianora should not speak so disparagingly to Chiara, the grand duke's *soror mystica*, their friend. But Isabella was alone in the center of the cosmos, and said nothing.

After a moment Chiara stood up, curtsied without a word, and went out of the room.

Fool, Babbo whispered. *Fool, to ever think the Medici are your friends.*

Her head pounded.

They're the fools, she thought, to eat food from their own kitchen. It's the grand duke himself who's having something put in the food, I know it is. Medici plotting against Medici. No one else would dare, and there's no other explanation for these bouts of sickness, over and over.

Does he simply mean to frighten them?

Or will I find them dead one day soon, lying in their beds with their silken cushions and velvet coverlets, and sweet red wine spilled all around them?

CHAPTER EIGHTEEN

The Boboli Gardens

28 FEBRUARY 1576

O n the last day of Carnival, between a fine banquet in the afternoon and a magnificent masked entertainment planned for the evening, the grand duke and Bianca Cappello stepped out of the Palazzo Pitti into the magnificent gardens that stretched behind it. It was cold and damp, with a lacy veil of mist. Off in the distance, the grand duke could hear fireworks.

"Leave us," he said to the courtiers who attended them. "Madonna Bianca and I would walk alone for a little while."

The gentlemen and the ladies melted away, probably thinking that a warm fire and a cup of sweet spiced wine before the entertainment would be much more pleasant than a walk in the gardens in February. Bianca Cappello pulled her mantle more closely around her body. It was made of dark green velvet quilted and embroidered with gold and pearls, lined with lustrous marten fur and clasped with jeweled gold martens' heads. Marten fur increased a woman's fertility, and the grand duke knew that even after nine childless years Bianca still prayed every night to bear him a son.

It was time he had a son, one way or another. Time the whispers about his ability to sire a male child were silenced forever.

"In the summer," he said, as they walked past a fountain and into the sunken court of the amphitheater, "we will mount spectacles here. I am pleased, Madonna, with your management of the Carnival celebrations, and in particular with your personal banquet. You did well—everyone said so."

"Thank you, my lord," Bianca said. It was her own voice, lower in timbre, adult, with a faint tinge of a Venetian accent. She held her head high, proud, a great lady. He was willing to allow her to enjoy her moment of triumph, because she would become his Bia again whenever he commanded it.

"I have a reason for allowing you to present yourself so openly as my mistress, and the first lady of the court."

That intrigued her, excited her, he could tell. She said, "What reason, my lord?"

"I will tell you when we reach the center of the labyrinth."

They walked on, and climbed a steep terrace. Amid plantings that would bloom when the weather became warmer, there was a water basin with a fountain in the center. It was dominated by the figure of Neptune standing on a great rock, surrounded by Nereids and minor sea gods crouching in niches, submissive under his power. The grand duke stopped, putting out one hand to stop Bianca as well. He looked at the statuary for a long time. One Nereid in particular appealed to him, a naked girl on her knees with one arm thrown up over her head, as if in fear or supplication.

"I do not like this fountain," Bianca said. She sounded petulant. "Neptune himself is well enough, but the other figures are unnatural. Perhaps they should be replaced, my lord."

"I think not."

She paled a little. She knew him well enough to know the thought behind the spoken words: *just because I allow you some public recognition, do not get above yourself.*

After a while they turned to the west and made their way to the edge of the main cultivated area. A fine labyrinth of hornbeam and yew trees had been constructed over the past year or so, with rose canes and bittersweet twining among the trees' branches. An iron gate with the Medici device of the shield and balls prevented the casual wanderer in the gardens from entering.

The grand duke unlocked the gate and stepped into the labyrinth confidently—and well he might, as he had designed it and knew its secrets. It was much larger than the mosaic set into his laboratory floor, but it was the same design, down to the last cusp and curving arc. He beckoned for Bianca to follow him.

"Come in," he said. "I would have you walk the labyrinth with me."

"I am cold," she said. "Please, my lord, let us go back."

"Do you not want to know the secret at its heart?"

She wrapped herself even more closely in her fur-lined mantle and stepped reluctantly into the labyrinth. The grand duke thought of the girl Chiara Nerini, his *soror mystica*—that first night, she had stepped confidently into the labyrinth in the laboratory, and walked its path with grave determination. Of course, it had not been hedged with such plants as this one was. He locked the gate behind them.

"By the lion of San Marco," Bianca said, reaching out to touch one of the rose canes. "I have never seen such thorns."

"Do not touch it." The grand duke paused. "These are unique plants, and they are dangerous."

"Dangerous? How?"

"They have been watered with *sonnodolce*, the elixir of Tommaso Vasari."

"What is that?" Bianca stepped into the center of the labyrinth's path, collecting her mantle and skirts close about her so they would not touch the plantings on either side. "Tommaso Vasari? Is he the fellow who built the Vasari Corridor?"

"No. He was an alchemist in my father's employment, who disappeared mysteriously around the time of Carnival in 1566. He left behind a formula he called *sonnodolce*, sweet sleep—a unique poison, quick, sure and undetectable; superior, even, to the cantarella supposedly used by the Borgias. I found the formula by chance, written on a page torn out of a lost book, among my father's papers."

It was not quite the truth, but it was close enough. He himself had torn the page from the book, after overhearing his father and Messer Tommaso talking about the *sonnodolce*, its efficacy and its strange effects. And it was fortunate that he had torn the page out when he did, because a week later Tommaso Vasari and all his books and alchemical equipment had disappeared. His father had refused to be questioned, and so in retaliation Francesco had kept the torn page as his own secret.

"I have been experimenting with it for some years," he said, "and interestingly enough, it does not kill plants. If it is used judiciously, they thrive on it. Come, turn this way."

Bianca followed him. He could see her trembling, very slightly; the shifting glitter of her diamond earrings gave her away. She was keeping close to him, her head no longer high and proud. She was afraid, knowing that he had such a poison in his possession, and that he was not afraid to use it. By the time they reached the heart of the labyrinth, she would be his Bia, fully and completely.

"There is still work to be done," he said calmly, continuing to walk along the paths, taking each turn without hesitation. "See the flower beds under the hornbeam trees? Last autumn I had them planted with lily bulbs, particularly treated, and I hope the flowers will be doubly poisonous—a substance distilled from the stamens of a particular red lily is part of the formula for *sonnodolce*."

"Francesco—Holy Mother, you are mad."

"Not at all. It is an experiment, a matter of science. Flowers and herbs have been used to convey poisons for centuries, with the poison applied to the leaves or petals as a liquid or a very fine powder. I am developing plants that carry the *sonnodolce* within their very veins, so a puncture from a thorn, even a small scratch, is instantaneously fatal."

As he spoke, he casually took a pair of heavy leather gloves, workman's gloves, from his belt and put them on. They were thick enough to protect him if he chose to break off one of the poisoned rose canes. Bianca watched him. Her earrings trembled more noticeably.

"But whom do you wish to poison, Francesco? Whom do you wish to trap in your maze?"

"It is a labyrinth, not a maze."

"Are they not the same?"

"A labyrinth has a single path—if you follow it confidently you will ultimately reach the end. A maze has many paths, many blind alleys."

"Very well. Whom do you wish to trap in your labyrinth?"

"Come with me to the center, and I will tell you."

The center of the locked, poisoned labyrinth, of course, being the safest place in Florence to speak of secret things.

They walked on. She seemed to shrink with every step. Her rich clothing and jewels looked more and more like a costume, awkward and unnatural. At last he led her into a rosette-shaped clearing. At the center of the clearing, the geometrical center of the labyrinth itself, rested an oblong stone, half-buried, the width of two hands, the length of three. There were round holes on its surface, as if it had once been hot enough to boil, and bubbles had risen to its surface.

"This is the center of the labyrinth. The heart of knowledge. Do you see that stone, my Bia?"

"Yes, Franco."

"It fell from the sky a thousand years ago. Now it belongs to me. It is full of iron, but even so I had it carved—the arms of the Medici and the lily of Florence, my own *impresa* and my secret glyph, my device as an alchemist."

He was proud of the stone, its uniqueness, its value, its meaning, what it concealed. He could see that Bia did not understand. She was bored and shivering.

"I think you should put off that fine mantle you are wearing," he said to her, "and remove your sleeves, and open the front of your bodice."

"But it is so cold." The Bia-voice, high and sweet. "Franco, I shall be cold."

"Good. You have been quite heated and comfortable at the Carnival banquets and entertainments, wearing fine clothes and jewels that do not belong to you, drinking in the admiration of every man in Florence. Now you shall feel the cold bite into that fine flesh of yours, and beg me to allow you to be warm again."

Slowly she reached up and unfastened the jeweled martens'-head clasps. The mantle fell in a heap of velvet and fur. She shivered again.

"Perhaps I should help you with the rest."

He drew his dagger and cut the laces at her shoulders. She tugged the embroidered silk sleeves down her arms and dropped them on top of the mantle. She was wearing a white silk camicia with sleeves that reached her wrists, but it was thin, thin as a whisper. Even so— He cut the camicia's sleeves away, leaving her arms bare. Her smooth, rosy skin contracted into gooseflesh as he watched.

"C-cold," she whispered.

He went behind her and cut the laces of her bodice. The boned and stiffened fabric was so thick with gold thread and jewels that it retained its shape when it came away from her body, like some fantastic insect's shell. She let it drop. He went back in front of her and cut the drawstring of her camicia, then pulled the gathered neckline to loosen it. One breast was entirely exposed, the nipple tight with the cold. The other was half-covered by the sheer white fabric. The sun was setting behind the labyrinth and a wash of pink-gold light made her flesh glow.

He did not touch her. He did not have to. She was trembling, but it was no longer entirely a result of the cold. She was aroused, his creature in that moment, there in the heart of the labyrinth. He could tell her anything, and no one else would ever know.

"Even with the perfect poison," he began, as calmly as if she were fully dressed and warm, "it is difficult to poison someone and avoid scandal entirely. Any sudden death creates whispers. Slow deaths are—slow. Consider, for instance, my youngest brother's wife. Eleonora di Garzia di Toledo. Dianora."

Bia nodded. "She did not attend my banquet. I mean, Donna Bianca's banquet. She claimed she was sick."

"She was sick. Just not sick enough."

"Franco. Are you—is the grand duke having her poisoned?"

"And if he is?"

Bia laughed. It was a jarring and unexpected sound. She had wrapped her arms around herself for what warmth they provided. "She deserves it. Everyone knows she was up to her neck in Orazio Pucci's conspiracy. Everyone knows she has had dozens of lovers. And she has been rude to Donna Bianca, over and over. Thinking she is too good for her brother-in-law's mistress."

The grand duke nodded. "It would be quicker and simpler," he said, "if there were proof she had a lover now. Then my brother would be entirely justified in killing her openly, to preserve his honor."

"She dances and whispers with half a dozen men. I do not know if she has actually taken a new lover in the present moment."

"Donna Bianca, now that she is taking the lead in court activities, is uniquely placed to learn such things. She could cultivate Donna Dianora's friendship, or if that does not suffice, pay bribes to her serving-women."

Bia looked at him. The cold was beginning to show on the skin of her breasts and throat and cheeks, the rosy flush becoming mottled with violet. Her eyes were wide and dark with self-surrender. He wondered what it would be like to put her out into real cold, cold with ice and snow, completely naked. Would her skin turn that deathlike violet color all over her body? What would it feel like to have her when she was half-dead with cold?

"That is why, then," she said. "Why Donna Bianca was queen of the Carnival this year."

The grand duke smiled and nodded. "That is one reason. She will discover the specific details of how Donna Dianora is dishonoring my brother. And for that matter, she will discover Donna Isabella's secrets as well. The Duke of Bracciano is also careful of his honor."

"Your own sister?" Bia sounded genuinely shocked.

"She is importuning me for money, telling everyone our father meant for her to have a substantial inheritance. She has nothing in writing and I am tired of her demands."

The sun had dropped below the top of the labyrinth's trees, and the light had faded. Cold mist swirled. In a husky voice, between chattering teeth, Bia said, "And the grand duke's wife? Is there some reason, perhaps, that he could kill her as well, or put her aside?"

The grand duke pricked her exposed breast with the tip of his dagger. She sucked in her breath and stepped back. He pricked her again. She stepped back again, and then realized that another step would press her exposed back and shoulders against the poisoned thorns of the rose canes. She whimpered softly and stretched out her arms, embracing the cold and the knife, the danger and his pleasure. With lingering care he cut three lines over the curve of her breast with his dagger's point; they were not deep but bright blood beaded up. She groaned but did not move.

"Your marten skins"—he gestured with the point of the knife to the mantle on the cold ground—"have not brought you a child, have they, despite the fact that you have been my mistress for what? Nine years? My wife may produce only daughters, but she at least is fertile. She has borne me six children, and three of them live. The youngest is thriving. I still have hopes of a half-Imperial son. Do not dare bring my wife's name into this."

"I am sorry," she whispered. Even under the cold-mottled color of her face he could see the flush of shame. It was her great failure, that she could not bear him a son.

"Only this month, the emperor recognized me at last as the Grand Duke of Tuscany—my wife's brother, my own brother-in-law. Do you think I would throw away his favor?"

"No, Franco."

"Very well. You understand what you are to do, then? You will discover evidence of dishonor against both Donna Dianora and Donna Isabella, and you will give that evidence to no one but me."

"Yes, Franco."

He said nothing for a moment. Her teeth chattering with cold, she said, "Franco? You said it was one reason. Why Donna Bianca was the queen of the Carnival. What is the other?"

"I still have hopes of a half-Imperial son," he repeated thoughtfully. "But a son—any son—would once and for all silence the whispers that I am less than a man."

She said nothing. He could read her expression—she feared he meant to take another mistress. She knew about his whores and did not care— they were only whores. But if another noble mistress bore him a son, even Bia would not be enough to hold him.

"Once Lent is over," he said, "during the Easter celebrations, you will begin to show symptoms of being with child. You will make a point of this—hiding the evidence of your courses, producing sickness in yourself in the mornings, feigning a growing belly. You may take that old woman of yours into your confidence, the one you brought from Venice with you."

"Caterina Donati."

"Whatever her name is. She will do anything for you, will she not?"

"Y-yes."

"In fact, she was willing to help you practice this very deception on me—a pretended pregnancy and a changeling child."

Bianca turned white. The violet mottling of cold looked like a lace veil over her skin. "No. No, I never intended to do that. I never told Caterina that."

"Do you think I am a fool? I know everything you do. I know everything you think and hope for. I would have killed you, my Bia, if you had tried to deceive me like that."

"But now—now—now you yourself want me to do it?"

"I do. I will manage the details, and far better than you could ever have done. I will have a son, legitimate or not. If my wife bears nothing but daughters, I will legitimate him and make him my heir."

"And I will be his mother?" Bianca flushed suddenly, her skin turning rosy despite the cold. "The mother of your heir?"

"The mother of my son, at least. Assuming that you have the courage and tenacity to carry it through."

"I will. Oh, Francesco, I will."

He gestured to her. "Cover yourself. We will return to the palazzo. The costume you have planned for the entertainment tonight—you will have to wear a scarf, I think, to cover those unfortunate cuts. How clumsy you were, to stumble into the thorns while we walked."

"I was clumsy," she whispered. Her voice was soft and acquiescent but there was a dark glitter deep in her eyes, joyful and secret. He had commanded her, and she would obey him. And the whispers about his manhood would be silenced forever.

She gathered up her bodice and sleeves. The grand duke picked up the marten-fur mantle and wrapped it around her. She grasped the rich fur and pulled it close.

"Let us go in, Madonna," he said. "It is growing colder. Even so, do you not agree? It has been a fine evening for a walk in the garden."

"A fine evening," she repeated. "And this fur is wonderfully warm. Even after nine years, my lord, there is always the chance of a miracle."

CHAPTER NINETEEN

Ruan left his apartment in the Casino di San Marco in the black of night, on foot and alone.

As he made his way through the silent streets—*and you, Magister Ruanno, will have time to meet secretly with your messengers, who run back and forth to London at your direction*—he thought of the arrests, the executions, the disappearances. Whispers of treason had been everywhere in the months since Orazio Pucci had lost his handsome head in the dark cellars of the Bargello. What had he confessed? Who was next?

The faintest and most dangerous whispers of all concerned Isabella and her reckless young sister-in-law Donna Dianora. They were sick. They were not sick. They were being poisoned. They were poisoning each other. He did not particularly care about Dianora's fate, although she was a beautiful creature and it would be a sin against God's creation to destroy her. But he cared about Isabella, very much.

Over the past months he had argued with her. Tried to convince her to leave Florence, travel to Rome where her brother the cardinal lived in state and comfort. To do something, anything. She had laughed at him. She was the grand duke's sister. The same Medici blood ran in both their veins, and to the Medici, blood was everything. How could her own brother harm her?

Sometimes in the nights he had thought of abducting her, taking her away by force. He had loved her once and that had marked her for him, marked his own heart. She was in danger and he would protect her, as he had not been able to protect—

Stop it, he admonished himself. You were six years old.

He needed a spy. A watcher, in the heart of the Medici women's secrets, to warn him if the situation became truly dangerous. He could not stand directly between Isabella and her brother's menace, but he could watch, and collect information, and eventually compel her to believe in her own danger.

It was the best way, the only way, to protect her.

He needed someone—

The softest scuff of a footstep behind him in the dark.

He stepped to one side just in time. The upward thrust of the stiletto, aimed for the small of his back, sliced through his doublet and stung the skin over his ribs on his left side. He turned, pulling his own knife out of his right boot in the same movement. The assassin, carried forward by the momentum of his failed thrust, stumbled slightly. Ruan brought his own knife down into the man's back, just below his shoulder blade, and pulled hard to the side, following the space between the man's ribs. The man collapsed with a grunt of shock and agony.

Kawgh an managh.

Ruan cleaned his blade on the man's short black cloak and turned him over. He was masked. He pulled the mask away and swore again. The man's skin was fair and high-colored, his hair was reddish-blond—he knew him. He had seen him before, in the employ of the English ambassador. And the ambassador was expecting him. In his pouch he had another hundred gold scudi for the English ambassador to send on to London, after taking his own share as a commission.

Had the ambassador sent this fellow, with an eye to keeping all the gold for himself instead of just a percentage of it? Or had the dead Englishman learned of the meeting and decided on his own to make his fortune?

Ruan put his knife back in his boot and walked on. He felt no particular remorse over killing the man—it was not, after all, the first time he had killed a man with a knife. If he had been half a breath slower, it would be his body lying dead in the street. The quickened heartbeat and quivering muscles of after-fear, yes. Repugnance, yes. Anger, yes. But not remorse. The watch would find the body and shrug their shoulders that an unwary foreigner had been stupid enough to walk the streets at night, and that would be the end of it.

It was a dangerous business, bribing men at the English court. Necessary, yes, and he would keep doing it. But dangerous.

Almost as dangerous as living with the grand duke's instability and mad suspicions in Florence.

He needed someone who could tell him the secrets of Isabella's household, so he could protect her from her brother.

After that Ruan kept to the laboratory, working on a new process for extracting silver from the ore of the Bottino mine. Most people believed alchemists could make gold and silver in their laboratories; metallurgists knew better. But there were ways to make a given amount of ore produce more metal than it had produced before. Science, not magic—although sometimes the line between the two was not easy to discern.

For practical purposes, though, increasing the mine's yield meant he could demand increased commissions from the grand duke, and he needed gold; buying influence at Queen Elizabeth's court in London was like feeding gold into an endless furnace. Damn the grand duke, anyway, for being caught up in his own plots and counterplots and not making a fresh start on the *magnum opus*. The *Lapis Philosophorum* would solve everything, not because it would magically turn base metal into gold, but because the grand duke would fling wide the doors of his treasury if he believed he had achieved it.

Whatever it cost, one day he, Ruan Pencarrow of Milhyntall, would kill Andrew Lovell and ruin his family. Only when they were poor and ragged and homeless, as he and his mother had been, would his revenge be truly achieved.

"Magister Ruanno?"

He looked up.

It was Chiara Nerini.

"Soror Chiara." He carefully set his reagents aside, the copper of Calais, sulphur and lead, orpiment and oil of Spanish radish.

She stepped farther into the laboratory. She was not wearing her *soror*'s habit, only an ordinary gown and a dark mantle, but he could see the glint of the silver chain around her neck, just inside her collar; she was wearing the moonstone. Her hair was neatly braided and coiled, with the silver strands over her left ear mostly hidden. She looked thinner. There was a hollowness around her changeable eyes and under her cheekbones that had not been there since the days when she had first joined the court.

She had reasons to be thinner—she was in Isabella's household, after all, and that was a dangerous place. It made her look more adult—more desirable, if he were to be strictly honest with himself, and at the same time more fragile. He did not want to hurt her or distress her.

"Your man brought your message," she said. "What do you want, Magister Ruanno? Can I help you with your experiments?"

"No." He poured clean water over his hands and dried them on a towel, taking his time about it. "You are intimate with Donna Isabella and Donna Dianora, are you not? You serve them, share their secrets?"

She folded her lips in and frowned. "I won't spy on them for you, if that's what you want."

He smiled. She was direct. He was not used to that; the intermediaries, informers and conspirators he was accustomed to dealing with never said what they thought in two words if they could dance around it in ten.

"I mean them no harm," he said.

"Perhaps not. Even so, I will not betray them."

So. He had hoped it would not be necessary to compel her.

"The times are unsettled." He stepped out from behind his worktable. She took a step backward. "Most of those connected with the Pucci conspiracy have been arrested, but not all. Pierino Ridolfi, for example. He is in Germany, they say, although the grand duke's agents continue to pursue him."

The girl said nothing. Her eyes had widened when he said Ridolfi's name.

"The grand duke knows that Donna Isabella helped Ridolfi escape Florence. He knows she provided him with Donna Dianora's necklace to pay for his flight, and a fine horse. What he does not know, not yet, is the means by which she passed these things into his hands."

"No one knows that."

"I know. It was you."

She turned so white he was afraid she might have one of her falling-spells. "Stop. Please. Do not say any more. What do you want? I will do anything you ask, if you will do something for me in return."

It had been little more than a guess, that Isabella had used this girl as a go-between. Who else who served her had no other ties or loyalties? Who else was young and foolish enough to do such a dangerous thing? His guess had apparently been spectacularly correct.

He said, "You are hardly in any position to bargain."

"Even so. Please."

What was it about her that touched him? He had not thought there were any soft places left in his heart, and yet here he was, struck to the quick by the thought that she would never trust him again. Angry at himself, he said, "If you swoon away, I swear I will leave you here on the floor and go straight to the grand duke with what I know. Very well. You will serve as my eyes and ears in Donna Isabella's household. Tell me what you wish me to do in return."

She steadied herself with one hand against a heavy cabinet filled with books. "Nonna," she said, as if that explained everything. Actually, it did. *The Nerini are supporters of the old republic*, she had told him the day they went to the booksellers' quarter to retrieve her father's equipment, *as well as being respectable.* That wild-eyed grandmother of hers had carried her support for the old republic far beyond respectability, and was probably up to her neck in Pucci's treasons. She might even have helped Ridolfi escape.

"Help me get them out of Florence for a little while," Chiara Nerini said. Her eyes were dark with fear and anguish. "Nonna and my two little sisters. If you'll do that, I'll tell you everything I see and hear in Donna Isabella's inner chambers."

"She helped Ridolfi escape."

She resisted for a moment longer, then nodded. One small terrified nod.

"Does anyone else know?"

She whispered, "No. I don't think so."

He looked at her for a moment. I should not agree to this, he thought. It is too dangerous. And yet even as the warning formed itself in his mind, he heard himself saying, "Very well, I will manage your fool of a grandmother's escape. Do you not think to ask that I keep silence about your own involvement?"

"You can't denounce me and at the same time use me as a spy."

Neatly reasoned. And true. He smiled at her, a baring of his teeth, nothing more.

"Say I get them out. Where will they go?"

"Nonna has a sister in Pistoia. It's to the west, not very far."

"I know where it is. Will this sister take your Nonna in? Hide her, if necessary?"

"I think so. I hope so. I only met her once. They aren't booksellers—Prozia Innocenza's husband is a locksmith and toolmaker."

"The better to lock your Nonna up if she dabbles in any more treason. What about the shop?"

"I'll speak to the master of the Arte and arrange for a caretaker. Nonna will never stay in Pistoia for long—she is Florentine down to her bones, and will come back as soon as it is safe."

"Perhaps it will never be safe."

"This is home," she said simply. "She will come back. I would come back, if it were me."

This is home.

He thought of Milhyntall House looking out over Mount's Bay, and he understood her.

"Very well," he said. "It is in the grand duke's interest that the shop remain as it is—there may be more small pieces of your father's equipment. More books, hidden. Who knows what may be there?"

That made her eyes flicker away for a moment. There was something hidden in the shop, something she had not told him about. He had suspected as much the first time they had gone there. Well, there would be time to deal with that later.

He said, "Tell your Nonna of the danger, and persuade her to go to Pistoia for a little while. I will arrange for suitable papers."

"You can do that?"

"I can. You go back to the Palazzo Medici and keep your promise. I want to know if there is any hint that Donna Isabella is in danger. Get word to me particularly if either the grand duke or the Duke of Bracciano require her to leave the city for some isolated place."

"I'll help you with Nonna's escape. I'll—"

"You will do as you are told. I want no suspicion attached to you."

"Will you let me know when they are safely away? Please?"

"I will let you know." She looked so desperate that he took pity on her. Again. A bad habit to get into. "It is not a dangerous thing, Soror Chiara, if properly managed. The less you know about it, the better."

"How soon will they be able to come home?"

"It will depend on whether or not Ridolfi is captured, and if he is, what he confesses."

"Donna Dianora's sick more often than she should be," she said abruptly, as if she felt she owed him some immediate payment. "One moment she thinks she is being poisoned, and the next moment she shrugs it off and drinks wine straight from the kitchens."

"Isabella?" he said.

"I'm not sure. She's sad, because Don Troilo Orsini has fled. But I don't think she's being poisoned. She's more careful."

"Good. That is the sort of thing I want to know. Now off you go. Tomorrow I will provide you with a cipher and a supply of invisible ink—your messages to me, and mine to you, must remain a secret."

She looked at him. Her eyes had lightened to a deep greenish-gold color, with brown in a distinct ring around the iris. They had the clarity that signified a water sign. He wondered if she knew what her birth date was, and what her sign would be if he cast her horoscope.

"Thank you," she said. "You could have forced me to help you, without helping me."

"I know." *I am a fool*, he thought. *How did she become another woman with her mark upon my heart?* "Do not forget your promise."

"I won't forget."

CHAPTER TWENTY

Texts of a series of secret messages from Chiara Nerini to Magister Ruanno dell' Inghilterra in the spring of 1576, written in the Trithemius cipher and using an invisible ink compounded from a dilute solution of blue vitriol and sal ammoniac in water, which becomes visible only when heated:

Third day of April. Isabella and Dianora were out in the city yesterday with alms-boxes, collecting alms for the poor as a Lenten penance. They are laughing about it. All is well.

Feast of San Marco. Dianora has been sick again. Isabella is worried because there's no natural cause for her symptoms. Thank you for your assurances regarding the three persons traveling to the northwest.

Last day of April. Dianora's health is better. Bianca C. has been here twice.

Tenth day of May. Dianora has been receiving secret letters and poems from a man whose name you know. She reads the poems aloud to Isabella, and too many people hear them.

Ascension Day. At Cafaggiolo with Isabella. She is safe, I think, because the Duke of B. is not here. Dianora remains in the city with only her servants. She writes that Bianca has become her fast friend, and helps her with her secret letters.

Day after Trinity Sunday. Back in Florence. Isabella is well. Dianora was sick again, but she is better now.

Twenty-seventh day of June. Bianca C. has discovered the letters and poems from Dianora's lover, hidden in a footstool. She gave them to the grand duke. Dianora's lover has been strangled in prison.

A final message, not delivered because Ruanno dell' Inghilterra was not in his customary apartments at the Casino di San Marco, and was in fact nowhere to be found:

Eighth day of July. Isabella's husband has arrived in Florence, as I am sure you know. We are preparing to travel to the Medici villa at Cerreto Guidi for hunting. Dianora and her husband are not coming with us, but have gone separately to the villa at Cafaggiolo. You must act if you can—I am afraid for us all.

Cerreto Guidi, west of Florence

16 JULY 1576

"**M**adonna Isabella," Chiara said. She straightened the embroidered silk coverlet, careful not to touch Donna Isabella herself where she lay curled in the great bed. "Won't you get up, eat a little bread? You have been crying all night."

They had been shut up inside the villa for what? Six—seven—eight days? Chiara didn't know for sure, because the time had run together in a shadowy blur of terror and prayers and contradictory mad entertainments with Isabella's pet dwarf Morgante dancing and singing. No one was allowed to go out or in. The Duke of Bracciano did nothing but eat and drink. Was Magister Ruanno outside, trying to find a way in to save Donna Isabella, save them all? Chiara didn't know if her last secret message had reached him. When she prayed, she imagined him, dark and inscrutable, looming on Lowarn's back. She imagined his whip uncoiling and wrapping around the locks on the doors, tearing them loose, setting them all free.

Then yesterday—could it have been only yesterday?—a messenger wearing the grand duke's colors had come and had been allowed in. Donna Isabella had been summoned into her husband's sodden presence. She had come back with her eyes like burned holes in the paper-white oval of her face, and thrown herself into her bed in tears.

Dianora was dead.

Eleonora di Garzia di Toledo, wife of Pietro de' Medici, beautiful careless sensuous unfaithful Dianora. The grand duke had written to tell his brother-in-law that Dianora was dead at Cafaggiolo, suffocated by accident in her bed and her body hastily carried back to the city, entombed in a crypt under the Basilica of San Lorenzo with no mass, no ceremonies, no mourners.

Although of course her death hadn't been an accident. Who suffocates herself accidentally in her own bed?

And why would the grand duke write such a letter to Donna Isabella's husband, now, when they were all trapped at Cerreto Guidi?

"I do not want to get up," Isabella said. Her voice was hoarse. She had been crying and screaming all night. "I will not move."

"Do you want me to call Father Elicona?"

"No. What good can a priest do? She is dead."

Chiara crossed herself. "He can pray for her, Madonna, and you can pray for her too." I sound like Nonna, she thought.

"I told her," Isabella moaned. She turned her face away. "I tried to warn her. The letters and poems that whore Bianca discovered—they were the last straw. She had too many lovers, too many plots. And it is partly my fault. I helped her arrange Pierino Ridolfi's escape. Francesco never forgave her for that."

And I carried her necklace and put it in Pierino Ridolfi's hands, Chiara thought. I'm guilty, too. Saints and angels, will I be the next to suffocate in my bed? What if they've arrested Magister Ruanno and tortured him? He could tell them what I did, and what Nonna did, and how he helped them escape. Why did I think I was safe, just because I am the grand duke's *soror mystica*? He has conspired in the murder of his own cousin, his brother's wife. Who will be next?

"Donna Isabella," she said. "We must go away. Somewhere, anywhere. Surely Don Paolo cannot prevent you if you surround yourself with all your household and demand to go back to the city, in front of everyone. Once you are out of Cerreto Guidi you could run away—"

"Run away where? And how? I have no money."

"You have your jewels."

"They will not take me far. And what about the children? Paolo would keep them from me—I would never see them again."

"Isabella." Chiara did not dare touch her, but she caught hold of the top coverlet and tried to pull it away. "Listen to me. No matter what Don Paolo says, Dianora was *murdered*. You know it, and I know it. She was taken to an isolated villa with her husband and the next thing anyone heard, she was dead. You are in an isolated villa with your husband. You must find a way to escape before you end up dead as well."

There. She'd said it. *Before you end up dead as well*. And before I end up dead too, she thought.

"Don't be ridiculous." Isabella pushed Chiara's hands away and curled up among the cushions and coverlets. "I am a princess of the Medici by birth and blood. Pietro, yes, I can see my brother killing his wife in a rage—he has always been difficult, unstable. But Pietro is a Medici—he is one of us. Dianora may have had great Spanish connections, she may have been my mother's niece, but she was not a Medici by blood. She had lovers, and my brother's honor was touched."

Chiara stared at her. "She was your cousin, your sister-in-law. She was your friend. She loved you and looked up to you—she modeled her life on yours."

Isabella threw back the coverlets. "How dare you? Fetch me hot water. Fetch me bread and wine. I am a *Medici*. Francesco and I may argue with one another over money, but we are brother and sister—blood is everything. My husband is an Orsini, an outsider—he would never dare to touch me. Francesco would never allow it."

She got out of bed and wrapped herself in her night-gown, rich sky-blue velvet with silver embroidery, glistening with sapphires and pearls. Just at that moment there was a scratch at the door, and one of her waiting-women came into the bedchamber.

"Your husband requires your presence, Serenissima," the woman said.

"I am not dressed."

"He said to tell you that you are to come to him at once, whether you are dressed or not."

Isabella laughed. "There, you see? He wishes to make love to me. Death has that effect on people sometimes—they are overwhelmed by the desire to make new life."

Chiara stood back, unconvinced. She and the waiting-woman looked at each other, and the waiting-woman shrugged. Isabella swept out of the room as if she was on her way to one of her grand entertainments. She'd always put Grand Duchess Giovanna in the shade with her brilliance, and the grand duchess had yielded, sunk in melancholy as she was, sad and homesick and pious, unpopular with the Florentines who saw only her Habsburg pride and not her private kindnesses. Until this past Carnival season, Isabella had reigned unchallenged. Until this past Carnival season—

Bianca Cappello.

The grand duke loved only two things, women and alchemy. And for him, "women" had shrunk and shrunk until it had become one woman. Donna Bianca.

Treason and honor were all very well, but if both Dianora and Isabella were gone, Donna Bianca would reign supreme.

Paolo Giordano Orsini could claim his honor had been touched as well—his wife's lover was Don Troilo Orsini, his own kinsman.

"Isabella!" Chiara cried. "Come back!"

She ran after the grand duke's sister. Isabella had paused for a moment in the room that separated her bedchamber from her husband's. She was speaking to the poet-priest, Father Elicona; the dwarf Morgante was in the room as well, doing somersaults, watched by a handful of ladies. Chiara went straight to Isabella and did the unthinkable: she put her hand on Isabella's arm.

"Don't go in," she said. "Stay away from your husband, and think of a way to go back to Florence."

Isabella frowned and pulled her arm away. She didn't like to be touched unless she had invited such a familiarity. "You presume too much, Mona Chiara," she said. Her voice was cold and her expression was stiff with pride, as it always was when she was imagining herself at the center of the cosmos. Nothing bad could happen to her, because if it did the cosmos itself would blink out of existence. "I am sad for my little cousin's death, but Pietro was justified. I will support my brothers, as I have always done. My husband, well"—she looked around at all of them and shrugged a little—"I have always been perfectly capable of managing my husband."

She walked on. Chiara watched her. They all watched her, in deathly silence.

She didn't scratch on the door to her husband's private chamber. She simply opened the door, and walked in, and closed the door behind herself.

There was a pause, and then the click of a lock.

The dwarf did three more somersaults, and ended just outside the door. He pressed his ear against the carved wooden surface. At the same time there was the unmistakable sound of a slap, the crack of a hand against flesh.

All of them, Chiara, the priest, the ladies, ran to the door and struggled for the best listening spots. Chiara pushed one of the other ladies away and put one eye against the crack between the door and the wall, just under one of the hinges. She could see only a tiny slice of the room. Wherever Isabella and her husband were, they weren't in that tiny space.

"How dare you lay your hand on me?" It was Isabella's voice. She didn't sound afraid, only angry. "I am going to return to Florence. Get out of my way."

"You are going nowhere." Don Paolo sounded as if he had been drinking wine, even though it was barely midday. "I have things to say to you."

"I do not wish to listen. I—"

Her words were cut off with another slap. She did not cry out in pain, but in anger. Chiara saw a brief flash of the blue night-gown, and then the door-handle rattled violently.

"Unlock this door!" Isabella shouted. There was an edge of fear in her voice.

"You will listen," Don Paolo said. "Do you not want to hear the things your brother's messenger told me, things the grand duke did not choose to commit to paper?"

The door creaked. Isabella was leaning against it. The dwarf Morgante growled like a wild animal. He loved his mistress, Chiara knew, and would have given his life to protect her. But the door was locked on the inside, and there was no other key.

"She fought hard, Donna Dianora did." Chiara saw an enormous blob of black velvet pass across the crack in the door. Don Paolo, so fat no horse could carry him. His voice was conversational and chilling. "She bit your brother's hand like a mad dog, and almost took off two fingers. Fortunately he had a pair of fine fellows from the Romagna in the room with him, to help him."

"I will not listen to you. Let me out."

"They threw her on the bed and held her down. Your brother was swearing, his hand bleeding. He said that if she wanted to bite him like a dog, she could die like a dog."

The handle of the door rattled frantically. Uselessly.

"He sent for a dog's leash—the servants were too frightened to disobey him. The two *teppisti* held her down, however much she struggled and screamed. A man brought him a leather leash, not one of the embroidered silk ones she liked to use for her own little hounds, but a good stout leather strap like the ones used to hold mastiffs. It was muddy—it had not been cleaned since the last time the mastiff hunted."

"For the love of Mary Virgin, my lord, stop." Isabella sounded genuinely frightened now. "I do not want to hear these things."

"No?" There was a sound of ripping fabric, and a sob from Isabella. "You will listen for as long as I choose to speak. And I want to tell you everything, all the details your brother told his messenger to share with me."

"Francesco would not wish that!"

"Oh, but he does. Where was I? Yes, the mastiff's leash. While the two men held her down, your brother wrapped the filthy leather strap around her lovely neck. Her clothes had become torn and disarranged in her struggles, and her throat and breasts were naked. He wrapped either end of the leash around his fists and jerked it tight."

Two of the ladies at the door had begun to cry. The priest was praying, his eyes closed, his fingers counting the beads of his rosary. Morgante had scratched grooves in the wood of the door, snarling. Chiara was frozen, unable to move, unable to cry, hardly able to believe the devil's tale she was hearing.

"Her face began to turn blue," Don Paolo went on. He was savoring every word. "She had such fine, clear skin, thin as silk. Your brother said he could see the veins beating beneath it. Her eyes started from her head, and her tongue from her mouth. He took his time about it, throwing the names of her lovers in her face while she could still hear them. How they were all dead. How he didn't believe the little boy, Cosimino, was his own seed, and would send him after his mother in a few weeks' time."

"You are a monster," Isabella sobbed. "You are making this up—none of it really happened."

"It happened. Just as I have described it. With the dog's leash cutting off her breath at last, she scratched the two men a little, and kicked her feet, and then it was over."

There was silence. Chiara could hear Isabella panting. She looked down at Morgante. The dwarf was curled on the floor, shaking. If he was crying, he made no sound. The priest and the ladies had shrunk away from the door, and were huddled together in the middle of the room.

Someone had to do something.

Someone had to fight back.

Santa Monica, Chiara prayed silently, patron of mistreated wives, pray for us all. Then she took a breath.

"Don Paolo!" she cried. "We are listening, all of us. You must let Donna Isabella come out. If you harm her, we will hear it."

Isabella's husband laughed. "Listen away," he said. "You will hear only a man taking back his honor. Massimo, help me. I don't want this one biting my fingers to the bone."

Massimo?

"Coward!" Isabella shrieked. "Coward, coward, to have a hired bravo under the bed—you cannot even attempt to murder your own wife? You have never been good for anything but consorting with whores and spending my family's money. No! Do not touch me!"

The blue night-gown flashed by Chiara's eyes again. There were screams, grunts of effort, slaps and blows, gasping struggles for breath—it was impossible to tell who was making what sound. Frantically Chiara tore at the crack between the door and the doorjamb. She knew it was useless— some part of her knew—but all she could think of was that she could hear them, through the crack, and she couldn't reach them. How could it be real that she was so close and she could hear them and she couldn't reach them?

She shouted—*leave her alone, leave her alone*—but her voice was lost in the cacophony.

Then all of a sudden there was silence.

Silence for a long time, long enough to say the Pater at least three times. No one in the room moved.

Then the lock rasped, and the door was abruptly pushed open. The edge of the wood, swinging back, crushed the fingers of Chiara's left hand—she had never known such pain, pain that took her breath away so she couldn't even scream. She tried to pull her hand free but it was caught. The pain sharpened her senses. She heard Morgante scrabbling back on his hands and knees, a man's heavy panting, her own animal whine of agony.

"One of you women." It was Don Paolo, then. He wheezed, trying to catch his breath. "Fetch some vinegar, quickly. Donna Isabella has fainted while washing her hair in a basin."

The women scattered. Chiara knew they were not running to fetch vinegar—they were running for their lives. The priest was already gone.

Don Paolo went back into the bedchamber and closed the door. Oh, God, blessed cessation of pain. Chiara snatched back her hand and cradled her fingers against her breast—the skin was sliced open, she was bleeding, were the bones broken?

Did it matter?

Had Isabella truly fainted?

She ran into Isabella's own bedchamber. Let it be true, let it be true, let her only have fainted. One-handed she threw open a chest, dug through the pots and bottles, and found a glass-lined silver flask of vinegar. She ran back to Don Paolo's bedchamber, with Morgante behind her. He was the only one of Donna Isabella's household to remain faithful. They went in.

Isabella de' Medici was sprawled half on her knees beside the bed, the coverlets still clutched in her hands as if she had been trying to climb up into the immense feather mattress. There was an empty basin on a table beside the bed. Her hair had come free from its loose nighttime braids and spilled wildly down over her shoulders, haphazardly drenched with water— any fool could see that the water from the basin had been thrown over her after she had fallen. Her head was bowed, her face hidden. She might indeed have fainted from terror or fury.

Don Paolo was standing bent over, gasping to catch his breath. The other man, the one he had called Massimo, stood on the far side of the bed. He was dark—that was the only impression Chiara had, dark hair, dark clothes, dark evil. She stumbled to the bed—please please let her be only in a faint—and knelt beside Isabella. With her teeth she opened the flask of vinegar and with the heel of her wounded hand she gently tilted Isabella's head back.

She was dead. Her flesh was still warm, but it had the inert claylike consistency of dead things.

Her face was mottled with purple, and her eyes half-closed, with the whites glimmering between the lashes. Her mouth was open and her tongue thrust out. There was blood—she had bitten her tongue in her desperate fight for her life. Her beautiful sky-blue velvet night-gown, all glittering with jewels, had been pulled off her shoulders, and one of her breasts was terribly bruised and ruptured, as if it had been crushed. Around her neck, there was the reddened imprint of a cord.

The looped cord lay on the floor beside her. It was red silk, with tassels on the ends.

Chiara put the vinegar flask down. For a moment she thought—will he kill me too? She lay her hand lightly over Isabella's eyes, pressing down the lids. *You presume too much, Mona Chiara.* Then she stood up and faced the Duke of Bracciano. A widower, now, by his own hand.

"Why did you bother to call for vinegar?" she said. She was astonished at herself, that her voice was so calm. "You knew it would do her no good."

He grinned at her. "For the others to hear. They will report that she fainted, nothing more, and then died of a sudden sickness. That she drank too much cold water when she was overheated. That she fell and struck her head on the basin, while she was washing her hair. Who cares? But you—" He looked at her more closely. He had scratches on his fat cheeks and down his own throat, and one of his eyes was half-closed with bruising. Isabella had fought for her life. "What is your name?"

Chiara looked back at him. It was probably stupid to say it but she didn't care. Clearly she said, "I am Chiara Nerini."

"By the balls of Christ," he said. "The grand duke's pet sorceress. Well,

Chiara Nerini, the grand duke himself knew what I intended to do, and gave his consent. My wife betrayed me with my own kinsman, and it was my right to kill her, to avenge my own honor, and the honor of the house of Medici, which she also despoiled with her lewdness."

It sounded as if he had written it out beforehand, and committed it to memory. Chiara said nothing.

"So say what you want. No one will believe you, and even if they do—it is a man's right to defend his honor."

Morgante had crawled over to Isabella's body and was stroking the soft blue velvet of her night-gown. He said nothing, but whimpered like a child.

"Who would I tell?" Chiara said at last. She could hear the bitterness in her own voice. It was like Babbo's voice, after Gian was killed. It was like Nonna's voice, when she talked about the Medici. Bitter as tears and blood and death. "If it was the grand duke's will that she die, who will listen to me?"

"Get me some wine," Don Paolo said. "Cavaliere Massimo—go get the coffin. Call some of the men from the stable, and they will put her in it."

Chiara walked out of the room. She didn't look back. She was dizzy with shock and pain and horror, and the only thing she could think to do was get back to Florence and take the last book, her father's most precious book, out of its hiding-place in the wall of the bookshop's cellar. It was valuable. She would take it with her to Pistoia, so she did not have to arrive empty-handed.

She was finished with the Medici, with or without the *Lapis Philosophorum*. She was finished with courts. Finished with alchemy. She'd find her way to Pistoia and Nonna and the girls, even if she died trying. They'd stay there for a while, until the grand duke forgot about them, but not forever. No, not forever. They were the Nerini and they'd lived in Florence for two hundred years. They'd find a way to come home, and everything would go back to the way it was before she ever went out in the rain to sell a silver descensory to Francesco de' Medici.

Nothing will ever go back the way it was, Babbo's voice whispered gleefully. *Remember the labyrinth on that silver descensory? You're trapped in the labyrinth of the Medici, and you'll never escape. Never in this life, or in any other.*

CHAPTER TWENTY-ONE

Florence

19 JULY 1576

She went home with Donna Isabella's body and the rest of her household the day after the murder. She had no other choice—she couldn't walk all the way to Florence without food or water and she'd have been easy pickings for bandits if she'd tried to steal a horse and ride alone. Her broken fingers turned purple and green and black and throbbed with every beat of her heart. She tried to wash them—*wash a wound with wine and comfrey root to drive out the evil humors*, Nonna always said—but it hurt so much she couldn't manage it on her own. The broken skin puffed up and turned red and shiny.

As they traveled, she kept far away from Don Paolo in his enormous litter, from the dark Cavaliere Massimo, and most of all from the makeshift coffin. The July heat was unrelenting and Isabella's body had been tumbled into the box with no embalming, not even a shroud or the traditional bathing and dressing by her ladies. Father Elicona had been dragged from his hiding-place and compelled to give her a conditional unction, so at least there was that. Was her soul at peace? How could it be?

As they traveled, Chiara began to feel sick and feverish. Her whole arm ached. The voices whispered, whispered, whispered—Babbo and the demons and now women's voices, too, Isabella's and Dianora's. *We had lovers, pleasures; we shuddered and screamed, and now we are dead, dead, dead. We died for our delights.*

It was the middle of the night when they entered the city at last, through the Porta di San Frediano. They went directly to the old church of Santa Maria del Carmine, next to the Carmelite convent. Don Paolo did not make the effort of descending from his litter, but directed brusquely that the coffin be taken into the church.

"And Massimo?" he added. He might have been giving instructions for a basket of offal to be thrown to the kitchen-yard pigs. "Open it. Leave it open. I want everyone in the city to see her, and know that I have regained my honor in full."

The dark man and three others wrestled the coffin from its cart and carried it into the church, handling it roughly and carelessly. Two other men lighted their way with torches. Chiara looked away.

"You, sorceress."

Chiara turned her head slowly. She was dizzy. The moon was waning and with the torches gone inside the church, she could not see Don Paolo's face. There was only the suggestion of a hulking figure in the darkness of the litter, like a demon in a pit of hell.

"Go in and look at it," he said. "Look at it well. In fact, all of you, her household—you, priest—you, dwarf—all of you women. Go in. Look at it. Look at what happens when you offend against the honor of the Orsini."

The women began to whisper. Some of them started to cry. Clinging together, they climbed down from the carts and went into the church, too frightened to disobey. Father Elicona followed them, his eyes cast down. Morgante the dwarf alone seemed to have regained his good spirits, or perhaps he had gone mad with shock and grief. He walked on his hands, waving his feet, grinning. Chiara followed last of all, barely able to walk. She wanted to defy Don Paolo, but what good would it do?

Donna Isabella is gone, she told herself. Her soul is in Purgatory, suffering for her sins but safe. What this monster does with her poor earthly flesh means nothing to her.

In the church, the men had flung the coffin down in a small chapel in the south transept. The walls were covered with frescos, figures of people appearing to twist and whisper in the torchlight. On the right wall there was a man crucified upside down. He was screaming. Above him, a little to the right, a woman in grave clothes sat bolt upright, her arms crossed over her breast. The sound of the coffin nails being drawn out sounded like devils shrieking.

"There," one of the men said. The coffin lid was tipped up and cast aside with a crash. "By the ass bones of San Martino, she stinks."

The women began to scream and sob. They pushed each other, trying to be the first to flee the chapel. The priest gabbled a prayer and went out. Chiara stood with Morgante the dwarf, the people on the walls closing in around them, and looked.

Saints and angels. She turned around and vomited helplessly.

"Principessa, principessa," Morgante sang. "Lady true, all in blue, color of the sky, falling down to die."

"Lift up her skirts, Emiliano," one of the men said. "I've never seen a princess's private parts before."

"Her legs are still white. Well, mostly white. What happened to her tit? It looks like it's been smashed."

"Massimo says her husband sat on her to hold her down. Fat as he is, that would've been enough to kill her in itself."

"Look at her face."

"That's not a face, it's a big black rotten melon with two holes punched in it where the eyes would be."

They all laughed. Chiara pushed past them and ran to the door of the church, gasping for the clean fresh air of the night. She couldn't move her left arm at all. Her head hurt and she was dizzy and she fell to her knees, and that was the last thing she remembered.

PART III

Giovanna

A Faithful Union

CHAPTER TWENTY-TWO

The Palazzo Vecchio

ASSUMPTION DAY, 15 AUGUST 1576

"Her name is Vivi," Chiara said. "From *vivacità*. Because she's so bright-eyed and lively."

She had an eight-week-old puppy in her lap, a daughter of Donna Isabella's Rina crossed back to the grand duchess's fine dark-eyed hound Rostig. The baby had the long, silky russet-colored ears of its breed, a white muzzle, and patches of black and russet on its plump little body.

"A fine name," the grand duchess said. "It fits her."

Rina, at least, had come out of the holocaust of Donna Isabella's household unscathed; with Donna Jimena's help, the grand duchess had seen to her safety and that of her newly born puppies. Isabella's children had joined the grand duchess's household as well, five-year-old Nora and four-year-old Virginio Orsini. Their father was claiming they weren't his anyway. Their father was claiming all kinds of things, including any Medici property he could get his fat, grasping hands on.

Little Don Cosimino, Dianora's three-year-old son, was not there. He was dead. A fever, some said. Dysentery, said others. Don Pietro roistered through the whorehouses of Florence, uncaring.

Chiara knew all these things only because Donna Jimena had told them to her. She herself had spent three weeks raving with fever, unconscious of anything going on around her. When she had awakened, the world had changed. She and Donna Jimena, like the dogs, belonged to a new mistress.

"She kept you alive, I think." Donna Jimena was sitting in a chair across the room, one hand resting on Rina's head. Rina was watching her puppy anxiously. Donna Jimena looked as if she had aged a thousand years. Her cheeks were no longer round as last season's apples, but sagged with empty sorrow. Her whole world had been balanced on her love for Isabella, child and woman. What would she do now?

"We despaired for you, Chiara," she said, "when Father Elicona brought you here. Your arm was swollen and your fingers were black and you were raving with fever."

"Indeed," the grand duchess said. "You cried out over and over about people from the wall of the church coming down, and—well, better not to speak of it. The priests from San Stefano brought the Sacra Cintola to Florence and placed it in your hand, that the Holy Virgin herself might heal you."

"With some help from the grand duke's physicians," Donna Jimena said. "They applied the French method, treatment with turpentine and oil of roses, just as they do with soldiers on the battlefield."

"*Das terpintin*, bah," the grand duchess said. "It was the Holy Virgin."

"And Vivi." Donna Jimena continued to pat Rina's head. "It was like another miracle when I put her into your arms. You stroked her ears and began to get better."

"I remember, Donna Jimena, your voice telling me I had to take care of her." Chiara tried to smile but didn't quite manage it. It felt as if it was wrong to smile. It felt almost as if it was wrong to be alive. Maybe she wasn't really alive, and all this was a dream. "I'm so grateful to you, and to you, Serenissima, more than I can say."

"You will remain in my household," the grand duchess said. "My husband, he agrees. He—came to my apartments last night, and we spoke at some length, about many things."

She colored up as she spoke. How little it took, Chiara thought bleakly, to touch the emotions under the stiff Austrian pride. How unexpected that there were emotions to touch, after eleven years of misery and loneliness, homesickness and humiliation.

"He spoke of you, Signorina Chiara. He was pleased the physicians had saved your life, and restored the use of your hand."

Chiara looked down at her left hand, resting on the puppy's fat little body. The second and third fingers were crooked and discolored and the nails had fallen off, but she could move them. Their ability to feel, sense hot and cold and textures, was returning. Vivi's puppy fur, for example, was warm and soft.

Was she really feeling it?

She was fortunate the grand duke wanted her to be alive, she knew that. So many of the people connected to Donna Isabella had disappeared. A lady who had sometimes looked after the children. A merchant who had sold her silk—and possibly passed on secret messages. Her gardener at the Baroncelli villa—his crime was that he had suddenly begun to wear fine clothes, too fine for his station. A chirurgeon and a cesspit-cleaner—saints only knew what crime they had connived in. Chiara couldn't remember all the names and all the people. Some were in prison and some were dead.

She was alive. Because the grand duke loved alchemy. No other reason.

Without any real sense of caring or urgency she said, "Does he intend to continue the search for the *Lapis Philosophorum*?"

"You wish to know, of course, if you are still bound by your vow. The answer is yes." The grand duchess nodded in a brief, decided manner. "The English alchemist is still in the Bargello, but I suspect in the end he will be released—he has skills and knowledge no other man has."

So the three of them, the grand duke, Magister Ruanno, and herself, were still a mystical triad, connected by the work they had done and the stones they wore. She'd heard the servants talking in the days since she'd recovered her lucidity—Ruanno dell' Inghilterra had been imprisoned a day or two before the murders of Donna Isabella and Donna Dianora. Obviously the grand duke had taken no chances that his pet alchemist might attempt to save either of the ladies. Had Magister Ruanno received her messages? All of them? Some of them? Had the grand duke intercepted them, and did he know it was she who had sent them?

Pain and fever had brought back the voices and the headaches, worse than ever. It had also brought a strange dreamlike state, a sort of not-caring. She was safe enough, here in the grand duchess's own household.

Magister Ruanno was safe enough, wherever he was. Nonna and Lucia and Mattea were safe in Pistoia. The grand duke had the city in an iron grip of terror, and escape now would be impossible anyway.

She stroked Vivi's ears. They were warm and silky, with a scent like milk and *frittelle*. Her paws particularly, with their pink puppy pads, had the sweet *frittella* smell.

"I am going to the Palazzo Medici today," the grand duchess said. "The grand duke is selling Donna Isabella's jewels and possessions to pay her debts, and I wish to collect a few things for her children before everything is gone. It is important, is it not, to have *andenken*, keepsakes, of one's mother?"

Chiara thought of her own mother, dead so soon after Gian's death. She had had no jewels, no trinkets. Her mother's few clothes had been cut down for the little girls and worn out. There was nothing left to remind her. Even her mother's face—sometimes it wouldn't come to her.

Her father's equipment, she knew where that was, at least. It was all in the grand duke's laboratory.

All but the book.

A representative of the Arte had been taking care of the shop since Nonna and the girls had fled. Had he gone down into the cellar? Had he looked closely at everything? What had become of the one ancient book with Babbo's handwritten notes, which she had wrapped so carefully in waxed silk and locked in an iron box and plastered into the wall?

"My own mother died a few days after I was born," the grand duchess was saying. She liked to talk in private. No one who saw her in public, stiff and silent, would ever guess it. "I never knew her, but I have her portrait. I have some of her jewels. I brought it all to Florence with me, and sometimes I look at her face and draw strength from it."

"There are portraits at the Palazzo Medici," Chiara said. "There's one in particular, of Donna Isabella with her children—it's very good."

"You shall come with me. You have been up, walking in the garden, have you not? You are strong enough. It would be good for you to go out."

"Serenissima. I beg you. I don't want to go back to the Palazzo Medici. Donna Jimena can find the portrait for you."

"You must face the things that cause you pain." The grand duchess rose. Chiara and Donna Jimena rose as well, Chiara cradling the puppy in her arms. The grand duchess looked at them for a moment, and then she said again, "You must face the things that cause you pain. I know that to be a true thing."

Chiara bowed her head. If the grand duchess could endure eleven years of disappointment and homesickness and unhappiness, she could endure a visit to the Palazzo Medici. It didn't matter anyway. She said, "Yes, Serenissima."

CHAPTER TWENTY-THREE

There was a coach in the street outside the front door of the Palazzo Medici. The driver lounged on his box at the front, wearing the red, blue and gold colors of the Medici. The coach itself was painted red, with ornate gilded carvings of laurel leaves and feathers around the edge of the roof and outlining the doors. On the door panel itself there was a white circle with a painted device: a traveling hat with two strings.

"Do you wish to pass by, Serenissima?" Donna Jimena recognized the device, just as they all did—the *cappello* of the grand duke's Venetian mistress.

"No." The grand duchess gestured that the door to her own coach be opened. "I am here. I will go in. Accompany me."

She stepped out. Donna Jimena helped her with her skirts. Chiara followed them. How did the grand duchess manage to appear so erect, her back so straight, her head so high? She wore steel corsets and padded dresses to disguise her twisted back, but there was more to it than that. It was the pride of a daughter of emperors and queens, pride that created a special quality in the air around her, despite her plainness and melancholy and the Habsburg deformity of her chin.

The palazzo's great door was opened for her—Medici guardsmen jumped to do her bidding, despite the fact that they had arrived with her husband's mistress. She passed through without a word, into the inner courtyard. Pillars of white stone supported arches to create airy colonnades, and above the arches there were carved stone medallions, classical scenes interspersed with the Medici balls. The walls were decorated with niches, and within the niches stood magnificent statues of gods and goddesses. Orange and lemon trees in pots gave the air a faint piquant scent.

"Where is this portrait you described, Signorina Chiara?"

The grand duchess had settled on "Signorina" as a suitable form of address—superior to the guildswoman's "Mona" yet not as high in status as the noblewoman's "Donna." Details like that were important to her. She didn't acknowledge the title of *soror mystica* at all. For her, a sister was a nun, vowed to the religious life; the use of the Latin word as part of a title for an alchemist's assistant was blasphemous to her.

"It's upstairs, Serenissima, in Donna Isabella's—in the salon that was Donna Isabella's private music room."

They went upstairs. The palazzo was quiet, with no sounds but the faraway splashing of water in the garden fountain. Where was Bianca Cappello? With her coach outside the palazzo so openly, surely she was somewhere inside. There were so many chambers and salons and elegant rooms for writing and studying.

Everything Chiara saw brought back a memory: the fruit trees; the graceful, neatly laid out garden where Donna Isabella would walk at twilight; the silken tapestries; the gold and silver vases; and the books, everywhere the books, a fortune in beautiful books, old and new, that Donna Isabella had loved and pored over and discussed endlessly with her little court of ladies and gentlemen.

Lift up her skirts, Emiliano. I've never seen a princess's private parts before. Her legs are still white. Well, mostly white . . .

Chiara swallowed back nausea. The terrible men's voices had somehow connected themselves to her demons' voices, and wouldn't go away.

"This way, Serenissima," she managed to say. "The music salon, it's at the end of this corridor."

They started down the hallway with its black-and-white tessellation of fine marble. At the same time Bianca Cappello stepped out of a chamber on the left side, just opposite the music room. She froze, midstep; her waiting-woman, walking behind with bundles of clothing and linens, almost stumbled over her. The grand duchess stopped as well. The two women looked at each other in awful silence.

The grand duke's mistress had a belly. Round and high, only four or five months' worth, but definitely a belly.

The grand duchess didn't move. She gazed at her husband's pregnant mistress.

Bianca Cappello broke first. She sank into a curtsy, spreading out her amber-colored velvet skirts. Her oversleeves were slashed to show off silver satin undersleeves, embroidered with gold in a barred pattern. She wore rich rings and pearls around her neck and jewels in her braided hair. She looked like an actress in one of the new commedia dell'arte companies, dressed up as a lady, compared to the severe and inborn dignity of the grand duchess.

"Serenissima," she said. Her voice trembled a little.

The grand duchess made her wait. Then she said coldly, "You may rise, Signora Bianca. What are you doing here, in my sister-in-law's palazzo? Stealing her clothes, I see. Her very underclothes."

Bianca Cappello straightened. She was quite beautiful, if you liked a lot of lush, velvety flesh. She had strongly marked brows and red-gold hair that obviously owed a good part of its color to henna, chamomile, and a powdering of gold dust. Her eyes flashed. She had her pride as well, it was plain to see, and these days she wasn't used to being addressed as plain Signora.

"I have the grand duke's personal authority, and his own guardsmen to escort me," she said. "And his permission to take what I please. What are you yourself doing here, Serenissima? Surely Donna Isabella's possessions are so suggestive of worldly pleasure that they could only disgust you."

Yes, she had her pride. What would the grand duchess say to that? Chiara held her breath.

"On the contrary. Even in worldly possessions, I recognize elegance and refinement." The grand duchess swept her eyes up and down Bianca's figure, the yards and yards of amber velvet, the embroidered sleeves, the opulent bosom, the thickened waist. She looked at the waiting-woman with her bundles, like a rag collector. The waiting-woman, at least, had the grace to blush.

The grand duchess said, "I recognize its lack, as well."

"Elegance and refinement are overrated," Bianca said. Her eyes glittered—tears?—but her mouth was drawn back over her fine white teeth. She arched her back, deliberately thrusting her belly forward. "Men, particularly, often find too much refinement—tedious."

Chiara saw the grand duchess flinch. It was such a small movement, so quickly and rigorously controlled, that only someone standing as close as she was, close enough to touch the grand duchess's slight figure, would have noticed it.

"How fortunate for you, then," she said. Her voice was like the flavored snows sometimes served at court banquets, ice-cold and sweet. "No man would ever fault you for over-refinement. You have my permission to leave my presence, Signora Bianca, and take yourself out of this place."

Bianca Cappello's heavy brows slanted together over her nose, and she took a step forward. "I will tell him what you have said to me," she said. "He will be angry that you have been discourteous."

The grand duchess did not move. There were centuries of breeding in her immobility. She said nothing.

Bianca walked toward them, her waiting-woman following her. The grand duchess looked through her, as if she were not there. Bianca stopped, two steps away, her color high.

"Donna Jimena," she said. That startled them all. "Will you be discourteous, too? You are lower than I—you should curtsy to me as I walk past you."

"I would sooner curtsy to one of the potted trees in the courtyard." Every one of Donna Jimena's sad deflated wrinkles quivered with outrage. "I am vastly your elder in years and an Osorio by blood, the first lady-in-waiting to the Princess Isabella from the days of her childhood. It is you who are the lower, Signora. Being a great man's mistress and the mother of his bastard does not give you that great man's rank."

Bianca sucked in her breath. The grand duchess continued to stare straight ahead.

"You, then." Bianca looked straight at Chiara. "I know who you are— you are Francesco's alchemist girl. You at least should curtsy in my presence—you are nobody, a bookseller's daughter he picked up in the street."

Chiara felt as if she were underwater—there was that sense of something clear and heavy drifting between her and Bianca Cappello. It was a shocking impropriety for her to refer to the grand duke by his Christian name, in public, before his wife. But then, everyone knew how the grand duke cosseted her. How they play-acted together like children. How she was the only person in all of Florence who could coax him to smile.

What was she, Chiara Nerini, daughter of guildswomen and supporters of the Florentine republic, doing standing in the Palazzo Medici, caught between the grand duke's furious big-bellied mistress and his steel-proud Imperial wife? A month ago, two months ago, three months ago—how long had it been?—she would have been excited, proud even, to be at the center of such a moment. What did she feel now? Nothing. I should probably take a few moments, she thought, work out all the possible consequences of what I do. But the consequences didn't matter.

She met Bianca Cappello's eyes and thrust out her chin in the way Nonna hated. She bent her knees the tiniest fraction, so tiny as to be more insulting than no curtsy at all. She smiled, curling her left hand with its misshapen fingers into a fist. Then she made her eyes look through the grand duke's mistress as if she was not there, just as the grand duchess had done.

"You will be sorry for that," Bianca hissed.

She stormed away. The waiting-woman dropped one white silk camicia, embroidered with black work and faceted jet beads. Her face red as fire, she came back and gathered it up, then followed her mistress. After a moment the front door slammed.

"Signorina Chiara," the grand duchess said. Her voice was composed. Her back was straight, or might as well have been. "Let us continue. I particularly desire to collect the portrait of Donna Isabella with her children, and any other *andenken* that will help to make their grief less, as they grow up without her."

CHAPTER TWENTY-FOUR

The Palazzo Bargello

20 AUGUST 1576

Ruan had not been held in the dungeons under the Volognana Tower. He had not been stripped, manacled, tortured or starved. The grand duke's guards had taken him the night of July seventh, four of them coming at him from behind as he locked the door of the laboratory at the Casino di San Marco. From that day to this he had been shut up in one of the small rooms at the back of the second story of the Bargello, given food, wine, water to wash with, books and paper, pens and ink, if he wished to read or write in the hours of daylight. Nothing more. No one would speak to him. The grand duke did not visit him, although clearly it was the grand duke who had arranged his imprisonment.

There was one small window, which looked out to the east, away from the Palazzo Vecchio, away from the Casino di San Marco. Away from everything in Florence that tied him to the Medici. He knew why he had been arrested in such a secret fashion—the grand duke had decided to move against Isabella and Dianora, and wanted no interference from his English alchemist, his sister's one-time lover.

Isabella was dead. He knew it. He could feel it. As with the sublimation of iodine, the direct change from an ordinary solid to a glorious violet mist, his sense of her had been transformed from earthbound flesh to numinous spirit. And all the while he had been locked in this room, safe, well-treated, and entirely helpless. It was worse than any torture, and Francesco de' Medici knew it.

Francesco de' Medici.

I will kill him, Ruan thought. Perhaps not today, or tomorrow, or even this month, this year. I will bide my time, gain my freedom, use his laboratories and resources to create a *Lapis Philosophorum* that will astonish him, blind him, and extract from him the riches I need. But I will kill him in the end, for what he has done to Isabella.

Ruan waited. Using the paper and pens, he wrote equations and formulas. He had never seen beauty in written words, letters or plays or poetry. He saw beauty in numbers and chemical symbols.

He waited. They had not taken his amulet, the chunk of hematite on its iron and copper chain. He himself had taken it from around his neck for the first time in years, and put it on the table. It was a reminder—this is what you were, a creature of the Medici. This is what you are no longer.

It also made him think of the girl, Chiara Nerini. He wondered if she was still wearing her amulet, the moonstone. Had the grand duke intercepted the messages from her? If he had, she was imprisoned too, or dead. The thought disturbed him, more than he would have expected. He imagined her carrying the silver sieve filled with water. Walking the arcs and double folds of the labyrinth on the floor of the laboratory, her dark hair loose to her hips, the moonstone glimmering on her breast. She was ordinary-looking, sharp-chinned, plain, even, but for that magnificent hair and those changeable, changeable eyes. He had coerced her into sending him the messages. If she was dead, he was responsible.

He did not want her to be dead. He was surprised, a little, by the intensity of his need for her to be alive. By the fact that he could not bear the thought of not seeing her again.

Forty-four days after he had been imprisoned, just as the light through his window was fading, the lock scraped, the door opened, and the grand duke walked into the room.

"Ruanno," he said.

Ruan did not allow himself to show surprise. He said nothing.

The door remained open. There were guardsmen outside. Francesco de' Medici was taking no chances with his prisoner.

"What is done, is done," the grand duke said. He was richly dressed in dark blue velvet. He held a pomander in one hand, an orange studded with cloves and cured in ground cinnamon bark and orrisroot powder. Ruan wondered if he had expected to find an unwashed, gibbering maniac, broken by forty-four days of solitude.

"Isabella is dead," the grand duke went on. "She deserved to die—she dishonored her husband and the house of Medici by taking lovers, and involved herself in Donna Dianora's treason. Even you cannot argue that."

"I do not argue the lovers," Ruan said. "It is no particular secret that I myself was one of them. I do argue her death at your hand."

He did not bother to address the grand duke with titles or honor. In his own ears, his voice sounded rusty from disuse.

"My hand?" the grand duke said. He tossed the pomander from one hand to the other and back again. "No. The Duchess of Bracciano died by misadventure, while washing her hair."

"*Re'th kyjyewgh hwi.*"

"Whatever that means in your barbarous language, it changes nothing. However she died, Ruanno, she is dead."

"And Donna Dianora?"

"That is a different matter. Don Pietro our brother took her life, as was his right, for her treasons and her unfaithfulness."

Ruan said nothing.

"As long as you stay here," the grand duke said, "you are nothing but a nameless prisoner—not a metallurgist, not an alchemist. And another thing—you cannot continue the plots you have afoot."

"I have no plots."

"No? I know you have been buying influence at the English court, with the intent to ruin the Englishman who now owns the manor and mine where you grew up. I could arrange—"

Ruan stopped listening. He closed his eyes and saw Mount's Bay, the mystical island of Saint Michael's Mount itself rising in its center. The granite and serpentine cliffs and the drowned forests under the sea, trees turned into stone, of unimaginable antiquity. He saw the vast marshes, smelling of salt and life, the herons, the twining of mallows and moonflowers. Moors and stone-hedged fields where tough, shaggy ponies grazed, and just beyond, Milhyntall House itself, sturdy and square with its center courtyard. Apple trees, the gillyflower apples tasting of cloves. A few miles farther, the winzes and shafts of Wheal Loer.

Home. Land saturated with the blood of his father and mother, his grandparents, his family for longer than anyone could remember. He would take it back from Andrew Lovell, whatever it cost him, and he would never give it up again.

Suddenly he realized what the grand duke was saying. He opened his eyes.

"I could arrange to purchase influence of my own. Support for the Englishman. His name is Andrew Lovell, is it not? All the lands around Marazion"—he pronounced the name of the market town in English, awkwardly—"were confiscated after the Cornish rebellion in 1549. The English queen is sensitive, I think, on the subject of rebellion, and might be persuaded the estate should remain in loyal English hands."

Ruan said nothing.

"I know everything about you," the grand duke said. "Ruan Pencarrow of Milhyntall. You should be called Ruanno della Cornovaglia, should you not? I have chosen to allow you to keep your secrets, because you are a metallurgist like no other, and an alchemist with knowledge that is valuable to me. I also know how you came by that knowledge."

"Do you now." In his heart, in Cornish, Ruan was repeating, *I will kill you. Perhaps not today, or tomorrow, or even this month, this year. I will bide my time, gain my freedom, use your laboratories and resources. But I will kill you in the end, for what you have done to Isabella.*

"I do." If the grand duke divined his thoughts, he gave no sign. "Your family were loyalists, captured after the siege of Saint Michael's Mount. They were imprisoned for months at Launceston by mad rebels who wanted to say their prayers in their own barbarous language. When they came out, the rebellion had been crushed and all the lands in Cornwall had been parceled out to Englishmen—even the lands of loyalists were given away. Andrew Lovell was a fine and trusted lieutenant of Sir Gawen Carew, and so obtained your father's estates."

I will kill you in the end.

"Andrew Lovell wanted no displaced Cornishmen to dispute his ownership, and so he had your father murdered. Your mother hid herself among the miners and dared not reveal her true name or yours. She died when you were five or six, and you went into the mines, working from dawn to nightfall for crusts of bread and a place to sleep."

I will kill you.

"You would be there still, but under your dirt and calluses you were a handsome boy, were you not? The German metallurgist certainly thought so. Konrad Pawer, his name was, no? He called himself Conradus Agricola, trading upon his uncle's famous name. Andrew Lovell wanted to improve his mine's production, and thought Agricola's nephew could help. What Pawer helped was the warmth of his own bed, by taking you into it."

"When one is not born a prince," Ruan said, "one has to seize the opportunities that present themselves."

The grand duke laughed. It was unpleasant. "You became his catamite. He took you back to Vienna, allowed you to educate yourself, and in time the student surpassed the master."

"I was not unwilling. As you say, without him I would still be carrying rocks in the mines of Cornwall."

"And without hope of taking revenge on the Englishman who usurped your estates and killed your father."

"That also." Ruan shifted his position and stood up.

"In Vienna, in fact, you became notorious, both for your own talents and your master's excesses. Your name came to the attention of the emperor himself."

"He wished to exploit the gold mines of the valley of Rauris," Ruan said. "Konrad Pawer was a charlatan—he had none of his uncle's knowledge."

"How convenient, then, that he died as he did. Leaving all his uncle's papers to you."

Ruan met the grand duke's eyes steadily. He had never told anyone what had happened the night Konrad Pawer died.

"You were certainly willing enough to leave Austria, when the emperor invited you to join the Archduchess Johanna's household. He knew of my interest in alchemy, and meant to amuse me by sending you to me."

"I was hardly invited."

"Invited, ordered, to emperors it makes no difference. You left Austria willingly enough. Who knows what crimes you left behind you?"

"You were pleased enough to have me, crimes or not."

The grand duke stepped closer. Ruan could smell the sharp, spice-sweet scent of the pomander. "I was pleased," he said. "And you did not disappoint me. Ruanno, give up this mad determination to hate me over my sister's death. I will give you any woman you want. Take your place at court, as you were before. Return to the laboratory. Put your amulet around your neck again."

Ruan said nothing.

The grand duke stepped closer still. He said, in a very quiet and intense voice, "I cannot create the *Lapis Philosophorum* without you, Ruanno, and you cannot create it without me and the resources I provide."

"That," Ruan said, "is true enough."

"You cannot pull the strings of your plots while you are here, like this."

"True also."

"Will you give it all up, then, for the death of one woman?"

For a moment Ruan thought he saw her, not the restless, sensual voluptuary she had become but the young Isabella he had loved so passionately, straight and shining, beautiful as an angel with her magnificent red-gold hair and her eyes brilliant as stars in the night. He saw her laughing, running—running away from him. Not looking back. His heart broke to see her go, and at the same time ached with anguish that he had not protected her as he should have done.

"The amulet," the grand duke said. "Put it on again, Ruanno."

What to do?

He might be able to kill the grand duke with his bare hands before the guardsmen standing outside the door cut him down. A quick revenge for Isabella, yes, but then Andrew Lovell the Englishman would live and die at Milhyntall House and take the riches of Wheal Loer, forever. He would pass them on to his sons and the Pencarrows would be forgotten.

If he waited, though. If he waited.

Demosthenes had said it: *The man who retreats shall fight again.*

If he waited, pretended to surrender, he could gather his strength and choose his own time. He could continue the quest for the *Lapis Philosophorum*, continue to amass gold of his own, continue his intrigues to take back his home. And in the end, in the end—yes, he would see Francesco de' Medici dead at his feet.

Slowly he picked up the amulet and put it around his neck.

"Vow upon the amulet that you will give up your hatred. That you will bend all your mind and skills toward our alchemical experiments. Do that, and you will have endless gold. Do that, and I will help you obtain what you desire in Cornwall."

Ruan took the chunk of hematite in his hand. In the past it had always felt warm to him, a piece of the living earth, bound with chains of purified ore from the earth's heart. Now it felt cold. The life, the connection, were gone. He could swear upon it, and the vow would have no meaning.

"I will give up my hatred," he said, his tongue smooth as silver. "I will say nothing more of your sister. I will return to the court and to the laboratory, and take up our experiments again. I vow it, upon this amulet."

The grand duke gestured to the guardsmen outside the door, and they went away. That was as much a vow as any words. Ruan could have killed him with his bare hands—even after forty-four days confined, he had the strength and weight. But he needed the grand duke's gold.

"Our *soror mystica*," he said, "the girl Chiara Nerini—she is well? She will work again with us?"

The grand duke placed his own hand over his chest. Under the velvet doublet and the fine silk shirt, Ruan knew the double rose-cut diamond lay, the sun to his hematite's earth. To complete the triad, the moonstone was necessary.

"She is well enough," the grand duke said. "She was at Cerreto Guidi when—when my sister suffered her unfortunate accident. In attempting to be of service, she herself was injured, the fingers of her left hand crushed."

"Crushed?" So she had tried to help Isabella, tried to do what he could not. She had courage, his quick-witted *soror*. Well, he had known that from the first moment he had seen her, fighting off two guardsmen in the rain. "Will she be able to do the work required of her?"

"Yes. I had one of my battlefield chirurgeons treat her, following the methods of Ambroise Paré. A fever almost took her, but in the end she recovered."

What had she done, to get herself wounded so badly? He would have to find a way to ask her. Perhaps she, too, would have a desire for revenge. At the very least, she would know the truth of Isabella's death.

"She has been assigned a position in the grand duchess's household," the grand duke went on. He put the pomander to his nose and breathed deeply. He was clearly pleased that everything would be as it was.

Although of course it would not.

"Once she has settled into her new place, she will help us begin the *magnum opus* again."

CHAPTER TWENTY-FIVE

The Villa di Pratolino

LATER THAT SAME NIGHT

"She was insolent!" Bianca cried. She was flushed with anger and agitation. "She would not curtsy to me as she should have done—is she your mistress, Francesco, for all your talk about vows of virginity?"

The grand duke drew back his hand to slap her. He was disgusted by her reddened face, her shrieking voice, the overly decorated lavishness of her night-gown, embroidered as it was with gold thread and citrines. It was unfastened, and under it, like a slattern, she wore only her camicia. She had taken her pretended pregnancy as a license to eat too many sweets and drink too much wine—she had put on enough genuine flesh that padding was hardly necessary.

To his amazement she ducked out of the range of his palm and ran to the other side of the room.

"I will *not* be your Bia today! I am so tired of Bia—tired of Franco—tired of it all. You are the Grand Duke of Tuscany, one of the greatest men in Italy. I wish to be acknowledged as your mistress, a great lady, the first lady of Florence, with your heir inside me."

The grand duke paced slowly across the room, his steps light and careful. The scheme about the child had changed everything. He had imagined his Bia placid and motherly at her hearth, sewing tiny shirts and swaddling-bands, softer and gentler than ever. Instead it seemed he had put an unexpected weapon in her hands, a weapon she used every day to batter him with her presumed dynastic importance. It was almost as if she herself had come to believe she was truly with child.

End it? Force her to feign a miscarriage? That would put her back in his power.

On the other hand, the image of himself with a new baby in his hands, undeniably and triumphantly male, was sweeter than any siren's song.

"The grand duchess is the first lady of Florence," he said. He made his voice even and soft, the tone that warned Bianca to expect violence. As he spoke, he picked up a pitcher, lead-glazed white pottery from France. The handle was formed in the shape of a curved tree trunk, from which emerged a winged dragon with a lion's face. It was a beautiful and valuable piece. He had chosen it particularly for the Pratolino, the new villa he had built—was still building—so his Bia would not have to go out in the streets of Florence where people threw stones and rotten fruit at her carriage.

"The grand duchess was never the first lady of Florence when your sister was alive!" Clearly Bianca was too much beside herself to be warned. "She is ugly and tedious and does not care about anything but God and her children. She—"

The crash of the pitcher shattering on the floor at her feet cut her off. She stared down at the broken pieces for a moment, then looked up at the grand duke. Her face had turned pale.

"I liked that pitcher," she said. It was not Bia's voice, but at least it was quieter and more reasonable.

"You should not have defied me. Now. Let us begin again."

She clasped her hands together and took a deep breath. "Your alchemical maidservant," she said. "She accompanied the grand duchess and other members of her household to the Palazzo Medici, where I—where I happened to be."

The grand duke nodded. "I have already collected her jewels and other valuable objects," he said. "You were quite welcome to the rest of her clothes, if you wished to have them."

"The grand duchess did not agree. She ordered me out."

The grand duke shrugged. "If she ordered you out, you should have done as she asked."

Bianca's lower lip thrust out and her eyes flashed. The grand duke picked up another piece of the white pottery. This one was a shallow stemmed cup, a tazza, with decorations similar to those on the broken pitcher.

"I did as she asked," Bianca said, swallowing her anger. "I paid homage to her. But her women—particularly the little alchemist, who is nothing but a bookseller's daughter—they did not show me the proper respect as I passed by."

"Very well. I shall speak to Soror Chiara." The grand duke put the tazza back on the table, gently. He was pleased he had not been compelled to destroy it. "Tell me now, what else were you looking for at the Palazzo Medici?"

Color rushed up into Bianca's face again. She pulled the velvet nightgown more closely around her lush body. "Nothing," she said.

"Nothing?"

The grand duke took a thin leather letter-case out of his belt. He laid it on the table beside the tazza and opened it. Every movement was slow and deliberate. Bianca watched him. Only her eyes moved, following his hands. He took out three letters, one at a time. He unfolded them. The crackling sound of the paper was the only sound in the room. The writing on the pages was large and round, with loops and underlinings.

"These letters, perhaps?" The grand duke's voice was pleasant. He had her under his control again.

"Yes," Bianca whispered. Her voice came out in a rush. "You have them. Oh, God be thanked, you have them. When I could not find them—"

"Do not be so sure that you are safe. These letters—they are proof, beyond any doubt, that four years ago you conspired with my sister to have your own husband attacked in the street and murdered."

He had been perfectly well aware of the foolish conspiracy between his mistress and his sister to assassinate Pietro Buonaventuri. He had been more than willing to let it go forward, because even though Buonaventuri had worn his cuckold's horns willingly, he had been reckless enough—or stupid enough—to involve himself in an intrigue of his own, with a young widow attached to the Ricci. The Ricci were not pleased about that. Roberto de' Ricci had turned to his good friend and patroness Isabella de' Medici, and Isabella, damn her for always involving herself in scandals and conspiracies, had happily arranged for a band of stout fellows to assist Ricci in murdering Pietro Buonaventuri.

"But—Francesco—surely you would not use those letters against me?" Bianca was trembling. "Isabella swore to me you knew. You wanted me, all for yourself."

"I had you, all for myself. Your husband meant nothing to me, alive or dead. Do you have any idea why Isabella would do such a thing for you, arrange your husband's death?"

"His mistress—she was related to one of Isabella's fine friends." Bianca faltered. "She was much above him in rank, and by giving herself to him, she had besmirched her family's honor."

"Rather like you, in fact."

Bianca said nothing. She did not take her eyes off the letters.

"Ah, my Bia. You are such a fool. My sister arranged the murder of your husband to put you in her debt. After my father died, *di felice memoria*"—he crossed himself; it was a measure of how terrified Bianca was, that she did not do the same—"she pressed you to support her in her demands for money, did she not?"

"Y-yes, but—"

"But nothing. She used you, my Bia. She hated you and the influence she believed you had over me."

"We were friends!"

The grand duke laughed. "Hardly friends. She kept these letters when a true friend would have destroyed them. Who knows what she ultimately intended to do with them?"

"Francesco," Bianca said. "Franco. Please."

Franco.

"That is better." He re-folded the letters, put them back in the letter-case, and tucked it into his belt again. "Now, take off that abominable over-decorated night-gown and serve me a cup of wine in your camicia, as a proper big-bellied wife would serve her husband."

He took off his own jacket and sprawled comfortably in a leather chair. What a pleasure it was to slouch like a workman and stretch his legs out before him. How many times had his tutors berated him when he did not sit up straight? How many times had his father rebuked him? How many times had his mother made him kneel on the prie-dieu with the peahen and the chicks? *You are the prince*, they had said to him, over and over. *You are the heir. Your life is not your own to live.*

Here, at least, his life was his own.

Bianca let the night-gown slide off her shoulders, although she did not drop it. She folded it carefully and placed it in a chest with her other fine clothes. Then she went into the next room and after a moment came back with a cup. Her naked flesh gleamed like mother-of-pearl through the thin white fabric of her camicia.

"Will you take a cup of wine, Franco?" she said. It was her own voice, husky and adult. She bowed before him, offering the wine and at the same time a voluptuously unreserved view of her breasts and belly where the deep round neckline of the camicia fell away from her body. She did have more flesh, a lot more. It was pleasant to receive homage from her in that fashion, as if the workman Franco had seduced and debased a fine lady of the court. She was Bia and at the same time she was Bianca as well.

"I will," he said. He took the cup and drank. "I am pleased."

She sank to her knees before him. "Will you allow me to please you further?"

"Who am I?"

"You are Franco, a laborer."

He smiled and unfastened the laces holding his codpiece in place. He did not remove any other piece of his clothing. She crept closer, on her knees, pressing herself between his legs. He did not look at her. He took another swallow of his wine, looking straight ahead.

She touched him with her hands first, her fingers working deeper into the fabric of his breeches and cupping his cods, caressing them, squeezing lightly, running her fingernails delicately over the tightening skin. Then she bent forward, tilted her head, and kissed the very base of his *cazzo*, where the shaft joined the cod-sack. She licked and pressed with her tongue.

He drank more of his wine.

You are Franco, a laborer.

It excited him. She was all the more his possession and his plaything, for being—well, not herself, exactly. When she was herself she was too shrill, too demanding. But this woman—this Bianca—he could imagine the workman Franco having drunk a little too much wine, perhaps, and abducted a lady of the court from her fine coach. Rolled her in the mud of the gutter while she begged for mercy. Brought her home to his laborer's hovel and stripped her to her fine camicia. Ordered her to please him, if she wished to see the morning's light.

She flattened her tongue and ran it up the underside of his *cazzo*, dragged it slowly like warm, wet velvet. Then she made her tongue a point and flicked at the sensitive spot, just under the ridge beneath his foreskin. He felt himself swelling, stretching his foreskin and beginning to thrust out of it.

"Franco," she whispered. He could feel her breath, warm and cool at once, against the wetness her mouth had left on him. His hand shook as he lifted the cup of wine and drank.

A little at a time she took the whole length of him into her mouth.

He put the cup of wine down and sank his fingers into her red-gold hair. Every sense in his body focused itself, like light through a lens, into the softness at the back of her throat.

After she had finished, he picked up his cup of wine again.

"Franco," she said. She had retied the laces of his codpiece. Her cheek lay lightly against his thigh, her hair spread out and tangled.

"What?"

"I am happy, so happy that I am with child."

He actually believed it at first. In the haze of his pleasure he had separated her so completely from Bianca Cappello, the grand duke's mistress. Bianca Cappello, who had been the grand duke's mistress for ten years and more, and never quickened. Then with a shock he came back to himself.

She was only pretending to be with child. He himself had arranged it, and when the time came he would arrange for a strong baby son to appear. A male child at last. She was pretending—and yet she was coming to believe it was true.

All the better.

"Yes," he said. "You are with child. My seed is swelling your belly with a son."

She looked up at him. There was something in her eyes but he could not read it.

"It was the marten skins," she said. "I had them made into a coverlet, and slept wrapped in them every night."

"That is superstition."

"Even so, Franco." She lifted her head. "Even so, Francesco. Francesco de' Medici, Grand Duke of Tuscany. I slept wrapped in marten skins, and now I am going to bear you a son."

CHAPTER TWENTY-SIX

The Palazzo Pitti

A WEEK LATER

"For the occasion of my marriage," the grand duchess said, "I chose a pair of turtledoves as my device, with the motto *Fida Conjunctio*, a faithful union."

She was embroidering a white dove on an altar-cloth, a symbol of the Holy Spirit. Chiara was working on the border, where exquisite skill in needlework wasn't as important. A good thing, since her left hand still didn't always do what she wanted it to do. The fingernails were beginning to grow back, at least.

She hoped the Holy Spirit would be more faithful to the grand duchess than the grand duke had been.

"I remember it, Serenissima," she said. "I was only a little girl, and not a part of the court, but there were so many celebrations in the streets. Duke Cosimo was still alive, of course. His men threw coins and I had a fight with my brother Gian over some silver *quattrini* we both wanted."

A sharp pain flashed in her temple as she thought of Gian. Her father's voice whispered, *He should be alive and you should be dead.*

"I did not know you had a brother," the grand duchess said. She knotted her thread and held out her hand for a new needle, freshly threaded with the white silk. A sewing-woman had one prepared. The grand duchess took it and continued her stitches. Chiara wondered what it had been like, to grow up never having to thread your own needles.

She was part of the grand duchess's inner circle now, a special pet, like Donna Isabella's little hound Rina and Donna Dianora's Leia. It turned out the grand duke had taken a dislike to one of the grand duchess's German ladies, her closest friend from childhood, and bundled her unceremoniously back to Vienna; the dogs and Chiara were the lonely grand duchess's new playthings. It was just as well, because Donna Jimena had withdrawn, more and more, her faithful heart broken by her beloved Isabella's death. When she spoke at all, she spoke of entering the convent at Le Murate.

Barring all the praying—and there was a lot of praying—Chiara was content enough to drift through the days in the grand duchess's household. Vivi followed her everywhere and with Nonna and the little ones so far away—would she ever see them again? Surely one day they would come home—it was good to feel as if she had a living creature who loved her and needed her. Her reading and writing lessons had begun again, with some of what the tutor called computation now, numbers and formulas. Magister Ruanno had been released from the Bargello, although she hadn't seen him. She dreamed of him sometimes, although she remembered only flashes. His arm around her throat, squeezing just hard enough. His hand on her wrist, not caressing, just resting there. His scarred palm against her sleeve, making her feel as if she were protected. She dreamed of the laboratory. Maybe one day the three of them, the grand duke, Magister Ruanno and herself, could begin again on the *magnum opus*.

Or maybe not. Did it matter? Did she even care, anymore?

"Signorina Chiara? Are you all right?"

She came back to herself. "Yes, Serenissima, forgive me. My brother was killed in—in an accident."

"May God have mercy upon his soul. Your father and mother are dead as well, are they not?"

"Yes, Serenissima."

"Perhaps one day, when the grand duke sees fit to release you from your vow, you will marry and have children of your own. They are a great comfort, children are. I myself—"

She paused as she took tiny stitches, outlining the white dove's wing.

"I have hopes of another child of my own," she said at last. A flush of color mounted in her cheeks. "It is hardly a private matter, with all the court watching and counting the occasions upon which the grand duke honors me with—his presence in the night. Perhaps if God sends me a son this time, the grand duke will take *Fida Conjunctio* as his motto as well."

"I pray it will be so, Serenissima," Chiara said. A thousand prayers, she thought even as she said it, a prayer for every single star in the sky, won't make the grand duke a faithful husband. Not with Bianca Cappello stepping into Donna Isabella's shoes before they were fairly cold, inviting everyone to her entertainments and pretending to be a patron of poets and musicians. Not with Bianca Cappello flaunting her belly for everyone in Florence to see.

"I met him for the first time in Vienna." The grand duchess's stitches slowed and stopped as she remembered. "We—we were—congenial, he and I. He brought me gifts. I liked him better than the Duke of Ferrara, who was to marry my sister Barbara. They were in Vienna at the same time that summer, and their gentlemen actually came to blows—the Duke of Ferrara contested with Duke Cosimo for years over which one was to take precedence."

Chiara also stopped sewing. Her left hand ached and she was glad for a chance to rest it.

"I thought I would be—content, at least. Mistaken, I was. Did you know, it was during the wedding celebrations here in Florence that he met—her—for the first time?"

"No, Serenissima. I didn't know."

"I did not know either, for a long time. They kept it a secret, and I suppose I did not wish to see it. But then a few years ago one of my Florentine ladies dared to tell me the truth."

She looked down at the altar-cloth, the pristine white dove. One dove, not two. Chiara wished she could think of something comforting to say. After a moment, the grand duchess took another stitch, and another, filling in a feather on the dove's wing.

"Magister Ruanno, your alchemist," she said. "Did you know he came to Florence from Austria in my household?"

"No, Serenissima." Chiara felt the prickly warmth of color creeping up into her face. "I thought he was from England. Well, somewhere in England. He speaks in a language sometimes that doesn't sound like English to me."

"He was born in England, in a place called Cornwall—Cornovaglia, it is, in Italian. It is known for tin and copper mines, and the boy, Rohannes as he was called in Saxony, was born with metal in his blood."

It was strange to hear Magister Ruanno spoken of as a boy. He seemed all of a piece, as if he'd just appeared in a laboratory, a grown-up man, scars and all. She'd never thought about it before, where the scars on his hands had come from, or how long he'd had them. It was impossible to imagine him without them.

"He was an apprentice to Agricola's nephew, and a brilliant student of Agricola's sciences. Do you know who Agricola was?"

"Yes, Serenissima. I've read a little of his writing in my lessons. He wrote a great book about metals and mining."

The grand duchess nodded. "My brother the emperor knew the grand duke—the prince, as he was then—was interested in alchemy, and so arranged for young Rohannes to come to Florence."

Chiara took more stitches in her border. She didn't know what to say, or why the grand duchess wanted to talk about Magister Ruanno.

"He found a great love in Florence, and was foolish enough to think he would be happy. Just as I was. He was only fifteen or sixteen when I first saw him, dark and rough-looking. Isabella was older—twenty-three, twenty-four, I am not sure. She seduced him, I think, as an amusement. She was already tired of her husband, and casting about for new sensations. With the boy Rohannes, she found more than she expected. For a while, at least, she loved him too."

"I didn't know you knew Magister Ruanno so well, Serenissima."

"Oh, I do not. But I watched him, and Isabella. They first saw each other on my wedding day, you see. An unlucky day for them, and for me. I know that you—"

"Your Imperial and Royal Highness."

They both jumped. It was one of the grand duchess's remaining German ladies, addressing her as always with her full titles in every correct detail. The lady continued, "Your brother-in-law the Cardinal Prince Ferdinando de' Medici is here, and desires an audience."

"Ask him to come in, if you please." The grand duchess put her needle down. "Bring some wine and sweet cakes. No, Chiara, remain. I would like to ask the cardinal to bless you."

The grand duke's brother stepped into the room. The two priests who accompanied him bowed to the grand duchess and withdrew.

"Peace be with you, my sister," he said.

Anyone less likely to bring peace, Chiara couldn't imagine. He had the Medici look—swarthy, bearded, his closely cropped black hair receding on either side to create a point in the center of his forehead. But unlike the grand duke he was fleshy, his cheeks round and pink, his mouth sensual. His robes were the traditional robes of a cardinal but cut and embroidered with worldly richness. He wasn't tonsured. How could he be a cardinal, Chiara wondered, if he wasn't a priest?

Because he was a Medici, of course.

How many mistresses did he have in Rome?

On the other hand, the day of the old grand duke's funeral, he had looked up at the grand duchess where she stood at the window, and signed a cross to bless her. Chiara remembered thinking that his connection with his sister-in-law was not of the flesh, but of the soul.

A complicated man, then. A man of contradictions.

"My lord cardinal," the grand duchess said. She rose to her feet and bowed, then knelt before him and kissed the enormous cabochon sapphire he wore on his right forefinger. When she straightened she took his perfumed white hand in hers, a surprisingly intimate gesture from the Austrian emperor's daughter who never touched anyone. "My brother. Come in, sit down. Have a cup of wine and some sweets."

If she was anybody but who she is, Chiara thought, I'd say they were lovers. She had risen too, and curtsied, and remained standing. Neither one of them paid her the slightest attention. She might have been a chair or a table or a candlestand.

The serving-woman returned with a tray; the grand duchess and the cardinal sat down and took cups of wine and plates of small spiced cakes scented with apricots and sparkling with crystals of grated sugar. When they were comfortable and their first appetites were sated, the grand duchess said, "Signorina Chiara. Come here."

Chiara stepped forward and curtsied again. She wasn't sure if she should kiss the cardinal's ring, but he didn't extend his hand and she certainly wasn't going to reach for his sugary fingers.

"Ferdinando, this is Signorina Chiara Nerini, the girl Francesco chose to be his alchemical *soror mystica*. She was in Isabella's household, but of course—well, we had to find a place for her. And so here she is."

Chiara felt a little dizzy with all the Christian names, used so lightly.

"Younger than I would have imagined, my dear Giovanna." The cardinal looked her over with a very un-cardinal-like eye. "So, Signorina Chiara, you assist my brother with his alchemical experiments? I would not think he would want a young girl for such a task."

"He required her to take a vow of virginity," the grand duchess said. "He convinced the priests at the Cathedral of Santo Stefano to lend him the Sacra Cintola for a night, and she put her hands upon it when she swore."

"A virgin, hmmm?" The cardinal's eyes brightened even further. Chiara felt as if he was looking right through her clothes, bodice and skirts and camicia and all. "Tell me, signorina, why did my brother do such a strange thing?"

The prince wishes you to be vowed as a virgin to satisfy his wife and his mistress. Only if you are proclaimed to be a virgin and vowed to remain a virgin will they accept you.

Magister Ruanno's voice, calm and straightforward. But of course she couldn't say such a thing in front of the grand duchess.

"An alchemist's *soror mystica* is always a virgin, my lord cardinal," she said. A lie, but surely the cardinal and the grand duchess didn't know about Perenelle, the wife of Nicolas Flamel. "She represents the moon, the labyrinth, water and silver, symbols of virginity and the feminine principle, and brings the power of those elements into the creation of the *Lapis Philosophorum*."

"There, Ferdinando, do you see?" the grand duchess said. "Francesco is dabbling in magic as well as alchemy. I fear for his immortal soul, and for Chiara's as well. That is why I have asked you to bless her."

Her sincerity shone through the heavy Germanic consonants in her voice. Whatever else people said about Giovanna of Austria, the Grand Duchess of Tuscany, her piety was pure and heartfelt as a saint's.

"Come here, *ragazzina*," the cardinal said. "Kneel before me."

There was a glint of carnal humor in his dark eyes, and Chiara knew he was imagining her kneeling for things that had nothing to do with blessing her. She stepped in front of him and knelt, tucking her skirt under her knees. She was close enough to see that his black cassock was made of fine silk, not coarse wool, the edges piped with the scarlet of his rank. His short cape was violet silk with a moiré pattern woven into the fabric, and his pectoral cross was heavy gold set with pearls and amethysts. She crossed herself—perhaps that would lift his mind out of the gutter—and closed her eyes as if she were praying.

He put his hands on the crown of her head. She could tell he was assessing the texture of her hair with a connoisseur's fingers. Well, there wasn't anything special about it, barring its length and the few silver strands that marked the scar over her left ear. It was brushed straight back and braided in a single thick braid, the braid looped and pinned with plain silver pins.

"Mary immaculate, ever-virgin, advocate of Eve," he said, his voice slow and deliberate, "watch over this girl, protect her purity, and turn her thoughts away from magic and worldliness."

She heard the grand duchess whispering the words after him.

"In the name of God, Father, Son and Holy Spirit, amen."

He traced a cross on her forehead with his thumb. It lingered just a fraction of a second too long, and her headache stirred. The scar on the side of her head hurt, even though he hadn't touched it. He withdrew his hands.

"Thank you, Ferdinando," the grand duchess said. "You always know the right things to say."

"For you, my dear Giovanna, it is easy to know what to say." His expression changed when he looked at her. No sly sensuality. Only warmth, affection and admiration.

It's a sad thing, Chiara thought suddenly, that he couldn't have been the oldest son and married her himself. They could have been happy together, and the grand duke would have been happier as the second son, left alone with his alchemy and his gaudy mistress. It made her uneasy to think that the grand duke's brother, a prince of the church, felt such particular affection for his brother's wife. But if one took the time to know the grand duchess, it was easy to feel affection for her. Easy for anyone except the grand duke and his mistress.

There was a white dove embroidered on the cardinal's sleeve. The holy spirit, of course. But still—it was so much like the white dove the grand duchess was embroidering on her altar-cloth. *I chose a pair of turtledoves as my device. . . .*

"Thank you, my lord cardinal," Chiara said. She got to her feet, looking away from the doves. Her headache pulsed gently behind her eyes. "Thank you, Serenissima, for taking such kind care for my soul."

CHAPTER TWENTY-SEVEN

The Palazzo Pitti

A FEW DAYS LATER

Two spools of the scarlet silk, the grand duchess had said, and one of the sky blue, from the store-closet at the end of the corridor. One skein of gold thread, too, from the locked casket on the uppermost shelf. It was real gold, the thread was, gleaming metal wire pounded fine as the finest silk. Chiara tucked the key back in her pouch and picked up her lamp.

"Come, Vivi," she called softly. She turned to leave the closet.

Magister Ruanno dell' Inghilterra stood in the doorway, with the slanting afternoon light at his back. She knew him—well, how did she know him? She just knew him. His height, perhaps, and the workman's breadth of his shoulders.

"Magister Ruanno," she said. She hadn't seen him—except for her dreams, which she tried not to think about—since that night in the laboratory, when he had agreed to help Nonna and the girls escape to Pistoia, in exchange for her secret messages about Donna Isabella and Donna Dianora, may they rest in peace. How long ago had it been? Five months, six months? It felt like a lifetime.

"You frightened me," she said. "What are you doing—"

He stepped inside the closet and closed the door behind him. The tiny flame of her lamp wavered in the movement of the air and went out.

Chiara was afraid and not afraid, at the same time. In the darkness she could hear him breathing, and hear herself breathing. She took a step backward. There was no room to take more than the one step. He loomed over her. Sensation stabbed deep in her belly, in a way she'd never felt before.

"I heard you'd been r-released," she stammered. It was the only thing she could think of to say.

"I have. Light your lamp again, if you please. I wish to speak with you privately, but not in the dark."

Chiara put the threads back on the shelf, took out her tinderbox, and struck a light. She was used to doing it in the dark, by touch alone. How many times had she been the first to rise and light the lamps, while her mother and Nonna tended to the little ones? She was awkward about it, with her damaged fingers, but at least she got the lamp lighted again.

Magister Ruanno's figure emerged from the blackness, dressed in plain dark breeches and doublet, clean-shaven, his hair neatly cut. He looked gaunt and—at first she thought he looked sad, but that wasn't it, not quite. He looked grieved to the bone, yes, but it was an angry grief. A frightening grief. She wondered what he'd promised to the grand duke to regain his freedom. Whatever it was, he still wore the piece of red hematite around his neck, set in its copper and iron chain.

Vivi was at his feet, standing on her hind legs, stretching her front paws to the top of his boots. He picked her up and petted her.

"What do you want?" Chiara's knees felt shaky. She was annoyed with Vivi for going to him so easily, annoyed with him for responding, and that made her want to strike out. "We made our bargain and I sent you the messages. I did my part. You can't blame me that they are dead."

"I do not blame you. The grand duke told me that you were injured at Cerreto Guidi."

Involuntarily she put her left hand behind her back. The crooked fingers were ugly and she didn't like people looking at them.

"Show me."

Reluctantly she held her hand forward.

"How did this happen?"

"My fingers were crushed in a door." She didn't try to explain any further.

He put one of his hands under hers, very gently, and lifted the poor fingers to his lips. It wasn't a passionate kiss at all. It was an acknowledgement that she had cared for Donna Isabella too, in her way, and that she had tried to protect her. That their terrible failures made a bond between them. Her fear melted away and she would have started to cry again, if she'd had any tears left.

"Can you tell me what really happened? The grand duke claims it was an accident, and the gossip around the city tells a hundred different stories."

"It wasn't an accident."

He waited, still holding her hand. Vivi, snuggled in the crook of his other arm, made a happy sound in her throat, almost like the purr of a cat.

"She went into a chamber where her husband had called her. They shouted at each other, about Donna Dianora being murdered, about the grand duke conspiring with Don Pietro, telling him it was his right to kill her. About the grand duke—conspiring in it all. Then her husband struck her. There was another man in the chamber, one her husband called Massimo. I could hear them struggling, but I couldn't see. I tried to see, I tried."

He stroked her hand with his thumb. "I know."

"Her husband threw the door open. I had my hand between the door and the wall. That—that's when—I didn't really feel it, not right away. He told us to fetch vinegar, that Donna Isabella had fainted."

"Had she?"

"No. She was dead when I went in. Her throat was marked, so clearly anyone could see it. One of them strangled her with a cord, a red silk cord. Or maybe they did it together."

"Some of the gossipers claim her body was abused after her death."

Walls covered with frescos, figures of people appearing to twist and whisper . . . a man crucified upside down . . . a woman in grave clothes sitting bolt upright, her arms crossed over her breast. The sound of the coffin nails being drawn out sounded like devils shrieking. . . .

"I don't remember. I had fever, I don't remember."

"Shhh. Chiara. That is enough, you do not have to remember."

By the ass bones of San Martino, she stinks.

Lift up her skirts, Emiliano. I've never seen a princess's private parts before.

She gulped and jerked her hand away from him, turning around to cover her mouth. All she could think was, don't let me vomit, not here, not in the grand duchess's special store-closet.

"Chiara."

She heard the click of Vivi's claws on the floor. He had put her down. Then she felt him put his arms around her, very gently.

"Shhh," he said again. "I needed to know, but even so I am sorry I asked you to remember."

His voice was deep and soft. The calm warmth of his arms steadied her and expected nothing in return. His body behind hers was hard and strong enough to lean on, and for a moment she closed her eyes and leaned. It was what she wanted, in her shattered heart of hearts, his strength to lean on. Forget, she thought. Forget. Slip back into that numb, watery haze where none of it matters.

He is going to kill you. It was one of the demons' voices, sudden and startling in the quiet darkness. *He says he doesn't blame you for Donna Isabella's death, but he does.*

You have escaped death twice, Babbo whispered. *You should have died, you should be dead. There will be a third time and you will not escape.*

You dared to touch me, Isabella put in. *You closed my eyes. And then you looked upon me when I was dead and rotting. How could you? How could you?*

He is going to kill you. You can tell the grand duke he helped Nonna escape, Nonna who was involved with Pierino Ridolfi. Why else did he come here secretly, to this tiny dark closet, but to kill you, kill you, kill you. . . .

The fear rushed back. She pushed his arms away and turned to face him again. Her heart felt as if it would burst out of her chest.

"The grand duchess is waiting for her silks," she said. She hardly had enough breath to speak coherently. "She will send someone to look for me."

Maybe it was just the flickering light from her small lamp, but the terrible sadness in his eyes seemed to darken and settle into every line and plane of his face.

"Perhaps," he said. "Perhaps not, not for a long time."

"Let me pass by."

He didn't move. "We are not finished, you and I."

Vivi whined and pressed against her legs. *Pet me, pick me up, love me.*

"What," Chiara managed to say. "What—do you want—of me?"

He put one hand on her neck, just where it sloped into her shoulder. He wasn't wearing gloves. Skin to skin—it was the first time he'd touched her like that, his bare skin against hers. His fingers lay lightly against the back of her neck. She could feel each individual fingertip. After all her dreams she should have felt pleasure, but she didn't. All she felt was terror rushing through her, from her neck to her toes.

He is going to kill you.

"You want it too, I think. Even if you are hiding it from yourself."

She closed her eyes. The voices crackled and scratched inside her head. She whispered, "What? What do I want?"

Very softly he said, "Vengeance."

She opened her eyes. The voices stopped, mid-whisper. For a moment there was absolute silence.

He moved his hand, slid it down over her shoulder. Then he took it away. Her knees gave way and if she hadn't been pressed back against the shelves she would have fallen. Vivi whined and pawed at her skirt.

"We can have vengeance," he said. "Both of us."

"But you're free," she managed to say. Her chest hurt, as if she had been running and running. "The grand duke let you go free."

"I made a vow to him," he said. "I swore I would pursue no vengeance, that I would become his English alchemist again, just as I was." He smiled. The wolf smile. "Unlike you, I have no intention of keeping my vow."

"Why are you telling me? I don't want to know. I don't want—"

"Hush," he said. "I am telling you because I do not want you to think I have submitted to the grand duke despite what he has done. That I condone—her death, or Dianora's, or any of the others."

"What does it matter what I think of you?"

He said nothing.

Her heartbeat and breathing began to feel steadier. After a moment she said, "So the grand duke wants to start again? With the *magnum opus*?"

"Yes. It is the only reason I am alive. The only reason he sent his best physicians to treat your fever and save your hand. We are bound to him, both of us, the earth and the moon to his sun. He believes it, that we must work together for the *magnum opus* to be successful."

"But you don't believe it."

"No. There is no such thing as the *Lapis Philosophorum*, at least not in the way he believes it to exist. But there are other things we can learn with alchemy, things that make ore from the mines richer, things that could even heal sicknesses. The grand duke's wealth and power provide us with the elements and equipment we need, and give us protection against those who would call alchemy witchcraft."

"Magister Ruanno," she said. She realized with a start that he had been calling her Chiara, just Chiara, not Mona Chiara or Signorina Chiara or Soror Chiara. What would it feel like to call him by his name alone? He had so many names, Ruanno, Roannes, Rohannes. Were any of them his true name?

"Ruanno," she said, testing.

"Ruan," he said. "My true name is Ruan."

"Ruan." It sounded right without the softening of the extra Latin and Italian syllables. "He killed them, I know. Not with his own hands, but he arranged it and he's protected both his brother and the Duke of Bracciano. Can you work with him, through the fourteen stages, and never once pollute the *magnum opus* with hate?"

"Hate will not pollute it. It will make it stronger."

"I don't believe that."

"It is true. I have hated all my life, and I am strong."

"Hated what? Who?"

He looked at her for a moment, as if he were balancing two sides of a scale inside his head. At last he said, "An Englishman in Cornwall. He had my father killed, and hounded my mother to death. He took my home, my estate, my birthright, before I was ever born. He put me to work in the mines when I was five years old. I hate him and one day I will kill him."

He is going to kill—

Not her. Someone else.

Her lantern began to sputter. She picked Vivi up—the puppy wiggled and tried to escape—and tried to push past him. He didn't push her back. He did reach out, hook one finger under the silver chain and pull the moonstone out of the bodice of her gown. It glowed, milky white with glimmers of green and blue and pink, reflecting the lamplight. He clasped the stone and touched it to the chunk of hematite around his own neck.

"We are bound together," he said again. "In life and in death. In vengeance and in—"

"No. Don't say it."

He held her moonstone for a few moments more, then let it go. "I will not say it now," he said. "But when the grand duke is dead, it will be just the two of us."

Her lantern went out. The closet fell into inky blackness. Even the moonstone was extinguished. Vivi dug her puppy claws into her neck, her plump little body trembling. Chiara's throat ached with wanting to say *yes, yes, the two of us*, but she couldn't make the words come out. The grand duke was too powerful. He would never be dead, no matter what they did, and that meant—

The door opened. Light from the corridor burst into the closet.

"Do not be afraid," Ruan said. "We will take our vengeance together, Chiara, and I will protect you from harm, as long as I live."

He left the closet without looking back. Chiara stared after him, the pain behind her eyes and at the side of her head suddenly so intense she could feel it even in the twists and knots of her braided hair.

CHAPTER TWENTY-EIGHT

The Villa di Pratolino

24 NOVEMBER 1576

The peasant woman crouched on the birthing stool, groaning in the moment of rest between her pains. Her camicia was gathered up around her waist, and her splayed thighs quivered as she labored. She had her hands thrust through two loops of twisted cloth that had been knotted to the back of the stool; her face was covered with a black hood and veil. Bianca Cappello stood behind her, wrapped in the rich mantle of dark green velvet and marten fur. An ancient midwife knelt in front of the stool, massaging the laboring woman's belly and exposed parts with lavender oil.

"Soon now," Francesco said. He moved a branch of candles closer so he could see the labor in all its detail. There was only a little blood so far, where the woman's inner membranes had torn. The top of the infant's head was visible, bulging from the joining-place of her thighs, dark red with a tracery of fine hair. He could smell her sweat, her fear, her helplessness.

"My Bia, come closer. Yes, lean forward. I wish to see your face instead of hers—I wish to imagine that it is you suffering here, bringing forth my son."

Bianca leaned over the woman's shoulder. She was pale as the wax of the candles. The jeweled gold martens' heads that clasped her mantle caught the moving candlelight, appearing to flinch and turn their faces away as she trembled; under the mantle her body appeared grossly thickened, as if she herself were to bear her child any day. Francesco had watched her wrap herself in silk-and-feather layers of padding, increasing it gradually. She had put on real flesh as well, a considerable amount of it. Everyone believed she was with child. It was a great satisfaction, to know that everyone believed it. They whispered about what a strong man he was.

The only thing left for him to desire was the whisper that he was the father of a strong son. His wife's six girls were not good enough. Sometimes he heard people laughing, or thought he did—*six girls and no son, six girls, six girls*.

To be a man, he needed a son.

"I know what childbirth is like," Bianca said. "I had my daughter, after all."

Another girl. Not even his, but still a reproach to him.

"Twelve years ago," he said. "When you yourself were little more than a child, and you were so mishandled in that birth that you have been barren ever since. Put your arms around her, Bia. Become one with her. This is to be our child, your child, if it is a son. I wish to see you experience the pains."

"I thought you were going to give her the anodyne. Is that not why you had your pet alchemists create it, to comfort birth pangs? Do you not wish to experiment with it, and see if it succeeds?"

He laughed. "God himself says that women are to bring forth their children with suffering, and anything that lessens their pain is the work of the devil. That is why I had the anodyne created—it has stirred so much talk about you being with child, and my fears for you, that no one thinks to question your sudden fertility after twelve years of barrenness."

"I would like to see if it works, though."

"Your birth pangs will be pretense, my Bia. You will not need the anodyne—although I will give it to you, for all to see, and you will act as if it eases you."

He could see by her expression that she was afraid. Was the anodyne real? Or was he intending to poison her, once he had a son everyone believed was his? It was pleasurable to let her feel uncertainty and fear. He would never let her go, but she did not have to know that.

"I do not want both of them in my chamber," she said. "I do not like your Magister Ruanno. The girl, the virgin—let her bring the anodyne. Let her offer it to me on her knees."

"I will choose the witnesses," Francesco said. "I will arrange every-thing."

The woman's contractions began again. She screamed, the sound deep and harsh at first, then higher and shriller as the pain grew worse. Her head thrashed from side to side; she dragged and twisted the loops of cloth, her body arching. Bianca crouched behind her, grasping the twisted cloth in her own hands, putting her cheek next to the woman's cheek. Francesco narrowed his eyes, looking through his lashes. With the woman's face hooded, and only the light of the candles—Bia's face beside hers, Bia's hands pulling the ropes—yes, it might have been Bia laboring there. Bia writhing and shrieking in agony as she brought forth the fruit of his seed.

The midwife supported the child's head as it emerged, turning it slightly so Francesco could see its profile. He had seen dogs whelp and horses foal but he had never seen a child born before. It was slick-looking, covered with mucus, streaked with something white and waxy. It did not look as if it was alive.

Giovanna was far too proud and modest to allow him in her birthing-chambers. In fact, she allowed no physicians, no males at all, only her midwives and one or two favored ladies. So be it. Bia—Bianca—Bia would do the same. It would make the whole complicated contrivance that much easier.

"Push again," the midwife said. "One good hard push, my girl, and the shoulders will be out, and the worst will be over."

The woman was sobbing and shuddering. Bia's face was twisted—she had sunk into the trance state he could always induce in her when he com-pelled her to do as he wished. She dragged on the loops of cloth and groaned as if she herself were truly expelling the child from her body.

The woman shrieked and strained one last time, almost lifting herself from the birthing stool. The midwife twisted the baby's shoulders expertly and supported it as it slid from its mother's body. It was attached to a puls-ing grayish-purple rope of flesh, as if one of the mother's entrails had be-come entangled with it. Francesco thrust the candlestand forward, careless of the dripping hot wax.

The midwife held it up by its ankles and smacked it smartly on the back-side. It wailed, a surprising loud and healthy sound. Its head was big, dispro-portionate to its body. Were all babies like that? He could not see its sex.

"By the piss of the Virgin," the midwife muttered. "A useless girl."

"No," Bianca said. "Oh no, no."

The woman had collapsed on the stool, half-fainting, hanging from the twisted loops that were still wrapped around her wrists. The midwife put the screaming child on her chest and began to massage her belly hard. "Still the afterbirth to come," she said.

Francesco put the candlestand aside. There was no more need to see clearly. "You, midwife," he said. "What about the others? Have you given them the potions to stimulate their labors?"

"Not yet, Serenissimo. There's only Gianna and me to tend them."

Four women, selected for their youth and health, the fullness of their bellies and the color of their hair, red-gold like Bianca's. Each had disappeared in broad daylight from their villages in the countryside around Florence, leaving husbands and families mystified and bereft; the power of the grand duke was such that he could arrange such matters with ease. The mercenaries who had performed the abductions had also vanished once the women were safely collected. They had been chosen, after all, with an eye to there being no one to wonder what had become of them.

Each of the women had been locked in a single, separate room in the cellars of the Villa di Pratolino, easy enough to manage with the villa still partly in the disorder of construction. They had been given the best food, the finest, softest beds to rest in. They had been promised gold, luxury, the restoration of their freedom once their babies were born. They had been promised their babies would end in their own arms, fat and happy. They were given no explanations; they had never seen the grand duke and so did not know why they had been abducted or why they were being fattened like Epiphany geese. Two women cared for them, the midwife Caterina Donati and the maidservant Gianna Santi.

All the promises, of course, were lies. The whole complicated plan was designed to produce one healthy red-haired baby boy. When that was accomplished, the women, the other babies, the midwife and the serving-woman, all of them would join the mercenaries in the dark depths of the Arno with garrotes knotted around their necks, the long loose ends drifting in the current.

This woman, the mother of the girl, she had been the first to begin her labor. She and her daughter would be the first to die.

"Do as you have been instructed with this one," Francesco said to the midwife. "When you are finished, give the next woman your potion, so her labor begins. Send the maidservant to us when she is ready."

"Yes, Serenissimo." The midwife had been promised gold, too. She had been part of the Cappello household in Venice, and had helped Bianca flee with her lover, all those years ago. She thought her years of faithful service made her safe.

"Come, my Bia," Francesco said. "We will have supper, and a little music, while we are waiting."

She shuddered as he took her arm, and drew her marten furs more closely around her body. Neither of them looked back at the woman. The baby had stopped squalling and was making whimpering sounds, looking for its mother's breast.

The passageways were like a maze. Before they even reached the first turning, the baby's whimpers had stopped. Francesco nodded, satisfied. Every detail was being attended to as he had ordered, and in the end no one alive would know the truth but he himself, and his Bia.

CHAPTER TWENTY-NINE

The Villa di Pratolino

26 NOVEMBER 1576

"Santa Margherita, help me, the pain, the pain!" Bianca thrashed her head back and forth, just as the woman in the cell had done. She was wrapped in half a dozen thick coverlets, so the actual shape of her body was well-hidden. Her face was flushed and swollen—she had drunk cup after cup of wine in her state of nervous hysteria, until he had ordered her servants to give her no more. Now she was clear-minded but miserably sick, and that just added to the verisimilitude. As he had instructed her to do, she was calling upon the patron saint of childbirth. All in all, the grand duke was pleased.

"You, midwife," he said. "Prepare loops of that silken rope—it will relieve Donna Bianca's distress if she has something to pull on."

The midwife picked up the coil of heavy silk cord and began to knot it into loops. It was the same woman, Caterina Donati, who had made loops of rough twisted cloth for the women in the cellars. The same woman who had smothered the first girl baby, and with the same matter-of-factness had sent him a message that a boy baby had been born. The other women in the cellars, well, they had been left to a mercenary assassin. After one more assignment—the deaths of Caterina Donati herself and the young maidservant and musician, Gianna Santi—the assassin would also disappear. Every trace of the plot would be eradicated.

Gianna Santi was not in the room. She was waiting in the proper place, for the proper signal. Other than that, the room was packed with people—two physicians, an apothecary, a priest, his own brother Don Pietro, half a dozen noble ladies. It was important to have witnesses. The grand duke was annoyed that his brother the cardinal had declined to travel from Rome to attend the birth, but of course Ferdinando had always been a great friend of the grand duchess's.

Other than the grand duchess herself, there were no great ladies of the Medici left to be present. Isabella and Dianora were dead, and good riddance to them. He had considered allowing his stepmother Cammilla Martelli out of her walled convent for the occasion, just for the sake of having a tenuously related noble lady in the room, but had decided against it.

"I must have lavender oil," Bianca sobbed. "I must have water—cold water, cooled with ice, please, please!"

"Calm yourself, Madonna Bianca." The physician was sweating. Fires burned high in both fireplaces and the room was stifling hot. "If you will allow me to examine you, I will be able to tell you—"

"No! How dare you! My lord, do not allow this man to violate my dignity. I wish only my own women about me, Gianna and Caterina."

She feigned fainting, clutching the coverlets around her, drawing up her knees as if to curl herself protectively around the child to be born.

"No man will touch you, Madonna, I swear it. Even I will leave you, and I will see that you do not suffer."

"It is a great sin to ease a woman's birth pangs," the priest objected.

The grand duke laughed. "I will buy indulgences enough," he said. "Even now, my alchemist is outside with an anodyne of my own creation."

The people in the room began to whisper, particularly the women. An anodyne for the pains of childbirth? What payment would the grand duke require, to share it?

"Soror Chiara." The grand duke raised his voice. "You may come in."

Every head turned. In the arched doorway stood Chiara Nerini, wearing her habit of pure undyed wool, her hair loose to her hips. The great moonstone in its silver setting glowed on her breast, and her eyes, clear and changeable as shot silk, brown to gold to green, met his with apprehension and defiance. The grand duke had not seen her, not even thought about her, during his preparations for the appearance of his son. He had left the creation of the anodyne to Ruanno, not thinking that a *soror mystica* would be required—but of course she would. The anodyne was meant to relieve a woman's pains, and according to the principle of correspondence it would require a woman's hand in the preparation.

And the plot required only women around Donna Bianca.

Soror Chiara carried a flask in her hands, a sphere of glass with a long narrow neck. The liquid that filled it was transparent and red as blood.

"Give me the anodyne," the grand duke said. "Donna Bianca is laboring to bring forth my son, and I would ease her pains."

The priest crossed himself but said nothing more. The physician scowled. Everyone in the room goggled as if their eyes would fall out. Good. All the talk would be of the anodyne, and the assumption that Bianca was indeed about to bear a child would be taken for granted.

Chiara Nerini paced forward, grave and graceful as a nun, and placed the flask in his hands.

"As you commanded, Serenissimo," she said. Her voice was formal, unlike her usual free-and-easy speech. He could tell she had memorized and practiced the words. "I have drunk of it myself, and it is safe and effective."

He examined the flask, trying to guess what was in the red liquid. Aqua vitae as a base. Oil of poppies, almost certainly. It had a sweet, sharp smell—oil of cloves? Something to sweeten it, and something—perhaps a pinch of vermillion, synthesized from mercury and black sulphur—to give it the red color. As he looked at the flask, he thought of ways to make use of Soror Chiara's unexpected appearance. She was known, she was a member of the grand duchess's household. She would make an excellent witness.

He handed the flask back to her. "You may remain," he said. "Physician, you may go."

"Serenissimo," the man said. "I beg you. If anything should go ill with your lady—"

"Go. Remain in the palazzo. If you are needed, you will be called."

With poor grace, the man went out.

"Soror Chiara, there is water on that table, cooled with ice. Please prepare a draught for Donna Bianca."

"Yes, Serenissimo."

He stepped back to Bianca's bedside. She had opened her eyes. They were huge and dark, as if she had bathed them with belladonna. She was deep in her play-acting, submissive to his will, believing what he wished her to believe.

"Francesco," she said. "Franco. Swear to me."

"Anything." He leaned forward so they could whisper together.

"If I die, swear you will make my son your heir. Swear."

"You will not die, my Bia."

"I do not want the priest here." She raised her voice. "He tried to give me the unction. He thinks I will die."

"All women in childbed are given the unction," the priest said. He was not used to being repudiated. "It is common practice. You cannot be sure you will pass through your labor safely, Donna Bianca, and surely you do not wish to die in your sins."

Bianca began to cry, writhing and screaming under the piles of coverlets. Soror Chiara went to her side with a cup and held it to her lips. Bianca stopped crying and looked up at her with those black, distended eyes.

"Drink," Soror Chiara said. Her voice was cool. "The anodyne will ease you."

The grand duke could tell from her expression that she hated Bianca, and he could tell from Bianca's expression that she hated Chiara Nerini in return. He remembered the story of how Soror Chiara had refused to show the correct respect at the Palazzo Medici. All the more reason to compel her to witness Bianca's triumph.

Bianca hesitated for a moment, looking to him, uncertain. He nodded, and she drank, deeply and thirstily. The priest began to pray in a loud voice, asking for God's mercy on daughters of Eve who fell into mortal sin.

"Enough." The grand duke stepped up to the priest, deliberately making it seem as if he intended to strike him. The priest scrambled back, clutching at his cassock. "You are dismissed, Father. You are all dismissed. The midwife will remain to tend Donna Bianca, and Soror Chiara will remain to witness."

He did not say, *to witness for the grand duchess's sake*, but that was what he meant. Everyone knew that was what he meant.

Soror Chiara did not move. She looked at him with those extraordinary eyes, different than he had ever seen them before. She said, "I wish to go with the others."

Suddenly the room was silent.

"I command you," the grand duke said, "as your temporal lord and as your master in the art, to remain and witness both Donna Bianca's labor and the birth."

What was she thinking? Something was happening behind her eyes, some weighing-up of action and reaction, defiance on the one hand and consequence on the other. After a moment she bowed her head and said, "I will remain, Serenissimo."

The room burst into sound and action, people shuffling, crowding toward the door, murmuring. He made a signal to Bianca. She pushed the cup away and said loudly, "I would like music to ease me. Send for my woman Gianna Santi, and her *mandolino*."

"I will fetch her myself," the grand duke said. "Midwife, I leave Donna Bianca in your hands. Soror Chiara, prepare additional draughts of the anodyne as may be required. Everyone else may go."

The people in the room went out, looking back over their shoulders, whispering among themselves. Chiara Nerini remained, unmoving, her eyes cast down. The anodyne rested on the table, the flask glowing red in the light from the fireplaces. The grand duke was the last to depart, and closed the door gently behind him.

The rest of the plan went off exactly as he had devised it. Gianna Santi arrived at the chamber carrying her Neapolitan *mandolino* with its vaulted bowl-shaped back; if it seemed heavier than such instruments usually were, neither the midwife nor Soror Chiara were musicians enough to notice such a detail. The grand duke went back into the chamber with her and closed the door again. Gianna Santi went around the bed and made a great show of tuning the *mandolino*'s strings. At the same time, the midwife lifted up the coverlets. That was part of the plan. No one, not even the grand duke himself, would see anything to indicate that the baby was not born from Donna Bianca's own body.

Bianca screamed, a high loud shriek.

A baby cried.

The midwife straightened, holding up the child triumphantly. It was smeared with blood and the white waxy substance, already beginning to dry and flake off. The cord had been tied and cut. The midwife went straight to a waiting basin of water and plunged the child in. It began to cry more lustily.

Bianca lay sobbing. The mounded coverlets concealed the state of the bed.

Gianna Santi began to pluck the strings of her *mandolino*. It sounded off-key, as if the sounding-board had been damaged.

"It is a son, Serenissimo!" the midwife cried.

The grand duke went over to the midwife and took the naked baby in his arms. The water made the blood look slick and fresh. The hair was reddish and the genitals were swollen. All the better to prove that he could, after all, father a son.

"You may go, Soror Chiara," he said. "You may tell what you have seen, to the grand duchess, and to anyone who asks you."

Her eyes were squeezed tightly shut. Was that her way of defying him, refusing to see? Good—all the more reason for her to believe what she had heard. She would see the baby in his arms, and that was enough.

"Soror Chiara," he said again.

She opened her eyes. For a long moment she looked at the squirming, howling baby. Then without a word she curtsied, turned around and went out of the chamber.

"Did she see?" Bianca cried. "Did she believe?"

"Shush, Madonna. All is well."

"I hate her."

"You will have your revenge, however little you may see it now." He bent his head to the baby. "Imagine how it will outrage her, that she has been the witness to our son's birth, and in honesty will be required to report it to all who ask her."

"I still hate her."

The grand duke laughed. To the baby he said, "I will name you Antonio, for the saint who discovers lost things. I had a brother named Antonio, who died in his infancy—you shall take up the name and carry it forward in the history of the Medici."

"Franco," Bianca said. Her voice was hoarse from all her screams and crying. With only the two serving-women in the room, it did not matter what she called him. "Did I do it as you wished? Are you pleased?"

He went over to the bed and placed the baby in her arms. "I am pleased," he said. "We have a son, my Bia."

CHAPTER THIRTY

The Casino di San Marco

6 DECEMBER 1576

Chiara stepped back from the great table and bowed to Magister Francesco and Magister Ruanno.

In the laboratory, after all, they were equal. She was willing to show them respect, as one practitioner of the great art to another, but curtsying like a maidservant? No, not anymore. So for the first time she bowed, her hands crossed over her heart, mirroring their own bows. Neither man said anything. She saw a glint in Magister Ruanno's—Ruan's—eyes that might have been admiration.

They had achieved the separation, the seventh stage of the *magnum opus*, and the next step was the conjunction, the recombination of the elements. It was like a man joining with a woman, Magister Francesco had explained. The female element was critical. Fire and air, those were male powers; water was the female power. When water surrendered itself to fire and air in the conjunction, an entirely new element was produced, like a child being born.

"Like a child being born," Magister Francesco repeated, lovingly, one word at a time. "We will be successful, I believe, because our art will mirror life."

The whisperers of the court had been quick to sink the devastating blade of the news into the grand duchess's heart: Bianca Cappello had borne a strong and healthy son. There were naysayers, naturally, as there always were, who pointed out Donna Bianca's age, the long years of her barrenness, and the fortuitous entry into her chamber of a musician with a large Neapolitan *mandolino*. Chiara couldn't be certain, either way. She'd been in the chamber, provided the anodyne for Donna Bianca's supposed pains, remained after the others had left, but out of defiance and anger she'd squeezed her eyes shut, choosing to see nothing. If she'd watched, she'd be able to speak fairly, for certain, one way or the other. But it was too late now.

"The powers of fire and air have manifested themselves within you," Magister Ruanno said to Magister Francesco. What a dissembler he could be when it suited him. "The feminine powers have surrendered, and a male child has been the result. It is the best possible sign."

"Indeed," Magister Francesco said.

He sounded smug as a barnyard rooster. How dare he give Bianca Cappello all the credit for ducal childbearing when the grand duchess herself was struggling through the early months of being with child? And for the seventh time.

"If I may be so bold, Magister Francesco," Chiara said. She knew she wasn't as polished a play-actor as Magister Ruanno was, and she could hear the edge of resentment in her own voice. "The grand duchess is with child as well."

"So she is," he said. "All the more a symbol of the power of the male element and the surrender of the female."

The air in the laboratory was thick with maleness and femaleness, as if it were a scent, a fleshly briny-sweet effluvium. None of the other stages of the *magnum opus* had created such an intense focus on the fact that Magister Francesco and Magister Ruanno were men, and she was a woman.

She had seen and spoken to Magister Ruanno—Ruan—any number of times since they had confronted each other in the grand duchess's store-closet. To look at him, to listen to him, you'd think none of it had ever happened. Well, maybe not entirely. His eyes were like deep holes in the earth, holes all the way down to hell, and they followed the grand duke relentlessly. Other than that, his face was as blank as a painted face in a portrait.

What would it be like, to be conjoined with him? Making the sounds that Isabella and Dianora had made together, on those lazy summer afternoons? Leaving the bed tangled and musky as the inside of a flower?

Saints and angels, she had to stop thinking such thoughts.

She had begun to look back on her first two years at the Medici court as if they had happened to a different person, a young, defiant, awestruck girl finding her way and losing her way, over and over, in a glittering maze of palaces and duchesses and conspiracies. She knew exactly when the path had started—the moment she took her first sip of the strong spiced wine in the grand duke's golden studiolo, with its hidden curiosity cabinets and its secret door. She knew when it had ended, too—in the grand duchess's store-closet, in the dark, with Ruanno dell' Inghilterra's arms around her.

When the grand duke is dead, it will be just the two of us.

For some reason, that moment had brought her back to life. The numbness that had overwhelmed her after her fever had gone. At the same time she had learned to be quiet. To be cautious. To see clearly, past titles and blood.

Most of the time, anyway.

Alchemy, alchemy. Focus on the alchemy.

"Combine the natron with the oil of vitriol," Magister Ruanno said.

Chiara poured a measured amount of white natron crystals into a new athanor. Magister Francesco then added the oil of vitriol, a large beaker of it, slowly and carefully. An intense blue color blossomed as the natron crystals dissolved.

"The aqua fortis is complete," Magister Francesco said. "The athanor is new and sound. Add the separated elements, and the aqua fortis will conjoin them."

Magister Ruanno added the elements, one at a time—the mystical analogs of fire, water and air. Then he sealed the athanor with copper seals imprinted with the mark of Solomon, two triangles representing fire and water, the conjunction of opposites.

"It is the night of the full moon," he said. "When the moon is full again, we will open the athanor and discover whether the conjunction has been successful."

"Amen," said Magister Francesco.

"Amen," said Chiara. She stepped back from the athanor and without a word turned to make her way to the door, not following the maze but walking straight across its double folds, its cusps and arcs. She wanted only to be far away from both of them—away from the grand duke because she was afraid of him, hated him, wished she could make him suffer somehow, the way he made the grand duchess suffer. The way he'd made Donna Isabella suffer. And away from Ruan—well, that was different. She wanted to be far away from him because if he ever touched her again, the way he'd touched her in the grand duchess's store-closet—

"Soror Chiara," the grand duke said. "You have not been given leave to go."

Chiara stopped.

"I wish to work on another alchemical process while we wait for the conjunction to take place. I would have both of you assist me."

For just a moment she considered disobeying him. Babbo's voice, dry and dark as ashes, whispered, *yes, walk away, girl, he'll come after you and kill you—you should be dead anyway and it will be one more mortal sin to drag the Medici prince down to hell.* She squeezed her eyes shut for a moment, fighting the voice, fighting the sudden sinking fear. Then she turned.

"Yes, Magister Francesco," she said. She compelled herself to be calm and deferential. She didn't look at Magister Ruanno. "What would you have me do?"

"I wish to create a fresh supply of *sonnodolce*, the elixir of Tommaso Vasari. When it is done, I would have it compounded with fresh rainwater, in a proportion of one part to one hundred parts."

"That is dangerous work," Magister Ruanno said.

At the same time Chiara said, "Create *what*?"

"Dangerous to you, perhaps," the grand duke said to Magister Ruanno. "Not to me. It is called *sonnodolce*, Soror Chiara, a sweet-tasting, unfailing and undetectable poison discovered by an alchemist in my father's employ, one Tommaso Vasari."

Chiara swayed. Neither of the men seemed to notice.

Sonnodolce.

Tommaso Vasari.

Babbo's book, the ancient book with Babbo's own notes in the back, plastered into the wall in the cellar of the bookshop. The first time she'd looked at it, she hadn't been able to read any of the Latin, and for that matter most of the Italian—Babbo believed good husbands wouldn't want girls if they could read anything more than the *Pater* and the *Ave* and maybe a recipe for roast veal. But she'd helped in the shop since she'd been tall enough to see over the counter, and she knew a signature when she saw one. On the first page, in fine black ink, had been the name *Tommaso Vasari*, clear as clear. The book itself wasn't printed but lettered by hand, its illustrations hand-drawn and colored. There were annotations throughout the book in the same fresh black ink as the signature. So presumably this Tommaso Vasari had found it, purchased it, used it, written his own notes in it. In the back, there were pages of Babbo's notes—she knew they were his because she had seen him writing some of them, when she watched him secretly.

She could close her eyes and see the page, headed with more Latin words and filled with drawings of strange plants, crystals, unidentifiable objects. Tommaso Vasari had added the word *sonnodolce* at the bottom. It had stood out to her because it was the only word on the page that wasn't in Latin, and she'd been able to sound it out. *Sonnodolce*, *sonno* for sleep and *dolce* for sweet. The other handwriting, Babbo's, had scribbled a few words of his own in the margin—some of it she could read but most of it she couldn't. The page opposite it, where the actual formula had been written, was torn out. The ragged edge of paper remained.

A poison?

How had her father come by such a book? Who had torn out the page with the formula, and how had the grand duke learned about it? Had there been some secret connection between her father and the old grand duke, long before the day when she'd gone out in the rain to sell the silver funnel to the prince?

Her father's handwriting—when she'd first looked at it, it had meant nothing. Scribbles. Lines and loops. A word or two, here and there, a name, that made sense. But now, now after two and a half years of endless lessons in Latin and calligraphy—now she could read.

She could *read*.

She blinked, and came back to herself.

"How can it be true that *sonnodolce* is not dangerous to you?" Magister Ruanno was saying. "One does not have to drink it. A few drops on the skin will be absorbed, and can be enough to kill."

"A few drops, yes. One drop, every seven days after taking the Sacrament at Mass, never twice on exactly the same spot of naked skin—that is not only safe, but will in time confer immunity to the *sonnodolce*. Because the *sonnodolce* is a mother poison, from which many others are compounded, it confers a powerful general immunity as well. It also—"

He stopped, as if he suddenly realized he had said too much.

"Mithridates of Persia is said to have compounded a universal antidote to poisons, in somewhat similar fashion," Magister Ruanno said. He sounded calm, uncaring, as if the *sonnodolce* was nothing more than a curiosity. "May I suggest that Soror Chiara's presence is not necessary? There is no need to expose her to possible accidental contamination."

"I wish to have her here," the grand duke said. "I have a reason for requiring the feminine element to be present in this particular distillation."

Chiara made her way back across the pattern of the maze. To Magister Ruanno she said, "I am perfectly capable of protecting myself from a poisonous distillate."

She looked directly into his eyes, for the first time since their secret exchange in the grand duchess's store-closet. He was thinking, *if the grand duke is to have a supply of this* sonnodolce *always at hand, then I am going to take some of it for myself and put a single drop upon my skin, once every seven days, to keep myself safe if the grand duke should decide he no longer needs me.*

She could read his thoughts so easily, because she herself was thinking exactly the same thing.

CHAPTER THIRTY-ONE

It was dark by the time the distillation was complete. As Magister Francesco removed his mask and cassock, he directed them to divide the distillate into one hundred parts, each part in its own separate vial, all one hundred vials in a silver rack in ten rows of ten. These would be combined with purified rainwater and applied to the roses and brambles in his private maze in the Boboli gardens one vial's worth every day. When he was satisfied his orders were being followed, he departed. Chiara and Magister Ruanno looked at each other without words, and carefully prepared one hundred and two vials. He took one of the extra ones. She took the other.

"Chiara," Magister Ruanno said. "Take care with that. No more than a single drop, and no more often than once every seven days."

Chiara put out her chin at him. "Do you think I'm a fool?"

"No. But I think you are young and impatient. I do not wish to lose—"
He stopped.

"You don't want to lose the grand duke's *soror mystica*." Chiara finished his sentence for him. She was hurt that he would think so little of her skill and care, and although she knew it wasn't true, she wanted to hurt him back. "You don't want to lose your chance at making him believe he's found the *Lapis Philosophorum*."

His eyes rested upon her, dark and endlessly deep and with an intensity she couldn't quite understand. After a moment he said, "That is true, as far as it goes."

"I'll be as careful as you will. Good night to you, Magister Ruanno."

She went into the small room next to the laboratory and took off her habit. As always, she had worn simple, dark clothing when the grand duke had called her to the Casino di San Marco; she put it on again. She strapped her leather belt around her waist and put the tiny, securely stoppered vial into her pouch. She went back into the laboratory—Magister Ruanno was gone—and from there out into the corridor. The guardsman in Medici colors who always accompanied her when she was called to the Casino di San Marco was waiting. He looked bored.

"I've been ordered to spend the night here, Rufino," she said. "To watch over one of the grand duke's experiments. I'll lock myself in. You can go home."

From the beginning she'd hated being watched over, and although she'd never actually slipped away from her guards before, she'd taken care to sweeten their feelings toward her with questions about their families and baskets of Nonna's cakes and *pasticci*. Rufino didn't wait to be told twice. He grinned at her and strode off whistling, sword-belt jingling.

She was alone. She had the night before her. Such freedom was rare and she was going to make the most of it.

She was going to see the book again, and read the things Babbo had written inside it.

With Rufino gone it was easy to slip past the grand duke's own night guards—they walked through the building, room to room, and she knew the pattern of it by heart. She kept to the shadows as she made her way through the narrow familiar streets, past the Duomo, to the booksellers' quarter to the northeast of the Palazzo Vecchio. The moon was full but mostly tucked away behind low gray clouds. It was icy cold, so cold her breath made a faint silvery plume in the night air. Had it really been a year and a half since she had ridden to the bookshop in the night, dressed in a boy's clothes, with a princess's necklace inside her doublet? A year and a half, and so much pain, so much terror, so much death. Her crooked fingers ached in the cold and dampness.

The shop looked the same. The door was locked, the windows were clean, the stones in front of the door were swept. Everything was dark and quiet. The caretaker didn't live in the shop, so it would be empty. She slipped into the alley and made her way around to the back door. It was locked as well. So it would have to be the secret passage. Santa Barbara, she whispered to herself, patron of diggers and stonemasons, help me. Let the passage be safe, let it be open, let the hatchway be undiscovered.

The passage came out in the corner of the yard, under what looked like a pile of stones left over from building the wall. She kilted up her skirts and mantle, rolled two stones aside and crawled into the passageway. It was dry and reasonably clear. Fortunately it was short and dark and she couldn't see the webs and filth and saints-only-knew-what-else she was crawling in. She came to the wooden hatchway and pushed, and glory be to God, it opened.

In the familiar cellar she could find her way by touch. The lamp was still on the shelf where it had always been; she could feel the layer of dust on the brass lid. The oil had congealed but the wick remained. She took her flint and steel from her pouch and struck a light.

The wall where the book was hidden was untouched. In fact, everything looked exactly as it had looked the day she and Magister Ruanno had come down into the cellar to look at Babbo's treasures the first time. If I break through the plaster, she thought, I'll have to take the book back with me, or find another hiding-place. I haven't got any fresh plaster to wall it up again.

Get it out, Babbo's voice whispered. Pain struck through her head like knives in her eyes. *Go ahead, you've come this far. Time for you to see what I've written about you and Gian and life and death and the Medici prince. . . .*

She had no tools, but there was a heavy stone mortar and pestle on the table; Babbo had used it to grind minerals but it was commonplace, not something Magister Ruanno had wanted. She grasped the pestle and began to pound on the plaster. It flaked and began to crumble. Her head felt as if it were about to burst with agony. Bigger pieces of the plaster broke away, and then there it was—the metal box she'd used to protect the book. A few more blows with the pestle and the hole was large enough. Carefully she took the box out of its hiding-place, opened it, unwrapped the waxed silk and laid the book on the table where the lantern's light would play over its pages.

The front and back covers were wood, studded with brass nails. Threads of red silk still clung to the nails, but the covering, whatever it might have been, had long since been worn away. The pages, in a dozen separate quires, were sewn to a woven net of braided linen cords, and the cords themselves were laced to the wooden covers. Holding her breath, Chiara turned back the cover.

The name *Tommaso Vasari* leaped off the first page, black and bold as she remembered it. The words written above it, which had meant nothing to her when she first saw them, now made sense to her. They were *Hic liber est meus*. This book is mine.

The satisfaction of reading for herself was like drinking spiced wine, that first spiced wine she had ever tasted, in the grand duke's golden studiolo. Hot and sweet. The words were more than ink and parchment. They had meaning. She understood the meaning. Until this moment she had never realized the power of knowing how to read.

She turned the pages. In the first section there were instructions for concocting the *Lapis Philosophorum*, different from the instructions that the grand duke followed. There were only four stages instead of fourteen, and each was identified with a color—*nigredo, albedo, citrinitas, rubedo*, blackening, whitening, yellowing and reddening. Each stage was described in detail. At the end of the descriptions she could pick out the words *alchimista solitarius*. A solitary alchemist. Using this method of four stages, was it possible for one person, working alone, to create the *Lapis Philosophorum*?

Thoughtfully she continued turning the pages. There were strange drawings, circles and lines with the positions of the planets drawn in, and the stars of the zodiac—horoscopes, then. She reached the place where the formula for *sonnodolce* had been torn out. The drawings now made sense to her. A black powder—some form of charcoal, it had been, although the grand duke had measured it out without identifying the wood it came from. White crystals. A golden-yellow powder. A red liquid. Only hours ago she had helped Magister Francesco and Magister Ruanno combine the ingredients, just as they were represented on the page. The sources and the exact proportions, those Magister Francesco had kept to himself. He was taking care that he was the only person who knew the secret of the *sonnodolce*.

Who had torn the page from the book? Magister Francesco, or someone else? Did someone else know? If so, who?

She turned to the last pages, where she had seen Babbo writing his own notes. They were there, just as she remembered, scribbled lines on the blank pages left over at the end of the last quire. The first page was neat, ruled with lines, and headed with a note:

Tommaso Vasari has been assassinated at an Austrian monastery. In accordance with my promise, I will use his equipment and books to injure the grand duke, and support the cause of the republic.

It was followed by a list, some of the items marked with checks and numbers set down beside them. The athanor from Trebizond was on the list, unchecked, as were the double pelican and the green glass alembic in the shape of the crescent moon. Even the little silver funnel was there—*one small silver descensory said to be a thousand years old, decorated with a design of a labyrinth.*

Chiara frowned. Had Babbo known the old grand duke's alchemist Tommaso Vasari, then? Or had Vasari chosen him by chance, because he sold books and curiosities and was known to have republican sympathies? She wondered if Grand Duke Francesco could tell her more about Tommaso Vasari, why he had left Florence, how he had come to be assassinated in a monastery in Austria. Or had only Grand Duke Cosimo known?

There was nothing more on that page. On the next few pages, more horoscopes—her own name jumped out at her, and Gian's. Giancarlo Nerini, born in Florence, the seventh day of August in the year 1557, under the sign of the Lion. Chiara Nerini, born in Florence, the twelfth day of November in the year 1558, under the sign of the Scorpion. She counted in her head. She had turned eighteen years old, then, a little less than a month ago.

After that, her father's handwriting changed, became fumbling and shaky.

I am teaching myself the things in the rest of Vasari's books. There are spells to bring back the dead. I will bring Gian back, even at the cost of my immortal soul.

So that was written after the accident. Chiara felt the hot spike of a headache driving into her skull from the crescent-shaped scar over her left ear. *Stop*, Isabella's soft, persuasive voice whispered. *Do not read any more. Put the book away, come back to the palace, lose yourself in comfort and lux-ury. Give yourself to Ruanno dell' Inghilterra—you know what he meant to say. He did not want to lose you, too. He wants you. You want him. Francesco will never know. . . .*

Chiara squeezed her eyes closed. Read? Don't read?

She opened her eyes and read.

The spell requires a sacrifice. Chiara watches me when I work—she thinks I don't see her looking through the stair-rail, but I do. She will come down willingly to help me when I ask her. I will cut her throat, and her virgin's life-blood will bring him back. She should have died instead of Gian, and it is only right she be the one to bring him back.

Chiara read the words over and over. They blurred before her eyes. It didn't matter. She would never forget them.

I will cut her throat.

Babbo had meant to kill her, in order to bring Gian back.

Necromancy. It was Magister Ruanno's voice, Ruan's voice, not a de-mon's voice but a real memory. They had been here in the cellar, in this very place. *Some necromancers . . .* Then he had stopped. Put his hand on her wrist, touched her deliberately for the first time.

It is nothing.

He had known about necromancy, and sacrifices. Had he guessed? Had he thought to protect her from the terrible knowledge that her own father had meant to kill her?

But Babbo had been the one to die, leaving behind poverty and misery and the unexplained hidden beauty of Tommaso Vasari's alchemical equip-ment. I would have known, she thought. I would have known all this from the beginning, if I had been able to read.

My greatest enemy was my greatest ally, Babbo's voice scratched and rus-tled in her head. *You thought I meant the devil. Stupid Chiara. I meant Duke Cosimo de' Medici, who did something terrible to Tommaso Vasari that made him flee from Florence in the middle of the night and leave all his knowledge and riches for the enemies of the Medici. For me.*

Then he laughed. And laughed and laughed.

Chiara put her face down against the book, trembling. Cry? No, she wouldn't cry. She wouldn't give Babbo the satisfaction.

You have the sonnodolce, he whispered. *Don't waste it with drips and drops on your skin. Drink it now, all of it. It's pleasant to the taste and you'll drift away quickly. You're the one who should have died, Chiara, and there's still time, still time.*

The grand duke had said that the drop was to be applied to the skin after taking the Sacrament at Mass. But she didn't want to wait. She took the vial out of her pouch.

One drop, no more, on the inside of your wrist where the skin is thin and soft, Isabella whispered. *It is not time for you to die. Put the one drop on your skin and think of Ruanno, here in this silent dark cellar with the lamplight flickering. He is a wonderful lover, hard and strong and exquisitely slow, and so gentle afterward. Live, Chiara. You and Ruanno must live to take revenge on Francesco.*

She opened the vial. The *sonnodolce* had a scent like honey, flowery with undertones of green leaves and insect wings. She thought of Ruanno—of Ruan—imagining him as he had been in the store-closet, close, a dark shadow looming. She could imagine his touch. He had taken a vial of the *sonnodolce*, too. One drop at a time, each one of them—and they would be immune to any poison, forever.

She let one drop fall on her left wrist. Then she put the stopper back in the vial. She thought about the secret instructions in the book that claimed a solitary alchemist could create the *Lapis Philosophorum* in four stages. Black, white, yellow and red. She thought about how easy it would be to rebuild a small laboratory here in the cellar, with equipment and elements stolen from the grand duke's storerooms.

She thought about Nonna coming home to Florence, with Mattea and Lucia, and all of them together again. Nonna would be happy to help her snatch the *Lapis Philosophorum* straight from under the grand duke's Medici nose. There'd been no news of Pierino Ridolfi but that didn't mean the grand duke's agents hadn't caught him. Was he dead? Had he confessed? Would Magister Ruanno know?

Magister Ruanno.

Ruan. Oh, Ruan.

As the *sonnodolce* took her, all the voices went away and she was alone with her thoughts, wonderfully alone. She imagined herself breaking her holy vow with Ruan, lying open under his weight and making the soft ecstatic groaning sounds Isabella and Dianora had made, in bed with each other on sweet summer afternoons.

. . . hard and strong and exquisitely slow, and so gentle afterward . . .

She imagined it all, from the beginning to the end, and with happiness afterward that was greater than any happiness she had ever known.

CHAPTER THIRTY-TWO

The Palazzo Pitti

6 JANUARY 1577

It had been hard to face Magister Ruanno at first, after that dark solitary hour in the bookshop's cellar. Did the *sonnodolce* increase the power of visions and fancies, bring hidden ones out into the light? Chiara felt as if she had broken her vow in truth, given herself to him, taken him, exposed herself to him with all the gasping intimacies of the flesh. If he noticed she was clumsy and tongue-tied in his presence, he said nothing.

She had brought Tommaso Vasari's book back to the laboratory and hidden it in the simplest possible way—by putting it in the cabinet with all the other books. She had also continued putting one drop of the poison on her wrist every seven days, alternating from one wrist to the other, choosing a different spot each time. Each time she felt desire for him. Was it the *sonnodolce*, or was it her own newly sensitized thoughts, feeding upon themselves? Surely he was using his tiny vial just as she was using hers. She wondered what, if anything, he desired, and wished she had the courage to ask him.

On Christmas Eve, the grand duchess had announced officially to her husband, with the support of her physicians, priests, and ladies, that she was once again with child. The city had exploded with delight, and the twelve days of Christmastide had been joyous like no other holiday Chiara had ever seen. Bianca Cappello was hated in Florence, by every woman, certainly, from the grand duchess herself to the humblest washerwoman.

Her much-vaunted son was a changeling, of course—even arrests and whippings in the street hadn't been enough to stop the whispers. What woman is suddenly fertile again, at the age of twenty-eight, after ten years as a barren mistress? Cold and unpopular the Austrian grand duchess may be, but at least she bore her own children. The city hummed with prayers for a half-Imperial son, to put Bianca Cappello's long Venetian nose out of joint once and for all. The Epiphany night celebration at the Palazzo Pitti was the glittering culmination of the holiday delights.

"I wish you a holy Epiphany, Signorina Chiara."

It was Cardinal Ferdinando de' Medici, the grand duke's brother, with his fleshy lips and his smoldering carnal eyes. He was robed in scarlet silk so heavily embroidered with gold thread, sapphires and amethysts that he might have been one of the Three Kings himself. Chiara knelt with every appearance of deference and kissed the ring he extended. His plump white hand smelled of musk, vanilla and cloves.

"Thank you, *sua Eminenza Illustrissima e Reverendissima*," she said, as she straightened. She would show him she had learned the proper way to address a prince of the church from a noble family. "Allow me to wish you a holy and joyful Epiphany as well."

"The processions were spectacular, were they not?" He gestured to the two priests who attended him, and with reverent bows they withdrew.

Why was he making an effort to talk to her, here among the noble and celebrated revelers in the grand salon of the palace? What did he want? Cautiously she said, "Indeed they were, Eminenza."

"And the star singers were charming. That is an Austrian custom, which reminds the grand duchess of her home. It is more important than ever, at this delicate time, for her to be happy and content."

"Yes, Eminenza."

"How cautious you are, my dear. I assure you, I mean you no harm. In fact, I can do you a great deal of good, if you will only allow me."

"Your blessings always do me good, Eminenza."

He laughed. "It is not another blessing I am suggesting. Come, over here—there is no better place to speak in private than in the midst of a large and boisterous crowd, do you not agree?"

"I am waiting for the grand duchess to return. She felt ill and withdrew for a little while, but asked me to wait here for her."

"I know. We will watch for her together. Come."

Chiara couldn't think of any more excuses, and he wasn't, after all, asking her to leave the grand salon. She followed him to the side of the room, slightly apart from the mass of revelers, into the small privacy offered by a window and its draperies. Outside light shimmered in hundreds of windows where people were dancing and exchanging gifts. The pattern of the city's streets was marked by torches, flaring and streaming in the cold night wind, lighting the way for the more raucous young men's processions.

"Now," the cardinal said. He leaned close, so he could lower his voice a bit. His breath smelled of sweet wine and rosewater pasticci. "Let us talk about this business of you being present to witness the birth of Signora Bianca Cappello's child."

Chiara looked down at her skirts, rearranging them slightly. They were the most amazing violet silk, new, richer than anything she had worn so far at court, with a foreparte and bodice embroidered with silver and knotted with a few small pearls, not quite perfect in shape. Her forehead was bound with a silver ribbon and there were silver chains and strings of crystals braided into her hair. The joy of being with child again and the season of the Epiphany had made the grand duchess generous with the ladies of her household. Chiara didn't want to repay that generosity with betrayal.

"I was in the room, Eminenza," she said, taking care with her words. "I did not see the birth."

"Indeed? How can that be so?"

She felt heat creeping up her throat and into her cheeks. How could a grown-up young woman of the court, eighteen years old, dressed in violet silk and silver and pearls, blush like a foolish child? Probably because she'd acted like a foolish child. In a low voice she said, "I was angry that the grand duke commanded me to stay and be a witness, and I squeezed my eyes shut so I would see nothing."

The cardinal stared at her for a moment, then burst into laughter. The people standing around them turned and looked, then whispered behind their hands. Who was the woman in violet silk, and what was she saying to the grand duke's brother to make him laugh in such an un-ecclesiastical manner? Chiara felt her blush get hotter.

"Well, my child," the cardinal said at last, when he had recovered himself. "What did you hear, then? And surely you opened your eyes before leaving the room, and did not stumble blindly out the door."

"I heard one of Signora Bianca's women come in. The grand duke was with her—they spoke to each other, too quietly for me to understand the words. I heard the sound of a *mandolino*'s strings, as if the woman was tuning it, but they sounded muffled and—well, not like music."

"How did you know it was a *mandolino*?"

"Later, after I opened my eyes, I saw it."

The cardinal nodded. He seemed pleased. "There has been a great deal of talk about that *mandolino*, particularly the size of it and what it might have contained. At least a dozen people were still outside the door, and saw the woman go into the chamber. Very well, go on."

"Signora Bianca screamed. Almost at the same time, the baby cried. I heard splashing—I think the midwife was washing it. Signora Bianca was sobbing. The other woman tried to play the *mandolino*, presumably to soothe her, but it sounded wrong, as if it had been damaged."

"And when did you open your eyes?"

"When the grand duke spoke to me. He was standing before me with the baby in his arms—it was naked and wet, and there were streaks of blood and patches of white material, like paste or wax, on its skin. The birth cord had been cut and tied with red thread. It was definitely a boy child."

"So it was genuinely a newly born child. I wonder what Francesco had to do, to assure himself of a healthy newborn baby boy at just the right moment."

Chiara had wondered the same thing. She said nothing.

"And after that, you went out of the room? You did not see what became of the *mandolino*, or the woman who played it?"

"No, Eminenza."

"Cast into the Arno, I suspect, the both of them. I have heard rumors that both the *mandolino*-player and the midwife have disappeared."

Chiara stared at him. The brightness and gaiety of the grand salon seemed to fade, like the colored sparks of fireworks blinking out and leaving trails of smoke against a black sky. "Disappeared? Both of them?"

"Some say one escaped. Even if that is true, perhaps it is your good fortune that you cannot say for certain what happened in Signora Bianca's bedchamber."

There was a stir among the people on the other side of the salon. The grand duchess came back into the room, making her way slowly to the dais with gentlemen bowing and ladies sweeping curtsies on either side of her. With dignity she resumed her seat beside the grand duke. His dark head bent toward hers, with some private words for her alone.

What had he done? Were Bianca Cappello's women murdered, their bodies eaten by fish, their bones tumbling slowly out to sea in the murk of the Arno? Had one of them escaped with her life? How could the grand duke eat and drink and receive gifts in these lavish Epiphany revels, bathed and perfumed, glittering with jewels?

"I must return to my place," Chiara said. "She may ask for me."

"A moment more," the cardinal said. "The English alchemist, Magister Ruanno dell' Inghilterra—you have worked with him, spent time with him, have you not?"

Oh, no. No. Not Magister Ruanno. Not Ruan, the dark secret lover who came to her in her *sonnodolce* dreams, who had saved Nonna and the little girls, who had given her the secrets she had needed to pass through her initiation. He would never abet the grand duke in conspiracy and murder. Unless—unless he was playing a double game, pretending to conspire while ensnaring the grand duke ever more deeply in evil, blackening his very soul in revenge for Donna Isabella's terrible death.

The cardinal must have seen the color drain from her face. He said, "You misunderstand, my dear—I have heard no whispers that Magister Ruanno was involved in the production of the changeling, or the disappearances of Signora Bianca's two women. I ask you about him because I have seen him look at you, and I have seen you avoid looking at him. Is he your lover?"

Yes.

No.

"No," she whispered. She could barely manage the single word.

The cardinal smiled. How could one smile be so full of amused and urbane lechery, as if he could see straight into her most secret thoughts?

"If you wish to be dispensed from your vow of virginity," he said, "I can arrange it. Quite privately, of course. The grand duke need never know."

"I would know." She took a long breath and steadied herself. She didn't want to be caught in whatever webs the cardinal was spinning. He hated

Bianca Cappello with a well-known and un-Christian hatred, and he didn't have much natural brotherly love for the grand duke, either. Better to stay well clear of him. "Thank you for your concern, Eminenza, but for the moment I am satisfied as I am."

He shrugged. "Very well, my dear," he said. "The grand duchess is looking our way, and I suspect she would like you to join the rest of her ladies."

"Thank you, Eminenza." She knelt again and kissed his ring. "Happy Epiphany to you."

"God bless you, my dear," he said. The plump flesh under his eyes crinkled as he smiled. "You may go, and good fortune to you."

CHAPTER THIRTY-THREE

"What were you and the cardinal whispering about?"

Ruanno dell' Inghilterra didn't look like himself, dressed in a courtier's padded doublet and paned trunk hose over tight-fitting canions, all in figured mulberry-colored silk, with a starched ruff at his throat and lace showing at his wrists. Apparently the grand duke had been generous to his household as well. Magister Ruanno—Ruan—looked like he wished he had his ordinary plain dark doublet and hose back again.

"Birth," Chiara said. "Death."

She had made her curtsy to the grand duchess, been kindly acknowledged, and waved away with a smile and a command to enjoy herself with the young people of the court. Bless her, the grand duchess made it sound as if she herself was a hundred years old. Chiara had kissed her hand with heartfelt admiration and withdrawn.

Straight into Ruan.

He had to have placed himself there deliberately—the grand salon was thick with people and yet there he was, right where she stepped. At least it was easier to talk to him when he was dressed up like a player in an Epiphany pageant. The unnatural courtier's clothing separated him from the primitive force in her *sonnodolce* dreams.

Is he your lover?

Yes.

No.

"Birth seems straightforward enough," he said. "Given that we are celebrating the grand duchess's happy news. But death? Whose death?"

"It was nothing, just talk."

She started to turn away and he put his hand on her wrist, below the edge of her sleeve where her skin was bare. It was a light, ordinary touch, no more than any other man might have done if he had wanted her to stay, talk further, dance, something, but it brought back the *sonnodolce* dreams—*Ruan grasping her wrists, spreading her arms wide, bending over her in darkness, saying something, his lips just barely touching hers as he spoke*—and made her whole body stiffen as if she had been touched by fire. She jerked her hand away. He started back at the same time. Surprise at her reaction? Or a reaction of his own?

"What is it?" He didn't try to touch her again but he moved, just a little, just enough to put himself between her and the rest of the room so no one else could see her.

"Nothing. Nothing. Let me go."

"That was not nothing."

She didn't dare say the word *sonnodolce*, not here where some passing courtier or laughing lady might hear the word and wonder what it was. But on the other hand, what better place to ask him? *There is no better place to speak in private*, the cardinal had said, *than in the midst of a large and boisterous crowd*. And that same crowd would protect her. From him. From herself.

She bent her head and said in a low quick voice, "The liquid. The drop on your wrist, one day out of seven. Does it—affect you?"

She wasn't looking at him but she felt him react. It was as if someone had struck him.

"You too?" he said.

She nodded, still not looking at him.

"I have—dreams," he said slowly. "They are more vivid that any other dreams I have ever had. I am at home, in Cornwall, walking along the cliffs and tasting the sea spray. I am inside Milhyntall House, where I was born, walking through the rooms—there are so many rooms inside the house that I have never seen, that I know only because my mother described them to me when she told me stories at night. I am going down into Wheal Loer, my father's mine, my mine, where there are veins of copper that go so deep they will never be exhausted, and I am not a nameless half-naked boy carrying rocks to the surface, but the lord of it all."

"You see your home." The house he described sounded like a great manor. And the mine—well, he had told her an Englishman had taken over his father's estate after a rebellion, and later put him to work as a child in the mine. Was that why he had always seemed to be half-workman, half-gentleman?

"Yes," he said. "I wonder if the—liquid—makes one see the thing one desires most in all the world."

She couldn't stop herself from asking. "Is that all you see? Your home?"

"Not all." He paused. She wondered if he also dreamed of Isabella, and his own revenge on the grand duke for her death. Then very gently he said to her, "What do you see, *awen lymm*?"

"What does that mean?"

"Nothing. Never mind. Tell me what you see."

If he didn't see her, she'd die before she'd tell him she saw him. And anyway, if it was true that the *sonnodolce* made you see what you wanted most, she'd be seeing visions of herself with her head clear and the *Lapis Philosophorum* in her hands. Herself as an alchemist as famous as Perenelle Flamel. Herself proving utterly and completely that Babbo had been wrong to cast her aside, wrong to think she was good for nothing but a sacrifice to bring Gian back.

"I don't remember," she said. "Just that there are dreams. Sometimes it's what I want most in the world, and sometimes it's—I don't know, what I'm most afraid of."

He didn't press her. Did he know she was lying? "I wonder what the grand duke sees," he said. He looked at Francesco de' Medici on the dais at the head of the salon and the lines of cruelty deepened at the corners of his mouth. "He has changed in the eleven years I have known him. He was always melancholy, and preferred to be alone in his laboratory with his experiments. But he was not—vicious. Not a man who would murder his own sister and cousin."

"When did he start—with the drops? Do you know?"

"I am not sure. I think from the time of his marriage. He made Bianca Cappello his mistress at about the same time, and he may have feared that

Imperial agents would poison him for bringing such shame upon the emperor's sister. The fellow who created the—the liquid we are speaking of—had supposedly fled to Austria, so the grand duke could have feared that particular substance."

"So for eleven years. I can believe it's driven him mad, after eleven years. What do you think he sees, in his dreams?"

"I do not know. I suspect he sees the *Lapis Philosophorum*, and all the power it would bring him. His mother and father begging his pardon for loving his brothers and his sister more than they loved him. All the world paying him homage."

"We should stop," she said. "It's not worth becoming immune to poisons, if the drops will do that to us in the end."

Ruan looked at her. She saw the terrible need in his eyes. Did he see the same thing in hers? Would she give up the overpowering and demanding Ruan who came to her and held her helpless after the drop of *sonnodolce* fell upon her wrist?

He said, "I will not stop. Not until I regain Milhyntall House and Wheal Loer, in truth and not only in dreams. Not until I see— until I have taken the vengeance I have sworn."

Not until he saw the grand duke lying dead at his feet. Even in the midst of a noisy crowd, there were some things that could not be said.

"In any case," he said, "there is still good reason for both of us to be immune to poison. The grand duke—"

A gasp and rustle ran through the room, as if everyone was turning and whispering at once. Chiara stepped to one side so she could see, and although Ruan didn't touch her, he put out one arm in front of her, as if to protect her.

Bianca Cappello stood in the center of the double doorway into the great salon, all alone. Her head was thrown back, as if overbalanced by the weight of her hair, braided and pinned, shimmering with gold dust and heavy with jewels. She was dressed in a gown of orange-scarlet satin lavishly laced with gold.

The grand duke looked at her. His face was flushed and black darkness surrounded him. The grand duchess sat like stone.

Bianca began to walk toward them.

A dozen people gasped her name at once, so the word *Bianca Bianca*

Bianca whispered and crackled and filled the air of the great salon like the sound of a flame. She walked the length of the room, slowly, deliberately, glorying in everyone's eyes upon her, her own eyes fixed on the grand duke's face and nothing else. She ignored the grand duchess. She ignored everyone in the great salon but her lover.

The father of her son.

Or so she claimed.

Men and women stepped back, making way for her. No one bowed or curtsied. After what seemed like hours she reached the dais and sank into a deep curtsy herself. The deepest, most perfect curtsy anyone could ever see. A graceful curtsy that the grand duchess could never perform with her poor twisted back, no matter how many steel corsets and padded dresses she wore.

Chiara saw the grand duke's lips move, although she couldn't hear what he said. From the look on his face, she wouldn't have wanted to hear it. Bianca was very still for a moment, then she straightened. An unnatural hush fell over the room. Everyone was suddenly being quiet because of course everyone wanted to hear what she would say.

"Surely, Serenissimo," she said, in a strong high voice, "you will welcome the mother of your son to your Epiphany celebrations."

More silence. Then slowly the grand duke rose to his feet, his darkness rising with him and swirling around him. "We have not commanded your presence," he said.

Anyone else would have crumpled and crept away. Bianca Cappello stood her ground, you had to give her that. To her own surprise, Chiara felt Ruan take her hand, his fingers slipping in between hers, his palm to her palm. She had a sense that he was preparing to pull her to safety somehow. What did he expect the grand duke to do?

"Is it so wrong, Serenissimo," Bianca Cappello said, "that I wish to join the revels at the court? The day for my churching has come and gone, and the rich public celebration you promised me has not been arranged."

The gasps and whispers rose to a fever's pitch. Sweat—or was it tears?—made streaks in the white ceruse on Bianca's face and the vermilion she had used to paint half-moons high on her cheeks. As much as she loved and admired the grand duchess, Chiara couldn't help feeling a flicker of sympathy. What had Bianca Cappello felt, sitting alone in her fine new villa at

Pratolino with her changeling child, her serving-women murdered, knowing her lover was leading his court in the dazzling Epiphany processions, masques, feasts and dancing, which would be talked about all over Europe? Epiphany revels to which she was pointedly not invited?

What did she expect the grand duke to do? Surely she wasn't fool enough to think he would smile and invite her to sit at his side on the dais?

He did smile. It was awful, like a skull's teeth. He looked around the grand salon in a leisurely manner, at his brothers, at his courtiers, at all the richly dressed noblemen and gentlemen celebrating the feast of the Three Kings with him. At last he said, very deliberately, "Magister Ruanno."

Chiara felt Ruan stiffen. His hand slipped out of hers as if he had never touched her at all. He stepped forward, made one of his stiff, economical bows, and said, "I am at your service, Serenissimo."

"I require that you travel with Donna Bianca back to the villa at Pratolino, and arrange that she remains there whether she desires to do so or not. You are detailed half a dozen guardsmen to assist you."

Bianca Cappello stood frozen. Her tears had vanished, transmuted to vapor, probably, by her fury.

"I will not go with him," she said. "He is a servant."

Ruan didn't move. His expression didn't change.

"As are you, Madonna," the grand duke said. "Go. I am not accustomed to repeating my orders."

For the space of a few breaths Chiara thought Bianca Cappello might defy him further. Then suddenly she swept around, with her head high and a great flouncing of her silken skirts, and walked out of the room. Ruan stood for a moment, then bowed again to the grand duke and followed her. At the door, the guardsmen formed up two-by-two and stepped after him.

Chiara turned to look at the dais. The grand duchess had not moved or said a word through the whole confrontation. The grand duke seated himself again and lifted his hand.

"Bring in the *befanini*," he said. "And more wine. We will refresh ourselves with the special cakes of the season, and then continue with the celebrations."

CHAPTER THIRTY-FOUR

A woman who has been crying for a night and a day, the grand duke thought, was hardly a creature to move a man's heart. Bia's face was blotched and swollen, her eyes little more than slits, her nose and upper lip so reddened they looked raw. Her hair was loose and tangled where she had dragged the jeweled ornaments out of it. One string of pearls and rubies remained, hanging in a forgotten loop like drops of blood alternating with milky drops of semen.

All this, because he had sent her away from the Epiphany revels. His wife had cried herself into an unrecognizable state after the deaths of her children, but that was different. Crying for a dead child was understandable, even if the child was a girl. Crying more than a pretty crystal tear or two over a court revel was beneath contempt.

"It was not the revel," Bia sobbed. "Do you not understand? You humiliated me. You promised me a grand churching and you did not keep your promise. You sent me away with a *servant* to escort me, in front of everyone."

"When we spoke of the churching," the grand duke said, "I did not yet know that the grand duchess would be with child. With her in such a condition, you can hardly expect me to throw your churching in her face."

"She has borne you nothing but daughters, and weak daughters at that—half of them have died."

"This time it may be a son. Take care with your words, my Bia."

She flounced over to the bed and threw herself down, sobbing like a madwoman. The grand duke poured himself a cup of wine, settled comfortably in the fine carved chair by the fire, and gazed out through the handsome glazed *portafinestra* at the snow-covered gardens. Snow. Wind. Darkness. He remembered that afternoon in the garden labyrinth, almost a year ago on Shrove Tuesday, how he had cut her dress and bared her breasts to the cold. How he had wondered what it would be like to expose her entire naked body to the cold, and then later have her when she was half-dead with it.

He sipped. After a while she stopped crying and sat up.

"I am so tired of it all," she said. "I do not want to be your meek little Bia anymore. I am Bianca Cappello, a noblewoman of Venice, and the mother of your son. I want to—"

"You are not the boy's mother."

"And you are not his father! I could publish that truth from one end of Italy to the other. I could write to the pope himself."

"So you could. But have you any proof that I am not his father?"

She stared at him. He sipped his wine calmly.

"It is perfectly possible," he said after a moment, "that I fathered the boy on another woman, and allowed you the pretense that he was yours, out of the kindness of my heart. All you know for certain, my Bia, is that another woman bore him, and that he was smuggled into your bedchamber in the bowl of a Neapolitan *mandolino*."

"But I saw," she said. Her voice was hoarse from all the screaming and sobbing. "In the cellars. I saw that woman—all the women. I heard your orders."

"Did you? There is no one to support your assertions. No one."

"Because you have killed them all."

"Tut, my Bia, that is slanderous. A bearing of false witness. I trust you will confess it, and do suitable penance."

Because of course I did not kill them, he thought. A few words here and there to selected fellows willing to take the sin of murder upon their own souls, well, that is a different thing altogether.

He watched her. He could see her thoughts pass across her face, just as clearly as if she were speaking them. *He is lying. Is he lying? Am I going mad?*

No, I know what I saw. It is another one of his games. He has played games with me from the beginning. Does he love me? Did he ever love me?

It always came to that. *Does he love me?*

She scrubbed the back of her hand across her face like a child. "Very well. He is yours and he is mine, and I am sorry—sorry for what I said. When will I have my churching, then?"

"I will arrange it here at Pratolino—the chapel is complete but for the final frescos."

"I do not *want* it here. I want it at the Duomo, for everyone to see."

"That is impossible just now. Be reasonable, my Bia."

"Because of her."

"Because of her brother. I need the emperor's good will."

She walked over to the table, picked up one of the wine cups, and held it out to him. After a moment he stood up and poured wine into the cup. She drank it down as if it were water, which was what he had been afraid she would do.

"You are the Grand Duke of Tuscany. The emperor has acknowledged you, and he cannot take it back. I want to be churched in the Duomo, and recognized by every man and woman in Florence as your favorite and the mother of your only son."

She held out her cup for more wine. He took the cup away from her and put it on the table.

"No," he said. "It is not possible."

She swung her arm at him, her fingers arched like claws. He was expecting it and stepped back, so calmly that the wine in his cup barely rippled. She lost her balance and stumbled over the hem of her loose night-gown, and only saved herself from falling by catching hold of the bedpost. She squeezed her eyes shut and cried—howled—screamed like a child.

"I *hate* you! You are like my father—he loved my stepmother more than he loved me."

"It is only right, my Bia, that a man love his wife more than his daughter."

"It was not right," she wailed. "He made me the mistress of the house, from the time my own mother died—I had beautiful clothes and necklaces and sweetmeats and all the leisure I wanted. The servants obeyed me, whatever I asked of them."

The grand duke finished his wine and put his cup down. He had become tired of her hysteria. He meditated on the snow blowing in the wind outside the *portafinestra*.

"Then he married again and she insisted I dress plainly and sit still for lessons and do needlework. She wormed her way into his heart and convinced him to let her change everything and I *hated* it, Francesco, I hated it. I was not born to dress plainly and sew shirts. I am not born to be hidden away here at Pratolino while everyone bows and curtsies to the emperor's sister."

"Bia," the grand duke said. "Be silent."

She wiped her eyes with her sleeve and sniffled, but put her shoulders back and stood straight before him. She had done that in response to his voice for eleven years.

"Strip yourself."

She began to take off her clothes, still sniffling. It was a simple task. She was wearing only the velvet night-gown the color of amber, crumpled and stained with her tears. Under the night-gown, a white silk camicia heavily embroidered with white and gold thread. Under the camicia, nothing.

He looked at her, the rich wealth of her flesh, the weight of her breasts, the sweet curve of her belly. Her hair was in wild disarray, with the single strand of rubies and pearls tangled in the strands. He felt his own flesh respond to her nearness, her scent.

Not yet. Later. It would be so much better, later.

"So," he said. "You do not wish to live quietly here at Pratolino, and serve me as my little wife Bia when it pleases me to require it?"

She arched her back and lifted her chin. She knew how she affected him.

"I do not," she said.

He caught hold of her wrist and jerked her toward the *portafinestra*. The casements opened like windows, both inward and outward. With his free hand he unlatched them, and without a word he pushed her through into the snow. She shrieked and staggered, her bare feet slipping on patches of ice, and fell to her hands and knees.

"If you do not wish to live here," he said, "then go. And take exactly what you brought with you that I did not provide."

He closed and latched the casements, went back to his chair, and sat down.

"Francesco!" she screamed. She got to her feet and flung herself at the glass panes. Everywhere her naked skin had touched the snow, it was reddened as if it had been burned. "For the love of God, are you mad?"

He poured himself more wine. She paced back and forth outside the window, her arms wrapped around her body, shivering and crying and screaming gutter imprecations. He wondered how long she could remain outside in the cold and snow, naked as an animal, without collapsing. He wondered what he would do if she collapsed before she surrendered.

"Francesco!"

Her breath crystallized on the glass panes, making shining patterns of ice. She was shivering violently now, uncontrollably. Her skin was losing its color even as he watched her, with the reddened patches turning to violet, and her lips and fingers taking on a blue cast. Her fingernails against the casements' glazing sounded like dead branches in a winter wind.

He sipped his wine. The fire crackled, pleasantly warm.

"F-Franco," she sobbed. Her teeth were chattering and she could barely form the words. "Your Bia will die in this cold. Please let your Bia in—she will obey you forever, she swears it."

He put the wine cup down on the table, stood up, and went to the *portafinestra*. He toyed with the latch, watching her eyes. The tears were freezing on her cheeks.

She sank to her knees. Her lips formed the word *please*.

He lifted the latch and opened the casements.

She fell back into the room surrounded by a gust of wet, icy air. He left her to lie sobbing and shuddering on the stone floor while he latched the casements again and pulled the draperies over them to help keep the cold out and the warmth of the fire in. Then he looked at her. Her skin was bluish-white, roughened with gooseflesh and gleaming with streaks of sweat, half-frozen to her flesh. As he stood over her, she turned her head and kissed his foot like a hound bitch who had been whipped.

"Ah, my Bia," he said. He lifted her and carried her to the bed. She sank into the deep warm down mattresses with a groan, and he piled comforters on top of her. She curled herself up like a child, whimpering.

In a leisurely fashion he took off his own clothes, enjoying the warmth of the fire against his naked skin. He took a last long swallow of wine. Then he lifted the coverlets and climbed into the bed. Holy Christ, but she was cold still. He gathered her into his arms and kissed her icy blue lips. Then he forced himself into her. She was cold everywhere. The sensation of his own swollen heat sunk deep in her cold flesh was beyond anything he had ever felt before.

She clung to him, whispering *Franco Franco Franco Franco* through her chattering teeth. He stroked her hair, brushing away the wetness of snow-flakes.

Having a son was all very well. In a few months he might even have the half-Imperial son he craved with every drop of Medici blood in his body. But even that was nothing compared to his craving for Bia's helplessness, Bia's obedience, Bia's sweet, sweet pleas for mercy.

However much she might anger him, in the end she always surrendered. She gave him more pleasure than anything else. Even alchemy. It was as simple and as inexplicable as that.

He would never give up his Bia.

CHAPTER THIRTY-FIVE

The Palazzo Vecchio

24 MAY 1577

To celebrate the birth of a legitimate Medici heir, the people of Florence went mad with fireworks, feasting and singing. Wine flowed from enormous barrels set up on the *ringhiere* of the Palazzo, all the way to the Ponte Vecchio, and even supporters of the old republic toasted the birth—free wine, after all, was free wine. The *potenze*, the workmen's holiday guilds, staged jousts in the piazzas and broke each other's heads with triumphant abandon.

What no one knew except the grand duke and the grand duchess themselves, the court physicians, the grand duchess's private chaplain and half a dozen ladies hand-picked for their ability to hold their tongues, was that the baby boy was frail and barely responsive. The soft spot at the back of his disproportionately large skull bulged in a frightening way, and his tiny limbs stiffened every few hours with seizures. But he had lived for four days now. He was a male. He was unquestionably the son of the Grand Duke of Tuscany and his wife, the grand duchess, the sister of Emperor Maximilian II.

The city celebrated.

"Will you drink a little wine, Serenissima?"

Chiara found herself whispering, because it felt like a sin to speak in a normal voice. The windows were covered and the bed-curtains were drawn. Propped up with dozens of cushions, the grand duchess looked like a child herself, her sunken eyes closed, her fingers moving from bead to bead of her rosary, over and over again. She was making a novena to the Holy Innocents, and she shook her head as she continued her prayers.

She would make herself seriously ill if she didn't stop praying and drink some hot spiced red wine and good stout meat broth. Chiara knew it was hopeless to insist, though, and she put the cup down on the table beside the bed.

"She wouldn't drink any of the wine, Messer Baccio," she said to the physician. "She just keeps praying."

"She is overwhelmingly melancholic, filled with black bile," the physician said. "Dry and cold. We must continue to press liquids on her, and spices to warm her from within."

Get her out of bed and give her a floor to scrub, Nonna would have said. *Let her nurse her own babe and wash its swaddlings. Noble ladies don't have enough work to do and it's no wonder their humors are disordered.*

"Yes, Messer Baccio."

"You may go, my dear. We may require you tomorrow or we may not—I will send for you if necessary."

Chiara didn't wait to be told twice. She had her own tiny, windowless cell at the Palazzo Vecchio, just as she did at the Palazzo Pitti and all the ducal palaces and villas. She was happy enough to have it, for all its lack of comforts. And she could always go to the Austrian kennel master's domain downstairs, where she and Vivi were warmly welcome.

And of course there was the laboratory. If she could only get to the laboratory—clean, bright, well-ordered, with its cabinets of books. Could she slip out of the Palazzo Vecchio and make her way to the Casino di San Marco? Probably not. The streets weren't safe, not with the *potenze* running rampant, the banquet tables set up in front of the Palazzo Medici, and the barrels of wine being refilled every hour. Banquet tables. Saints and angels, she was hungry. Maybe she could go down to the kitchen and—

"Chiara."

She stopped.

It was Ruan.

"I have been looking for you, *awen lymm*."

He was dressed for riding in his plain dark doublet and leather breeches, with his whip coiled over his shoulder—all workman tonight, no trace of the gentleman. She could smell wine on his breath. He had always seemed abstemious but with so much celebrating going on, apparently even the self-contained Magister Ruanno had downed a cup or two of the grand duke's free wine as he passed through the streets. She said, "I wish you'd stop calling me that. Or at least tell me what it means."

"Perhaps one day. How is the grand duchess?"

"I'm not allowed to say anything."

"The grand duke has asked me to create a compound that he believes will reduce the swelling of the little one's skull, while it is still soft. He also requires a syrup that is a specific for convulsions. From those things I can draw my own conclusions."

Chiara tried to control her expression but she couldn't. She felt her mouth twist and the sting of tears in her eyes. Poor little baby, so frail and helpless. Poor Grand Duchess Giovanna, to have her longed-for son at last and to have him—wrong, so wrong. He wouldn't live. He couldn't live. How could God be so cruel, to send him and then take him away again?

"I know," Ruan said. "They are cheering in the streets, pressing wine on every passer-by, and then I come here. It is like going from light to darkness in one step."

She gulped back her tears. "I don't want to talk about it. Why were you looking for me?"

"I want you to help me with the tasks the grand duke has assigned me, in the laboratory. I have two mounted guardsmen with me, and an extra horse. If you wrap yourself up well in a dark mantle and hood, we will be safe enough."

"I was wishing there was a way for me to get away from the Palazzo. I'd like to help if I can."

"You can. Get your mantle."

He had measured and arranged his ingredients, and laid them out in clean glass bowls and flasks. Chiara didn't recognize all of them. The clear, syrupy-thick liquid in the second flask had to be oil of vitriol—in itself it was dangerously corrosive, but it also had a strong dehydrating property. There was another clear liquid that looked like ordinary water, and four dishes with powdered minerals—two white, one yellow, and one a startling bright blue. A system of retorts and an alembic had been constructed, and a fire had been lit in a small burner.

"I have already made the measurements," he said. "I will combine the forces, if you will add each one according to my direction."

Neither of them had changed into their habits—without the presence of the grand duke and his fancies, it didn't seem necessary. Chiara had pulled the moonstone out from under her camicia, so she could touch it, and feel its weight against her breast. She said, "Yes, Magister Ruanno."

"Begin with the first white powder." He picked up a glass rod. "Pour it slowly into this retort."

For a little while they worked together, without speaking other than his quiet instructions. He seemed to be making a particular effort not to touch her, not even so much as a brushing of their fingers. Eventually he said, "Have you seen the baby prince?"

"Yes, but only for a moment."

"Tell me what you saw. You know the grand duke believes in observation as part of the scientific and alchemical method. I do not think he would expect you to keep silence in the laboratory, if your observations will help to formulate a treatment."

Chiara added another dram of the yellow powder, using a silver cochlear in order to measure carefully. "He didn't look—right. His head wasn't so much misshapen, like babies' heads are sometimes, as it was out of proportion, too large. The soft spot at the back of his head was swollen, and his poor little face— I didn't see him suffering the seizures, but the ladies—well, they talked among themselves."

Magister Ruanno stirred his compound in silence. The number of times the glass rod circled was important.

"What you describe," he said at last, "sounds very much like what Hippocrates called *hudroképhalon*, a collection of watery humors over the brain."

"Will this help?" Chiara gestured to the compound. The ingredients had been combined and were beginning to bubble gently over the fire. It had become a milky, bluish-green liquid, thick, looking for all the world like Nonna's spinach soup with cream.

"No. There is probably nothing that will help the child. All this can do is help the grand duke and the grand duchess believe they have done all they can to save their heir."

"And the syrup for the seizures?"

"Again, a palliative, not a cure."

"Where did you learn all these things?" Chiara asked. "What is that word you said, and who is Hippocrates?"

He smiled. "Hippocrates was a Greek physician and philosopher—he might well have been an alchemist too, or at least worked closely with alchemy. The word was also Greek—a combination of *húdôr*, the word for water, and *kephalé*, the word for head."

"Did you learn Greek at your home in Cornwall?"

His expression changed. "No. I learned nothing but misery and bitterness at my home in Cornwall."

"Then why do you want to go back?"

"Because Milhyntall House is mine. Wheal Loer is mine."

"Are those Greek words, too?"

He stirred the compound twenty-eight times. She counted the strokes with him. Twenty-eight was a perfect number, equal to the sum of its proper positive divisors, and it would help bring the compound to perfection. Then he turned the hourglass over.

"They are Cornish words," he said at last. "Wheal Loer is a tin and copper mine—loer means moon, and the first of the Pencarrows, generations ago, claimed to have seen the full moon when he first looked up from the mine's main shaft. Milhyntall means labyrinth. There is an old tale that there was a stone maze built on the spot where the house stands, long before there was any written history."

"Pencarrow. Is that your other name? Is that why you sign yourself *Roannes Pencarianus*?"

He looked surprised, as if he hadn't meant to speak the name aloud. Reluctantly he said, "Yes."

Chiara looked down at the black-and-white labyrinth inset into the laboratory floor. "Labyrinth House," she said. "You were born to be an alchemist, then."

"I was born to be Ruan Pencarrow of Milhyntall, and nothing else."

"Why did you leave?"

The sand in the hourglass ran out. He picked up his glass rod and again stirred the compound twenty-eight times. Apparently the consistency pleased him, because he removed the retort from the fire and placed it in the silver rack to cool.

"I did not leave of my own will," he said. The fire left deep shadows of sorrow in the hollows of his eyes and under his cheekbones. "Chiara, enough. Perhaps one day I will tell you the story, but I cannot do it tonight. There is already enough unhappiness for both of us."

She turned her face away and began to collect the glass rods and silver cochlears. It was easy to understand loving a place so much. She loved Florence, her home, her native soil, every street and alley, church and marketplace, bridge and tree and stone. The only home she had ever known was the bookshop and the rooms overhead and the cellar—

The cellar. Her new laboratory, all her own.

I can heal myself, she thought. I can get away from the court and be myself again, Chiara Nerini, Florentine, alchemist, sister in the art to Perenelle Flamel. I can call myself the daughter of Carlo Nerini and be certain that Babbo would be proud of me. Nonna can run the shop and I—

Nonna.

"Ruan?" She put the glass rods in a basin for washing, carefully, one at a time.

"What?"

"Do you think it's safe for Nonna and my sisters to come home to Florence? It's been a year and a half."

"The grand duke never forgets a betrayal. You know that."

Pain stabbed through her forehead. It surprised her, because her headaches had become less frequent. "He never knew it was Nonna who helped Ridolfi escape. Well, Nonna and me. If he knew, we'd both be dead."

"Perhaps."

"I miss her," she said. "I miss having my home to myself, without the Arte's caretaker. You of all people should understand what exile means, and having a stranger living in one's home."

She saw him stiffen. She was sorry she'd said it, but it was too late.

For a long time they stood without moving or speaking. The compound in the retort made soft crackling sounds as it cooled. The pain behind her eyes faded. Being in the laboratory always helped. Being in her own laboratory, in the cellar of the bookshop, would help even more.

"It is a risk," he said at last. "It must be done very quietly, and there will be bribes to pay."

"The grand duke's money should be enough. Twenty gold scudi per year. Has he been paying it properly?"

Ruan's mouth twitched in what might have been a fragment of a smile. "Are you only now wondering about that?" he said. "He has paid it regularly. Some has been allotted to the caretaker, and some of it has been sent to your Nonna in Pistoia, to sweeten the temper of her sister and buy Lucia and Mattea new dresses. Some of it has paid for your own expenses. Some of it has been put away safely. I will prepare you an account, if you want one."

"Of course not."

"Write a letter to your Nonna, then, and I will see that it is delivered. I am sure she will be happy to come home to Florence, and be the mistress of her own household again."

That made Chiara smile, in a wry sort of way—imagine Nonna, not the mistress, forced to defer to her sister in everything. She was probably desperate to come home. She would probably be willing to walk every step of the way. And she would help build and conceal the laboratory in the cellar. How she would laugh at the thought of stealing the grand duke's equipment and materials and using them to find the *Lapis Philosophorum* before he did. Even in the midst of all the darkness and sorrow, Chiara felt her heart lift.

"Ruan," she said. "Thank you."

He smiled, a real smile. "It is a small thing."

"It isn't. It's more than you know. It makes me want to—"

She stopped. She couldn't tell him about the *sonnodolce* dreams, how much she craved them, how they made her feel as if she was already his lover, even if she had never even kissed him.

"To what?" he said. He sounded amused and only mildly interested. He had turned back to his compound, bending forward to examine it carefully. His profile was sharp and clear against the laboratory cabinets full of exotic colors and shapes, the ancient books, the flasks of colored liquids, the crystals and the skulls. His thick dark hair was cut short enough to show the shape of his head and the fine musculature of his neck.

The air itself seemed to shift and darken, as if she were in a *sonnodolce* dream even though she knew she wasn't.

She laid her hands on his arm and pulled him around to face her.

"It makes me want to kiss you," she said.

He frowned a little, as if he didn't quite understand her.

She ran her hands up over his arms and shoulders and put her palms flat against his cheeks. His skin was cool, slightly rough where his beard would grow if he was not clean-shaven. His eyes had narrowed and his lips had parted a little. He didn't think she was going to do it. But she had already done it so many times in the *sonnodolce* dreams. She had imagined it during those summer afternoons, her first year at the Palazzo Medici, listening to Donna Isabella and Donna Dianora pleasuring each other. She had dreamed of men then and told herself they were faceless men, but in truth there was only one man and his face was Ruan Pencarrow's.

She stood on her tiptoes, closed her eyes and touched her lips very lightly to his.

One breath, hers and his together.

He pushed her away from him so hard that she stumbled, flailing with her arms for balance. One arm swept the hourglass from the table. It smashed on the floor, scattering glass and sand over the patterned black and white tiles of the maze.

She wanted to scream at him. She wanted to cry. She wanted to run away but her legs wouldn't move.

"Chiara," he said at last. His voice sounded as if it hurt him to speak. "Chiara, if you do that I cannot promise you I will not—"

He stopped. They stared at each other. Neither of them breathed.

He said something in Cornish. Then he said, "I cannot promise you I will not compel you to break your vow."

Chiara felt the blood flame up in her cheeks.

"I see you, Chiara," he went on, in that same husky anguished voice. "In the *sonnodolce* visions. I see Cornwall, yes, and Milhyntall House and the moon over Wheal Loer, but I see you beside me as I walk along the cliffs. I feel you. I taste you and breathe your scent."

She swallowed. She whispered, "I see you too. I count the days sometimes, until I can put the drop on my wrist and dream of you."

He said nothing for a long time. At last he said, "Chiara, it changes things. If we are to love one another, everything will be changed."

"I know."

"I do not share the grand duke's belief that an alchemist's *soror mystica* must be a virgin. You know that. But as closely as we work together, the three of us—if you and I were to become lovers, he would know. He is not a fool, and the *sonnodolce* has made him—unpredictable. I would fear for you."

"I understand." She felt tears well up in her eyes and blinked fiercely. It didn't work. The tears slid down over her cheeks. "We can't— We can't. Not now. After, though? After we find the *Lapis Philosophorum*? After you—take your home back? After you take your revenge on the grand duke?"

"Many afters. Dangerous afters."

"Even so."

He reached out and ran his thumb lightly under her left eye, then through her hair where the scar was printed into her scalp. She felt him rub it gently, making little circles.

"After those things are done," he said, "I will go back to Cornwall. Are you willing to leave Florence behind, leave your family behind, and come home with me?"

Leave Florence? Leave Nonna and her sisters? How could he ask her such a thing? She wanted to be with him, be his wife and his lover, work in a laboratory with him until the end of time. She wanted to see his Labyrinth House and his Moon Mine, yes. But she didn't want to go away forever. She wanted to come home in the end.

"Can we come back?" she whispered. "Have a home here, too?"

"No," he said. His voice was stark. "Listen to what you yourself have said, Chiara. I am going to take my revenge on the grand duke. When I have done that, I cannot ever come back here."

Chiara couldn't stop the stupid tears. She scrubbed them away and more kept welling up and spilling over. "What are we going to do, then?" she said. She knew it was stupid and childish but she couldn't help herself. "I know Cornwall is your home, but Florence is my home, just as much. How can we be together if you're there and I'm here?"

He ran his scarred palm over her forehead, brushing back a few loose strands of her hair. His touch was so gentle and so full of care that it broke her heart.

"We will be together," he said. "For now, we must wait."

She put out her chin at him. She felt it quavering. "Wait for what?"

"I do not know, *awen lymm*." He smiled at her, just a little. "But we are bound to each other, and in the end we will find a way, or I will die in the trying."

CHAPTER THIRTY-SIX

Carlo Nerini's bookshop

16 SEPTEMBER 1577

"Nonna!"

Chiara slid down from the horse and ran into her grandmother's arms. Vivi danced beside her, barking with delight at all the excitement.

"Look at you," Nonna said. She squinted her eyes as if it was hard for her to see clearly. "Riding a horse like you were born to it. I remember the days when you were so scared of horses you'd puke at the sight of one. Let me look at you, *nipotina*."

She took hold of Chiara's wrists and spread them wide, then let go of one and twirled her around with the other. Vivi jumped up and went round in circles as well.

"You look thin. You look older. Not so fresh and pretty, for all your fine clothes and pearls in your hair. How old are you now, anyway?"

Leave it to Nonna to say the things no one else ever said. "I'm eighteen—I'll be nineteen in a couple of months. As you know perfectly well. Living at the Medici court is enough to squeeze the freshness and prettiness out of anyone."

"Still keeping that crazy vow of yours? It's past time you were married—a good husband would perk you up a bit. Why are you riding about with only a guardsman in Medici colors? Where's your fine chaperone?"

"Donna Jimena? She entered the convent at Le Murate. It broke her heart, I think, the—" She was going to say *murder* but stopped herself at the last moment. "The death of Donna Isabella."

"Le Murate, eh? She can tell her beads with old Duke Cosimo's so-called widow, then. No one ever gets out of that place. Come inside, *nipotina*, and see your little sisters."

The bookshop gleamed with cleanliness. The caretaker had managed it well enough, but no one could clean like Nonna. Lucia and Mattea stood next to each other, scrubbed spotless and neatly dressed. In the year-and-a-bit they'd been in Pistoia, Lucia had changed from a gangly girl to a young woman. How old was she? In her head Chiara counted. Fifteen. The same age she, Chiara, had been when she'd gone out in the rain with an ancient silver funnel in her pouch.

Three and a half years ago. It seemed like a lifetime.

"Hello, Lucia," she said. "Hello, Mattea."

Mattea—if Lucia was fifteen Mattea had to be twelve, and she didn't seem to have changed at all—squealed and flung herself across the room for a hug. Chiara caught her up and swung her around, then kissed her on both cheeks.

"This is Vivi," she said. Vivi looked up at the sound of her name, her brown eyes bright with merriment, her long ears floating out on either side of her head like an angel's wings. "Grand Duchess Giovanna gave her to me when she was just a puppy, and she's a year old now, a little more. A grown-up dog, just as you two are grown-up girls."

Mattea instantly went down on her knees and began to stroke Vivi's ears, murmuring with pleasure. Lucia didn't move. She looked straight at Chiara with stormy eyes.

"How kind you are, Donna Chiara," she said, "to allow us to come back to our home."

Nonna cuffed her ear, not really hard enough to hurt. "It wasn't Chiara's fault that we had to go to Pistoia," she said. "It was mine, and you know it. If your sister's friend Magister Ruanno hadn't arranged for us to get out of the city I could've been arrested and tortured and hanged in the Piazza della Signoria, and where would you have been then? Orphans begging on the streets, that's where."

"It must be nice to have such friends at the court," Lucia said. The cuff hadn't sweetened her temper. "And to wear beautiful dresses, and have a dog that's a gift from the grand duchess herself."

"A sweet doggie," Mattea crooned.

"The grand duchess gave Vivi to me," Chiara said, "because I was sick and she was afraid I would die. See these?" She stretched out her left hand, displaying the ugly crookedness of the second and third fingers that she usually went to such pains to conceal. "They were broken by—by a duke. He crushed my hand in a door and didn't even care. There was no one to treat the wounds for days and they got infected and I'm lucky I didn't lose my arm. That's how *nice* it is to have friends at court."

"Shush, *nipotina*." Nonna was there, tucking the poor fingers into a safe curled fist and holding them warm against her heart. "I'm sorry you were left alone to suffer such things. Lucia doesn't understand—she only sees the pretty things you have, and that she had to leave her home and all her friends without even saying good-bye."

Lucia's face crumpled up with a combination of shame and dismay and anger and longing. Broken fingers or no, it was easy to see she envied the dresses and the names of the highborn. "Sorry," she said. It didn't sound as if she meant it. "I'm betrothed now, did you know that? Cinto's a booksell-er's son from Pistoia, and when we're married he'll be made a member of the Arte here. The shop will be his. His and mine. I'll have a husband, which is more than you can say, for all your dukes and duchesses."

"It's true," Nonna said. She patted Chiara's hand. *Let her have her mo-ment*, the pats said. *We need a man and a guild member to run the shop again. She is growing up and all this has been hard for her.* "His full name is Giacinto Garzi, and he's the second son of a good family, so this is an ex-cellent arrangement for everyone. He's a fine boy."

"I'm happy for you, Lucia," Chiara said. She meant it, too. "I truly am."

"There, now, we are all a family again." Nonna started through the doorway to the kitchen behind the shop. "Lucia, go and see your friends, and if you have a word to spare from stories of your *promesso*, remember to tell them we went to Pistoia to take care of your Prozia Innocenza in her terrible sickness. Mattea, play with Vivi, and take care she doesn't run off. Chiara, come into the kitchen with me, and help me cook our dinner."

What she meant was, *Chiara, come into the kitchen with me so you can tell me all the things you don't want your sisters to hear.*

A fat chicken was simmering on the stove, its rich scent punctuated with garlic, onions and sweet peppers. The cupboards were packed full of food, vegetables and fruit, oil and olives, long strings of noodles looped and knotted, dried peas and lentils in baskets and bags and jars. Two new loaves of bread awaited cutting, and a bottle of strong red wine had been uncorked to breathe.

"Now," Nonna said. "Tell me about your Magister Ruanno, and why he suddenly arranged for us to come home, and settled your Babbo's debts to the Arte once and for all, and filled the kitchen with so many good things."

"He's not my Magister Ruanno," Chiara said.

"I know when you're lying, *nipotina*. Go slice the bread with that fine new knife, if you please—my sight's not what it used to be and I'm not used to such sharp knives. While you're slicing, tell me what it is you're not telling me."

"It's true he's not my Magister Ruanno." Chiara picked up the knife and sliced the end off the loaf. The knife was so sharp it was like slicing butter. "I'm keeping my vow, Nonna, until I hold the *Lapis Philosophorum* in my hands. Until I can be healed, and—well, and some other things."

"What other things?"

She sliced off another piece of bread. The sweet yeasty scent made her mouth water. "Magister Ruanno is from a place called Cornwall, in England. His home is there, his father's estate and a mine, and they were stolen from him somehow. He won't tell me exactly how, but he wants to get them back."

"There's talk about him. He disappeared, people say, after Donna Isabella's"—she paused, just like Chiara herself had paused—"death. Then he appeared again, thick as two thieves with the grand duke. Some people say he killed them himself, the grand duke's sister and sister-in-law, on the grand duke's orders."

"That's a lie." Chiara put down the knife. If her hands were going to shake like this, she'd cut herself. "That's a terrible lie. I was there, Nonna, and I saw—well, I heard—Donna Isabella's husband beat her and strangle her. Magister Ruanno loved Donna Isabella, and his obedience to the grand duke is only a pretense so he can—"

She stopped.

"You have to be more careful, *nipotina*, in what you let people goad you into saying." Nonna spooned up the chicken's juices and basted its golden skin complacently. "I think your Magister Ruanno is a dangerous fellow to know, and it's just as well you're keeping your vow right and tight. Are you close to finding your Philosopher's Stone?"

Chiara picked up the end piece of the bread and nibbled on the crust. After a moment she said, "We're getting closer each time, but the process the grand duke has chosen, with fourteen stages—there are just too many things that can go wrong."

"So there are different ways to do it? Like different recipes for *ribollita*?"

"Yes." Chiara had to smile at that. "And Babbo had a book with a different—well—recipe."

Nonna frowned. "He had a lot of books. Your Magister Ruanno took them all away."

"Not all of them. Nonna, listen. I've learned a lot, working with the grand duke and Magister Ruanno. I think I can create the *Lapis Philosophorum* myself, if I follow the process in Babbo's book. But I need you to help me."

"Ah, now we get to what you're really hiding. Tell me, *nipotina*, if you do this thing, will it mean that the devil-damned Medici won't succeed in getting the Philosopher's Stone for himself?"

Chiara ate some more of the bread. She hadn't really thought of it that way, but suddenly the whole plan revealed itself in her head, perfect in every detail. Of course. The ultimate revenge. Make little mistakes, so tiny as to be unnoticeable, while helping the grand duke. Deny him the *Lapis Philosophorum* he lusted for. And at the same time, work as a single alchemist, not a *soror mystica* but an alchemist in her own right, in her own secret laboratory in the bookshop's cellar.

"Yes," she said. "That's just what it means. I can make sure the grand duke's process fails, and at the same time, if I can set up a laboratory in the cellar here, I can follow the stages in Babbo's book and achieve the *Lapis Philosophorum* for myself."

"You know what happened when your Babbo made the cellar into a laboratory."

"I know. I'll be careful. He was doing something bad, something against nature."

Her head throbbed. Babbo's voice whispered, *I will cut her throat, and her virgin's life-blood will bring him back. . . .*

But the sensation in her head wasn't as painful as it once had been, and the voice seemed to be coming from far away. Maybe it was part of being older, and not so fresh and pretty, that the headaches and voices weren't torturing her like they'd done before. She hadn't had a falling-spell for—well, she couldn't remember. Half a year? A year?

"I will practice only alchemy itself," she said, as if with the purity of her art she could keep every danger away. "Science, and not necromancy."

Nonna nodded slowly. "You scare me sometimes, girl. You know I don't believe the Philosopher's Stone really exists."

"It exists. I'll prove it to you."

"If it strikes a blow against the Medici, I'll help you. What do you want me to do?"

"Just keep the cellar locked. Make sure the girls don't go down there. Help me carry things down—I'll bring equipment from the grand duke's laboratory, and the materials I need. He has so much, he'll never miss it."

And I'll block the secret passage with stones, she thought, *and lock the hatchway with double locks. I won't need it anymore, now that Nonna is in charge of the shop again.*

"And your friend Magister Ruanno," Nonna said. "Are you going to tell him about your secret laboratory?"

After we find the Lapis Philosophorum? *After you take your home back? After you take your revenge on the grand duke?*

What was one more lie after all the others?

"I won't tell him now, because he'll try to stop me," she said. "He'll be afraid for me."

"Sensible man."

"I'm not afraid, Nonna. Magister Ruanno has secrets of his own and I don't want to break his back with another. I'll tell him after I've succeeded, because after—"

She didn't say what was going to come after. She couldn't put it into words, even inside her head, because the choice was too terrible. Ruan? Or home? How could she live the rest of her life without one or the other?

"After," Nonna said, "you're going to have to run far and fast, because the grand duke will want what you've made. He'll kill you for it, if he can catch you."

"He won't catch me," Chiara said. She wasn't sure if she believed it but she said it anyway. "And even if I have to run away for a little while, I'm a Florentine down to my bones just like you are, and I'll always come home in the end."

CHAPTER THIRTY-SEVEN

The Casino di San Marco

20 NOVEMBER 1577

The athanor had been the hardest part. Chiara had chosen a small one made of dark gray stone, hidden away at the back of one of the grand duke's cabinets. Even so it had been too large and heavy for her to carry out of the laboratory on her own. After studying how it was constructed, she took it apart, and carried it away one piece at a time: the base, the lower tower, the upper tower, and the cupola, which corresponded to the four elements of earth, fire, water and air.

From that point on it was easy—a retort here, a small alembic there, a few lengths of tubing, a set of silver cochlears and a box of glass rods, and of course the elements she needed for the four steps described in Tommaso Vasari's book. There were abundant stores of everything. She was just collecting containers of purified flowers of sulphur and elemental mercury, making sure each container was perfectly sealed before wrapping it in lamb's wool and packing it into a leather saddlebag, when the grand duke himself strolled into the laboratory as if he owned it.

Which of course he did.

"Soror Chiara," the grand duke said. His narrow dark face was half-in, half-out of the light and looked like the faces of a man and a demon put together a little crookedly. He had put on flesh in the months since little Prince Filippo had been born. "What are you doing here alone? I did not see your guardsman at the door."

She fumbled with the glass container of mercury. It was impossible to hide it.

"I am—looking at—counting—making an inventory of—of the laboratory's stores." She could feel her face burning. "We're going to start the *magnum opus* again on the winter solstice and I didn't want any of the elements to be missing. Or used up, or not enough."

The grand duke walked across the tiled labyrinth toward the table where she was working. Two gentlemen remained at the door, looking away as if they didn't want to see or hear what was going to happen.

"And this—inventory—that you purport to be taking," he said. "Does it necessitate lamb's wool for packing, and a stout leather saddlebag?"

Chiara said nothing.

The grand duke picked up the glass container of mercury and tipped it from side to side, watching the viscid silvery metal break up into bright droplets, roll about and then recombine. "You intend to sell this, I take it? Are you not provided with enough luxury as my *soror mystica*, you, a bookseller's daughter?"

Sell it?

Sell it, of course.

Oh, thank you, saints and angels. A lifeline. Stealing the elements for their value in money might be forgivable. Stealing them to set up her own secret laboratory—well, there'd be no forgiveness for that.

She came out from behind the table and knelt at the grand duke's feet, rather like she had knelt before his brother the cardinal. "Magister Francesco," she whispered, keeping her eyes lowered in penitence. "Forgive me. There was so much of it, and I never thought— I have every possible luxury, Magister Francesco, all by your generosity. The only thing I don't have is—well, actual money. And I wanted to purchase a gift. I wanted it to be a secret."

She dared to slant a look up at him. Before her eyes his expression softened. She had seen it happen often enough at court, men coaxed and manipulated by ladies pretending a pretty submissiveness. She had never thought to play the game herself. It was surprising and disconcerting to see how well it worked.

"And what gift is this?" he said. His voice was stern but it was pretend-stern, like someone playing a part. "I trust you are not exchanging gifts with men, when you are a vowed virgin."

"Oh, no, Magister Francesco." She looked up at him fully, opening her eyes wide. "I wanted a gift for the grand duchess, because I know her happy news, even if she has not yet made it publicly known."

He smiled. He had made no secret of the fact that he hoped for another half-Imperial son. That would make three sons in all.

"And what did you have in mind to give the grand duchess?" He reached out and ran one hand over her hair, where it was smooth and tight against her head, caught back in its braid. A ghost of a headache blossomed softly behind her eyes, like a blood-colored rose barely visible through morning mist. It wasn't bad, but thank the saints he had a glove on. If he had touched her with his bare skin she might have been sick all over his embroidered boots—

"Embroidered boots," she said, before she thought. Hastily she added, "Tiny ones, for the baby, to keep his little feet warm when he begins to walk. I meant to buy soft leather, and metallic threads, and precious stones—rubies and sapphires and topazes, for the Medici colors."

"A charming idea." The grand duke stroked her hair again, then gestured for her to rise. "But you should not be trying to sell alchemical elements in the street markets, my *soror*, without my personal protection. You could easily be taken up by the Dominicani for practicing witchcraft."

Chiara scrambled to her feet. The headache had dissolved away. "I'll put it all back, Magister Francesco," she said. "I swear I will. I'll think of another gift for the grand duchess. I'll—"

"Oh, no," he said. "You must buy your materials, and make the little boots you describe for the new baby. It will please the grand duchess a great deal." He reached into his pouch and took out a gold scudo, then another, then another. "Here. Be sure to take your guardsman when you go out into the markets. You will want only the finest of everything."

Chiara took the coins because there was nothing else she could do. "Thank you, Magister Francesco," she said. She didn't curtsy to him—he was playing at being simple Magister Francesco and that would have annoyed him. But she bowed her *soror mystica*'s bow, her legs straight, her hands crossed over her breasts. He seemed to believe her—please, let him believe her—and hopefully he would be further softened by the special mark of deference.

He was. He nodded. The spark of sensual consideration in his eyes made her stomach lurch, as if it wanted to jump out of her mouth.

"Now," he said, after a moment. "I have come to the Casino di San Marco to obtain some of Magister Ruanno's compound for little Prince Filippo's bandages. It has helped him considerably, I think, and our physicians' supply has run out."

"Magister Ruanno keeps it in his locked cabinet. He has the—"

Magister Francesco took a small silver key out of his pouch and held it out to her. It glinted in the candlelight, dangling on its chain. She had never seen that key anywhere but in Ruan Pencarrow's own hand.

"Magister Ruanno has left Florence," the grand duke said. "You may open the cabinet."

"*What?* Left Florence? When? Why?"

"Open the cabinet, if you please."

"But— Where has he gone? When will he return?"

Magister Francesco put the key in her hand and closed her fingers around it. "Perhaps he will return," he said. "Perhaps he will not. Why do you ask so many questions, Soror Chiara? It is nothing to you, vowed as you are, whether Magister Ruanno is present or not."

Horror made her dizzy. Surely the grand duke had not set his assassins on Magister Ruanno, scholar and scientist, miner and metallurgist, his brother in the alchemical art. Yes, he had imprisoned him at the time of Donna Isabella's murder, but Ruan had talked his way out of the Bargello somehow, convinced the grand duke to trust him again.

The grand duke never forgets a betrayal.

Perhaps not, but surely the grand duke still needed his English alchemist. Surely it was nothing more than a test, to see what she would do or say if she thought Magister Ruanno had gone. Surely when she arrived at the grand duchess's apartments, measured jar of healing compound in her hands, Magister Ruanno would be there, half workman, half gentleman, full of secrets as he always was.

Agree with him, she thought. Haven't you learned it's always safest to agree with him?

"I can't make the compound," she said. She fought to keep her voice steady. "That's all I meant—once it's used up, I can't make more by myself. Do you want to measure out the compound, Magister Francesco, or should I?"

"You may do it. The physicians desire enough for one week's applications. They have assured me that after one or two weeks more, the compound will no longer be necessary."

"Yes, Magister Francesco."

"I will see you shortly, then, in the grand duchess's apartments at the Palazzo Pitti. As you have come out without your own guard, I will leave one of my gentlemen to escort you."

He went out, with a single gesture indicating which of his followers was to accompany him and which was to stay. Chiara looked after him for a moment, listening for the footsteps to fade. She wanted to scream, wanted to throw something, wanted to fall down on the floor and crawl under the table and howl in terror. But the grand duke's gentleman was standing there watching her steadily and she didn't dare. She didn't dare let herself think of Ruan gone, Ruan dead, garroted like Donna Bianca's women, drifting in the dark currents of the Arno.

After a little while she collected herself. The grand duke's gentleman looked at her without expression or curiosity. Taking care with each step, she turned to the cabinet to unlock it and collect the jar of Magister Ruanno's compound.

He was not dead. He was not dead. What would he have done, Magister Ruanno, if he'd caught her stealing flowers of sulphur and elemental mercury from the laboratory? He would never have believed her garbled lie about boots for the grand duchess's new baby.

Her hands shook as she scooped out the thick greenish compound. So close to disaster, so close.

On the table the grand duke's three gold scudi gleamed.

He'll remember, she thought. He'll be waiting for me to present my gift. So now I'll have to make good on my lie, actually shop for the leather and thread and jewels, and make the baby boots. Serves me right.

How did you make baby boots, anyway?

CHAPTER THIRTY-EIGHT

Magister Ruanno was not in the grand duchess's apartments.

They were full of people, though, and blazing with light and warmth. A consort of strings played softly in one of the outer rooms, and the music drifted in the air with candle smoke and perfume, sweat and the rich scent of sugared fig pastries. Ladies in bright-colored silk sleeves and velvet overgowns whispered of lovers and babies; gentlemen in padded doublets and pansied trunk hose were as bright, if not brighter, than the ladies. At the center of it all sat the grand duchess in Habsburg black and gold, erect as always, aloof as always, yet at the same time glowing with a happiness Chiara had never seen before. Her two parti-colored hounds sat at her feet. Rostig's rich rust-colored face was turning white.

Chiara stepped forward with the jar of ointment in her hands and curtsied deeply.

"I have brought Magister Ruanno's medicament, Serenissima," she said.

"*Das is gut,*" the grand duchess said. "The grand duke informed me you would be arriving."

"Have you seen Magister Ruanno today, Serenissima? Surely he should supervise the application."

"I have not." She reached down and stroked the dogs' heads. "I was surprised when the grand duke told me you would be bringing the compound. Perhaps Magister Ruanno will arrive later, or perhaps the grand duke has assigned him some other task."

"Perhaps." The knot of fear and uncertainty in Chiara's belly pulled tighter. "Where is the grand duke, Serenissima?"

"He is consulting with the physicians. Come, I shall walk over with you."

She rose, gesturing to a little knot of men with long beards and the black academic gowns and hoods of physicians, standing to one side of the fireplace. The grand duke was at their center, his expression intense as he argued with one of them. Chiara stepped back to make way. All the other ladies and gentlemen did the same, as if opening up a magic pathway from the center of the room to the fireplace.

Next to the fireplace, surrounded by the physicians, stood a cradle. Well, a child was lying in it, so presumably it could be called a cradle, but it was enormous and elaborately carved in polished light brown wood. At the head it had a *baldacchino* draped with satin curtains in the Medici colors of red, gold and blue. The wood itself was incised with a medallion of the Holy Family and the legend GLORIA IN EXCELSIS ET IN TERRA PAX. All around the *baldacchino*, down the rails and around the posts, were carved flowers and fruit and fanciful animals, symbols of health and strength.

Poor little Prince Filippo was red-faced, hot and restless, swaddled with far too many embroidered blankets despite the fact that his cradle was so close to the fireplace. His head was wrapped in bandages, and because of their thickness it was hard to tell if the unnatural swelling had been reduced or not. On top of the bandages was pinned a heartbreakingly jaunty little blue velvet cap with a red feather.

Get that child out from under all those blankets and swaddlings and let him kick, Nonna would say. *Let him crawl if he can. He's six months old and needs air and exercise if his bones are going to grow strong and hard.*

"Signorina Chiara has brought the compound, my lord," the grand duchess said.

"Excellent." The grand duke took the jar and handed it to one of the physicians. "It is having a salutary effect, I am sure."

The grand duchess bent over the cradle and stroked her little son's cheek. He turned his head toward the touch and made a gurgling sound.

"See, he knows his mother," she said. "My lord, do you think he is too hot? Look how red his face is."

"It is of the greatest importance to avoid dry and cold humors," one of the physicians said. "Please do not excite him, Serenissima—too much stimulation will only cause his brain to swell further."

The grand duchess sighed softly and took her hand away. "My little son," she said. "Next summer perhaps you will have a brother, and the two of you can play together."

The physicians looked at each other. It was clear as clear that they didn't expect Prince Filippo to grow up and play with his brother.

"The physicians will take him now," the grand duke said, "and apply the compound. Come, Madonna, let us go into the other room and enjoy the music."

"Yes, my lord." The grand duchess turned away obediently, with only one last sorrowful look at her child. "I will join you shortly—I feel the need to withdraw for a moment. Signorina Chiara, attend me, if you please."

Chiara curtsied politely to the grand duke, avoiding his eyes, and followed the grand duchess into one of the inner rooms, and from there to a tiny private alcove fitted out with a shelf that held a basin, a silver ewer, and a stack of clean white towels. Beside it was a box—a chair, really, but with the space under the seat enclosed with carved panels. The back was upholstered in violet-colored velvet. The grand duchess lifted the seat to reveal a padded under-seat, pierced with a hole under which a silver chamber pot rested.

"Pour out some water, Signorina Chiara," the grand duchess said. She gathered up her skirts and seated herself on the chair. The arms, Chiara could see, were designed to make it easy for her to seat herself and get up again, even with the brace and padded bodices that disguised her twisted back.

"Forgive me, my dear," she said. "I wished to speak with you privately, and I could not think of any other way."

Chiara smiled. "I'm hardly embarrassed by all this luxury, Serenissima," she said. "I grew up sharing a single bedroom and a necessary pot with my Nonna, my mother, and my two sisters." She picked up the ewer and poured out some water for the grand duchess to wash with. "It was just a cheap earthenware basin on the floor, too, and nothing so beautiful as yours."

The grand duchess nodded. "Now tell me what you know about Magister Ruanno's strange disappearance," she said. "I promise you I will not tell the grand duke, if it is something you wish to keep secret."

"But that's just the thing, Serenissima. I don't know anything. The first I knew he was gone was when the grand duke came to the laboratory and told me. I thought he might be here, but he isn't."

The grand duchess looked thoughtful. "He could not leave Florence without the grand duke's permission—without papers, a passport. I suspect my husband knows where he has gone and why, and is keeping the knowledge to himself for some reason."

Ruan got Nonna and the girls out of Florence with no papers, Chiara thought. He could get himself out if he wanted to, and the grand duke would never know.

"I hope you're right, Serenissima," she said.

The grand duchess held out her hand for a towel. Chiara handed her one and discreetly turned away. When the rustling of skirts told her the grand duchess had finished and risen from her chair, she turned her head again. The grand duchess dipped her hands in the fresh water, and took a second fresh towel to dry them. Chiara expected her to nod a brief thanks—the grand duchess was always courteous, for all her stiff reserve—and step out of the room to return to her guests. But she hesitated. She looked down at her hands, spreading her fingers out as if to count the rings she was wearing.

"They do not like me to touch him," she said. "It has nothing to do with whether or not my poor little son is over-stimulated. The grand duke fears this new baby will be marked, if I touch Filippo, or hold him."

Chiara couldn't think of anything to say to that. Everybody knew babies could be marked by what a woman saw or touched or ate. Nonna had a hundred stories of women who'd been startled by an owl, or who'd eaten too many peaches, or who'd held a one-eared rabbit in their arms, and who'd borne babies with the marks of it.

In a very low voice, so low that even in the tiny closet Chiara had to lean close to hear her, the grand duchess said, "He blames me that Filippo is as he is."

What did one say to such a dangerous confidence from the Grand Duchess of Tuscany, the daughter and sister of emperors?

"I'm sorry, Serenissima."

"The physicians do not know if he will ever be—healthful, strong, if his mind will ever develop completely. There is one man who suggests cutting an opening in his head to let the excess humors out. He claims he has read instructions for such an operation in old writings. Have you ever heard of such a thing, Signorina Chiara?"

Saints and angels. Cut a hole in that pitiful child's head? Were they mad?

"No, Serenissima, I've never heard of such a thing."

"I am praying for another son. A fine strong son, like—the other one. They say she is keeping court at the Villa di Pratolino."

"She's at the Villa di Pratolino because people stoned her house here in the city. She's hated, Serenissima, especially since your own little prince was born."

"She knows I am with child again, I think—it is one of those secrets that is not really a secret. She is only waiting for me to die, so she can step into my shoes."

"You must not think such things, Serenissima, or you truly will mark your baby." Chiara could have shaken her, although of course one didn't shake grand duchesses. "You're not going to die. And the fine strong son, well, he's not hers. He's not the grand duke's, either. Everyone knows he's a changeling who was carried into the room in a Neapolitan *mandolino*."

The grand duchess smiled a little at that. "Ferdinando tells me you were there," she said. "You saw it."

"I did." It was a lie, or part of a lie, but who cared? "Serenissima, don't you want to return to your guests? They will be wondering—"

"I see her sometimes."

Chiara blinked. "Who, Serenissima?"

"Bianca Cappello. Here, at the Pitti, and at the Palazzo Vecchio, too. She dresses up in a servant's clothes and comes to spy on me."

"Serenissima," Chiara said. Her own voice sounded strange to her. "Enough. You will hate me tomorrow for hearing you say such things."

The grand duchess clasped her hands together and straightened. There would be no more confidences. Chiara wasn't sure if she was glad or sorry.

"You think I am seeing things which are not there," she said, in her precise, Imperial voice. "I assure you I am not."

"Of course not, Serenissima."

"I will never hate you, Signorina Chiara. And I have every faith in your discretion."

"Of course, Serenissima."

"Then let us return to my guests."

After supper the grand duchess's bedchamber-ladies undressed her and put her to bed. The grand duke disappeared, leaving whisperers to conclude— probably rightly—that he had gone to the Villa di Pratolino to spend the night with Bianca Cappello. Chiara wanted to slip away to the laboratory again but she didn't dare go out into the city alone, at night. Her one task was to take the dogs out to the garden on their embroidered leather leashes, and even for that she had to have one of the Austrian kennel master's assistants to accompany her.

"How have they been today?" she asked the boy as she attached the leashes to the dogs' collars. He was twelve or thirteen, with hair as coarse and yellow as straw and a gap between his two front teeth. His name was Rudi and he was a nephew or a cousin or some sort of relation to the kennel master.

"Fine, Fräulein Klara, fine. Rostig, a little stiff and sore, but he has eight years now and it's to be expected."

"Poor Rostig." Chiara stroked the old dog's soft ears and gave him a bit of dried meat for a treat. "We'll walk slowly. Anything else?"

They passed out of the back of the Palazzo and into the gardens. "That Vivi of yours," Rudi said. "She's a wild one, no mistake about it. She ran away from me earlier, when I brought them out here. Just pulled her leash right out of my hand and ran straight toward the Neptune fountain down there."

"How strange," Chiara said. "That's not like Vivi."

"It was as if someone was a-calling her. After a little while she came back, though."

"I would say she smelled a rabbit, but it's too late in the year for rabbits."

Rostig and Seiden, the grand duchess's original breeding pair from Ferrara, walked down the gravel path with the stately assurance of elder statesmen. The younger dogs, the four-year-old littermates Rina and Leia and then Vivi, not quite a year and a half, ranged from side to side, sniffing everything. They walked to the end of the path and then turned back.

"I'll take Vivi upstairs with me," Chiara said. "Please make sure the rest of them are warm and comfortable, especially Rostig."

"So I will, Fräulein Klara, and I'll be seeing you on the morrow."

When she had undressed in her bare little cell, she patted the pallet beside her and Vivi jumped up, pushing close for petting.

"What were you thinking, Vivi, to run away like that?" She stroked the little hound's rich russet ears, tickling her fingertips in the patches of soft puppylike fur behind them. "You are a lucky dog to have a home, with plenty of food and a warm bed. There are stray dogs in the street who would—"

Under the blue leather collar there was a tiny corner of paper. No one would ever see it if they were not holding the dog close and petting her. Chiara ran her fingers under the collar. The piece of paper was folded lengthwise, and attached to the collar with two loops of fine blue silk thread.

"What's this? Rudi said you ran as if someone was calling you—who were you running to, Vivi?"

She unfolded the paper. It was blank. She remembered the notes she had sent to Ruanno dell' Inghilterra in the terrible months before Donna Isabella's death, and scrambled down from the pallet to hold the paper over the tiny brazier that provided her cell's only light and heat.

I am required to return to England to address my affairs there. The grand duke has refused me permission or papers, so I am going secretly. Whatever he tells you, do not listen. Do not forget—we are bound to each other, and in the end we will find a way.

It was not signed, even with an initial.

So he was not dead. He had not left Florence forever. Her heart was thudding and her breath coming fast. I should have known, she thought. He is the one person Vivi would go to.

She crumpled the paper and put it into the brazier. Whatever reason the grand duke had for making such a mystery over Ruan's absence, she would pretend to believe it. She would wait. Maybe she would learn something useful.

Am I even still myself? she wondered, as she watched the paper burn. Ruan has gone, and I think only that I will wait and learn. Chiara Nerini, daughter of Carlo Nerini—troubled, fearful, awestruck Chiara Nerini, with her headaches and falling-spells and demons' voices—that Chiara Nerini would have been afraid. She would have struck out, flailed, lost herself ever more hopelessly in the Medici maze. But now—now. I have learned to be still, look about me, and choose my own path. I wait for Sundays, after Mass, when I can let a drop of *sonnodolce* fall on my wrist and show me visions of what I want most in the world. Even the headaches and the falling-spells have lessened, and I hardly ever hear the voices anymore.

You would be proud of me, Babbo, if you could see me now.

The last embers of the paper fell into ash.

Tomorrow, she thought, as she climbed back into her pallet. I'll collect the mercury and the flowers of sulphur tomorrow, and put them carefully away in my new laboratory. I'll take Babbo's book back from the grand duke's shelves at the Casino di San Marco and give it a place of honor. What would Ruan say, I wonder, if he knew about my new laboratory?

We are bound to each other, and in the end we will find a way.

After he comes back, I'll tell him all about the laboratory, and my plan to create the *Lapis Philosophorum* with the four colored stages.

And while I'm at the shop, I'll ask Nonna about making baby boots.

CHAPTER THIRTY-NINE

The Palazzo Vecchio

11 APRIL 1578

"*S*ie *sind charmant,*" the grand duchess said. She dangled the tiny pair of boots by their strings and looked at them first from one side, then from the other. "They are charming, Signorina Chiara. Did you make them yourself?"

"Yes, Serenissima. I'm afraid some of the stitching is a little crooked."

"Yes, but something one makes oneself, that is special, is it not? A short time more, and he will be born. You can put them on his feet yourself."

Easter had been early this year, and spring had swept into Florence like a lady wearing a ruffled cloak of blue skies, fresh breezes and flowers. Roses and irises were beginning to blossom in the formal gardens of the Boboli, and buttercups starred the grass along the paths. Ruanno dell' Inghilterra, on the other hand, had not come back to Florence. Well, it was a long way to Cornwall—wherever that was, somewhere in England—and winter was a bad time to travel. Maybe he'd arrive to greet the grand duchess's new baby, bearing exotic Cornish gifts of his own. Maybe the grand duke would forgive him for going away without permission.

There had been nothing but the simplest alchemical work at the Casino di San Marco since he had gone. The grand duke depended on his English alchemist more than he knew. Surely he would welcome him back. She herself would welcome him back with—

"I wish to go over to the Pitti today," the grand duchess said. "The gardens are so lovely, and it is warm for April. Put the leashes on the dogs, please, Signorina Chiara—we will take them with us."

"Yes, Serenissima."

While Chiara snapped the leashes on Rostig, Seiden and Vivi, the grand duchess turned to consult with Prince Filippo's nurse. Contrary to everyone's expectations the little prince had lived, and even begun to hold up his poor head a little. The bones of his skull had hardened and at almost a year old he had a mop of curly reddish-brown hair that grew down in a point at the center of his forehead, just like his father's. He had not begun to say words and he could not yet sit up on his own, but his eyes were bright and sometimes he smiled.

"Filippino," the grand duchess said softly. "*Mein liebste kleine prinz.* Are you going to be a good boy today?"

He made gabbling sounds.

"There," the nurse said stoutly. "He said 'Mama,' plain as plain. He's always a good boy."

The grand duchess smiled and ran her hand lightly over his hair. "Indeed he is. We shall take our dinner at the Pitti, and return this afternoon. Magdalena, the red mantle, if you please, with the fox fur. Chiara, are the dogs ready?"

"Yes, Serenissima."

"Then let us go."

They made their way down the stairs from the second floor to the first floor. The grand duchess took each step carefully. Her back always troubled her when she went up or down stairs, and the weight of the baby made it worse. Seven times she's gone through childbearing, Chiara thought, watching her slow progress. Eight times, it will be, counting this one. She's braver than the men who parade around with their swords and daggers, boasting of their exploits.

When they reached the first floor, the grand duchess stopped to rest. Rostig lay down on the cool polished marble and whined softly. His arthritic joints made the stairs as difficult for him as they were for his mistress.

"We should not have brought the older dogs, after all," the grand duchess said. "Poor Rostig. Magdalena, Anna, please take Rostig and Seiden back upstairs. Carry them, if you will. No, Chiara, you stay here with me to manage your Vivi. We will wait until Magdalena and Anna return, and I will catch my breath for a moment."

Anna, being the taller and stronger of the two, gathered Rostig into her arms. Magdalena picked up Seiden and the two women started back up the stairs. Vivi whined—partly to see her sire and dam go, Chiara thought, and partly just because she was anxious to go down the rest of the stairs to the courtyard, and outside into the sunshine. Chiara crouched down to quiet her.

The swish of a skirt.

A voice, familiar. "Good day to you, Serenissima."

Chiara looked up.

A woman in a plain dress and apron had come up to them, as if out of nowhere. Her hair was covered by a serving-woman's wimple and coif, and from a distance she would have looked like any one of the dozens of women who worked in the kitchens and laundry-rooms and sewing-rooms of the Palazzo Vecchio. Face-to-face, however, her strongly marked eyebrows and reddened, sensuous mouth were unmistakable.

I see her sometimes. Bianca Cappello. Here, at the Pitti, and at the Palazzo Vecchio, too. She dresses up in a servant's clothes and comes to spy on me.

Holy saints and angels, the grand duchess had been right. But of course the grand duke's mistress couldn't come openly into the Palazzo Vecchio, not as hated as she was in Florence, not when the grand duke himself required her to stay at the Villa di Pratolino. Her curiosity about the little prince and the grand duchess's condition must have been driving her half-mad. This play-acting was worse than madness.

"Signorina Chiara," the grand duchess said. She did not acknowledge her husband's Venetian mistress by so much as a flicker of her eyelids. "Perhaps we should go downstairs into the courtyard to await Magdalena's and Anna's return."

Chiara scrambled to her feet. "Indeed, Serenissima," she said. "Lean on my arm, if you will, and I will—"

"You will be silent, alchemist woman, and stand to one side while your betters speak together." Bianca pushed her, unexpectedly, one hand flat against her shoulder. Chiara stumbled back against the balustrade, her foot coming down on Vivi's paw. Vivi yelped, high and shrill.

Chiara went down on her knees and wrapped Vivi in her arms. The little hound pressed close to her, confused and frightened. At the same time, the grand duchess turned her head and slowly, with every ounce of Habsburg pride in her fragile twisted body, focused her gaze on Bianca Cappello. "Touch either Signorina Chiara or her dog again," she said, in an icy, even voice, "and I will make you sorry. What are you doing here, dressed in such mummery? Or has my husband disowned you at last, and put you to work in the kitchens where you belong?"

Bianca flushed, hot as fire. "The grand duke has given me leave to enter any of his palaces," she said. "And I wear whatever I choose—I do not need silks and jewels, or iron corsets to make my back straight."

"An iron bridle to control your tongue might be a fine thing."

Chiara put her face down against the sleek black-and-russet fur of Vivi's shoulder. It was not like the grand duchess to wrangle like this, but what woman could withdraw in dignified silence when her husband's mistress mocked her deformity? Even an emperor's sister would fight back.

"I need no bridle." Bianca Cappello's voice rose, and her Venetian accent became more pronounced. "You look pale, Serenissima. Thin. Uglier than usual. My astrologers tell me this child will be another girl, and that she will be the death of you."

At that Chiara straightened. She wasn't sure what she intended to do, but she had to do something. But the grand duchess lifted her hand—*Stop*.

"Your astrologers are fools," she said, quite calmly. "Stand aside."

"I will not stand aside. I have been standing aside for months now, caged up in the Villa di Pratolino. It is your fault, Serenissima, that I cannot come into the city unless I have disguised myself. You have turned the people of Florence against me."

"I do not consider that a fault, but rather a badge of honor."

"If so, it is the only honor you can claim. Your son is a monster—"

The grand duchess turned white.

"—while mine is strong and straight. He has taken his first steps already, did you know that? He knows a dozen words and more. 'Mama,' he calls me. And he calls the grand duke 'Papa.'"

"The more fool he, poor changeling child. Stand aside at once. You may be sure I will tell my husband you call his legitimate son a monster."

Bianca laughed. "I call it a monster?" she said. "Francesco himself calls it a monster, when you are not listening. He calls it—"

The grand duchess drew back her arm and struck Donna Bianca across the mouth, with all her small reserve of strength. It was so unlike her—Chiara had only a moment to wonder if she had ever struck anyone or anything before in the whole of her life. Then the arc of her arm made her lose her balance, and her foot slipped on the polished marble.

Chiara cried out and jumped to catch hold of her.

At the same time Bianca Cappello, blind with fury, struck back. Her blow—so much more practiced, how many of her serving-women had she slapped over the years?—glanced off the grand duchess's shoulder and pitched her headfirst down the staircase.

"No! No no no no!" Chiara skidded and stumbled down the stairs, trying to catch the grand duchess's skirts, her mantle, anything to break the fall. There was no human way she could be quick enough. The grand duchess turned over and over, in eerie silence, until she struck the stone floor at the bottom of the stairway.

Chiara fell beside her, knees and elbows bruised and skinned, sobbing. She was afraid to touch her, for fear she would hurt her more. She was not unconscious—her eyes fluttered open and her lips moved. She pressed one hand to her belly, and groaned very softly.

"Serenissima, Serenissima. No, do not try to move. Guards, help! Guards! Magdalena! Anna!"

As she screamed she looked back up at the top of the stairway. Vivi stood there alone, her tail tucked between her legs, her soft ears pinned back against her head with fright and misery.

Bianca Cappello was gone.

Word was sent immediately to the grand duke and the physicians. A litter was brought and the grand duchess was lifted—she screamed, high and anguished—and carried back up the stairs to her own apartments. There was blood on her skirt, and on the cheerful red velvet mantle with its rich fox fur. Chiara was pushed aside and ordered to take the dogs to the kennels. No one asked her what had happened. Everyone—guards, ladies, physicians—simply assumed the grand duchess had slipped and fallen because of her awkwardness and the weight of the child.

I'll tell the grand duke, Chiara said to herself as she ran back from the kennels. I have to tell someone the truth. Someone.

When she reached the grand duchess's apartments again, the doors were closed and two of the grand duke's personal guardsmen stood outside.

"I'm Chiara Nerini," Chiara said. "The grand duke's *soror mystica*. I was with the grand duchess when she fell. I must speak to the grand duke at once."

"No one's allowed in, *signorina*. Il Serenissimo's own orders."

From inside the apartments Chiara could hear a woman screaming.

"Please. *Please*. I was with her. I saw her fall. I saw—"

But no. It was too dangerous to speak aloud, to two ordinary guardsmen.

They did not answer, and did not move from their places. The screaming continued, and after a while faded to choking sobs.

Chiara waited, but the grand duke didn't come out. No one came out. No one went in. The guards refused to look at her or speak with her further. After a while she crept away, sick at heart. She went downstairs to the kennels again and sat with the kennel master and his family. They cried and prayed together. The dogs pressed close, as if they knew something terrible was happening.

Around midday the next day, one of the guardsmen came into the kennels.

"You, *signorina*," he said to Chiara. "Il Serenissimo requires your presence."

"The grand duchess," Chiara said. She ached all over with her own bruises. Her eyes were sticky and her mouth was dry and sour. "What has happened? Is she—"

"Il Serenissimo said only to fetch you."

She went with him.

The doors to the grand duchess's apartments were still guarded. The rooms were silent and empty. Chiara followed the guardsman through the receiving room and the reading room and the supper room, into the private bedchamber. It smelled of blood and death. The grand duke sat beside the bed in a heavy chair. His face was expressionless.

The grand duchess lay on the great bed, her body straight as a stone effigy, her hands crossed on her breast. She was covered with a black-and-gold velvet pall. Her face was white, but for a bruise on her cheekbone, sharp-edged and empty in death. The holy oil of the unction glistened on her eyelids and lips.

Chiara fell to her knees and made the sign of the cross over her breast.

"Her child was stillborn," the grand duke said. "He became twisted in her womb, the physicians said, when she fell. He was a fine boy, and would have been healthy in every respect."

He didn't say, *unlike Prince Filippo*, although of course that's what he meant. Poor sad little prince, not even a year old, motherless now.

"I will pray for his soul, Serenissimo."

"Her womb was ruptured. The physicians could not stop the bleeding. She lived long enough to make her farewells to the children, and to me, and to take the Viaticum."

Chiara said nothing. She looked at the grand duchess's profile, white as a paper cutout. How could it have no life in it, when yesterday she had smiled, and hoped, and planned to walk in the gardens at the Palazzo Pitti?

"I am told you were with her."

Slowly Chiara turned her head and looked up at the grand duke's dark face. He knew. Bianca Cappello had sent him a message somehow. If I speak the truth, Chiara thought, what will he do? *Your Venetian mistress was in the Palazzo Vecchio, dressed as a servant woman, spying on your wife and wishing her ill, calling her names, calling your son names. Yes, the grand duchess stumbled after striking her, but who would not strike a low, vicious woman who calls her son a monster? She stumbled a little and I would have caught her. It was your mistress striking her back that pushed her into the stairway. It was your mistress—*

He already knew. She could see it in his eyes, the downward curve of his mouth, the darkness always so close behind him. He knew, and he was waiting to see what she would say.

"We had come down from the second floor together," Chiara said steadily. "But the dogs, the old dogs—they couldn't manage the stairs."

"I understand she sent her women back upstairs with the dogs. You— were you there when she fell, or did you go upstairs with the others?"

What to say?

Tell the truth and die? Because if I accuse Bianca Cappello now, I will be floating in the Arno myself before nightfall.

Lie, and live?

What had Ruan said, in the grand duchess's store-closet? *I swore I would pursue no vengeance.* Then he had smiled the wolf smile. *Unlike you, I have no intention of keeping my vow.*

Unlike me then, perhaps. Not anymore. Now I understand.

"I wasn't there," Chiara said. She looked straight into the grand duke's eyes. "I went upstairs—the other women had gone before me, and didn't see me. It was only when I heard her scream and ran back down that I discovered she had fallen."

The grand duke nodded. He knew she was lying. He would kill her if she ever told the truth, and he knew she understood it. "Very well," he said. "You may go."

She curtsied deeply, then backed away. One last time she looked at the grand duchess's face. Good-bye, Serenissima, she thought. So much sadness and loneliness in your life, and yet you took time to be kind to me, a bookseller's daughter. I hope your soul has flown home to Austria, where you always wanted to be. Don't fear for your children. I'll watch over them. And I'll watch over your little dogs, too, forever and ever.

She went out of the room and closed the door behind her.

The guardsmen paid no attention to her. She clenched her fists as she walked down the passageway, and her crooked fingers ached.

"I'll make Bianca Cappello pay." She whispered the words aloud, her voice bitter as gentian. "I'll smile to her face and to the grand duke's, until the right moment comes. Then she'll pay for what she has done, I swear it."

PART IV

Bianca

The White Swan

PART IV

CHAPTER FORTY

The Villa di Pratolino

21 JUNE 1578

Followed by two wagons full of books, equipment and alchemical elements, Chiara rode past the red-roofed gatehouse and into the magnificent southern gardens of the Villa di Pratolino. Since the grand duchess's death, the grand duke had spent most of his time there, directing the ongoing construction, building a new private laboratory, and sating his senses with the overripe flesh of Bianca Cappello. Ruan had not returned to Florence, and that left Chiara as the only person in the grand duke's personal household who could tell an athanor from an alembic. She grasped the power with grim satisfaction.

At the Casino di San Marco, she supervised the men who packed boxes with equipment and elements and stacked them in wagons. It was an easy hour or two's ride to Pratolino for a good horseman on a hot-blooded horse, but for laden carts and draft mules it was slow and tedious. The first time they'd done it, it had taken most of the day. This trip, the third, had gone a little more smoothly. Chiara was tired of riding back and forth. At least once the boxes had been unpacked at Pratolino she would have food and drink and a place to sleep, before starting back to Florence the next day.

She was washing glass beakers and setting them out in the cabinet, arranged by size from the largest to the smallest, when the grand duke stepped into the lemon-house he had chosen as the site of his new laboratory. He gestured to his gentlemen to remain outside, and shut the door.

He looked different. He had put on even more flesh, but it was unhealthy flesh, the flesh of a man who no longer rode or hunted or went out in the sun. The darkness that had always surrounded him seemed to have crept inside the outline of his figure, making shadows where there hadn't been shadows before.

"The moon is up, Soror Chiara," he said. "If you work by nothing but the light of these lanterns, you will make mistakes."

She put the last beaker in the cabinet and picked up a white linen towel to dry her hands. It gave her a moment to put her hatred away in its dark cankered hiding-place at the center of her heart. "I am finished, Magister Francesco," she said in a pleasant voice. "The workmen are settled in the stables with the mules and the wagons. Is it your pleasure that I sup and sleep in the same room I used before?"

"All in good time. I wish to speak with you first."

One of the lanterns flickered and went out. The darkness deepened.

"Of course, Magister Francesco."

"I have had a letter from Magister Ruanno."

A moment passed. Chiara realized she had stopped breathing, and her hands had knotted themselves in the towel so hard that it made her crooked fingers ache. She loosened her grip on the linen slowly and carefully, and took a breath.

I am required to return to England to address my affairs there. . . . Whatever he tells you, do not listen.

In a way he had never been gone, because she had seen him so vividly, every week, in her *sonnodolce* dreams. She had felt his skin under her palms, slick with sweat, and his mouth over hers. . . .

"What did he write?" she said. Her voice was not quite steady. "Will he return soon?"

"He intends to. However, I am displeased with him—he went away without my permission."

The displeasure was all for show. He was the grand duke and he had to act angry when one of his household disobeyed him. But he needed his English alchemist. There was no one else with Ruan's skills and knowledge.

"Perhaps," Chiara said, "Magister Ruanno was called away in such a hurry he did not have a chance to ask for official papers."

"Perhaps."

"But he is well? He asks your permission to return?"

The grand duke smiled. "You are particularly interested in whether he returns or not? I would have thought you would be pleased he was gone, so you could be the only alchemist in my personal household."

Careful, Chiara thought. Careful.

"You honor me with your confidence, Serenissimo," she said.

Have you guessed, Serenissimo, that for each large chest and crate of materials I bring here, I take an inconspicuous small one to the bookshop where I am stocking my own laboratory in Babbo's cellar? Have you guessed that I am arranging things here in your fine new laboratory, so that every attempt you make to create the *Lapis Philosophorum* will end in failure? It's not difficult—a pinch of ground alum stone here, a drop of aqua fortis there. You will never notice anything, but the *Lapis Philosophorum* will forever elude you.

"Magister Ruanno is necessary for the completion of the *magnum opus*," the grand duke said. "I am fire and you are water, but he is earth, and earth is required." He picked up a glass flask filled with the alkahest of tartar, clear as water, and tilted it from side to side thoughtfully. Through it she could see his eyes, magnified into something terrifying. "In any case, he writes that he is taking ship from England, and as his ship cannot be far behind the messenger that brought me the letter, he should be in Florence within the month."

"I look forward to beginning our work again, Serenissimo."

"Say nothing of all this." The grand duke put the flask back on the table. "Welcome him back with courtesy. We will begin the *magnum opus* anew at the summer solstice. When we have been successful, perhaps you will wake one day to find yourself my sole alchemist—my *magistra*."

Magistra . . .

Yes, her dark heart cried. See, Babbo? I will be the grand duke's *magistra*, greater than you, greater even than Perenelle Flamel.

But only if Ruan is gone, Babbo whispered. *Only if Ruan is dead. Dead. Dead.*

The grand duke had restored him to favor once, in the terrible time after Donna Isabella's death. He wouldn't do it again. He'd allow Ruan to come back, oh yes, like a hunter drawing his prey into a trap. He'd make use of him, his skills, his power. And then he would kill him.

She made her gesture of respect, a bow from the waist like a man, with her hands crossed over her breast. A good way to hide her eyes and her mouth and the fact that she was lying through her teeth when she said, "All shall be as you desire it, Serenissimo."

The next morning she broke her fast with a piece of freshly baked bread, a few figs, and a cup of watered wine. At the Villa di Pratolino her small room had a window, and as she ate she could look out over the garden and marvel at the fanciful statuary, the topiaries and automatons that were so dear to the grand duke's hard mechanical heart. When she was finished she smoothed her skirts, stepped out into the corridor and started for the side entryway that led to the stables.

"Signorina Chiara."

A woman's voice, husky, imperious, with a breath of a Venetian accent.

Chiara stopped. Once she'd stopped, she was trapped—she couldn't walk on, pretend she hadn't heard the voice. The last time she'd heard it had been at the top of the stairs in the Palazzo Vecchio.

I call it a monster? Francesco himself calls it a monster, when you are not listening.

Bianca Cappello.

Say nothing. Smile. You have chosen the path of slow, cold revenge. Wait. Choose your moment. Remember what you hope to gain for yourself in the households of the Medici.

She turned and faced the grand duke's mistress.

Bianca Cappello was dressed in cream-colored summer silk with a loosely gathered skirt and full loose sleeves, a high ruffled lace collar and a deep square décolletage that revealed the cleft between her white breasts. Over this dress—hardly more than a fanciful camicia—she wore a crimson velvet jacket, sleeveless, embroidered and frogged with so much gold it was a miracle she was able to stand up straight. In her curled russet hair, she had pinned a circlet of red lilies.

Red lilies. The heraldic symbol of Florence. As if she had strolled into the garden in the dawn and said to herself, *oh look, red lilies, how pretty, I'll just pick a few and weave them into a crown for myself. . . .*

He must have married her. She never would have dared wear the red lilies of Florence if he hadn't, she, a Venetian and all the more hated for it.

But of course the marriage would be a secret, so Chiara was perfectly free to pretend she didn't understand.

"Signora Bianca." It was clear as clear the woman expected a curtsy, a deep and humble one to make up for Chiara's insultingly tiny bend of the knees that afternoon at the Palazzo Medici. Would she ever forget that? Probably not.

Chiara stood unmoving, her knees straight, her hands at her sides.

"The day will come," Bianca Cappello said, "when you will kiss the floor before me and beg my pardon for your discourtesy. Do you see the lilies I wear in my hair?"

"I see them."

"Do you understand what they mean?"

Chiara met her gaze steadily. "No," she said. "They are red flowers, nothing more."

Bianca's heavy brows thrust together in a scowl. "They are red lilies, you fool. The symbol of Florence."

"Indeed?" Chiara smiled. It was pleasant, she had to admit, to see Bianca Cappello so outraged, and so helpless to do anything about it. Clearly the grand duke had forbidden her to tell anyone about their secret marriage. As long as I remain blind to her red lilies, Chiara thought, I don't have to pay her obeisance and it will drive her mad. And she can't run to the grand duke to complain, because she's not supposed to be swanning around like a grand duchess. Not yet.

"They're pretty flowers," Chiara said. "I was looking out at the gardens this morning, and saw many flowers of every possible color."

Bianca's face colored up with anger until it was almost as red as the lilies she would still not dare to wear in public, or even in the grand duke's presence.

"I will make you sorry. I will see you cast into an oubliette, so you never see flowers again."

"Take care with your threats, Signora Bianca. You may be the grand duke's—mistress—but I am his *soror mystica* and the sole *magistra* of his laboratories."

"I am no longer his mistress." Bianca was so angry she could hardly talk. "I am his wife. Yes, his wife—his true wife, not his meek little play-acting wife anymore. That is what the red lilies mean, if you were not too stupid to understand it."

"And this is to be announced in the city—when? Sometime soon?"

"You know it cannot be made public until a year has passed. A year of mourning for poor ugly Giovanna of Austria. I am to have my own apartments in the Palazzo Pitti and the management of her children, what do you think of that? Eleonora is eleven and may resist me, but Anna is only eight and Maria only three, and of course Filippo is barely a year old and an idiot. In the end they will love me more than they ever loved her."

The children? Oh, no, Chiara thought. You will never have her children. I will find a way to put a stop to that.

"Keep your vicious tongue off the grand duchess and her children," she said aloud. "She was a greater lady than you will ever be."

"You think so? Wait until you see me enter the city in a chariot drawn by golden lions, and with the red lily crown upon my head."

"The wait may be longer than you think. Cammilla Martelli was old Duke Cosimo's wife, and she had no grand coronation, or any coronation at all. Look at her today—walled up in a convent, all her property stripped away from her, seeing her friends, such as they are, through a grille in the nuns' parlor. Being a wife is not the same thing as being a grand duchess."

"For me it will be." Bianca had become calmer, and seemed to be realizing how foolish she had been to reveal her clandestine wedding. "You will say nothing to anyone about this matter, Signorina Chiara. Even the grand duke himself would order you to keep silence."

"As he ordered you to keep silence, for all the good it did him."

Bianca reached up and took the red lilies from her hair. She held them to her lips for a moment and appeared to breathe their scent. Then she looked up. Her face had changed—it was pale and cold. Her eyes were the color of storm clouds. Chiara actually took a step backward, she was so startled by the change.

"You have been silent about the day the grand duchess died," she said. "You told the grand duke you were not there. Why did you do that, Signorina Chiara? Did you think to keep what you know to yourself, and one day use it against me?"

Lie, Chiara thought. Lie like you've never lied before.

"I would not blacken the grand duchess's name," she said, "by speaking it in the same breath as yours."

"Perhaps," Bianca Cappello said. "Perhaps not. And perhaps I will find a way to make certain your breath speaks no one's name, ever again."

CHAPTER FORTY-ONE

Chiara burst through the front of the bookshop and ran into the kitchen behind it. "Nonna," she said. She doubled over, trying to catch her breath. Vivi danced around her, claws clicking on the scrubbed wood floor. "Nonna, he's married her."

Nonna looked up from the soup she was stirring. The cloudiness of her eyes was becoming more visible every day. The kitchen smelled of roasted chicken and fennel and garlic.

"Who's married who?" Nonna said.

"The grand duke. He's married Bianca Cappello."

Nonna tasted her soup and added more salt. "Can't be more than gossip. Even Francesco de' Medici wouldn't be stupid enough to marry his Venetian whore with the emperor's sister hardly cold in her tomb."

"It's not gossip." Chiara slung her leather bag on the table and began to take out bottles of white and red crystalline powders. "I've been to the Villa di Pratolino, taking equipment and supplies for the grand duke's new laboratory there. I saw Bianca Cappello."

"She lives there." Nonna dipped a piece of bread in the soup and held it out to Vivi. The little hound sat up on her haunches with her white front paws tucked neatly against her chest, and when Nonna threw the morsel of bread she jumped up and snapped it out of the air.

"I spoke to her." Chiara began to arrange the bottles in groups, by color. "May she be damned to hell for all eternity. It's supposed to be secret, of course. In public he's still pretending to be a grieving widower."

"All the better for you the Medici devil's occupied, coming and going with his powders and potions like you do and taking whatever you please. What's all that?"

"The red crystals are cinnabar—it's a sulphide of mercury, although you'd never know there's a silver metal inside it, by looking at it. The white powder is called philosopher's wool—it's zinc ores that have been burned in air."

Nonna made the sign of the cross, then the *corna*, the two down-pointing fingers like horns that warded off the evil eye.

"It's not black magic, Nonna."

"Best to be safe, either way."

"I wish it was magic, and that I knew how to use it. Bianca Cappello threatened me—she boasted to me that she was married to the grand duke, and afterward she regretted it. She told me she could have me silenced forever."

"Keep out of the affairs of the Medici, *nipotina*. I worry that you spend so much time alone with the grand duke, without your Magister Ruanno."

"The grand duke says he's coming back to Florence. We're going to start the *magnum opus* again at the summer solstice, and if we succeed . . . I don't know, I think Magister Ruanno may find an assassin's dagger between his shoulder blades."

Nonna looked at her thoughtfully. She seemed to be weighing whether or not to do something. After a moment she said, "Just so there are no daggers in your own back from that bitch of a Venetian. Have you been to see the kennel master today?"

Nonna held up another tidbit of bread and made a circling motion with it. Vivi went round and round in circles, then again caught the bread when Nonna tossed it. Nonna did love dogs and had clearly spent hours teaching Vivi her tricks.

"Yes, I saw him. Rostig and Seiden are grieving for the grand duchess, refusing to eat, lying by the door all day, watching and hoping. The kennel master's wife takes care of them, and Rina and Leia too, but they're lonely—there's no one left to love them."

"What about the children? I'd think they'd want their mother's pets."

"I don't know if anyone's asked them. They're at the Palazzo Pitti, and the grand duke has put them in the charge of Bianca Cappello. I'm going to ask him to put me in the children's household too—someone has to keep an eye on the grand duchess's children, because the Venetian will poison them all to make her changeling boy the only heir."

Nonna sniffed. She could express more scorn in one sniff than Chiara herself could do in a week's worth of words. "I can't help you with the children, *nipotina*, but bring the old dogs here. I'll make sure they have good dinners and folded blankets in the warm sunshine, for your grand duchess's sake. She was good to you, for all she was married to a Medici."

"And I could take Rina and Leia to the Pitti—the grand duchess's daughters could take them out into the gardens for their exercise. I promised her, Nonna, that I would watch over them all."

After she was dead, perhaps, but still. A promise was a promise.

Nonna reached down and ran her hand over Vivi's head. "Just be careful," she said. "I don't like all this talk about assassins, and the grand duke's Venetian whore threatening you. We've had enough trouble with the Medici, and we don't need any more."

Chiara dipped a piece of bread into the soup and ate it herself. "I want to keep my place," she said. "I can become a *magistra*, Nonna, an alchemist in my own right. I can show Babbo that I'm worthy."

"Your father's dead and gone. You can't show him anything."

"He meant to—"

I will cut her throat, and her virgin's life-blood will bring him back. She should have died instead of Gian, and it is only right she be the one to bring him back.

She stopped herself just in time. It would break Nonna's heart anew to know what a deadly sin her son had planned.

"He meant to do a lot of things," Nonna said. The wrinkles in her cheeks seemed to deepen with sadness. "I wasn't sure if I should give you this, *nipotina*, but if you're bound to stay at court with the devil and his whore, you need all the friends you can get. Your Magister Ruanno, he's different."

She went to the box where she kept fresh bread, opened it, and took out a packet of paper, folded together and covered with wax seals. The seals had been broken. Chiara took it and saw that it was addressed to the bookshop of Carlo Nerini in Florence, nothing more. The handwriting struck her to the heart, with its tall, narrow letters and sharp, straight, angular lines. She had seen it before in one short note, written in invisible ink and tied to Vivi's collar with silken threads.

"This is from Magister Ruanno," she said. "You opened it?"

"It was addressed to the shop, wasn't it? I'm not so blind that I can't read an order if I look close enough, and that's what I thought it was."

Chiara unfolded the paper. It was exactly as Nonna described it—an innocuous request for a book of Dante. The writing filled only half the space. The other half was blank.

Although of course it wouldn't be blank if it was held over a flame.

"I'm going to take this down to the cellar with me," she said. "I need to put these things away."

"Be careful with it, *nipotina*. Burn it when you're finished."

Nonna, who had survived how many anti-Medici plots and revolutions, who had been born during the first republic, who had been an ardent supporter of the second republic? Yes, she would know about such things as invisible ink.

"I'll be careful," Chiara said.

In the cellar she lit the lanterns and put the bottles of cinnabar crystals and philosopher's wool on the shelves in their proper places. Then she lit the brazier, unfolded the piece of paper, and held it over the fire.

I am taking ship in the morning. I have sent the grand duke a letter, but I know him well enough to expect an embrace in public and an assassin's dagger in secret, and will take care accordingly. The news of the grand duchess's death has reached me. May she rest in peace.

I have achieved what I desired, and at the same time I have lost everything. I have missed you, awen lymm. I will tell you more when I see you.

It wasn't signed, but then none of his messages had ever been signed.

I have missed you.

She tore the paper into shreds and fed the pieces into the brazier, one at a time. The fire burned up hotter, and the heat seemed to find its way into her flesh and her veins and her heart. She needed the *sonnodolce*—it had been only six days instead of the seven that were supposed to pass between doses, but she craved it and the dreams it would bring, the relief.

I have achieved what I desired, and at the same time I have lost everything. What did that mean?

And what about what she herself desired? What about the *Lapis Philosophorum*, which would heal her, quiet her demons, make her whole? What about her ambition to learn, to experiment, to be a *magistra* more famous than Perenelle Flamel? What about proving to Babbo, once and for all and forever, that she was worthy to be alive? Was she to leave Florence, give up everything she had struggled and suffered to achieve, for Ruan Pencarrow and his labyrinth house and his moon mine halfway to the end of the world? I love you, Ruan, she thought—yes, there, I said it, inside my head at least—but I'm not ready to go. Not yet.

She took the tiny bottle of *sonnodolce* from its hiding place—hidden even from Nonna—and looked at it for a long time. It was half empty. I have to be careful, she thought. I don't know when the grand duke will make more. I know something about the components but he's the only one who knows the exact ingredients and the proportions of the formula. So that's another thing I need to find for myself. I wonder if Ruan's been continuing to use it, or if being back in his Cornwall, his home, has been satisfaction enough. I hope he hasn't stopped. He needs protection from poisons if he is coming back to Florence.

She removed the stopper from the bottle and let one drop fall on her wrist—left wrist this time. The liquid remained in one cohesive drop for a minute or two, then seemed to sink into her skin. Like the water in the silver sieve, she thought. A thousand years ago.

Carefully she sealed the bottle again and put it away. Then she went to the narrow pallet she'd set up in the darkest corner of the cellar and stretched out on the straw mattress. She closed her eyes.

When Ruan comes back . . .

She was in the great salon of the Palazzo Vecchio, standing to one side, half in the shadows. The grand duke was seated on an elaborate throne, decorated with gold and studded with jewels. He was dressed in gold and silver, and wore the crown of Tuscany with its central red fleur-de-lis. In his right hand he carried the scepter, a gilded rod topped with a globe of the world. Light seemed to shine from all the magnificence he wore, and it intensified the black shadow behind him.

Slowly, slowly, Chiara turned her head.

At the other end of the salon, Ruan Pencarrow stood in an arched doorway. He was dressed in plain dark cloth and leather, his head bare, his whip coiled over his shoulder. On his left wrist perched a glossy black bird, like a crow but not a crow, its beak bright red, long and curved. Behind him there was a storm of light, bright as the sun.

He is the opposite of the grand duke in every way, Chiara thought, dream-slowed. Dark simplicity outlined with light.

"Welcome back to Florence, Magister Ruanno," the grand duke said. "You have come to kill me, I think, in revenge for my sister Isabella's death."

Chiara tried to scream. She couldn't.

"I have come to kill you," Ruan agreed. He took a step forward. "And to take our *soror mystica* away with me."

"You will never have her. She cannot live without the *sonnodolce*, and only I know the secret of its formula."

Two men with silver daggers stepped into the room from a side door. They went to Ruan. He did not move. The black bird screamed, and launched itself into the air. It flew up and up and up, and Chiara realized that in her dream the great salon was open to the sky.

"I will have her," Ruan said.

"You will not." A different voice, a woman's voice with a Venetian accent. Bianca Cappello floated down into the room wearing a white silk dress and a blood-red jacket. She had a rose in her hand, its stem thickly starred with thorns.

"I will stop her breath," Bianca Cappello said.

The grand duke gestured with his scepter.

The two men struck Ruan with their silver daggers. He fell. They continued to stab him, over and over, as he lay on the floor at the grand duke's feet. His blood spread over the polished marble. It was not ordinary red blood, but molten metal, copper and iron, metals from the heart of the earth.

"Ruan!" Chiara screamed. She tried to run to him but every move was unnaturally, terrifyingly slow, as if she were caught in a thick sticky web. "Ruan, Ruan . . ."

She opened her eyes. She was whispering, "Ruan, Ruan."

She was in the cellar, on her pallet. The brazier had gone out, and the lanterns were flickering. None of it had happened. It was only the *sonno-dolce*.

"Ruan," she said aloud. "He means to kill you. Hear me, wherever you are."

The cellar was silent. She was alone. And Ruan Pencarrow, wherever he was, couldn't hear her warnings.

CHAPTER FORTY-TWO

The Poisoned Maze in the Boboli Gardens

17 JULY 1578

Chiara floated up out of blackness with the taste of blood in her mouth and the scent of earth in her face. She was wet and shivering, although it wasn't cold. It was dark, so dark. At first she thought she'd been buried alive, but then she realized there were sounds around her, chirrings, rustlings, insects and leaves. There was air. There was the unmistakable scent of the Arno. She was lying face down on soft thick grass, mown as short and fine as velvet.

But where?

She turned over. The sky was black and clear, glittering with stars, the Via Lattea arching through the vault of the heavens like silver smoke. The moon was almost full, bright enough to cast shadows. She was in a circular clearing, surrounded by a wall of leaves, with some kind of stone in the center. But no. It wasn't quite circular. It was lobed, like a rosette with one, two, three—six petals. A rosette with six petals—the center of a labyrinth. A labyrinth made of small trees, clipped and manicured, with bittersweet and rose canes twining among their branches. Flower beds around them. It was too dark to see what kind of flowers were planted there.

She sat up. She was wearing ordinary clothes, her blue linen bodice and skirt over her white camicia, striped stockings and blue leather slippers, her hair braided and pinned up with plain tortoise-shell pins. Her head hurt— not a headache, and not a demon's voice to be heard, thank the saints—

just a hot painful spot at the back of her neck. She lifted her hand—a lump, swollen and throbbing. Had someone struck her? When? Why?

I was at the Casino di San Marco, she thought. Rufino was there—but wait, no, he wasn't. I came out into the street and he wasn't there with the horses and I looked for him—

And that's all I remember.

She gazed up at the stars. There, that was the North Star, just as Ruan had taught her. Her own stars, the curling tail and spread claws of the Scorpion, were on the opposite horizon, so that was south. Was the labyrinth itself aligned with the cardinal directions? If it was, the pattern of the arcs and double folds might be the same as the pattern of the labyrinth set into the floor of the laboratory at the Casino di San Marco.

She focused on the Scorpion and slowly moved her gaze straight down. And there was the darker shadow among the shadows, the break straight south between two petals of the rosette. The way out.

She pushed herself to her feet, using the central stone for support. It felt rough, pitted with sharp-edged indentations. Was it natural, or had it been carved?

There was only one person in Florence who had gardens vast enough to create a labyrinth so large out of trees and vines. And with the scent of the Arno in the air—she had to be in the Boboli Gardens, behind the Palazzo Pitti. Had the grand duke arranged for her to be abducted and abandoned here? Was it another one of his mad tests? It could hardly be an attempt to murder her—surely he'd realize that she'd come back to consciousness and eventually find her way out. A labyrinth, after all, was a single path, for all its doublings and foldings.

"Straight south," she said aloud. "Then east, and double back west at the first fold."

Some small animal rustled away at the sound of her voice. She stepped through the opening and between the walls of leaves, black-and-silver in the moonlight. The trees were hornbeam and yew, taller than the top of her head. Bittersweet vines, bramble bushes and rose canes grew thickly among the trees. At the first turning a thorn caught her sleeve and she heard stitches tear.

"Che palle," she said, under her breath. Now that she was out of the open rosette in the center of the maze, the pathway was narrow and the

moonlight slanted across the tops of the leaf-walls. Between the walls it was hard to see. She held out her hands, and only just in time, because her palms found thorns, long and sharp. She gasped and jerked her hands back.

Carefully she felt her way around the loop of the double fold and started back to the west. She rubbed her palms against her skirt—the prick-wounds were superficial but they stung. Was the path getting narrower? Another thorn caught her skirt, and when she turned south again she felt a branch of bramble-thorns gouge into her upper arm, tearing the fabric of her sleeve. She walked straight. If the labyrinth was built according to the same pattern as the one in the laboratory, here, at the end of the path, she was at the outer edge. But the shrubs and trees and bushes were entangled and impenetrable, and there was nothing to do but continue to follow the path.

She walked east and north, around the first arc. Something—something was making her dizzy. It was almost as if she had put a drop of *sonnodolce* on her skin. The thorns seemed to writhe and reach out to catch the fabric of her clothing. She pushed them aside and kept walking. A fold of the path, double back, keep walking. Keep walking.

Keep walking. I am here with you, and I will help you walk to the end.

She wasn't surprised to hear Ruan's voice. She wasn't surprised to feel his presence, see him even, if she glanced quickly out of the corners of her eyes.

"What's happening to me?" she asked. She kept walking. Double back again. A short arc, this time.

What do you think the grand duke wanted with one hundred small vials of the sonnodolce, *each vial to be compounded with fresh rainwater, in a proportion of one part to one hundred parts?*

Was it Ruan's voice, or her own thoughts?

She could feel the scratches of the thorns and brambles, throbbing with the beats of her heart. They were on her hands, her arms. A branch scratched her face, and pulled at her hair.

Keep walking. Around, double back, around again.

Compounded with fresh rainwater, such as might be used to water plants. He has been using it here—every thorn that pricks you puts sonnodolce *into your blood. If you had not been taking your small doses, if you were not immune—you would be dead, long before you reached the end of the maze.*

So it was an attempt to murder her.

And perhaps I will find a way to make certain your breath speaks no one's name, ever again.

Not Ruan's voice. Bianca Cappello's. The grand duke's mistress must have known the maze was poisoned, and she had arranged it all. Who would ever think to blame her, when it was discovered that the grand duke's *soror mystica* had wandered into a maze in the Boboli Gardens and fallen dead in one of the paths?

Each arc was getting shorter—she was closer to the center of the labyrinth again. Even though the poison wouldn't kill her, somehow she had to stay on her feet—the familiar dream state with its visions made her want to lie down, curl up, and dream forever.

You must walk the labyrinth, awen lymm, *all the way to the end.*

It was strange, that she could hear Ruan's voice as if he were standing beside her, when she hadn't heard Babbo's voice or the demons' voices for so long.

In fact, barely once or twice since you began taking the sonnodolce.

Had Ruan said that, or had she thought it for herself?

Was it true? She tried to remember. When had she last heard the voices?

Time twisted and folded back upon itself just as the path did. She was standing in the Piazza della Signoria in the rain. She was carrying a silver sieve, full of water. She was outside a door, her fingers in the crack between the door and the wall, trying hopelessly to pull the crack wider as Donna Isabella screamed. She was standing at the top of a marble stairway with Grand Duchess Giovanna. She was facing Bianca Cappello, who had red lilies in her hair.

She walked and walked. The moonlight glanced off the leaves and the thorns, the roses that looked black and white, the bittersweet and bramble berries like drops of blood. The flowers under the espaliered trees were lilies, touched with scarlet where the moonlight struck them. Were her feet even touching the ground? She wasn't sure. She was sure that Ruan was walking with her, although of course he wasn't really there. He was on a ship somewhere, coming to Florence, where the grand duke intended to use his knowledge and then kill him—

Suddenly she realized she had come out of the labyrinth. Before her there was a locked iron gate. She was tired, so tired, but at the same time she felt as if she'd been sleeping and had dreamed it all. Only the scratches on her hands and arms and face proved it had been real.

She could see a golden line above the buildings of the city in the east, across the Arno, where the sun would rise. Surely a gardener would come soon, and open the gate. In the meantime she would sit, holding tight to the ironwork, and close her eyes for just a moment.

"Soror Chiara," the grand duke said. He looked—what, angry? Partly, and partly surprised, and partly curious, and in a frightening way, satisfied as well. "So it is you."

"Yes, Serenissimo."

"And you were inside the locked gate. Inside the labyrinth. Is that correct?"

She'd been asleep when the gardener found her. He'd run off to find the key to the gate and had come back with an ironmonger—apparently the key was mysteriously missing. By the time the lock was broken and she was freed, the sun was high overhead and bells were ringing for Sext. She was taken inside the palace, given a cup of watered wine and a chance to withdraw for a few minutes to relieve herself, thank the saints. But the scratches on her face and hands had grown hot and swollen, and her clothes were dirty and torn, and there wasn't much she could do about that when she was taken straight to the grand duke without being allowed to wash her face or change her clothing.

"Yes, Serenissimo," she said. "Inside the labyrinth."

"And you are well? I see you have scratches, and I will direct my physician to attend to them shortly, but other than that—you are in normal health?"

So it was true. The plants in the labyrinth had been watered with *sonnodolce* and the grand duke couldn't believe she'd been scratched so badly and was still alive. Once he got over his amazement, he'd start wondering why.

"I'm well enough, Serenissimo."

"How did you get into the labyrinth in the first place? The lock is on the outside of the gate, and the key was missing."

"I don't know, Serenissimo. I was—"

Just then Bianca Cappello ran into the room, satin skirts rustling and jewels glittering. When she saw Chiara, she turned so white that Chiara expected her to faint. She clutched at her skirts—no, she was trying to conceal part of the finely worked gold filigree tassel of chains attached to her belt with an enameled medallion.

"Madonna," the grand duke said. He didn't speak to her as if she was his wife, but of course they were still playing their game of make-believe mourning. "What do you do here? I have not requested your presence."

"Serenissimo." She made a hasty curtsy. "I—I heard that—that a woman had been found in the maze, and—"

So she'd known the labyrinth was poisoned. She'd had to see with her own eyes when someone had told her the grand duke's *soror mystica* had been rescued alive. Because she had arranged it, the abduction, the labyrinth, all of it.

I will find a way to make certain your breath speaks no one's name, ever again.

She flushed bright red. "Nothing, my lord."

He let her stand there for a few seconds, then gestured wordlessly to the chair beside his own. She seated herself, clearly regretting she'd run into the salon and wishing she could run back out again. Chiara looked at her steadily, without any curtsy or acknowledgment. If the grand duke noticed the omission—and surely he did—he said nothing.

"Now, Soror Chiara," he said instead. "Continue."

"I was at the Casino di San Marco, Serenissimo, and had gone out to look for Rufino and the horses. That is the last I remember before waking up in the center of the labyrinth. I believe Rufino was either tricked or complicit or assassinated. I believe I was struck down from behind and abducted."

"And do you have any idea who might have done such a thing?"

Tell the truth? Lie? Or be silent?

It was too soon. As much as she hated Bianca Cappello, she didn't have the power to confront her openly. Wait, she thought. Wait. Don't attack until you're certain you can win.

Without expression she said, "No, Serenissimo."

"Indeed." The grand duke looked from her to Bianca. He was no fool, and Bianca had given herself away, rushing to find out how her victim could possibly have escaped from the poisoned maze, so obviously attempting to hide whatever it was she had attached to her belt.

"Tell me, Madonna," the grand duke said to his wife-who-no-one-knew-was-his-wife, "what have you there?"

"Nothing, my lord. My needle case, my scissors, a reliquary."

"Show me."

She didn't give him the medallion at once. The grand duke looked at her, intent and narrow-eyed. Then something strange happened. Her whole appearance changed—she lowered her eyes and hunched her shoulders slightly, as if she had changed from a proud Venetian noblewoman to a frightened kitchen maid. Her hands shook as she unfastened the medallion with its decorative chains and all the golden and jeweled objects attached to it. Without a word she handed it to the grand duke.

"That is better, my Bia," he said. "Now, let us see what we have here."

Bia?

A pet name, presumably, between two lovers.

"A needle case and scissors, yes. A thimble. A gold toothpick with pearls, a reliquary, a few keys. And what is this?"

He held up one of the keys. It was not gold, not ornamental. It was plain worked iron.

Bianca Cappello sat frozen. She might have been changed into a wax effigy of herself.

"An iron key. I know what key it is, because I am quite familiar with it—it is the key to the garden labyrinth."

Bianca said nothing. Why didn't she protest, deny any knowledge of the key, make up a lie? The Bianca Cappello I know, Chiara thought, would fight back. She would hold up her head with pride and claim that as a Venetian noblewoman she was above suspicion. Who was this meek Bianca, this Bia?

The silence lengthened.

"So," the grand duke said at last. "Here I have a woman who spent a night locked in my particular labyrinth. She is covered with scratches, some of them quite deep, and yet before me she stands, healthy and well. The only way this can be possible is if she has stolen something from me, something unique and valuable."

Chiara held her breath. Saints and angels, she prayed, please don't let him take the *sonnodolce* away from me. The only reason I'm not dead is that I've been taking the *sonnodolce*. I'm not dead, and I'm not having headaches and falling-spells and hearing demons. I have to have it, until I can create the *Lapis Philosophorum* and heal myself completely.

"At the same time," the grand duke went on, "I have a woman with a key in her possession, the key to that very same particular labyrinth, stolen from its hiding-place. Why would she want this key? To lock the first woman in the maze, of course, and expect it to be the death of her."

Bianca Cappello didn't look up or defend herself.

"Two thieves. The worst kind of thieves, who steal from their liege lord. How shall they be punished?"

"Serenissimo," Chiara said. By the Baptist, she was going to defend herself, even if Bianca Cappello wasn't. "May I speak?"

The grand duke nodded. "Please do."

"I confess to taking one tiny flask of the substance called *sonnodolce*." I won't call it a poison, she thought, even though they both know it. Nonna always says, if you don't speak a word, it doesn't exist. "I confess to using it as you described, the night I helped you create it—one drop on the skin, one day in seven. But of course you know this, because only the effect of this stolen *sonnodolce* kept me alive as I made my way through the maze."

"Indeed."

"The flask I took is barely the size of my thumb, and it's two-thirds empty. That's a very small amount, and in exchange, I am alive this morning. You continue to have a *soror mystica* to serve you."

"I do not begrudge you the *sonnodolce* itself. In point of fact, I am pleased that your experience proves beyond a doubt that the small doses will ultimately protect against a large dose. I do expect you to do penance, however, for taking something from the laboratory without my knowledge and permission."

If you only knew, Chiara thought. In a steady voice she said, "I will do penance, Serenissimo."

"And I will allow you to have a small amount of the *sonnodolce*, so you can continue to take it. I would have you safe against any further attempts."

Chiara said nothing. She couldn't have spoken if she'd wanted to, her relief was so great.

"I myself know," the grand duke went on, "that one cannot simply start and stop taking the *sonnodolce* at will." He sounded rather pleased about it.

"By continuing to take it, you will be bound more closely to me, and all the more willing to do whatever I ask of you."

I will find the formula, Chiara swore to herself. For that reason alone, I will find the formula so I can make it myself. I will be free of every tie—I will find a priest to absolve me of my vow of virginity as well. Not because of the virginity itself—oh, Ruan, Ruan—but because I will be free of the Medici in every way.

The grand duke continued. "Here is your penance, then. You will enter Donna Bianca's household, to serve her—"

"But—"

"Be silent. To serve her as you served the late grand duchess, and my late sister. It is my pleasure to have you close by, both here in Florence and at the Villa di Pratolino, so you will be readily available when I choose to work in my laboratories. In order to avoid scandal, it is necessary for you to be a member of a lady's household."

Bianca Cappello raised her head. For all her submissive mien, her eyes were stormy. "I do not want her around me, Franco," she said, in a little girl's voice. "She will be a constant reminder."

"A reminder, yes, my Bia, that you attempted to murder her and did not succeed. Every day you will look at her and know that if you had succeeded in your plot, you would have committed a mortal sin. And by my hand you would have suffered for it."

You're a fine one to be talking about mortal sins, Chiara thought. She might not have murdered me this time, but if we have to live in the same apartments and see each other every day, she'll try again. If I don't murder her first.

"You, Soror Chiara," the grand duke said. "Do you agree to these terms?"

Suddenly Chiara saw how she could turn the grand duke's so-called penance to her own advantage. Keeping her eyes down, she said earnestly, "I would serve your children, Serenissimo. You have placed them in Donna Bianca's household, after all, and if I were to care for them, it would give Donna Bianca all the more freedom for—other demands upon her time."

All the *Donna Biancas* made her mouth taste as sour as Nonna's apple vinegar. They worked, though. Bianca Cappello's mouth twisted in a self-satisfied smile at the thought of her enemy being reduced to the status of a nursemaid.

"An excellent suggestion," the grand duke said. "You are dismissed, Soror Chiara. Go to the children's apartments now, and I will order my physician to wait upon you there."

"Thank you, Serenissimo."

As she withdrew she kept her face turned aside, so Bianca Cappello wouldn't see she was smiling a self-satisfied smile of her own.

CHAPTER FORTY-THREE

The Palazzo Pitti

31 JULY 1578

"Maria!" Chiara called. "Come along, *principessina*, we are going inside."

"Doggies!" The stubby-legged three-year-old ran after Rina, laughing with delight. "Catch doggies!" Vivi, Rina and Leia romped over the grass, barking, their long russet ears flying. Clearly none of them had the slightest intention of being caught.

"She will spoil her dress with grass stains if she falls." Eleonora, the eldest of the Grand Duchess Giovanna's three surviving daughters, was eleven, dark and narrow-faced like her father but with her mother's devout and scrupulous character. "Call the dogs, Signorina Chiara—you are the only one they will answer to."

"Vivi!" Chiara whistled, something the dignified Eleonora would never do. Vivi responded at once, and when she ran up to Chiara the other two followed. Chiara snapped the red leather leashes to their collars. Maria pounded up behind them, laughing and sticky, her honey-colored curls tangled. Eleonora clicked her tongue disapprovingly.

"You look like a peasant girl," she said. "I do not envy your nurse's task, getting that hair brushed out."

Maria scowled at the thought of a hairbrush, and would have run away again if Chiara had not caught her hand firmly. They started up the broad steps to the palazzo, just as Maria's nurse and Eleonora's lady-in-waiting—at eleven she was far too grown-up for a nursemaid—came down to meet them.

"I'll leave you to go in, Donna Eleonora," Chiara said. "I'd like to walk a little longer with the dogs, until they calm down."

"Very well," Eleonora said. "We will look for you at suppertime."

The children had been cool to her at first, until she brought them the dogs. Starved for affection as they were, they'd welcomed Rina and Leia into their lives with delight. Anna, the middle girl, was too frail to run around in the gardens, but she particularly loved resting in a cushioned chair with Leia cuddled close to her. Filippo, of course—well, poor little Filippo was only a little over a year old and could barely sit up by himself, much less walk in the gardens. Somewhat to her own surprise, Chiara found herself loving them all with a fierce, Nonna-like protectiveness.

So the black canker of vengeance hadn't completely eaten up her heart. There was a warm, living place left for the children. And another for Ruan Pencarrow—Magister Ruanno dell' Inghilterra, who had still not returned to Florence. When was he coming? And when he did arrive, what would he do? What would he expect of her?

Eleonora and Maria and their attendants went into the palazzo. Chiara started back down the stairs with the hounds on their leashes. To her surprise three gentlemen came walking toward her. Where had they come from? She hadn't seen them before. It was almost as if they'd been concealing themselves deliberately, waiting for the children to go in.

"Signorina Chiara." One of the men stepped ahead of the other two and addressed her. His voice was familiar, and after a moment, to her astonishment, she recognized him as Cardinal Prince Ferdinando de' Medici, dressed not in the scarlet of a prince of the church but in fine, rather plain secular clothing.

"Eminenza," she said. "I didn't—"

"Shush. No titles, if you please. I am here in secret, and when I learned you had been placed in the children's household, I determined to find a way to speak with you privately."

More plots. I have enough plots of my own, she thought. I don't want to find myself tangled up in yours.

On the other hand, I know you hate your brother, and hate Bianca Cappello, and how can I help but be curious?

"It isn't very private here," she said. "Anyone could walk by. And I have the dogs."

The cardinal, the prince—whatever he wanted people to think he was—snapped his fingers to one of his gentlemen. The man took the dogs' leashes from her hands. The cardinal then wrapped his own princely fingers firmly around her elbow.

"Have you ever walked through the Vasari Corridor?" he said pleasantly. "It is quite private, as only the family uses it. The entrance is here, in the garden, just a bit farther on."

So what were her choices? Pull her arm free, make a scene, run back and demand the dogs' leashes from the presumptuous gentleman? Or go with him and find out what he wanted? Surely she wasn't in any danger, not from Cardinal Prince Ferdinando de' Medici, who had been Grand Duchess Giovanna's beloved friend. She was probably in less danger from him than she was from the grand duke himself.

On the other hand, he was a Medici, and they were all dangerous. Always.

"I walked through it a few times, with the grand duchess," she said. "Up over the city, all the way from the Palazzo Vecchio to the Palazzo Pitti. My Nonna says it's typical Medici—cut straight through ordinary people's houses and shops, all for their own privacy and luxury."

Prince Ferdinando—that's what I'll call him for the moment, she thought, since he's not wearing his cardinal's robes—laughed. "Ah, yes, your Nonna—Mona Agnesa Nerini, that is her name, is it not? A great supporter of the old republic. Here, here is the entrance."

Mona Agnesa Nerini, that is her name, is it not? How much did he know about Nonna? Had he found Pierino Ridolfi, far away in Germany, and learned the truth about his escape? It wouldn't matter to him one way or the other, but if he were to drop a word or two to his brother—

He guided her through an archway in the stone wall surrounding the garden. They walked up a good number of steps to a doorway; the single guardsman, recognizing Prince Ferdinando, unlocked the door and swung it open. A long corridor stretched out before them, full of light from the small square windows on one side and the round windows on the other. A few paintings hung along the walls between the windows; the ceiling was frescoed and the floor was tiled with polished russet-colored stone.

"My father and my brother have collected some fine pieces of art here, where only the family can enjoy them," the prince said. "Come, let us walk a way—I have the perfect spot in mind."

A short distance down the corridor a *loggiato*, a small balcony, looked out over the nave of a magnificent church. The prince gestured to the upholstered benches.

"Seat yourself, *signorina*," he said. He made himself comfortable and waited until she had taken a seat as well. "Now. I have heard one or two disturbing pieces of gossip regarding your new mistress."

"If you mean Bianca Cappello," Chiara said, "she is not my mistress." After a moment she added, "My lord."

The prince laughed again. Was all his laughing meant to disarm her? "Mistress or not," he said, "I am told she tried to have you poisoned."

Chiara said nothing.

"I am also told my brother has been mad enough to marry her in secret."

"I wish I could say that isn't true."

"Ah. I see. I have been writing to my brother from Rome, suggesting suitable princesses for a second marriage—and all the while he has been married to the Venetian."

"I don't see why he has to marry again at all," Chiara burst out. "The grand duchess is only a few months dead. Couldn't he wait a year, for decency's sake? Couldn't you wait, my lord, before you began suggesting new wives?"

"My dear," he said. No smile or laughter. He was sincere, if he could ever be sincere. "I loved Giovanna as if she were my own sister. I think you know that. I was shocked and saddened to hear of her death."

Chiara looked away, out over the church. She blinked hard. *If you only knew the truth about her death,* she thought. Aloud she said, "I know, my lord."

"There are two reasons, however, why I wished to arrange a new marriage for my brother at once, and I think Giovanna herself would have agreed with me. Firstly, to keep him out of the claws of the Venetian. Secondly, to breed up another true heir if possible—little Filippino is very fragile. If Francesco is fool enough to legitimate the Venetian's changeling brat, I will have the boy strangled. I will never allow a bastard without a drop of Medici blood to inherit our crown."

Chiara swallowed. "You're very frank, my lord."

"You will not betray me, will you?"

"Of course not."

Once, when she had been just herself, Chiara Nerini, the bookseller's daughter, she would have felt amazed and self-important and a little frightened that such a great man had opened his innermost heart and mind to her. Now—now, after four years at the Medici court, she had learned guile and she knew exactly why he had done it. To put her in his power. At any point, if what he told her became public—even if he himself started the whispers—he could blame her, and ruin her.

If she refused to do what he asked her to do—and of course he was going to ask her to do something, that was obvious—he could ruin her.

And ruin Nonna. Worse than ruin. That was why he'd made such a point to mentioning her full name.

So be it. If he wanted to play with her, she would play her side of the game.

"I would ask you a question, my lord." She made her voice gentle and innocent.

"And what is that?"

A tapestry in red and gold had been draped over the stone balustrade. Chiara traced some of the tiny stitches, the shield and *palle* of the Medici interspersed with the red lily of Florence. The great altar of the church, far below, gleamed with gold.

"Why do you make such confidences to me, my lord? You're a great prince, a secular prince by birth and a prince of the church as well. Surely there are people of your own rank who would be more suitable as confidantes."

"People of my own rank are all the more likely to have purposes of their own, and so to betray me. I must go back to Rome, and I need someone in the Venetian's household who will keep me informed. I think you loved Giovanna too, and for her sake will become my—correspondent."

"Your spy."

"A harsh word."

"I did love her, my lord. For me she was the one truly good person at the court. I've been happy to help to take care of her children, and her little hounds."

The prince laughed. "She did love those dogs," he said. "Where are the two old ones? I did not see them in the park."

"My grandmother has them. She's taking very good care of them."

"Turning them into four-legged republicans, no doubt." He smiled, his eyes dark and merry. He was like his brother in appearance, but seemed to be utterly unlike him in character. Did the difference go all the way down to his heart, or was it a game he played? A snake in a new skin, Nonna would say, is still a snake.

And for all his apparent friendliness, all his openness, there was that underlying threat. *Mona Agnesa Nerini, that is her name, is it not?*

"So what can I do for you," he said, "in exchange for your correspondence? My brother is already paying you generously, I think, for your services as his *soror mystica*."

What could he do for her?

She thought of her wish to be free of every tie to the Medici. If she asked him now to absolve her from her vow, would he guess her true desire, and refuse her? He wouldn't want her to be free, because he himself wanted to use her. But if he thought it was for a lover's sake—he would like that, sensualist that he was. He would want to imagine her in bed with her lover, and he wouldn't even think it was only for the sake of her freedom.

We are bound to each other, and in the end we will find a way.

Well, perhaps for a lover too. But the cardinal didn't have to know that.

She said, "I don't want gold, my lord. Only—are you a priest?"

She could tell she'd surprised him. "Not exactly," he said. "I am a lay cardinal, not ordained to one of the major orders, although I am in minor orders. Why?"

"Can you absolve a person from a vow? A vow taken on a holy relic?"

He tilted his head to one side. "What sort of vow?"

She looked out over the church again. What would it be like, to hear mass like this, high above the crowd of ordinary people? Did a priest bring the Body and Blood of Christ to them up a secret staircase?

"A vow of chastity," she said. "Not a religious vow—a secular vow, but taken with my hands on the Sacra Cintola of the Virgin."

"Ah. I remember—Giovanna mentioned the business with the Sacra Cintola, the first day I met you. Do you remember?"

"Yes, my lord."

"And my brother subjected you to some sort of pagan initiation, and imposed a vow of chastity upon you. You do not need a priest to absolve you of such mummery, my dear."

Now you must vow that you will remain a virgin while you are in my service, upon pain of death. The grand duke's voice, in the laboratory at the Casino di San Marco. *Magister Ruanno, the relic.*

She remembered thinking, relic? Pain of death? She remembered the rock crystal reliquary, cool and polished, the fluting of the scallop shell perfectly carved.

With my hands on the Sacra Cintola of the Holy Virgin, I swear I will remain a virgin, upon penalty of death, for as long as I am in the service of the prince.

"I feel as if I do." To her dismay and anger her eyes stung with tears. "It was a true relic, my lord, the girdle of the Holy Virgin herself."

He leaned forward and placed his hands on either side of her head.

"In nomine Patris, et Filii, et Spiritus Sancti," he said, his voice calm and low. "I relieve and dispense you from the bond of your vow of chastity made upon the relic of the Holy Virgin, now and forever. Amen."

It was so quick. Only a few words. But she felt her heart lighten.

"You are now free," he said. "Is there some particular reason why you wished to be free of your vow? Some particular person you—are attached to?"

She looked away from him, as if she was hiding something. It wasn't entirely play-acting. "No particular person," she said.

He chuckled. "Particularly not Magister Ruanno dell' Inghilterra?"

She said nothing.

"I will keep your secret, I promise you. But you must keep your promises to me as well."

"Thank you, my lord. I'll keep my promises and send you news of Bianca Cappello's household when there is any news to be had. For the grand duchess's sake, and little Prince Filippo's."

He stood up and gestured for her to go out of the *loggiato*. "Let us go back to the gardens, where my man is holding your dogs," he said. "It's very kind of your grandmother to keep Giovanna's old dogs. I shall have to send her a gift, to show my appreciation."

In other words, Chiara thought as she passed through the Vasari Corridor, high over the streets and houses where the ordinary people lived, I am to remember that you know my Nonna's name and where she lives, and that supporting the old republic is treason under the Medici.

CHAPTER FORTY-FOUR

The Villa di Pratolino

5 AUGUST 1578

The grand duke had made elaborate arrangements to receive his English alchemist into his presence again. Waiting-gentlemen surrounded him on the dais. Bianca Cappello sat at his side, richly dressed in rose-colored silk, attended by graceful ladies. Chiara stood a little distance away from the dais with her hands folded and her eyes cast down, plainly dressed, the moonstone hidden under her camicia.

The entire tableau vivant had been designed to show the grand duke's aloof indifference to alchemy, to his *soror mystica*, and in particular to Ruanno dell' Inghilterra and whether he came back to Florence or not. Everyone's face was expressionless. No one moved. Then Ruan stepped through the doorway, and Chiara felt as if a great burst of flame had sucked all the air out of the chamber.

His eyes met hers. There was one spark of joy and desire, so quickly damped that it might not have happened at all. He didn't smile, but he didn't have to. She managed to draw in a breath and looked away.

"So, Magister Ruanno." The grand duke sat back with insultingly informal ease in his fine carved chair. "You have decided to grace our city with your presence again."

"I can only beg you to have mercy upon me, Serenissimo," Ruan said. Chiara looked up again, unable to resist. He sounded different. He looked different. How? It wasn't his clothes. They were plain and dark, as they had always been. The heavy workman's muscles in his shoulders were the same. The difference was something in his face. Before, for all the endless sadness of his dark eyes, there had been certainty—certainty that what he wanted would ultimately be his. Now the certainty was gone.

I have achieved what I desired, and at the same time I have lost everything.

What had happened to him in Cornwall? Chiara pressed her hands together hard, to keep from reaching out to him.

"Mercy, Magister Ruanno?" the grand duke said. "I am not in the habit of rendering mercy to those who leave my household and my city without my permission."

Ruan didn't move. "My affairs in England were disordered," he said. "You, Serenissimo, were much occupied with the birth of your son and the heavy responsibilities of your position. I had no opportunity to apply for permission in the ordinary way."

"And the fact that you have returned—does that mean your English affairs are in order now, and you are prepared to remain in Florence until the *magnum opus* is completed and the *Lapis Philosophorum* is in my hands?"

"My English affairs are settled for the time being," Ruan said. His expression was unreadable. "I have come back to Florence indeed, Serenissimo, to help you create the *Lapis Philosophorum*, once and for all."

Since he doesn't even believe there is such a thing as the *Lapis Philosophorum*, Chiara thought, that couldn't be the real reason he has come back. Has he come back for vengeance? For gold? Is he running away from something?

We are bound to each other, and in the end we will find a way.

Has he come back for me?

"Very well, then," the grand duke said. He seemed to be staring at Ruan as intently as she was, but his eyes were oddly out of focus, as if he could not see clearly beyond the dais upon which he and Bianca Cappello sat. He often looked like that now, absorbed in himself and his mistress-wife and nothing else. However little he may have cared for the grand duchess, she had connected him to the outside world of emperors and kings. With her death that thread had been cut.

Would Ruan understand that?

"I will show you the mercy you ask," the grand duke was saying, "and reinstate you in your position as alchemist and metallurgist in my personal household. Apply to my secretaries for your wages and for the keys to the laboratories."

Ruan's expression betrayed a flicker of surprise. He thought the grand duke had given in too easily. The truth, of course, was that nothing the grand duke had done in his new laboratory had been successful. He believed it was because their triad, sun and earth and moon, had been disrupted by Ruan's absence. Let him believe it. Chiara wondered what Ruan would say when he learned that virtually every element in the laboratory at Pratolino had been cautiously and delicately adulterated.

"Laboratories, Serenissimo?" Ruan asked.

"Yes. The Casino di San Marco, of course. You will resume your residence in the apartments there. But I have installed a new laboratory here at the Villa di Pratolino as well. One of my guardsmen will take you there. Later today, perhaps, Soror Chiara and I will join you."

No, not *Soror Chiara and I*, Chiara thought with an intensity that frightened her a little. Just Soror Chiara. I will find a way to change your mind for you, Serenissimo, so I will be the only one to join Ruan, in the silent shadows of the lemon-house, with the scents of the fruits and the leaves all around us.

The grand duke rose and offered his hand to Bianca Cappello. She rose as well. They seemed to see no one but each other. The gentlemen and the ladies followed them as they went out of the room. Chiara walked last of all. She wanted to look back—oh, she wanted to look back so badly.

But she didn't.

It took nothing more than a whispered lie to Bianca Cappello that the grand duke had looked with favor on one of the other ladies that morning. The Venetian stormed off to the grand duke's private apartments, and Chiara was sure as she could be that no one would see either one of them again until morning. No one else would go to the lemon-house. The servants were afraid of the blasts and strange smells—brimstone, they whispered, from the depths of hell—that the grand duke's experiments produced.

She stepped into the laboratory and closed the door behind her. There was one lantern burning over the great table. Reddish light from the setting sun slanted up through the high windows. The lemon and orange trees in their tubs had been pushed into the corners, but their pungent scent still drifted in the air, mingled with the smells of saltpeter and sulphur. Babbo's athanor from Trebizond was on the table, with alembics and pelican flasks lined up beside it. In the cabinets the ranks of glass jars were filled with liquids and powders and crystals of every imaginable color.

"Chiara."

Ruan stepped out of the shadows. He had taken off his jacket and his white laced shirt shimmered in the half-light. The skin at his throat was darkly tanned against the white, but of course he had been outdoors on his Cornish estates, on ships and horseback as he traveled. "The grand duke?" he asked.

"Safely occupied. No one else will come."

For a moment they looked at each other. Then he held out his arms, a gesture half-questioning, half-demanding. She went straight to him as if she had been doing it all her life.

"Awen lymm." He bent over her, embracing her as if he would set her apart from the rest of the world forever. She could feel the words in the outflow of his breath.

"Tell me what it means," she said. "Please?"

"I am afraid you will not like it."

"I don't care. Tell me."

"It means sharp jaw."

She had to laugh, pressed against him. She wasn't sure what she'd been expecting but that wasn't it. *Does the grand duke not like his bedmates with their ribs sticking out and their chins as sharp as a kitchen-knife?* Nonna's voice, the day Ruan had taken her back to the bookshop for the first time. Did he never forget anything?

"But in Cornish the word *awen* means also inspiration. So you may have a sharp jaw, but you are also my keenest inspiration." He curved one hand over her head, gently, so gently, stroking her hair. "Did you get my letter?"

"Yes. Nonna gave it to me."

He put his hands on her shoulders and pushed her gently away from him. She made a wordless sound of resistance but he compelled her to step back. "We must take care, Chiara."

"But Ruan—Ruan, please don't push me away. No one will come."

"You cannot be sure of that. Not here, in a villa belonging to the grand duke himself."

They stared at each other.

"I feel as if you've never been gone," Chiara whispered. "The *sonnodolce*. The dreams. Oh, Ruan, you said we would be together, and I've been waiting and waiting and *waiting*—"

He caught her up in his arms again with a harsh sound, half-groan, half-curse. "Do you think I have not waited?" he said. "I have waited, and taken such care—*re Dhyw am ros*, I am tired of being careful."

He pressed his open mouth to her eyebrow, and then her temple. Every muscle in his body was trembling. She felt him pull one of the silver pins out of her hair. The delicate scrape of the pin's point against the scar over her left ear made her shiver with a desperation she'd never felt before.

"I have a pallet," she said. It was hard to breathe and hard to talk. "Over there. For the nights when I have to watch over something in one of the athanors. I swear to you, no one will come."

"I do not care if anyone comes." He pulled out another hairpin, and she felt the heavy braid of her hair uncoil. She put her head down against his chest, breathing his scent, feeling the pulse of his heart. It felt strange to have her hair loose. It was like that first day, in the rain, in the Piazza della Signoria. She wanted him, but she was—what? Afraid? Not really afraid, not of the act of them coming together. Afraid of what it meant. How it would change everything.

He stroked her head again, then took hold of her braid and tugged her head back so he could look into her eyes. It hurt a little, and at the same time it overwhelmed her with desire more intense than any of the dreams had ever been.

"*My a'th kar,*" he said. "My love, my love."

She wrapped her arms around his waist and held on to him tightly. Did he really taste of lemons, or was it just the scent of the lemon trees? Slow, so slow—she heard herself groaning very softly with the pleasure of kissing him, tasting him, breathing his breath. After a little while he lifted her, cradled her against his chest, and carried her to the shadowy corner where her pallet was, behind the trees in their tubs, where she couldn't see the cabinets or the alchemical paraphernalia. There he put her on her feet for a moment while he spread his cloak over the straw. His own fine dark blue cloak that smelled of his skin and his hair and the sea.

Ruan . . .

Without taking his mouth away from hers, he unlaced her bodice, untied her skirt and overskirt, stripped it all away, the fabric and stiffened stays and the embroidered lace. He left only the great moonstone on its silver chain. It seemed to tremble as her heart pounded, but of course that couldn't be true.

"Even if someone looks into the lemon-house, they will not see us here," he said. "Lie back."

She let herself fall back, drowning in her own senses—the way his scarred hands felt against her naked flesh, flesh no man had ever touched, flesh so responsive it frightened her a little. She could hear herself keening with helpless delight, hear his breathing, uneven with the effort of holding himself back. His skin tasted like salt and copper.

"We are breaking your vow," he said softly.

"No. I have been absolved."

He drew back. In the lemon-scented dimness she could just see the glint of surprise in his eyes. "When? How? Does the grand duke know?"

"No. Don't talk, Ruan. Please don't talk."

He said nothing more. She closed her eyes and gave herself up to him. He didn't rush her or press her. One touch at a time, one intimacy at a time, he learned her secrets and revealed his own to her. It was like the *sonnodolce* dreams and at the same time utterly unlike them, because real flesh had real heat and tastes and scents, more head-swimming than anything any drug could ever give. It had real shape and size and weight, real sweet silkiness, real ferocity, real overpowering completion.

It didn't hurt, not really, not the way the young women at the court were always whispering it did. It was strange, but it wasn't terrible at all. I've done this before, she thought—I've put two elements together, male and female, dark and bright, earth and moon, let them mingle and burn until the whole room blazed with heat.

After a little while he turned her face back to his and touched his lips gently to the spot just between her eyebrows. "The headaches? The voices? Do you still have them?"

"Not so much. Not at all, really, not anymore."

He kissed her eyelids, first one, then the other. "Mystery after mystery. I cannot tell you how much I have thought about you."

"*Sonnodolce* dreams?"

"Sometimes." He kissed the thin fine skin under her eyes, then the place where her scar was, under her hair above her left ear. "Sometimes just my own thoughts—memories—your hair, loose down your back as it was for your initiation. The way you looked at me, when you ground the *caput mortuum*, wearing the silk mask—you knew, without being told, how dangerous it was. In the grand duchess's little store-closet, in the dark. I wanted you so in that moment I was almost afraid to ask you to strike the light."

"Oh, Ruan. I've missed you so much. I knew—I knew when you came back—I knew."

"So did I." He ran his hands through the masses of her hair, twisting strands of it around his wrists. "You have such beautiful hair. There are copper ores deep in Wheal Loer that are just this color—brown, but so dark as to be almost black, with glints of blue and violet."

"It's just hair."

He laughed softly. "It is your hair, and that is what makes it unique. Like your eyes, which change from one moment to the next. One day I will cast your horoscope—do you know what your birth date is?"

"Yes—it was the twelfth day of November, in the year 1558. I found it in Babbo's book."

"Babbo's book?"

"I have a book I kept back, when I showed you the other books."

"I knew it," he said. "Will you show me?"

"Tomorrow. Or the day after. I want you to tell me everything," Chiara said. "I'll tell you everything too."

He helped her dress again, and braided up her hair as deftly as any maidservant. They stood on either side of the great table—I need to be apart from him now, Chiara thought, for a little while at least, so I can be my own separate self again. Even so, the connection between them was like the strange force she had observed between a lodestone and an iron nail, intrinsic and inescapable.

"Do you think the grand duke will guess?" she said.

"No. You may not see it—but you have seen him every day, or close to every day, for the past eight and a half months, have you not? When I saw him this morning, after being away for that long a time, I was struck by the change in him. He is so lost in his own pleasures now that other pleasures, other people, no longer exist for him."

"Then we are safe?"

"I would not go so far as that. He is still dangerous, and we will have to be careful. I will find a place for us, a secret place, where we can be together."

She nodded. "But for tonight we are safe here."

"We are safe."

"We can talk for a while, then," she said. "Begin at the beginning."

CHAPTER FORTY-FIVE

"There was a rebellion in Cornwall in 1549," he said. His voice sounded like Nonna's when she told one of her old fairy tales. "The year before I was born. It was over religion and the prayer book—the young English king of the time was a Protestant and wanted everyone to pray in English. The Cornish wanted their Catholic prayers in Latin, as they'd prayed them for a millennium."

"And they had a war over that?"

He smiled ruefully. "Many wars are fought for religion. The new prayer book started it, but it grew and grew and suddenly the rebels wanted to kill all the gentlemen as well. My father and mother—"

He stopped. The dark depths of sorrow and remembered cruelty welled up in his eyes, and he stepped back, as if he did not want the story to touch her. The increase of distance between them hurt, as if he were pulling her heart out of her breast.

"My father and mother were loyalists," he went on, "imprisoned by the rebels in terrible conditions. The English used mercenaries to put down the rebellion, and when it was over, they did not take time to sort out who had been loyal and who had not. Estates and land were given away wholesale to Englishmen, as rewards. One of them was given the gift of my father's estate—Milhyntall House and the mine, Wheal Loer."

Chiara wanted to put her arms around him and hold him forever, but she knew she dared not touch him now if she wanted to hear the rest of the story.

"His name was Andrew Lovell. He paid to have my father killed in cold blood. He hunted my poor mother like an animal, for all that she was heavy with child. With me. Andrew Lovell wanted no true heirs to Milhyntall born, to contest his ownership. If a miner's family had not taken her in and hidden her name and rank and concealed me as one of a dozen hungry and dirty miners' children, I would not stand here this moment."

"Oh, Ruan."

He made a gesture, short and hard. *Do not say you are sorry. I could not bear it.* After a moment he went on.

"I was six when she died. I was put to work in the mines with the other children. I would still be there if—"

He stopped.

"If what, Ruan?"

He picked up a glass retort and looked at it. His hand was shaking. Chiara huddled inside herself and waited for him to throw it.

He put it back on the table, very gently. "I have been using the grand duke's gold," he said, "and my own reputation, such as it may be, to convince the English crown to give Milhyntall back to me. The queen's advisor John Dee has spoken to her on my behalf."

Chiara wondered if he would ever tell her what had happened to get him out of the mines. She wondered if she wanted to know. She said, "Is John Dee an alchemist too?"

"Among other things. He is the one who sent me word here in Florence—I thought the matter had been arranged, but Queen Elizabeth's fancy turned to another petitioner. She is a great one to reward her favorite gentlemen with gifts, is Elizabeth Tudor."

"Apparently you arrived in time to change her mind."

"Only just."

"So you took it back from the Englishman? Your home?"

He walked across the room to the other window. Dusk's fading light made him nothing more than an outline, all darkness with none of the detail that made him Ruan. He said, "I rode up to Milhyntall House between its rows of lime trees, breathing their scent, thinking of how my father and his father and his grandfather before him must have played along the lane. It felt as if—as if it had been bred into my bones, to love those trees. To love the house. It is nothing special, just an old cobbled-together house built through the centuries in different styles, weathered by the sun and rain and sea winds."

"Home."

"Yes. Home. You have lived in your own home all your life. My home—my home was never mine, not until that day."

"What happened?"

"Andrew Lovell was waiting for me at the end of the lane with ten mounted men. I had the queen's commission and two dozen German mercenaries riding with me. It was hardly a fight—Lovell's men surrendered immediately, rather than give up their lives."

"But Andrew Lovell didn't?"

"No. He swore that Milhyntall was his, no matter what the queen said, and that he would die before he gave it up. The men on both sides stood back and left the fight to the two of us, sword to sword."

Chiara said nothing. She wondered about Andrew Lovell, about his family. He had lived at Milhyntall for what, twenty years? He would have thought it was his, and his son's after him.

"It was not a fair fight," Ruan said. His voice was hard. "I was twenty-five years younger, a handspan taller. But it was not a fair fight in the days after the rebellion, when my father faced three of Lovell's mercenary roughnecks and held them off just long enough for my mother to escape, before they killed him."

"You killed Andrew Lovell."

"I killed him. Milhyntall House and Wheal Loer are rightfully mine again, as they should have been from the moment of my father's death."

"I'm surprised you came back to Florence at all."

He turned at last and faced her.

"The grand duke owes me a death," he said. "And I would have come back for you, in any case. But as I wrote to you—I have achieved what I desired, and at the same time I have lost everything."

"What does that mean?" She held out her hands to him again. Did it frighten her, disgust her, that he had killed Andrew Lovell? That he had planned it, risked his own life for it, and ended it deliberately with a sword thrust through his enemy's heart?

No. It didn't. It was vengeance, quick and clean. She understood vengeance.

"It means that Andrew Lovell took everything valuable out of Milhyntall House," he said, "right down to the furniture and the paintings and the very tiles on the floors. He drove the miners to overwork the mine, without opening new shafts or adits—it is stripped down to the bare rock, and even the machinery has been sold. The miners are starving, the very families who protected my mother and me, and now they look to me to bring back their livelihood."

"But you—"

"I beggared myself to buy the English queen's influence. I need gold again, a great deal of it. However much I hate him, I need Francesco de' Medici and his obsession with the *Lapis Philosophorum*."

He leaned toward her and put his hands in hers. The sensation was as if the piece of iron had attached itself to the lodestone at last, with an almost audible sound like the click of a lock.

"Help me," he said. "The grand duke will pay anything if he thinks we can create the *Lapis Philosophorum* for him. It will be part of our revenge—to lead him to think he will have what he wants, and to deny it to him in the end."

"I've thought the same thing," she said.

"You have?"

"I've been making changes to certain substances in his laboratory, so his search would never, ever succeed."

That surprised him. "Ingenious," he said. "Dangerous, as ingenious things often are."

"There's a place where everything is pure. A secret laboratory. I know you don't believe the *Lapis Philosophorum* exists, Ruan, but I do, and I will find it—I will be an alchemist in my own right, greater than Perenelle Flamel. I will show Babbo he was wrong to—"

I will cut her throat, and her virgin's life-blood will bring him back. She should have died instead of Gian, and it is only right she be the one to bring him back.

She couldn't say it. Ruan couldn't say what had happened to take him out of the mines. Would they be able to tell each other all their secrets one day? Or not?

"You amaze me, *awen lymm*," he said. "You have faced so much and changed so much, in the time I have been away."

"The grand duchess's death changed everything."

He leaned over and kissed her mouth, a gentle kiss, comforting. "I am sorry," he said. "I know you loved her."

"I don't know what I felt. I admired her. She didn't deserve to die as she did, and Bianca Cappello doesn't deserve to be in her place."

"How did you end up in her household, of all places?"

"She tried to kill me."

"She *what*?"

She kissed him again. "It doesn't matter. I'll tell you later. Ruan, what will we do in the end? After you have the gold you need, and after we make them pay for what they have done? What will we do?"

"We will go home to Cornwall. We will be safe there."

Her heart seemed to shrink and grow cold within her breast. She said, "Your home, Ruan. Not mine."

He looked down at their hands, clasped together. After a long pause he said, "Can you make it your home, for my sake?"

"I don't know. I'm not a lady and I don't have a fine house or a mine or property. But this is where I was born, and my mother and grandmother and great-grandmother before me, all back through I don't know how many grandmothers. I'm a guildswoman of Florence, in my blood and bones, and I can't even think of what it would be like, a life somewhere else. It would be like going to live—in Trebizond, or at the bottom of the sea."

He withdrew his hands from hers. "What do we do, then?"

She swallowed. I won't cry, she thought, I won't cry, I won't cry. "I don't know."

A long time passed—she could have said the *Pater* and the *Credo* and half a dozen *Aves*. "We do not have to decide now," he said at last.

"No," Chiara said. "We don't."

He smiled at her. Her heart came to life again with a painful jerk. "Decision or no decision, I love you, Chiara. It is too dangerous for us to marry, because I do not trust any priest to hold his tongue. But I will vow myself to you, if you will vow yourself to me."

"I vow myself," she said. "Now and always."

She stood up and put her arms around him again. As she leaned against him she could feel the hardness of his flesh against her own softness. After a few moments she said, "Ruan, maybe we really will find the *Lapis Philoso-phorum*. Maybe it will—I don't know, give us a way to be in Florence and in Cornwall, at the same time."

He smiled. "I think not," he said. "There is no such thing, my dearest love. In the end, you will have to choose."

She leaned back and put one palm on his chest, over his heart. "One of us will have to choose," she said.

CHAPTER FORTY-SIX

An apartment of two rooms on the Via di Mezzo

15 AUGUST 1578

Chiara opened her eyes. Bells were ringing. She counted them. Nine—midafternoon, then. At first she didn't know where she was. Then Ruan shifted beside her and put his arm around her, and she remembered.

"In these rooms," Ruan had said, as he unlocked the door, "I am a petty nobleman from Siena, and you are the unhappy young wife of a very rich banker here in Florence. We are carrying on a clandestine affair, and find opportunities to meet when we can. The dyer's widow who rents out the rooms is transported by the romance of it all, and of course by the gold I have paid her. She swears she will keep our secret."

And then they had come into the bedroom, and—

"I fell asleep," Chiara said. She stretched out her arms and legs. "I don't know if I ever want to get up again."

Ruan smiled. "We have a little time still," he said. He lay one hand over her belly, caressing the smooth taut skin. "The more we meet here, the more careful we must be that you do not conceive."

"Nonna always says there are ways, but only wicked women use them."

He laughed. "Wicked women," he said. "And intelligent ones as well. There are secret formulas in the ancient books, which are probably safer than your Nonna's old wives' remedies."

"Give me the formulas, then. I will make them myself—they're for women to use, so they'll be more effective if they're created by a woman's hand."

She knew he didn't believe in such correspondences, and said it only to tease him. That was the most amazing thing of all. When they were in these rooms, they laughed. They teased each other. They acted as if they were ordinary people.

It was heaven.

He grinned, rolled out of the bed and pulled on his shirt.

"I am hungry," he said. "And the apricots will be juicier if peeled by a man's hand."

Chiara scrambled out of the bed as well and slipped her arms into her camicia. "You'll have to tie my laces when I put on my bodice and sleeves and skirt," she said. "But that can wait."

The other room was simply furnished with a chest and two chairs. The walls were whitewashed. On a table under the window rested a jug of wine, a fresh loaf of bread in a napkin, and a basket of apricots. The fruits were a rich golden color blushed with red, their velvety skin stretched to bursting with ripeness. Their scent filled the air, sweet with an elusive edge of bitterness.

He picked up one of the fruits, took out his dagger, and began to pare it. The velvety skin fell in spirals on the scrubbed wood of the table. Juice dripped in the slanting sunlight, gleaming and sweet.

"Tell me," he said, "about Donna Bianca trying to kill you."

The change from teasing to seriousness was so unexpected Chiara didn't know what to say at first. Then slowly, haltingly, she told him all of it—how Donna Bianca had been in the Palazzo Vecchio, how she had struck the grand duchess and meaning it or not sent her to her death. Later, how Donna Bianca had gloated about the secret marriage and threatened to silence her, Chiara, forever. And then how she had awakened in the heart of the labyrinth under the moon, with the *sonnodolce*-poisoned thorns glinting all around her. There was no reason to whisper with just the two of them in the room eating apricots, but saying the words aloud, all of them, for the first time—it frightened her. At the same time it was an agonizing relief, as if she had put one of Nonna's hot poultices on a deep, deep wound and drawn out all the poison.

When she was finished, Ruan said something in Cornish. It sounded ugly. Then, more gently, he said, "So the grand duke also knows you have been taking the *sonnodolce*."

"Yes. And there's something else—he told me you can't just stop taking it, once you've started. I've craved it, but I thought— I thought it was only—".

"Only what?"

"Well, only that it made me dream of you. And that it—I don't know, somehow it's made me better, stopped the headaches and falling-spells and demons' voices. It's good as well as bad. The grand duke promised I could have as much as I needed—"

She stopped.

Ruan laughed softly. "He would. Because as long as he is the only person with the formula, it binds you to him."

"I may be bound by the *sonnodolce*, but I'm not his creature."

Ruan leaned over the table and kissed her mouth, a long and lingering kiss that shivered through her nerves like a silver thread and tugged itself into an intricate knot in her belly. He tasted of apricots. "No," he said. "You are no one's creature, not even mine. You have learned a good deal of court politics, for the daughter and granddaughter of republicans."

"I haven't had much choice." She kissed him again, feeling the thread of sensation quiver. Then she leaned back. She had talked enough about herself. What Babbo had written in his book about the sacrifice? Her secret ambition to become an alchemist in her own right, like Perenelle Flamel? Those things could wait for another day. "Ruan, how did you end up in Austria? I want you to tell me."

He didn't move for a moment. Then he stood up and ran one hand over his left arm, just below the shoulder. There was a scar there, she knew—she had seen it. She had seen every inch of skin on his body, every mark and scar, and she wanted to know everything about them all.

"When I was only a boy, I worked in the mine. The Warnes hid me that way, among all their own children. They were the family who gave my mother and me shelter after my father was killed."

Chiara nodded.

"Andrew Lovell wanted Wheal Loer to produce more. He hired an Austrian metallurgist, a man named Konrad Pawer, to inspect the mine for new lodes."

"Konrad Pawer," she said. The name meant nothing to her.

"You have read Agricola's book, *De Re Metallica*."

"Some of it."

"Agricola is a Latinization of Pawer."

"Like you sometimes sign yourself Roannes Pencarianus."

He smiled. "Yes. Konrad Pawer was Agricola's nephew. He was a charlatan, but he traded on his uncle's famous name."

"How did he end up taking you to Austria?"

He rubbed the place on his arm again. "I wanted to learn," he said. "I was too young to realize he knew nothing."

"And then—"

"He took me to Austria with him," he said. "I was fourteen years old. Angry and terrified and wild with the wildness of a boy who is not quite a man. You have seen the scar on my arm—it is where Konrad Pawer's knife went through and pinned me to a table."

Chiara said nothing. The sweet juice of the apricot had turned bitter on her tongue.

"He shouted at me—swore he would not stand by while I surpassed him in the emperor's estimation. Swore he would kill me first. To him I would never be anything but a pretty Cornish mine-boy."

"So you were defending yourself."

"Even so, I killed him."

"And then—?"

"I made sure his body would never be found. I told the emperor he had gone off on a journey to the east, along the Silk Road to Cathay, in search of rare substances. A year later I was sent here, to Florence with the Archduchess Johanna's household."

Without a word she held out her own hands. After a moment he put his hands in hers. They were warm and perfectly clean, with the exception of some stickiness from the apricot juice.

"We've eaten all the apricots," she said.

He looked at her. After a moment he nodded. This was what it was, then, to love someone? This acceptance, whole and complete?

"And it is time to go back to the Palazzo Pitti," he said. "The children will be looking for you."

She stood up and went back into the bedroom for the rest of her clothing. He helped her put her bodice on, and laced it up, and tied her sleeves. She said, "Ruan?"

"Hmmm?"

"Your formulas? They won't keep me from conceiving, ever in my life, will they?"

"No, *awen lymm*."

"I'd like to have children of our own. I love taking care of the princesses and poor little Prince Filippo."

"We will have our own children one day, when we can marry and it is safe."

"As long as the grand duke is alive, it will never be safe."

He had re-braided her hair and was pinning it up again. She could feel the silver hairpins against her scalp, and she knew what he was thinking. *It will never be safe in Florence while the grand duke is alive, but far away in Cornwall, after he is dead—*

Don't say it, Ruan, she begged him silently. Please don't say it. Not now.

He didn't. He pressed his lips to the side of her throat, just under her ear, and said quietly, "The grand duke will not live forever."

CHAPTER FORTY-SEVEN

The Palazzo Pitti

29 MARCH 1582

"Prince Filippo's soul has fled to heaven," the priest said. "You must let him go, Serenissimo—clinging to his abandoned flesh is unseemly, as if you would deny the will of God."

Francesco de' Medici ran his hand lightly over his four-year-old son's forehead. It was still warm and moist with the sweat of his final throes. His curly hair—his mother's hair—lay in damp ringlets. His cheeks were flushed—true Medici blood under his delicate child's skin, mingled with Imperial blood by means of a legitimate union. So much joy, so much hope, centered on this single fragile boy child. What was under the high forehead, the bulging skull, that had brought all the joy and hope to nothing?

"A moment longer," Francesco said.

The priest bowed and withdrew. The physicians had long since fled. Seventeen days—seventeen *days*—the little prince had suffered with fever and convulsions. None of the physicians' medicines or remedies had helped. Even Magister Ruanno's compound had lost its efficacy. In the end Francesco had known it was hopeless, and that the physicians were probably doing more harm than good.

His son. His one true-born heir. And he was yoked to the barren Bianca now, so there would be no more. There was only Antonio, so rudely healthy that sometimes he had wanted to slice him in half like a Sicilian orange, squeeze out the juice of his health and give it to Filippino to drink.

If I had only known, he thought, *how much I would love him, and how much it would mean to me that he was a true son of my blood.*

"My lord."

Bianca's soft voice. Bianca's presence, warm and thick-fleshed and rustling with silk, her perfume overwhelming. He wanted the smells of the sickroom for a little longer, the purgings, the voidings, the last smells of his son.

She knelt beside him. "My lord, my heart aches for you, but we must let the serving-women into the room, to wash him and prepare him."

"The grand duchess washed the bodies of her own dead children. Can I do less?"

He waited for her to protest. *I am the grand duchess now.*

He had given her a sumptuous public wedding, once his year of mourning had passed, a spectacular coronation. She had made her procession through the streets of Florence in a chariot drawn by lions and heaped with red lilies—the lions being less than cooperative, but managed reasonably well by his menagerie-keepers. On either side had been drawn floats lined with silver, decorated with more lilies and filled with water, upon which white swans swam with graceful bad temper; because of her name, Bianca, she had chosen the white swan for her device.

He himself had anointed her with the holy oil and placed the coronet upon her head. The Venetians had suddenly discovered it in their hearts to forget her elopement, her theft of her father's jewels, her years of shame as his mistress—in fact they had hastened to create her as a true and particular daughter of the republic. Her brother and his minions had flocked to Florence for favors, and the courtiers had truckled to her.

Florence itself, the guilds, the people in the streets, and most particularly the women, hated her. Sometimes Francesco thought that he had come to hate her, too. He hated the Grand Duchess Bianca, at least. He loved his Bia still, but since Bianca's coronation he had seen less and less of her. He did not understand how the marriage—a few words by a priest, a few days of celebrations—could have changed things so completely. For twelve years she had been his mistress and he had been obsessed with making her his wife. The moment she had become his wife, everything had changed.

He hated the Grand Duchess Bianca, the white swan. That was the truth of the matter.

"Let me bring in the serving-women to help you," she said. Her voice was soft and gentle—Bia's voice. "They are waiting, with everything you will need."

"Is Soror Chiara with them?"

"No." Her grand duchess voice now. Silks rustled as she stood up and stepped away from him. "Why do you want her?"

"She has been in his household all his life, and she loved him. She loved his mother. She has been faithful, all this time—Giovanna cannot be here, but if there is anyone who can prepare him with a measure of his mother's love, it is Soror Chiara."

"I loved him, too," Bianca protested. "I will help you. Does he not deserve a grand duchess to wash him and wrap him in his shroud, and not a bookseller's daughter?"

The grand duke laid his son's body back on the bed, stood up, and swung his arm around in a single movement, from the gentlest of gentleness to the most violent brutality. His blow caught her across her mouth and made her stagger to one side. Once, such a blow would have knocked her down, but she had put on a great deal of flesh. His own increased flesh made him slower, and it was not as easy to strike her to the ground as it had been.

Once, such a blow would have excited him. The reddened skin around her mouth would have given him pleasure. This morning, he felt nothing.

She rubbed her hand across her mouth, her heavy brows slanting low over her eyes. She seemed to feel nothing either, other than the sting of the blow itself. "Very well, my lord," she said in a flat voice. "I will fetch your sorceress. Be it upon your own soul, to have her touch Prince Filippo's body."

She went out, trailing her overripe clouds of perfume. Francesco knelt by the bed again. A little while later, Soror Chiara came in.

"Serenissimo," she said. He heard fabric rustle, and he knew she was curtsying. Outside of the laboratory, she curtsied like any other court lady. At one time, she had done it awkwardly, like the guildswoman she was. Now she curtsied as if she was born to it.

Softly she said, "May I be of service to you, Serenissimo, and to the prince?"

He looked up at her. Her expression changed for the space of a breath—

widened eyes, parted lips, surprise and uncertainty to see him alone, un-washed and disheveled. That was one thing she had never learned in the—how many years had it been? Since just before his father's death, so eight years—she had been connected to the court. She could not always keep her face from showing her feelings.

Everything else about her was different. Her character, which at first had been barely suggested in her features, had been finished and polished and refined by adulthood and sorrow. She said very little, but her eyes spoke for her, clear and changeable. She wore the moonstone between her breasts every day—he could see the thin silver chain against the smooth skin of her neck. She took the *sonnodolce*. She had secrets and unlike any other woman he had ever known, she never spoke of them. *Qui vult secreta scire, secreta secrete sciat custodire,* she had shouted out to him on the day she had come to him with her silver descensory. *Whosoever would know secrets, let him know how to keep secret things secretly.* Sometimes he won-dered if his *soror mystica*, chosen and initiated on a whim, had not become a greater alchemist than he himself would ever be.

"I would have you help me bathe him. I have instructed the physicians to open his body, particularly his head. I wish to know—"

His voice failed him. She said nothing, but only looked at him with such sadness in her eyes.

"I wish to know what it is that has made him this way, and also to be certain that his death was—not unnatural."

"I will help you, Serenissimo." She stepped to the door and gestured to the serving-women waiting outside. Again he was struck by the authority she had taken to herself. The women brought in ewers of hot water, a basin, washing-cloths and towels and fresh sheets, and a clean folded nightshirt. Although not really a nightshirt. A shroud. Murmuring among them-selves, they went out.

"If you will lift the prince, please, Serenissimo, I will arrange the bed."

He gathered his dead son up into his arms. She began to remove the soiled sheets from the bed and lay out fresh ones. She did not flinch from the terrible sights and smells of death, of seventeen days of sickness, and God be thanked, she wore no perfume of her own. She poured water into the basin, with as much exquisite care as if she were in the laboratory. It was faintly scented, some herb, astringent and not sweet.

"Let us wash the prince now, Magister Francesco," she said.

It gave him a way to escape—to stop being Francesco de' Medici, Grand Duke of Tuscany, whose only true son was dead. Magister Francesco the alchemist, adept in the arts of the laboratory, was above such things as sons by the way of the flesh.

"I have no heir," he said. He untied the shirt the little prince was wearing and slipped it over his head. His body was so thin, his little limbs so frail. I could put my thumb and first finger around his arm, he thought. Or perhaps he said it aloud.

"There is Cardinal Prince Ferdinando," she said. She dipped a cloth into the basin, twisted it to wring out most of the water, and handed it to him. Then she dipped another cloth for herself. As gently as if the little prince were still alive, she began to wash his body. "And Prince Pietro as well."

"I will never allow the crown to go to either one of my brothers." Francesco washed his son's dead face. He was careful to leave the marks of the Holy Viaticum on his eyelids and lips and ears. "I will legitimate Don Antonio, before God and man. He will become the prince."

She took another towel, a dry one. "The people will not accept him," she said. There was an edge to her words, like a dagger sliding between his ribs to satisfy a *vendetta*. But of course that was only his imagination. His own sins were making him hear things that were not there.

"The crown is mine," he said. "It will go to Prince Antonio. I will compel the people to accept him."

"And your brothers?"

She handed him the clean nightshirt. He slipped it over Filippino's head and drew it down to cover his body, his arms and legs, all the way to his feet. His toes were so perfect and even. Why could he not have had crooked toes and a perfect head?

"Ferdinando is a prince of the church. He has no authority in secular matters—he will remain in Rome and continue his intrigues there. Perhaps he will be pope one day."

She said nothing to that. Did she believe it? He did not really believe it but he repeated it to himself over and over, trying to convince himself. Ferdinando will remain a cardinal. Ferdinando will accept Antonio's right of succession. Ferdinando is my younger brother and he will do as I wish.

"Prince Pietro?" she said at last.

Pietro, who had murdered his beautiful young cousin-wife Dianora. Pietro, spendthrift and rake, who had left Florence and never come back, as if there were ghosts in the very streets that cried for revenge.

"Pietro is not suitable."

She did not persist, but handed him a single napkin, snowy-white. He unfolded it and very gently laid it over his son's face.

"*De profundis clamavi ad te, Domine,*" he recited. He remembered saying the psalm over his father's body, for no reason other than to appear pious to the outside world. This time, every word felt as if it was tearing out a piece of his heart.

"*Domine, exaudi vocem meam. Fiant aures tuae intendentes.*" Soror Chiara's voice joined his. "*In vocem deprecationis meae. Si iniquitates observaveris, Domine, Domine, quis sustinebit?*"

From the depths, I have cried out to you, O Lord. Lord, hear my voice. Let your ears be attentive to the voice of my supplication. If you, Lord, were to mark iniquities, who, O Lord, shall stand?

Her voice was clear and intense.

If you were to mark iniquities, who shall stand?

CHAPTER FORTY-EIGHT

The bookshop of Giacinto Garzi,
formerly the bookshop of Carlo Nerini

THE NEXT DAY

The last stage—*rubedo*, the reddening—of the *Lapis Philosophorum* was sealed inside the athanor. The fire was as low as Chiara could keep it. On the table beside the athanor she had pinned a piece of parchment with a record of the fuel added to the fire and the times and directions in which the athanor had been turned. Under that there was a chart of the days and the phases of the moon. Days were neatly checked off—twenty-four of them. In three more days, if all went well, the *Lapis Philosophorum* would be hers at last.

Footsteps. Chiara looked up, expecting Ruan. Instead it was Giacinto Garzi, Lucia's young husband from Pistoia, too tall for the narrow walled steps and too thin to fill out his quilted *farsetto*, the gown and hose of a prosperous bookseller. Lucia's dowry—paid for with the grand duke's gold, although no one else but Nonna knew that—and Cinto's election to a place in the guild on the day after their wedding, had rather gone to his head. The secret room in the cellar, kept under lock and key by his wife's unmarried older sister, was an affront to his position.

Or so Lucia was egging him on to believe. Chiara was sure as sure that Lucia was behind it all.

"Cinto," she said. "How did you get a key to the cellar?"

"I took it from your Nonna's ring, while she slept. The shop is mine now, and all the keys should be mine as well."

Lucia's words, coming from his lips.

"No," Chiara said. "The cellar is mine alone. Give me the key."

"I won't. The shop belongs to me now—"

"—and you agreed, upon marrying Signorina Chiara's sister and pocketing her dowry, that the cellar would not be considered part of the shop." It was Ruan, coming down behind him. "Give Signorina Chiara the key, if you please."

The boy's lower lip thrust out, but he had always been afraid of Ruan, older and stronger, the grand duke's own English alchemist with his whip looped over his shoulder and his hands scarred by the good God only knew what magic and sin. He threw the key to the floor at Chiara's feet.

"Get out of my way, then, *straniero*," he said. "Have your secret room and your sorceries."

Ruan stood aside with a mocking gesture, and the boy went back up the steps. His guildsman's gown trailed behind him like a Carnival costume made for a larger man. With his own key Ruan locked the door again, behind him.

"Maybe we should close off that door permanently and open the secret passage again," Chiara said. She bent down and picked up the key from the floor. "The last thing we need is Cinto meddling down here. Ruan, listen— the little prince is dead."

He came down the rest of the stairs, uncoiled the whip and laid it aside, and put his arms around her. She lifted up her mouth for his kiss, careless and comfortable as a wife. Well, for all practical purposes she was his wife. "The rumors are already out in the streets," he said. "I am sorry, my heart. Were you there?"

"No, not when he died, but just afterward. The grand duke called for me to help lay out his poor little body."

"He knows you love all the children."

"The girls are heartbroken. I fear for Anna—she is not strong to begin with. She had a special bond with Filippino, I think, because they were both in fragile health."

"Poor little boy. May he rest at last in his mother's arms." Ruan crossed himself. Chiara did the same. Then she went over to the table and looked at the athanor again. The heat was at a perfect level. The athanor was solid stone and couldn't possibly be pulsing gently, but even so it looked as if it was.

"Three more days," she said. "It has been hard to keep watch over it properly, with Filippino's lying-in-state and entombment, and the girls needing me."

Ruan stepped over to the table and looked at the parchment with her calculations. "And if this attempt fails," he said, "will you want to wait longer, and try again?"

There was an edge to his voice. It seemed as if there had been an edge to his voice for a long time.

"I couldn't leave the little prince," she said. "He was so sick."

"And before that, it was Nonna's blindness. Before that, Lucia's wedding. Before that, your first attempt at the *Lapis Philosophorum*. You have made excuse after excuse for over three years, and I have come to the end of my patience."

She looked at him. He looked worn and tired. With a shock she realized there were a few silver threads in the coppery-dark thickness of his hair. He was only just back from another of his trips to the mine at Bottino—he had traveled there a dozen times in the past three and a half years, each time spending weeks attending to the tasks the grand duke had set him. Each time she had been afraid he would never come back, but each time he did.

They had attempted the *magnum opus* twice, in the first year after Ruan's return, and both times it had failed. Not surprising, considering the fact that she'd adulterated the grand duke's alchemical elements with her own hands. To her surprise, though, the grand duke had withdrawn into a fit of dark petulance and turned his attention to other things—to the automata in the gardens at the Villa di Pratolino, to the workshops of the court artists and artisans at the Uffizi, to his collection of curiosities in the hidden cabinets of his golden studiolo. It was as if he'd achieved what he wanted in Ruan's return and submission—apparent submission—and didn't care anymore.

Well, he'd achieved what he wanted in his marriage to Donna Bianca, and he didn't seem to care about her anymore, either.

In between the trips to Bottino, she and Ruan had snatched moments—too short, too few—of happiness. Every day it had seemed as if something would happen, and yet somehow every day had slipped away. How had three and a half years passed?

"I'm sorry," she said. "I'm sorry. I don't know what else to say."

"You must choose."

"Now?"

"Now. At the end of your three days, and no later. Jago Warne has Wheal Loer running again, and Milhyntall House is in good enough repair for us to live there. I have gold enough, which I have transferred to my London bankers today. Chiara, it is time to go."

"I need the *sonnodolce*," she said.

"I will force the grand duke to give up the formula before I kill him."

"If you will just give me time to create the *Lapis Philosophorum*, I won't need any more *sonnodolce* to keep back the voices and the headaches. It will heal me, completely and forever."

He bent his head and kissed the side of her throat. She felt tension in his muscles, as if he was resisting her at the same time that he was kissing her. "Better to have the formula, just in case."

"I wish—" She tilted her head back, her eyes closing, letting the pleasure of his mouth on her skin pulse through her, matching the deep half-imagined contractions of the athanor. "Oh, Ruan, I wish—"

"Wish what?" He ran his hands over her shoulders and down her arms. The tension had dissolved away. They had become so accustomed to each other that the slightest touch, the slightest change of body temperature or position, had meaning.

"That you would give up your determination to kill the grand duke. Leave it to the cardinal. Now that the little prince is dead, the grand duke is determined to make Don Antonio his heir, and the cardinal will never allow that to happen."

He stepped back. As warm as the cellar was, it made her feel cold all of a sudden when his body was not close behind hers.

"Have you forgotten Isabella's death? Forgotten how he allowed her body to be abused? Forgotten Dianora's death as well?"

"No. But—"

"And the grand duchess? Have you forgotten how he shamed her, and in the end how his mistress was the instrument of her death? Have you forgotten the tales of how he got his changeling brat, with who knows how many people dead to conceal the plot?"

"No. Ruan—"

"Have you forgotten the Pucci conspiracy and the months, the years of terror that came after it? Have you forgotten your own Nonna, escaping from Florence by the skin of her teeth?"

"No!" She turned to face him, tears starting from her eyes. "I haven't forgotten and I'll never forget. How can you think that? The grand duke will pay for his sins—he'll burn in hell forever with Bianca Cappello beside him, and he'll pay in this world too, see if he doesn't. The cardinal—"

"I do not care what the cardinal intends. I have sworn to kill Francesco de' Medici with my own hands, and I will keep my promise."

He stepped back again, farther away from her. The shadows gathered around his face, giving his eyes their old look of bottomless black sadness. The sound of the fire hissing inside the athanor, faint as it was, seemed to fill the cellar.

"Ruan, it has been so long," she whispered. "I'm different, you're different. I'm just—I'm afraid for you."

"Afraid for me?" His voice became harder. "I will tell you just how easy it will be. He considers himself to be safe at the Villa di Pratolino—he and Donna Bianca go about with only a guard or two, or no guards at all. I can have them both dead in bed and be gone long before their bodies are discovered."

She stared at him open-mouthed.

"You think I have not planned it, over and over, while I have been waiting for you to make your choice? It has been three years and more, Chiara. And if you fear for my immortal soul, well, there is already blood enough on my hands."

He held out his hands, ridged with the scars of his childhood in the mines. The flickering light of the lanterns played over his palms. There was no blood on his hands, despite his confessions. Only hardened, flexible skin that had stroked over her own skin, over every secret place of her. Only warm skin that had caressed and coaxed her to heights of pleasure she never knew existed.

She couldn't think of anything to say.

He stepped closer and put his hands on her shoulders again. He waited. For what? Did he expect her to shudder with hatred and push him away? Did she want to push him away? Blood on his hands there was, and more blood there would be, the grand duke's blood unless the cardinal got to him first. Even so—even so, saints and angels, she loved him so much.

Remember, Babbo's voice whispered. She hadn't heard it in so long, and it wasn't a demon's voice anymore, just Babbo's voice, sad and faint. *Remember. You yourself swore to take vengeance on Bianca Cappello, for her part in the grand duchess's death. You are not so different from him.*

"We are what we are," Ruan said. He put his hands under her arms and lifted her, swung her around to press her against the rough stone of the cellar's wall. "Tell me to stop if you can."

"Never," she gasped. She clung to his shoulders, sinking her nails into the workman's leather of his doublet. He pulled up her skirts as if she was a woman of the streets, in a hidden alleyway. She didn't care. "If we burn in hell, we'll burn together. Ahhh—"

She threw back her head and cried out with sensation as he thrust himself into her. Her body shuddered with ecstasy. He bent his head and sank his teeth into her neck as he jolted her hard against the wall, over and over, every breath hoarse with effort. She screamed, and screamed again.

"Ruan. Ruan. Holy Mother of God, Nonna and Lucia will think you're killing me."

"They know what I am doing to you."

"Cinto, then."

"If he so much as rattles the lock on the door I'll whip him through the streets."

He lifted her higher. The stone wall scraped her back, and she felt one of her sleeves tear away from the bodice of her gown. It didn't matter. Nothing mattered. She wrapped her legs around his waist and gave herself up to him.

"My a'th kar," he said, soft and harsh, deep in his throat. "Always and forever."

The athanor smoldered on the table, making its faint hissing sound. She heard it, and then she didn't hear it anymore.

"I wish I could be perfect for you," he said after a while, when the first frantic violence had passed and they were moving together, gently and sweetly as two waves curling around each other to make a whirlpool, slow and deep in the brine of the ocean. "Without flaw, sinless and good. But I never was. Even as a child, I never was."

"I know."

"I will wait, for three days and no more. I will speak to the cardinal if

I can—surely he will return to Florence to console his brother upon this terrible loss. But I cannot promise you, Chiara, that I will not take my vengeance with my own hands. I have waited for it too long."

"I know. I understand."

"I have waited for you, too."

"You have me."

"No. Not completely."

She closed her eyes and imagined herself leaving Florence. Oh, the scent of the Arno, the marketplaces on the bridges, bright with color, noisome with fish and fruit, loud with bargaining and the crying of wares. The tall tall bell tower of the Palazzo Vecchio, and the dome of the Basilica, rose-red in the sunrise and frescoed inside with the Last Judgment in a hundred thousand different colors. The streets and piazzas, each one unique. The shop with its secrets and sorrows. Nonna, blind now and frail, wishing every day that her Lord would come for her. Lucia and Mattea, yes, even Lucia and Mattea, her sisters, her blood.

All of it, all of them, on one side of the scale.

On the other side, Ruan.

What would she choose?

"We are what we are," Chiara said softly, her lips against his throat. "I wouldn't want it to be different."

CHAPTER FORTY-NINE

*The bookshop of Giacinto Garzi,
formerly the bookshop of Carlo Nerini*

TWO DAYS LATER

Rostig and Seiden—Nonna called them Ruggi and Seta, their names in Italian, but Chiara could never think of them by anything but the names the grand duchess had given them—lay curled together in the patch of morning sunlight streaming through the shop's front door. She crouched down for a moment and stroked Rostig's sun-warmed fur. They were white-faced and ancient, both of them, and Seiden was as blind as Nonna was, but Nonna took good care of them, berating Cinto fiercely every time he said dogs had no business being in a well-run shop. And they were always together. They had each other.

This is Rostig. Rust-red, in your language, for the color of his head and ears. His mate is Seiden, silky one.

The grand duchess's voice, the day of old Duke Cosimo's funeral. Not a demon-voice, just a memory, bittersweet. That had been the day she herself had first met both the grand duchess and her hounds. Isabella had been there too, weeping for her father. Dianora, whispering about her lovers. Eight years ago. Saints and angels, how much had happened since then? And yet here were Rostig and Seiden. They were all that was left of that day.

Rostig opened his dark eyes and looked at her sleepily. He moved one paw, pushing her hand to continue petting him. She did. He sighed, contented, and closed his eyes again.

"I'm glad you're here, Chiara." It was Mattea, who was standing behind the counter. In the past year she had shot up a handsbreadth in height, grown womanly curves, and been betrothed to Simone di Jacopo, a wool-dyer's son who lived on the Via dei Calzaiuoli near the guildhall of the Arte della Lana. "I must run to the market to buy a fish for our dinner. Will you watch the shop?"

"Where's Cinto?"

"I don't know. He and Nonna were quarreling, and I think he went down into the cellar. Lucia and Nonna—"

I think he went down into the cellar.

"Go get your fish," Chiara said. "I'll manage things here."

She walked through into the kitchen. Nonna was standing by the window, her hands bundled up in her apron, outrage and misery and humiliation—humiliation? why?—in every line of her body. The cloudy whiteness had almost completely blotted out the sharpness of her eyes. Lucia faced her, holding a half-peeled onion in one hand and a knife in the other.

"What are you doing, Lucia?" Chiara said sharply. "Where's Cinto?"

"It's none of your business," Lucia said. "None of it—what I'm doing, or what Cinto's doing. The shop is ours now, all of it, from the attics to the cellars. I'll cook what I please for dinner, and Cinto will go where he pleases in his own shop. Go back to your palaces, Chiara, and leave us alone."

"Nonna? What's the matter?"

Slowly Nonna drew her hands out of the folds of her apron. Her right wrist was twisted at an unnatural angle. Already bruising and swelling were beginning to come up.

"He took the keys away from me," she said. "He went down into the cellar. Chiara, I couldn't stop him. Forgive me."

He went down into the cellar.

And there was only one day left. One day.

"Che infido sdraiato stronzo," Chiara said under her breath. "Nonna, I'm sorry for swearing. I'll fetch you the grand duke's own physician to put your wrist right, and I promise you he'll never touch you again. I promise."

She picked up Nonna's broom—that long-ago night, Pierino Ridolfi doubling over with a grunt of pain as Nonna rammed her broomstick into his belly, where was Pierino Ridolfi now?—and started down into the cellar. Behind her she heard Lucia shouting, "He'll touch whoever he pleases, and don't you dare call him such names! It's our shop now!"

The lanterns in the cellar were lighted. It smelled of damp earth and wood, acids and alkalis, metals and powdered minerals and hot stone. Chiara looked over the wall and saw before anything else Babbo's book spread out on the table. Then she saw Giacinto Garzi with his back to her. He might have been a collection of sticks in a fine robe. He should spend less time picking out expensive clothes and letting Nonna and the girls wait on him, she thought, and more time doing the heavy work of the shop. She tightened her grip on the broomstick.

"Cinto," she said.

He turned around.

He'd opened the athanor and taken the nascent *Lapis Philosophorum* from it with nothing more than his bare hands. It was melting into his flesh. For one endless moment they both looked into the heart of the universe. Then the cellar disappeared in a sheet of flame.

PART V

Chiara

The Red Lily Crown

CHAPTER FIFTY

*The Monastery of the Santissima Annunziata,
called Le Murate*

15 SEPTEMBER 1582

Chiara stretched a coarse cloth over the tub of laundry and tied it down to each of the six rings around the rim. Her hands were red and chapped and her knuckles were swollen. She scooped wood-ash from a basket and spread it over the cloth. Dipped up a panful of boiling water from the cauldron. Poured the water over the ashes. The water would leach out the lye, and the lye would soak through the heavy linens and burn out the stains and then—

"Chiara."

She jumped. She dropped the dipper.

It was only Donna Jimena. She wore the white wimple and veil and plain dark tunic of the lay sisters of Le Murate, but Chiara had never quite managed to think of her as Suor Jimena. Whatever she was called, she was pretty much the only person who ever talked to Chiara. The nuns kept silence, and the other lay sisters and servants made signs against the evil eye when they passed near.

"Suor Maddalena told me you would not eat or say your prayers this morning," Donna Jimena said.

Sick all the time, that one, the sisters whispered to each other, not caring if Chiara heard them or not. Possessed, some of them claimed.

After a moment, she said, "Yes. I think—I remembered—some things."

Donna Jimena's poor wrinkled face crumpled together all the more with sadness and apprehension. "Leave the laundry for now," she said. "Let us walk in the cloister."

Chiara untied her laundry-apron and took it off. She didn't wear a habit or a veil herself, just an old wool gown, patched in a dozen places, with an apron and a coif over what was left of her hair. She didn't remember her hair being cut but Donna Jimena had told her—they'd cropped it off in the first days she was at Le Murate because they hadn't been able to make her talk sense, and everyone knew it cured madness to cut the hair close to the scalp and bind the head with poultices of valerian leaves.

The valerian hadn't helped. Her hair had grown back but it wasn't silky and dark anymore—*so dark as to be almost black, with glints of blue and violet*, someone had said once, in another life. Now it felt like an animal's pelt, matted and sticky, short and straight and coarse. There was a raised half-moon shape over her left ear. When she touched it, her head throbbed with pain.

She walked out into the small cloister with Donna Jimena. The air was clean and cool. It was good to be outside. For a while they simply walked, with Vivi pacing beside them. Vivi was always with her. How Vivi had come to be at the monastery, and Rostig and Seiden who were so old and frail and cosseted by the affection-starved nuns—that was part of what she had remembered.

"It's nice out here," she said. "I don't walk in the cloister very often."

"The fresh air is good for you, whatever the infirmarians might say about evil humors. Chiara, my dear, if you have remembered— Tell me. I will tell you what I know, if you are able to listen."

"I remember," Chiara began. Then her thoughts cut off. They did that sometimes. She'd be thinking something or saying something and everything would just stop. She shook her head and said again, "I remember."

Donna Jimena said nothing. They reached the end of the cloister walk. An apricot tree was espaliered against the old stone of the wall. It was heavy with fruit, red-blushed golden apricots, their scent sweet with a faint green edge of bitterness.

The velvety skin of an apricot falling in spirals on the scrubbed wood of a table. Juice dripping in slanting sunlight, gleaming and sweet.

Ruan.

She drew in her breath and clenched her fists and said, "I remember Ruan."

There. The word had been said.

"Magister Ruanno dell' Inghilterra," Donna Jimena said gently. "He brought you here, my dear—is that what you remember?"

"A little. I remember the dogs, Vivi and Rostig and Seiden. He brought the dogs."

"He did."

"I remember screaming. My head hurting."

"And before that?"

"I don't know."

Donna Jimena took a deep breath and closed her eyes for a moment. Then she said, "There was a great blast like cannon fire that utterly destroyed your brother-in-law's bookshop. Magister Ruanno said it was as if someone had fired a bombard from the cellar straight up into the upper floors of the building. The front of the shop was untouched, and the two old dogs not even scratched."

Suddenly Chiara remembered Cinto—who was Cinto?—with a light in his hands.

"I saw it," she said.

"Yes. You were apparently thrown backward by the force of the blast. Magister Ruanno said it was the only thing that could explain how you survived, and that he had seen such things happen to gunners sometimes."

"I remember a light. I remember Cinto. Who is Cinto?"

"Cinto was your brother-in-law," Donna Jimena said gently. "Giacinto Garzi. He was married to your sister Lucia."

"Lucia," Chiara said. The shape of the name on her lips and tongue was familiar. "I remember her shouting. Shouting at me, and at Nonna—"

She stopped.

Don't be sad, nipotina. Nonna's voice. Not like the demons' voices. It was kind. There was love and even laughter in it. *It was Cinto's fault, not yours. I was standing there, listening to Lucia shriek at you and wishing I had two good wrists to shake her, and then all of a sudden I just wasn't in my body any longer. My wrist didn't hurt anymore, and none of my joints ached, and I could see. I could see like a young girl again.*

Nonna.

Nonna was—

Nonna was dead.

Suddenly Chiara's knees wouldn't hold her anymore. She collapsed to the graveled pathway and put her face down in her arms and wept.

"Oh, my dear, my dear," Donna Jimena said. "I knew this day would have to come and how hard it would be for you. Yes, they are all gone, Cinto and Lucia and your Nonna. Your family's shop is gone, and everything in it. Your younger sister Mattea—her betrothed's family broke off the arrangement because of all the talk, and she has gone to live in Pistoia."

Chiara choked into her folded arms in her anguish. Vivi pressed close, making a soft whining sound in her throat.

After a while there were no more tears. Chiara's eyes were swollen and her throat was raw. She straightened and wiped her nose on her sleeve like a child.

"Ruan?" she whispered. "Can I see him? It feels like it's been forever since—since I came here."

"Five and a half months, since the first day of April. Chiara, when he brought you here, you and the dogs, he gave the nuns gold to take care of you. He came back every day for three days."

He came back for three days.

Five and a half months had passed.

"So after three days he went away," she said. Her chest ached, as if her whole body was breaking apart. "He went home—home to—to Cornwall. A labyrinth house and a moon mine."

"No," Donna Jimena said. "I saw his face when he carried you into the infirmary, Chiara. He loved you, and if he never came back, it can only be because he is dead."

Which was worse? For him to be dead, or for him to have abandoned her?

"Dead how? Why?"

"I do not know, but— How much do you remember about the grand duke? The Medici?"

"I remember—" She stopped. Her head felt as if it was—well, what? A dry, cracked garden patch that had suddenly been watered and stirred up with a sharp rake. Inside the soil, seeds were cracking open and pushing their leaves and stems up into the light.

Poison stems. Poison flowers.

Where had she seen poison flowers?

"I remember the taste of hot spiced wine," she said slowly. "A moonstone the size of an egg, on a silver chain. A necklace, rubies and pearls, and riding a horse alone at night. A book—my Babbo wrote things in the back, in his own handwriting. A laboratory in a lemon-house—"

So many pictures crowded her mind so quickly she couldn't keep track of them. They overwhelmed her. Some of them were beautiful. Some of them were terrible.

"The grand duke," she said, in a voice that didn't sound like her own. "Yes, I remember him. And Ruan—"

Ruan lying on the floor at the grand duke's feet. His blood spreading over the polished marble like molten metal, copper and iron, metals from the heart of the earth.

Was that real? Or had it been a dream?

"After the three days, one of the grand duke's physicians came instead. It was as if he knew Magister Ruanno would not come back."

Ruan had wanted to kill the grand duke. Had he tried? Had he failed?

"The grand duke's physician brought the medicine," Donna Jimena said. "He instructed me—"

"The medicine?"

"The clear liquid I put on your skin on Sundays after Mass. He said it was very strong, and that I should put one drop on your skin, no more, once every seven days. I have done it every week, after those first three days—well, you know that."

One drop, every seven days after taking the Sacrament at Mass, never twice on exactly the same spot of naked skin.

It was one of the poison-flower thoughts. A demon whispered *sonnodolce*, sibilant as a snake.

One cannot simply start and stop taking the sonnodolce *at will. By continuing to take it, you will be bound more closely to me, and all the more willing to do whatever I ask of you.*

Her thoughts stopped. Her throat burned with hatred. Did she hate the grand duke? Why?

"Yes, the grand duke himself. Chiara, listen to me. You are a prisoner here at Le Murate. The grand duke's prisoner."

"Why?"

"It is something to do with what happened at the bookshop. There was no natural explanation for it, and the grand duke believes you were practicing alchemy."

Chiara said nothing.

"I have not questioned it, Chiara—I have been so happy to have you here and take care of you. You are all I have of the old days, you and Vivi, Rostig and Seiden." Her faded eyes filled with tears. "All I have of my dear Isabella."

Isabella. Another seed cracked and another tall spindly plant reached for the light. Isabella de' Medici, the grand duke's sister, in a sky-blue velvet night-gown. Isabella, dead, murdered—

Chiara closed her left fist. The two crooked fingers. That was why she had the two crooked fingers. That was why she hated the grand duke.

Why did he keep her here, a prisoner of the *sonnodolce* as much as the monastery walls? What did he want from her? Had he killed Ruan, or had Ruan gone away?

And Nonna was dead.

It was all too much. She felt sick and dizzy. She pushed herself to her feet and said, "I don't want to remember any more."

Donna Jimena put her arms around her and held her close. "You do not have to. You do not ever have to remember it all. You will be safest if you do not—the grand duke will leave you alone, and I will take care of you."

You will be safest. The grand duke will leave you alone.

Had there been a time when she had lied and intrigued and contrived her way through the grand duke's court, the palaces and laboratories and gardens, the great entertainments and secret alchemical transmutations? Was there a reason why the grand duke was keeping her a prisoner here at Le Murate and not throwing her in an oubliette or having her killed?

There had to be a reason.

If she could remember it, she would have one small scrap of power. If she could remember it, and keep the grand duke from knowing she remembered it, perhaps she could—

Could what?

What did she want? To be free? Free to do what?

She took hold of Donna Jimena's shoulders and pushed herself back, as gently as she could. "I don't want to remember any more today," she said. "But I will remember, in a week or a month or a year, or in all my life if it takes that long. One day, when I'm strong enough, I'll remember everything."

CHAPTER FIFTY-ONE

The Monastery of the Santissima Annunziata, called Le Murate

19 DECEMBER 1584

"The grand duchess is here," the portress said. She was flushed and her eyes were bright with self-importance. "The grand duchess her very self, and she demands to speak with you."

Chiara's first thought was *but the grand duchess is dead.*

From the Grand Duchess Giovanna her mind jumped to Rostig and Seiden, who had slipped away quietly within a day of one another in the warm days of high summer. Safe with their mistress now, who had loved them so dearly. The old dogs led her thoughts to the shop, and Nonna—oh, Nonna—and Ruan. From there she worked her way back to the rooms on the Via di Mezzo and the lemon-house at the Villa di Pratolino, and at last she reached Bianca Cappello.

"She can demand all she wants." Chiara turned back to folding clean tunics. It was so cold in the laundry she could see her breath when she spoke. Vivi had made herself a warm nest in a basket of linens waiting to be washed. The head laundress hated it when she did that, and Vivi had learned to do it only when Chiara was alone in the laundry. "I won't go."

The portress went away. After a few minutes she came back with two of the lay sisters, the biggest and strongest.

"The grand duchess demands to speak with you," she repeated. "If you do not come, you will be taken."

Chiara finished folding the last tunic. Refusing to go wasn't worth being dragged off like a sack of meal. She shrugged and followed the por-tress. She had never been to the parlors, not in the whole—two years? three years?—she'd been at Le Murate. Time ran together and blurred when the days were all the same, with only the Sundays and the *sonnodolce* to look forward to. The grand duke's physician brought a new bottle from time to time, and at first he'd asked questions, sharp ones, about alchemy and the *Lapis Philosophorum*. The last time, though, there'd been no questions, as if suddenly the grand duke didn't care anymore.

Or couldn't care anymore.

She remembered almost everything now, from the rainy morning she'd offered the grand duke Babbo's silver descensory, to the moment she'd stepped down the first few steps into the bookshop's cellar and seen Cinto with the heart of the universe in his hands. She hadn't told anybody, not even dear Donna Jimena, that she'd remembered so much.

Vivi jumped out of her warm pile of laundry and followed them down the flagged corridor, her claws clicking on the stone.

In the parlor, Bianca Cappello sat upright in a cushioned, gilded chair, with another cushion for her embroidered slippers to rest upon. Fires burned in two braziers, giving warmth and light. An iron grille separated her from the single low, roughly made bench on the nuns' bare, cold side of the parlor.

She was dressed in white-and-gold satin, and wrapped up warmly in a mantle of green velvet quilted with gold thread and embroidered with pearls. It was lined with some kind of glossy dark fur and clasped with jeweled gold animals' heads. Her hair was red, unnaturally bright, bound up with more pearls and ruby clips worked in the shape of red lilies.

Chiara didn't sit down. She didn't say a word. Vivi sat beside her.

"How gaunt and worn you look, Mona Chiara," the grand duchess said. She sounded pleased about it. "Ten years older, at least. I would not have known you, if it were not for your little hound."

Chiara said, "What do you want?"

"No curtsy? No Serenissima? I have been told you lost your reason after your injuries—do you even know who I am?"

"I know who you are."

"Do you know why I am here?"

Chiara said nothing.

"Well, then," the grand duchess said, leaning back in her chair and stretching like a fleshy, glittering, henna-haired cat, "I will tell you why I have come. I want the stone you call the *Lapis Philosophorum*."

"I wondered when someone would ask again," Chiara said. "I don't have it."

"Oh, but you do. You created it, in the cellar of your father's bookshop, and with it you killed your grandmother, your sister, and your brother-in-law."

"I didn't kill them," Chiara said. Her hands started to shake, and she put them behind her back. Vivi shifted slightly, gathering herself. "And I didn't create anything."

Cinto with something unimaginably bright in his hands, melting into his flesh. His eyes wide, his mouth screaming.

The world ending.

I did, she thought. For a few seconds, anyway.

"That is a lie," Bianca Cappello said. "You stole elements and materials from the grand duke's laboratory at the Villa di Pratolino. He told me the story—how he came upon you in the very moment you were doing it. You told some foolish lie about a gift for the Grand Duchess Giovanna's new baby, and he believed you at the time. But when you created such an unnatural blast? When you walked away from it untouched? He knew then what you had done."

"I wasn't untouched," Chiara said. "You said it yourself—I lost my reason. I look ten years older, at least."

The grand duchess leaned forward. "Even so. You should be dead and you are not. The wreck of your shop has been searched and searched again, and every inch of the monastery. You have hidden the stone by some magical means, and I require it, Mona Chiara. I require it now."

"Why?"

"So you do have it."

"I didn't say that. I just wondered why you wanted it. Why the grand duke's own physician stopped asking for it, and why you're asking for it now."

"I can have you beaten until you tell me. Le Murate is under the patronage of the Medici, and the abbess will do whatever I direct her to do."

"Beat me all you want. I don't have it."

The grand duchess stood up and paced back and forth in the little parlor, her heavy brows slanting down over her eyes in anger—and terror? Why terror? Her velvet and fur and silk made wild-animal rustling noises. Watching her through the grille, Chiara thought suddenly that it was the grand duchess who was in a cage. Why did she want the *Lapis Philosophorum* now?

"He is sick," the grand duchess said. "The grand duke."

Chiara's thoughts stopped. They still did that sometimes. She closed her eyes for a moment, gathering her strength. Part of her wanted to go back to the laundry-room where everything was simple and clear, wood-ashes and hot water and lye and heavy wet linens, over and over again until the day she died. But another part of her wanted to cultivate her renewed memories, even if they were poison. Even if they did draw her back into the deadly labyrinth of the Medici.

"It is not a secret at the court," Bianca Cappello said, "although you would not have heard it here, walled in as you are. Yes, he has had a few small strokes of apoplexy, as his father had before him. He is perfectly well now, but I must have the stone to be certain that he remains well."

She was lying when she said he was perfectly well. If he was perfectly well, she would not have come.

"When he dies," Chiara said, "the people of Florence will drive you out of the city, crown or no crown—you and your changeling son."

The grand duchess came up close to the grille and grasped the bars with her hands. She had two or three rings on every finger. Her fingernails were bitten down to nothing. Even the skin of her fingertips was ragged and reddened.

"Prince Antonio is the heir," she said. "He has been legitimated—it is legal and finished. He will rule after his father, and even the cardinal can do nothing about it."

If Francesco is fool enough to legitimate the Venetian's changeling brat, I will have the boy strangled. I will never allow a bastard without a drop of Medici blood to inherit our crown.

Another memory. The Vasari Corridor, of course. The loggia looking out over the church. Cardinal Prince Ferdinando de' Medici with his pink cheeks and merry eyes, who had forced her to spy for him and absolved her from her vow of virginity, all in the space of half an hour.

"You might be surprised," she said, "what the cardinal can do about things. If you're so sure your boy will succeed, why do you care if the grand duke dies?"

Suddenly the grand duchess shook the grille as if she had gone mad. It was ancient and it rattled. Flakes of rust fell off. Vivi came to her feet and barked.

"Will no one ever *believe*," Bianca Cappello said, "that I love him?"

Chiara didn't believe it. She said nothing.

"Oh, not the grand duke. Not Francesco de' Medici. But Franco—tell me, Mona Chiara, as intimate as you once were with both of us. Do you know who Franco is?"

"It's a pet name you call the grand duke."

"It is more than a pet name. Franco is—a different person. Franco is—what the grand duke might have been, if he had not been born to wear the red lily crown of Tuscany."

"Is it Franco who whips you?" Chiara said viciously. "Ties you up like a lamb to be slaughtered? Makes you crawl to him like a gutter whore?"

Bianca Cappello let go of the grille and stepped back. The rust had left reddish-brown marks on her fingers, like old scars.

"Yes," Chiara said. "I know. I lived in the Palazzo Pitti, in your own household. How could I help but know?"

"She has done many wicked things," Bianca Cappello said. It took Chiara a moment to realize that she was talking about herself. "She deserves to be punished, to make fair payment for her sins."

Skidding and stumbling down the polished stone stairs in the Palazzo Vecchio, trying to catch the grand duchess's skirts, her mantle, anything to break the fall. The grand duchess turning over and over, in eerie silence, until she struck the stone floor at the bottom of the stairway.

"There is no fair payment for your sins," Chiara said. "Whatever you call yourself. No fair payment but death."

Bianca Cappello stared at her for a moment. A shudder ran through her, as if she felt cold despite the fires and her sumptuous furs. She pulled her mantle closer around her body. "The stone," she said. "That is all I want from you, Mona Chiara. Give it to me, and I will see you have comforts in exchange. Leisure. Luxuries. Books."

Not, Chiara thought, freedom. But then I just threatened her life. She said, "I told you. I don't have it."

"Your conspirator, your lover, the Englishman. Suppose I were to tell you the truth about what happened to him."

Chiara's heart stopped. Everything stopped. She couldn't breathe. How much time passed? She never knew.

In a voice that didn't sound like her own she said, "He abandoned me and went home to Cornwall. That's what happened to him."

"Perhaps not."

"Then he is dead."

"Perhaps not."

Ruan holding out his arms, half-questioning, half-demanding. She herself running straight to him as if she had been doing it all her life. His arms around her as if he would set her apart from the rest of the world forever . . .

Her eyes filled with tears she couldn't control. They spilled over and streaked down her cheeks like fire. For a moment she couldn't speak at all. All her hard-won strength, her recovered memories, her determination to be herself again, seemed like dust in her hands. She whispered, "Tell me. Please."

"Give me the stone."

"I can't. I don't have it."

The grand duchess went to the door and knocked once. It was opened immediately by one of the lay sisters.

"Send a messenger if you change your mind," she said. "If you do not give me the stone, Mona Chiara, you will live out your dreary life as a washerwoman here in Le Murate. And you will never know the truth about the grand duke's English alchemist."

CHAPTER FIFTY-TWO

*The Monastery of the Santissima Annunziata,
called Le Murate*

9 SEPTEMBER 1587

The abbess of Le Murate was not one to allow pearls, however insignificant, to be cast before swine. When she learned Chiara could read and write—not only read and write, but read and write *Latin*, and why had no one told her this before?—she removed her from the laundry-room and set her to assisting the copyist nuns in making the hand-lettered psalters and books of hours that brought the monastery a good part of its income. At first Chiara's work was poor, because her hands were so badly damaged by her work in the laundry. After a year or so, with warm wrappings in the winter and liberal applications of goose grease every night, her skin became soft again and her fingers—barring the broken ones—flexible.

Vivi missed the baskets of laundry where she had liked to make snug nests. She was eleven years old now—in the copyists' room Chiara finally had access to calendars—and not as lively as she had once been. The copyist nuns remembered Rostig and Seiden, and were delighted to have a russet-eared hound in their midst again. They made beds from folded blankets, and brought treats from the refectory. As Vivi's face grew whiter, her little body grew plumper. She did her tricks for the nuns, and slept every night curled at the foot of Chiara's own pallet.

The grand duchess didn't come to Le Murate again.

The rumors of the grand duke's strokes of apoplexy simmered and simmered and eventually bubbled over, even inside the monastery. His right hand was contracted into a claw, one nun whispered, and when he signed his name he produced an unreadable scribble. Another added that her sister had seen him with her own eyes, and his face appeared to droop on the right side. Still another, citing her cousin's shoemaker who was also the grand duke's personal shoemaker, swore the grand duke wore a special shoe on his right foot to allow him to stand upright.

Chiara lay awake at night, making and unmaking plans. Send a message to the grand duchess agreeing to give her the *Lapis Philosophorum*. Give her an ordinary stone from the cloister walk, find out the truth about Ruan, and somehow, before the deception was uncovered, work out a way to escape. But then—then what? She had nowhere to go. She had no *sonnodolce* of her own, and she would die or go mad once and for all without the drug. She couldn't leave Le Murate without Vivi, and how would she take care of her? How could she leave Donna Jimena, growing older and frailer, whose only pleasure in life was to talk about the old days and her beloved Isabella?

Time slipped away. Donna Jimena died and no one but Chiara cared. No one was left to care. So much for the noble blood that had been Donna Jimena's pride and joy. She was buried beneath the apse of the church in the communal crypt where the lay sisters were commonly buried. Her name wasn't engraved anywhere. She was simply gone.

I am Donna Jimena Osorio, related by blood to the late Duchess Donna Eleonora of Toledo. She invited me to Florence to manage her daughter Donna Isabella's household, and so I have done with all my heart, for thirty years and more. . . .

Every Sunday after Mass Chiara knelt in the apse and prayed for her. She prayed for Nonna and Lucia, for Grand Duchess Giovanna and little Prince Filippino, for Isabella and Dianora, so long in their graves. So many dead. She prayed for Ruan Pencarrow, too—whether he was alive or dead, she loved him and she still dreamed about him. When she was finished with her prayers, she let a drop of *sonnodolce* fall on her skin. That was one thing that never varied—the grand duke's physician appeared two or three times a year with a fresh supply.

She began to believe that she would live out the rest of her life in Le Murate.

One warm September morning she was copying a psalm into a psalter.

In deficiendo ex me spiritum meum, she wrote carefully, *et tu cognovisti semitas meas. In via hac, qua ambulabam, absconderunt laqueum mihi.*

Though my spirit may become faint within me, even then, you have known my paths. Along this way, which I have been walking, they have hidden a snare for me. . . .

Two of the lay sisters came into the copyists' room. Neither one said anything. One of them picked Vivi up without taking any care not to hurt her, and Vivi yelped in surprise and pain and outrage. Chiara jumped to her feet, scattering pens and ink pots, but the second lay sister caught hold of her arms and held her back as the first one walked out of the room with Vivi under her arm. The copyist nuns sat stunned, their mouths open, without a sound.

"You can't take her!" Chiara shouted. "What's the matter with you? She's doing no harm. Bring her back at once, and don't you dare hurt her or I'll go to the abbess."

"Abbess's own orders," the lay sister said. She pushed Chiara away, hard enough that Chiara stumbled against the writing-table and fell to her knees. "Grand duchess is here and wants the dog. Says you can see her in the first parlor, if you want."

Chiara scrambled to her feet, ducked under the lay sister's meaty arm, and ran out of the room. The first parlor was on the other side of the cloister walk. *You can't have her you can't have her you can't have her*, she sobbed through her clenched teeth as she ran. She burst into the nuns' side of the parlor and flung herself against the grille.

On the other side, the grand duchess was just buckling a new leather collar on Vivi's neck, gilded and painted with red and blue stripes and red fleurs-de-lis. Vivi's ears were pinned back and her tail was tucked between her hind legs. When she saw Chiara she howled, a hoarse pitiful cry unlike anything Chiara had ever heard before.

"You can't have her," Chiara panted. "May you be damned to hell, Bianca Cappello, she is all I have left—you can't have her."

"As you yourself can see, Mona Chiara, I can." The grand duchess clipped a leash on Vivi's new collar and sat back in her chair. "Now, let us talk again about what you did in the cellar under your father's bookshop."

Chiara closed her eyes and tried to breathe. Screaming and shaking the grille wouldn't help. Think, think—what was different? Why had the grand duchess suddenly come to the monastery again, after all this time? Why was she so desperate that she would stoop to taking a little dog—

Desperate.

Chiara opened her eyes and looked, really looked at Bianca Cappello. It had been almost three years since she had seen her last, in this very parlor, and the grand duchess had aged badly. She had lost her lush plumpness and her face sagged under its thick layer of pink-and-white ceruse. Her hair, dressed in a high elaborate style with ropes of pearls, was too perfect. A wig, then.

His right hand was contracted into a claw . . . his face appeared to droop on the right side . . . he wore a special shoe on his right foot to allow him to stand upright.

Chiara said bluntly, "Is he dying?"

"I will not let him die," the grand duchess said. "He is a young man yet, ten years younger than his father was when he died, and his father died before his time. He will live, my Franco, because you will give me your stone."

"Serenissima," Chiara said. She was willing to give Bianca Cappello the form of address that meant so much to her, if it would get Vivi back. "I would give you the stone if I had it, I swear by all the saints and angels."

"It is not the apoplexies," the grand duchess said. Her voice shook. "Those come and go, and although he has some ill effects, they are not enough to kill him. But this summer—it has been wet and hot and his tertian fever is worse than I have ever seen it. He has no strength to fight it, and it breaks my heart to see him suffer so."

She wasn't just saying it. She meant it. For all her sins and selfishness and cruelty, she loved her Franco.

"His brother is coming from Rome. The cardinal. He writes that he wishes to make amends with Francesco for their differences, while they both still live. I am afraid of him."

As well you should be, Chiara thought.

"Francesco must regain his health. That is the only answer. The physicians are useless. The other alchemists are useless. You, Mona Chiara, you are my only hope."

"I can't help you. Vivi can't help you. Please, Serenissima, give her back to me."

"When you give me the stone. Only then."

Chiara looked down. She didn't want the grand duchess to see her eyes and guess what she was about to do. Carelessly, as if it meant nothing, she said, "If anyone has created the *Lapis Philosophorum*, it is the grand duke's English alchemist."

"Francesco has questioned him, over and over. He—"

She stopped.

Chiara looked up. She felt as if she could burn through the grille with her eyes alone. "So he is alive," she said.

The grand duchess stood up and jerked Vivi's leash tight. The little hound choked and whimpered. "The unnatural blast," she said, her voice hard again, "was in your father's bookshop. You stole valuable elements from the grand duke and created it. The grand duke believes the English alchemist helped you, and that is why he has kept him a prisoner and questioned him endlessly. But I think he is wrong. I think you created the magical stone, Mona Chiara. You, and no one else."

And here I am at the end of the circle, Chiara thought. That was my dream. To show Babbo. To be known and acknowledged as the greatest female alchemist since Perenelle Flamel. Now I've achieved it and it's going to cost me everything.

Unless—

Unless I can do it again. *Nigredo, albedo, citrinitas, rubedo.* Black, white, yellow, red. Babbo's book is gone but it was an old formula. I might be able to find it again in another book, in the grand duke's library. If I can find it, I might be able to make the *Lapis Philosophorum* again. I might—

"Don't hurt Vivi," she said. "Don't let the grand duke do harm to Magister Ruanno. The stone that I made in the bookshop's cellar is gone, but I can make another one. All I need is the grand duke's library, so I can find the formula again. Then a laboratory, and equipment, and elements. I need to be released from Le Murate, and I can make the *Lapis Philosophorum* again."

The grand duchess looked at her steadily. After what seemed to be an eternity she nodded.

"I will make the arrangements," she said. "Do not think you can deceive me, Mona Chiara. You will be watched every moment, and if you do not create that stone for me, I will see that you regret it."

She went out. Vivi struggled with the leash, crying. Bianca Cappello struck her sharply with the doubled-over end of the leash to make her obey.

Chiara watched them go, helpless and with murder in her heart.

CHAPTER FIFTY-THREE

*Villa Seravezza, near the silver mine at Bottino,
northwest of Florence*

10 OCTOBER 1587

"I would have gone mad," Ruan said, "if it had not been for the miners. They talked to me, brought me lamps and oil so I was not left in the dark, their own food to supplement what the guards gave me. Books and papers for calculations. Johan Ziegler, the mine master—I would like to arrange a rich reward for him, both in money and in advancement."

Cardinal Prince Ferdinando de' Medici lounged comfortably among cushions in a chair on the other side of the room. He was not wearing his cardinal's scarlet. Ruan wondered if he would ever wear it again.

"I did not know what I would find," the cardinal said, "when Francesco let slip amidst his ravings that he had you imprisoned in the mine at Bottino. It has been what, five years? I half-expected a gibbering maniac, naked and filthy and overgrown with hair."

"So I might have been, but for Johan."

The first months of his imprisonment were a blur of nightmare images. Being in an underground cell carved from the bare rock, with no opening but the grating overhead. Being without the *sonnodolce*. Knowing Chiara was hurt and alone in Le Murate. If he had known he would be arrested, he would not have taken her to a place where the grand duke had such power.

Weeks of madness. *A gibbering maniac, naked and filthy and overgrown with hair.* Yes, for a while. Then a little at a time he had fought his way to sanity again.

His first wish upon being freed had been for news of Chiara. When the cardinal had assured him she was still at Le Murate and safe, he had asked for a bath, a barber, and fresh clothing from the skin out. For all his pacing—the cell had been eight paces in one direction, ten in the other—his deliberate working of his muscles against the stone walls and his daily ritual of jumping to catch hold of the iron grating in the ceiling and pulling himself up as many times as he could manage, he had lost flesh and strength. It would be a long time before he was himself again.

"I am surprised your miners did not dig you out," the cardinal said.

"The grand duke's new prefect watched them closely. It would have taken days to dig out the grate without blasting, and if they had blasted, they would have killed me."

The cardinal turned over a page in a ledger that lay on the table in front of him. "The production of the mine has increased in the last five years. My brother imprisons you under the harshest of conditions, and from your hole in the rock you use your knowledge and skill to improve his mine's workings?"

"It was for the miners, not for the grand duke. And to maintain my own reason. Nothing more."

"Indeed." The cardinal turned over another page. "So you no longer consider yourself the grand duke's man."

"I consider myself," Ruan said, "the man who is going to kill him."

The cardinal smiled. "You will be pleased when you see him, I think. He has had a series of apoplectic strokes, and is partly paralyzed. At the moment he is at his villa in Poggio a Caiano, suffering from a serious attack of tertian fever. One way or another, he will not live long, and what life is left to him will be unpleasant in the extreme."

"I take it you intend to succeed him?"

"I do. My brother's attempts to legitimate Prince Antonio are immoral and illegal by both church and secular law—the boy is a bastard unrelated by blood to the Medici. I have a written confession from one of the women who assisted them in the deception."

"I will not kill a child."

"The boy is eleven years old. He has been raised to believe himself the heir. A snake fresh from the egg will bite, just as much as an adult."

"Put him into a religious order. After all, the church will soon be short a cardinal."

The cardinal laughed. "Very well, Magister Ruanno. We will see."

Ruan pushed himself to his feet and walked across the room. His eyes were still sensitive to the light, but oh, the astonishing delight of looking out a window and seeing gardens, the mountains, and the sky. He said, "I am not sure why you have gone to the trouble of freeing me, Eminenza. Surely it would have been simple enough to accomplish your brother's death yourself, with no one else to find out."

"And if anything goes wrong, and people do find out? A person to blame is a necessary thing, Magister Ruanno, and you are the perfect scapegoat. You have every reason to hate my brother. And when the thing is done, you will go home to Cornwall. I will make a play of pursuing you, but I am not my brother, obsessed with revenge."

Home to Cornwall. Ruan wondered what had happened with Wheal Loer and Milhyntall House in the past five years. Had Jago Warne kept the mine working, at least, so there had been a living for the miners? Had the English come back and taken Milhyntall again?

"You are frank," he said to Ferdinando de' Medici.

"I know you are not a fool. I have another reason to free you as well, you and the woman Chiara Nerini."

Ruan felt a flicker of apprehension. "What reason?"

"In my brother's fevered ravings, he speaks over and over of something he calls *sonnodolce*. He seems to think it is the most valuable thing he possesses. I am not sure what it is, whether it is a poison or an aphrodisiac, but either one would be useful to have."

It is more than you guess, Ruan thought. He said, "What does that have to do with me, or Chiara?"

The cardinal chuckled. "Come, come, Magister Ruanno," he said. "I am not a fool either. My brother associates both your name and Signorina Chiara's with this *sonnodolce*. You both know something about it. Surely it would be a small thing to share with me, in return for your freedom."

"A small thing," Ruan repeated. He was tiring from the activity and the light and he could not think clearly, although even in his weakened state he was not fool enough to believe that the cardinal did not design to kill him in the end. Kill him and Chiara. "Eminenza, I desire to see Chiara before anything else."

"She is safe and well at Le Murate. The abbess found out she could read and write Latin, and has put her to work as a copyist, so she has easy work and some comforts. I want her at Poggio a Caiano as well, because she witnessed Giovanna's death, and I intend to send for her at the proper time."

Ruan closed his eyes. He wanted to say *send for her now* but he knew he would have to lie down before he fell down. He heard the cardinal's fingers snap, and after a moment two gentlemen were there to support him on either side. He sagged against their arms.

"We must leave for Poggio a Caiano tomorrow, or the next day at the latest," the cardinal said. His voice sounded far away. "Rest. Try to eat."

"Chiara?"

"You will see her soon enough. Think on this, Magister Ruanno—you will be face-to-face with my brother again in a few days, and I promise you, you will have your revenge at last."

CHAPTER FIFTY-FOUR

The Villa del Poggio a Caiano, northwest of Florence

17 OCTOBER 1587

Ruan stepped into the grand duke's bedchamber. The day before, when he and Ferdinando de' Medici had arrived at the villa, it had smelled of sickness, with medicaments and basins of water and stinking slop jars everywhere. Today it was clean again. Two maidservants were just going out, carrying between them a basket heaped high with soiled linens. Inside, the cardinal sat in a fine chair beside his brother's bed, dressed in a night-gown of rich brocaded crimson, not a cardinal's robe but much the same color. He still wore his ring of office, and the great cabochon sapphire smoldered darkly in the wavering candlelight.

There was a table set between the cardinal's chair and the bed. On the table lay two rings of keys, a few papers, a seal matrix with an elaborately engraved golden handle, and its counterseal, a gold ring with the arms of Tuscany engraved on a black onyx stone.

The grand duke was asleep. The worst flush of fever had gone. He was freshly shaved and what was left of his hair had been combed. There were things a recovery from tertian fever could not achieve—the right side of his face still did not quite match the left, and his right hand was still contracted like a claw—but he looked better. He turned his head from side to side and clutched at the richly embroidered coverlet, as if he were struggling with evil dreams.

As well he might be. Dreams of the devil coming to claim his own.

"The fever has gone?" Ruan asked.

"As you see." The cardinal gestured. "The physicians say he is better. What report do you have of Bianca Cappello?"

"She is still shut up in her bedchamber. She knows he is sick, of course, and knows you are here. She is terrified, because other than your brother she has no one to protect her from the vengeance of all the people who hate her."

"Good. And the rest?"

"I have told her women that she is sick as well, and already two or three of them have slipped away. They will find their way back to Florence and spread the tale."

"Good. I had hoped the fever would carry Francesco off last night—it would have simplified matters. He knew how sick he was. He gave me his keys and his seals, without reservation."

"So I see."

"He will die tonight, one way or another." The cardinal took a small glass vial from a pocket inside his robe and put it on the table. It contained a clear greenish-blue liquid. The candlelight licked and shimmered over the glass and struck rainbow reflections from the liquid itself.

"Wake him," the cardinal said.

Ruan looked thoughtfully at the grand duke's face. He could see his eyes moving, under his eyelids. Had he continued to take the *sonnodolce*, even after suffering the apoplexy that had crippled him? If so, the cardinal would have a surprise when he gave his brother the liquid in the glass flask. The intense greenish-blue was the color of arsenic combined with an acetate of copper. It was a terrible poison, but it would not kill a man who had been taking *sonnodolce*.

He grasped the grand duke's shoulder and shook him hard.

"Wake up, Serenissimo," he said. "Wake up—your brother is here."

The grand duke coughed and shuddered in a brief convulsion, then slowly opened his eyes. Ruan watched, and saw the precise moment when his senses came back to him.

"Ruanno dell' Inghilterra," he said. His voice was weak and hoarse, not like his own voice at all. "What are you doing here?"

"You no longer have the power to keep me imprisoned."

"You no longer have any power at all," the cardinal said. "You will die tonight for your sins, Francesco. Do you understand that?"

The grand duke turned his head and looked at his brother. After a moment he pushed himself up on his left elbow. His right shoulder and arm were twisted and too weak to support his weight.

"You would be happy if I were to die, brother," he said. His voice was stronger and clearer. "But I think not just yet. I will live long enough to take back the keys I gave you in the depths of my sickness. To see Prince Antonio publicly proclaimed as my successor. You thought you had the red lily crown within your grasp, but I will keep it for myself a little longer."

"You will not. I have a written confession from the woman Gianna Santi—you are surprised? Well you might be, as you sent a troop of hired bravos to kill her on the road to Bologna. She escaped with her life, at least long enough to dictate her confession, and when you and Bianca Cappello are dead I will make that document public. The boy Antonio is related by blood to neither of you."

"The woman lies."

"I do not think so."

"I am better. I am not going to die tonight."

"Magister Ruanno may have something to say about that."

The grand duke turned his head and looked at Ruan. Sick he may have been, crippled he may have been, but he could still call up the authority that ran in his Medici blood. After a moment he smiled and lay back against his pillows. "Neither of you would dare to harm me," he said. "Where is my Bia? She will take care of me."

"Bia?" The cardinal acted as if he had never heard the pet name before. "If you mean Bianca Cappello, you will not see her again in this life. She is already dead, Francesco."

Ruan had not expected that. Some men, he thought, did not need racks and thumbscrews to torture other men.

"I do not believe you," the grand duke said. "She is the Grand Duchess of Tuscany, crowned and anointed. You would not dare."

"It is true. Magister Ruanno here strangled her, just as Paolo Giordano Orsini strangled our sister Isabella. Just as our own brother Pietro strangled our cousin and sister-in-law Dianora. Do you remember how you wrote to them, to Pietro and to Orsini, and gave them your authorization to commit their murders? How you welcomed them back into your presence afterward, and helped them excuse themselves?"

The grand duke pushed himself up once more, this time struggling to a full sitting position. "It is not true," he said. "Ruanno?"

Ruan said nothing.

"I will tell you this as well," the cardinal said. "I admired the Grand Duchess Giovanna with all my heart. I used to think, sometimes—what if I had been the elder son, and she had been my wife? Did you even know that she took a pair of turtledoves as her device, upon her marriage, and *Fida Conjunctio* as her motto? A faithful union. She was faithful to the end, to a terrible death, and if I had been her husband, I would have been faithful too."

"Giovanna," the grand duke said. He sounded genuinely baffled. "What does she have to do with any of this? What does she have to do with Bia?"

"What does she have to do with it?" The cardinal rose, his robe like a sheet of blood. "She died at your Bia's hands. Oh, yes, I know. Magister Ruanno knows. You may have thought you silenced the woman Chiara Nerini, but you did not. She will testify against your Bia, that she struck Giovanna, and caused her to fall."

"Giovanna struck Bianca first. It was a quarrel between two women, that is all—Bianca never intended to push her."

"So she may have said. She will say nothing more. I saw her face turn blue, and her filthy tongue swell up—that is what it looks like when you strangle a woman. You do not know that, do you, Francesco? You have always commanded others to commit your murders for you."

For the first time the grand duke's conviction seemed to waver. Tears welled up and streaked down over his cheeks. "Bia," he said again. He stiffened and shuddered with another of his seizures.

"Serenissimo," Ruan said sharply. Even those recovering from tertian fevers sometimes died suddenly in the course of such a seizure. "The formula for the *sonnodolce*. Where is it?"

The cardinal leaned forward, listening.

"The *sonnodolce*." The grand duke opened his eyes. They were clear again. "It is safely hidden where you will never find it. Bring my Bia to me, alive and well, and I will tell you where it is."

Ruan looked at the cardinal. The cardinal gathered his gown and seated himself again. He twisted his ring of office on his finger, as if he was making certain it would be easily slipped off when the moment came. He thought for a moment, then raised one hand to Ruan.

"Go," he said. "Fetch the Venetian woman. Let us learn where my brother has hidden his secrets."

CHAPTER FIFTY-FIVE

Ruan expected to find Bianca Cappello reduced to a welter of tears and hysteria. To his surprise she was kneeling at an old prie-dieu, her eyes red and swollen but her expression composed. People forgot, he thought, that she was a Venetian noblewoman by birth. They remembered only her sins and excesses.

"He is dead?" she said. Like her eyes, her voice bore signs of tears within its calm. She had taken off all her jewels but for a single pin that held a white veil over her hair. There were diamonds decorating its head, and the arms of Tuscany impaled with the arms of the house of Cappello.

"Come with me," Ruan said. He gave her no name or title.

"If I am to die too, I would die as the Grand Duchess of Tuscany."

"That is for the cardinal to say. Come with me."

She crossed herself and rose. "I did not push her," she said. "I have confessed all my sins, and done what penance I could do, shut up as I have been. All I have left to say is this one thing. I did not push her."

Was she play-acting, as she had done throughout her life with the grand duke? There was only one other person alive who knew the truth—Chiara, who had been there. He took Bianca Cappello's arm as if she were a prisoner, and walked with her back to the grand duke's bedchamber.

"Here is your Bia," the cardinal said, when they stepped into the room. "She is alive and well, as you can see—you will excuse my small jest regarding her death. Now keep your promise, and tell us where to find your secrets."

The grand duke got to his feet. He could not stand straight without the special shoe that he wore on his twisted right foot, but he held his head with dignity. For the space of several breaths he just looked at Bianca Cappello. She looked at him steadily in return. What were they thinking? Had it been worth it, their long obsessive love for each other and all the death and destruction and misery it had caused?

"The hiding-place is at the center of the labyrinth," he said.

"The labyrinth?" The cardinal frowned. "Where? Which labyrinth?"

"Chiara Nerini will know."

Images flashed through Ruan's mind—Chiara naked with her hair loose, down to her hips, little more than a child on the night she had passed through her initiation. Chiara older, a woman, in her pale habit with the moonstone on her breast, gravely pacing through the labyrinth set into the floor at the Casino di San Marco. Chiara telling him how Bianca Cappello had hired an assassin to leave her in the center of the poisoned labyrinth in the Boboli Gardens—*she never guessed I'd be immune to the poisoned thorns.*

There were so many labyrinths, all associated in one way or another with Chiara. Which one?

The cardinal looked from his brother's face to Ruan's, and back again. Then he gestured. *Allow him to embrace her.*

Ruan released Bianca's arm so she could walk across the room to her lover. With the white veil pinned over her hair, she looked like a nun. The grand duke embraced her, and she bowed her head against his shoulder. He ran one hand gently over her veiled head.

"Have courage, my Bia," he said. "I will not die tonight."

The cardinal picked up the vial of luminous greenish-blue liquid. For a moment it seemed to absorb all the light in the room.

"But you will," he said. "I give you the opportunity, brother, to choose your death—which is more than you gave Isabella, or Dianora, or the women you abducted to provide yourself with an heir, or the men who dared to whisper conspiracies against you. Which is more than your Venetian whore gave to the Grand Duchess Giovanna."

Bianca Cappello cried out wordlessly. The grand duke stroked her head again. "Be calm, my Bia," he said. "And what choices do you offer me, brother?"

The cardinal held out the vial. "Poison," he said. "A dignified death, as Socrates died. Or Magister Ruanno's blade."

Ruan said nothing. He thought of all the times he had sworn he would kill the grand duke with his own hands. Now he was not sure he would have the physical strength to do it.

The grand duke smiled. "It amuses you to jest with life and death, brother," he said. "Well, then, I propose a wager to amuse us all. If I drink your potion and do not die, you will take Magister Ruanno's blade for yourself, and die on it as Roman generals died. Swear it."

So he has been taking the *sonnodolce*, Ruan thought. He is immune to poisons. Even arsenic, which whatever the cardinal says is hardly a dignified death, will not touch him.

"Eminenza," he said. "I must warn you—"

"I swear it," the cardinal said. "Magister Ruanno, your blade, if you please."

Too late, then, for objections. Ruan drew his dagger and offered it to the cardinal, hilt first. It was a workmanlike piece, with a blade of tempered steel, a pommel and guard of bronze, and a carved black horn handle. The cardinal took it in his right hand. With his left, he removed the stopper from the vial and handed it to his brother.

The grand duke did not bother to sniff it or taste it, but drank it down quickly, as if it was a fine ice-chilled wine on a hot summer day. He put the empty vial on the table.

"Not particularly pleasant," he said. "A rather sour, metallic taste. From the color, I would guess it is a compound of arsenic and copper."

"Franco," Bianca Cappello said. "For the love of God, I beg you—cast it up. No one can drink such a large dose of arsenic and survive."

"Be calm, my Bia," the grand duke said. "You must prepare yourself to witness my brother's death, which will be unpleasant for you. For me, however, it will be—"

Suddenly he doubled over, choking. Saliva ran from his mouth, and a ghastly scent of rotten garlic filled the room.

"Hold the woman, Magister Ruanno," the cardinal said. "I want her to watch. So, brother, you thought you had become a god, and were not subject to the natural laws of poisons?"

Ruan stepped forward and grasped Bianca Cappello by the arms. She was white and shaking with horror. For a moment she struggled weakly, then subsided.

"I will—not die," the grand duke gasped out. "I am immune—for years I took—the *sonnodolce*—a mithridate. I have seen proof that it is—efficacious—"

He fell to his knees, retching violently. Sweat stood out on his forehead like drops of oil of vitriol.

"A mithridate?" The cardinal grasped his brother's hair and pulled his head up. "A universal antidote? God's blood, is that true?"

"A drop—every seven days—no poison will ever—" He began to vomit. The cardinal jumped back, disgusted.

"But you have not taken it for almost two years," Bianca Cappello cried. "Ever since your last stroke of apoplexy—the physicians—Francesco, you have not taken it."

"It does not—matter—the effect lasts—"

He began to convulse. He lost control of every function of his body. As much as Ruan hated Bianca Cappello, and despite the cardinal's order, he turned her away from the grand duke's suffering and forced her head down against his chest.

After about a quarter of an hour, the cardinal said, "It is over. He has died of his own hubris, and fortunately, Magister Ruanno, I can return your blade to you unbloodied."

"Fortunately, Eminenza," Ruan said. He took the dagger.

Ferdinando de' Medici smiled. "Address me as Serenissimo," he said. "I am the grand duke now. As for Donna Bianca—"

The doors to the chamber burst open. They both turned their heads.

In the doorway, flanked by four guardsmen in Medici colors, stood Chiara Nerini.

CHAPTER FIFTY-SIX

Chiara thought: how many things can a person see all at once?

Ruan. Alive. White as a specter, his bones showing through his skin, his eyes suddenly aflame.

Bianca Cappello in his arms. A white veil. Swooning? Dead? Oh, please God, not dead, not yet.

The cardinal, smiling. His merry eyes turning toward her. A red night-gown, embroidered with gold. Keys and a seal on a table beside him.

On the floor, sprawled in a horrifying welter of blood and vomit and feces, the grand duke. His night-cap had fallen off to reveal that he had lost most of his hair.

How many disconnected details, frozen between one moment and the next? How many things that were not what she expected?

"Ruan," she managed to say.

Time jolted forward again. The cardinal spread out his arms and said with authority, "This room is to be sealed. You, guard, find a priest. You, find servants to wash the grand duke's body and lay it out properly and clean the room. You, take Donna Bianca to her own chamber and lock her in. Magister Ruanno, take Signorina Chiara to the library where you can speak with her privately. I will see you in the grand salon in an hour."

The guards scattered to their assignments. Ruan stepped forward and held out his hands.

"Chiara," he said. *Keer-ah*, as he had always said it, not *kee-ah-rah*. "*Awen lymm*, my inspiration, my dearest heart."

His voice was the same, low and precise, the voice of a man who spoke many languages and sometimes had to think before choosing a word. There were new lines at the corners of his mouth. His eyes were still hollow and dark and bleak with endless sadness.

She tried to say his name again, but she couldn't.

"Come with me," he said.

She didn't take hold of his hands. She was still shaking with shock and confusion. The guardsmen in their Medici colors—she had believed them to be from the grand duchess. She had expected to be taken to a laboratory, cool and quiet, filled with athanors and alembics, elements neatly labeled, books set out for her to study.

Instead—death. Horror. Nothing as it should be. And Ruan. Ruan—

He walked beside her to a room furnished as a library, with polished tables and cushioned chairs and magnificent books laid out on reading stands. A harpsichord stood in one corner, its lid propped open, the inner surface gilded and painted with red lilies and milk-white swans.

Gently he said, "Will you sit down?"

She sat down in one of the chairs. She clasped her hands in her lap so he couldn't see them or try to take hold of them.

He seated himself in another chair, on the other side of the table. She heard him let his breath out, as if it had taken the last of his strength to walk so far.

"I love you," he said, without preamble.

—*I love you*—

It made her feel sick. Anger, fear, joy? She wasn't sure. She didn't know if she believed him or not. If it was true, why had he left her at Le Murate for so long? Why hadn't he found a way to escape from the grand duke and come for her?

"I knew you were alive," she said at last. "I tricked the grand duchess into telling me. Where have you been?"

"I was arrested three days after I took you to Le Murate. I have been walled into an underground cell at Bottino, from that day until seven days ago."

So that was why he was so white. Why he looked insubstantial. One cell, underground, all this time? At Le Murate she'd had the laundry to do, at least, and then the copying. She'd had the cloister to walk in, with Donna Jimena. She'd had Vivi.

How had he kept from going mad?

How could she be angry with him?

"One day," he said, "when we have more time, I will tell you about it. The only thing that matters now is that every day I was there, I thought of you. I thought of what we said to each other, that afternoon in the cellar, and how we were at odds—I would have changed it, if I could."

Her heart contracted. "How did you get out?"

"The cardinal came for me. The grand duke was sick with one of his tertian fevers, and in his ravings he revealed—" He stopped. After a moment he said, "Revealed many things."

"When the guardsmen came for me," Chiara said, "I thought they were from Bianca Cappello. She visited me at Le Murate." Her voice began to shake, out of her control. "Ruan, Donna Jimena is dead and Bianca Cappello took Vivi. She took her and she *hit* her and I want to kill her but not until I have Vivi back."

He frowned. "Gently," he said. "We will find your Vivi and make sure she is safe. Start from the beginning."

He laid his hands on the table, palms up. When she saw the familiar white scars she felt a quaver of response, as if he had touched her.

"Will you put your hands in mine?" he said.

She unfolded her hands, finger by finger. Each small movement seemed to matter so much. She lifted them and lay them flat on the table in front of her. The crooked fingers, the ink stains and calluses from holding a pen day in and day out. She had become so used to her hands she hardly saw them anymore, and seeing them now shocked her, as if they weren't her own hands at all. Ruan didn't move or say anything. After a while she felt strong enough. She lifted her hands again, and put them into his.

Warmth and strength flowed from his skin to hers, as if between them they were somehow performing the first step of a distillation, the application of heat to extract vapor.

A distillation. The laboratories, in the Casino di San Marco, the lemon-house at the Villa di Pratolino, the bookshop, in the cellar, her own laboratory where—

"I saw it, Ruan," she said. "The *Lapis Philosophorum*. It was finished, or so close as made no difference. Cinto took it out of the athanor, and it was—like looking at—like looking at—"

She couldn't think of anything it was like. She could remember the moment but there were no human words to describe it.

"It lasted for only half a breath," she said. "And then it was gone."

He closed his hands gently over hers.

"It was not your fault, Chiara."

"He broke Nonna's wrist, taking the key to the cellar away from her. She was crying."

"They didn't know. Any of them. It was a blast like no one had ever seen before, over in an instant. You must have been on the stairs, with the wall to protect you."

The wall—

"You took me to Le Murate," she burst out suddenly. She didn't mean for it to sound like an accusation, but it came out that way. *You took me to a place where they walled me up for years and years—*

She pulled her hands free. She remembered how red and raw they'd been when she worked in the laundry, how swollen her knuckles had been with damp and cold. How it had taken a year of goose grease and warm wrappings to make her fingers flexible again, and then how she'd developed new cramps and calluses from copying psalms, day after day after day.

"We could not wake you," he said. His eyes didn't waver from hers. "I did not know if anyone would ever wake you. I knew Donna Jimena had been your friend, and I knew the Benedictines had famous infirmarians. I never thought I would be arrested—I would not have taken you there, Chiara, if I had known."

How many things would they both have done differently, if they had known? His hands were changed, too. She remembered them as sunbrowned and strong. Five years in an underground cell had made them pale and thin, the joints prominent. She unclasped her hands and laid her palms against his again.

In a gentler voice she asked, "Why did he arrest you?"

"You know how mistrustful and suspicious he had become. The blast was an unnatural thing, it was at your family's bookshop, and I went a little mad, I think, with my fear for you. I was not careful to hide what I said and felt. He put those things together and he deduced—"

"That we had broken my vow."

"Yes. And more than that, that we were performing secret alchemy, a *magnum opus* he did not know about."

"Bianca Cappello thought I was doing it alone."

He smiled, just a little. It changed his face. "You were," he said. "The grand duke did not believe a woman could be an alchemist in her own right. I suppose it is a good thing he thought I had been directing you, because that is why he kept me alive."

They sat quietly together for a little while. Suddenly she remembered once thinking that she and Ruan were like a lodestone and iron—when had that been? Whenever it was, it was still true. Her fingers interlaced themselves with his, and for a moment she could not quite tell where her flesh ended and his began.

Then slowly, so slowly, he stroked the inner surface of her right wrist with his thumb. Her wrist, where the *sonnodolce* liquid dropped. He said, "Do you remember taking the *sonnodolce*?"

"I am still taking it."

She could feel his surprise—his thumb stopped for a moment. He said, "How did you obtain it in Le Murate?"

"A physician brought it four times a year. It was one way the grand duke made sure I would not try to escape. He knew and I knew I would go mad without it, and only he could give it to me. I don't know what I'm going to do, now that he's dead—he kept the formula a secret."

Ruan put his head down for a moment, his forehead against the backs of her hands. She lifted one hand and ran it lightly over his hair. That, at least, felt the same as it had felt before—thick and crisp. Ruan had never used scented pomades on his hair, as most of the men at the court did. She wondered if his mouth would feel the same against hers. If his hands would feel the same when they weren't holding hers, but sliding sweetly over her naked skin.

After a moment he lifted his head. "You will not die or go mad without it," he said. "He gave me none after he imprisoned me, and although it was bad for a while, I survived. It will probably be easier if we can give you smaller and smaller doses, instead of stopping it suddenly, between one week and the next."

"But you didn't have—" She pulled one hand free and pressed her fingers to the scar over her left ear.

"I know. If you need the *sonnodolce* because of that, we will find it. The grand duke told us, before he died, that he had a secret hiding place at the heart of the labyrinth—"

"Which labyrinth?"

"He said you would know."

She closed her eyes. Labyrinths. Think of the labyrinths.

The large and beautiful design traced out in black and white chips of stone on the floor of the laboratory at the Casino di San Marco. The smaller, cruder one set in terra-cotta tiles in the lemon-house at the Villa di Pratolino. Were there others? She had never been in the grand duke's private apartments in any of his palaces. He could have had dozens of them.

And then there was the poison labyrinth in the Boboli Gardens, behind its locked iron gate. An exact match to the black and white labyrinth but a dozen times its size, created with hornbeam and yew, rose canes and bittersweet and masses of red lilies. She had been in the center of it only once, in night's blackness and moonlight, and the last thing she'd been looking for was a secret hiding-place. Even so—what better place? And the center had been marked with a strange pitted stone, covered with what might have been carvings—

She opened her eyes. "The poison labyrinth in the Boboli Gardens," she said.

He pressed his lips to her fingers again. "I think you are right," he said. "Chiara, I do not trust the cardinal, but if we can reach this hiding-place first, it will give us a chance to bargain with him."

She thought about that. Once, when she had been a different person, she had struck such bargains, for life and death. Now the very thought made her sick and shaky. She said, "Ruan?"

"What?"

"Will things ever be the same again?"

Will we ever be strong again? Trust each other again? Will we ever love each other the way we used to? Will we even be alive, tomorrow and the next day?

"Not the same," he said. He stood up and walked around the table. She shrank back in her chair but he grasped her wrists firmly and gently and pulled her to her feet. They looked at each other. He put his arms around her. She pressed her hands against his chest and tried to push him away at first, then all at once with a wordless cry she threw her own arms around his neck and clung to him as if she was falling and falling and he was the only thing in the world she had to hold on to.

"Not the same," he said again. She could feel the warmth of his breath on her cheek. "But we are meant to be together, *awen lymm*, and we will find our way back. Will you come home to Cornwall with me now?"

"Yes."

"We will have to be married before we leave Italy. There are no Catholic priests left in England, or at least none who dare practice their faith openly."

"But the banns—"

"A few gold scudi will take care of the banns. Now quickly, before the cardinal sends for us again—what happened with your Vivi?"

"The grand duchess took her. She wanted me to make another *Lapis Philosophorum* to heal the grand duke, and she thought she could use Vivi to force me. We have to make her tell, Ruan."

"We will."

"Is the cardinal going to kill her? Bianca Cappello, I mean?"

"Yes. But he is not the cardinal anymore." He kissed her cheek, and then the corner of her mouth. His lips did feel the same. Her whole body shuddered with its need for him.

"He is going to take the crown for himself?"

"Yes. And we must fight, my dearest heart, so he does not kill us too."

CHAPTER FIFTY-SEVEN

Guardsmen escorted them to a room at the end of a corridor. Two of them stepped forward and threw open the doors.

The cardinal was there. He was standing to one side, half in and half out of the pool of light from the candle-branches. How much he looked like his brother sometimes, particularly in the play of light and darkness.

In the center of the room, the candlelight spilling over her in golden pools, Bianca Cappello knelt at a prie-dieu made of light-colored wood, well-worn, carved with the peahen device of Eleonora of Toledo. Her face was swollen and shiny with tears. Her head was covered with a white veil, pinned with a diamond pin, and her hair had darkened. Or had she simply stopped treating it with bleaches and sunlight and gold dust? She was no longer beautiful, no longer sensuous, but at the same time she had more dignity.

I never thought I'd see dignity, Chiara thought, when I looked at Bianca Cappello.

The rest of the room was empty.

"Here are the English alchemist and the woman Chiara Nerini, Serenissimo," the leader of the soldiers said. "As you commanded."

Serenissimo.

She had seen Grand Duke Francesco lying dead, yes, but even so, hearing his brother addressed with the grand-ducal title shocked her. He was truly gone, then, Francesco de' Medici, who had bought a silver descensory with a labyrinth pattern around the rim and changed her life forever. Francesco de' Medici, alchemist and prince, his favorite room at the Palazzo Vecchio a golden studiolo with metals and earths, crystals and acids and bones, concealed in compartments behind priceless paintings. Would anyone else ever find them? Would they find the secret door? It was like him, that room—a rich exterior with a hundred hidden things, some of them beautiful, some of them ugly, some of them terrifying.

Well, may his soul sink down into the fires of hell where it belonged. Perhaps the prayers of the Grand Duchess Giovanna in heaven would save him one day, because for all his wickedness she had never stopped loving him.

"Signorina Chiara," said the cardinal. The grand duke now, although she wasn't sure she'd ever be able to think of him that way. "Good. I require your witness against this woman, that she might be punished for her sins as she deserves."

"I will speak the truth as I saw it, my lord," she said. "But I beg you—"

"The truth is all I desire," he said.

Chiara nodded. She didn't look at Ruan.

"Now," the cardinal said, turning his attention to Bianca Cappello. "My brother is dead and can no longer protect you. I wish to—"

"Your brother is dead because you poisoned him." Bianca Cappello's voice was flat and husky, as if with tears and screaming.

"So you say," the cardinal said. "The symptoms were the symptoms of advanced tertian fever, were they not? The seizures, the vomiting, the purging? The doctors have been treating him for such a fever for a week now, and will witness to that fact when his body is opened."

"You poisoned him," Donna Bianca said again. "Magister Ruanno was there."

Chiara looked at Ruan. His face was shadowed and without expression. He didn't move. He didn't have to. It was enough that he was there.

"You poisoned him," Bianca Cappello said for the third time. It was as if she still could not quite believe it, and was trying to convince herself. "You have hated him and wished him dead from the day he married me. Wished both of us dead."

"From the day he married you?" the cardinal said. He might have been arguing a fine point of theology with a roomful of bishops. "You are mistaken. I have hated you from the day you polluted the Grand Duchess Giovanna's wedding day with your presence and first set your snares for my brother."

"I did not—"

"Do not insult us all with your lies. You made the grand duchess's life an agony of sorrow and humiliation, and you caused her death in the end."

Chiara saw Donna Bianca's hands twist together, where they lay on the prie-dieu. "I did not push her," she said. She turned her head and looked straight into Chiara's eyes. Chiara stepped back involuntarily. "You were there," Donna Bianca said. "If you tell the truth as you say you wish to do, you will bear witness to that. I did not push her."

"Well, Signorina Chiara?" the cardinal said. "You were threatened by my brother, and so you held your peace. Now he is dead, and there is no one to hurt you. Tell your story, from beginning to end, the truth without omission."

So. Here it was. The moment she had dreamed of, longed for, given up hope of ever seeing. There was life and feeling in the moment still—she wanted Bianca Cappello to pay for all the anguish she had caused with her ambition and selfishness. She wanted to bear public witness to the Grand Duchess Giovanna and how kind she had been. How she had loved her children. How she had loved her little hounds. How she had loved God. How, somehow, she had loved her husband, for all the misery and shame he had brought her. All that love, hidden behind the steely pride of her Imperial blood.

But even so—to say words that would bring about another woman's death? Even if they were true words? Even if the other woman deserved the death a hundred times over? Even if she had doubled a leather leash and struck Vivi hard enough to make her yelp with fright and pain?

Some people said revenge was hot. Some said it was cold. In truth it was dry and bitter as ashes.

"The grand duchess wished to go to the Palazzo Pitti that day," Chiara said slowly. The images welled up in her memory, clear as clear. The grand duchess's voice. *The gardens are so lovely, and it is warm for April.* The dogs barking as their leashes were snapped on. "We set out to take the dogs with us. The grand duchess spoke to little Prince Filippo. The nurse told her that he had said the word 'Mama,' and that he was a good boy."

The room was utterly silent. The cardinal and Ruan were like ghosts, in front of her and behind her, one scarlet, one black. Chiara saw only Bianca Cappello, kneeling in the candlelight.

"We started down, but the old dogs couldn't manage the stairs. The grand duchess sent her other women—" She closed her eyes for a moment, visualizing. The memories were flooding back, and they made her head hurt so much. She needed time to sort them out and put them in the proper order. "She sent them back upstairs with the two old dogs. I stayed, because I had Vivi with me. And I didn't want to leave the grand duchess entirely alone."

The cardinal moved, distracting her. She looked at him and saw that he had bowed his head and put his hand over his eyes.

"A woman came up to us and spoke to the grand duchess. She was dressed as a servant, but when I saw her face I knew her. It was you, Donna Bianca."

"I confess it freely," Bianca Cappello said. "I was there."

"You were there to spy upon her."

"I confess that as well."

"She didn't acknowledge your presence. She asked me to help her walk down the rest of the stairs. You pushed me aside, and when I stumbled I stepped on poor Vivi's paw. She yelped with pain. That made the grand duchess angry, that you would push me, and that Vivi would be hurt."

Touch either Signorina Chiara or her dog again, and I will make you sorry.

"It was only a dog."

Chiara could feel anger welling up in her heart. "Only a dog? She feels pain, just as you do. I haven't forgotten that you struck her when you took her away from Le Murate."

Donna Bianca looked down and didn't answer. Chiara waited for a moment, to calm her temper.

"The grand duchess asked you why you were dressed as you were," she went on at last. "You told her you didn't need silks and jewels to prove your worth, or an iron corset to keep your back straight."

The cardinal lifted his head. "Venetian *sgualdrina*," he hissed.

Donna Bianca turned and looked at him. "You call me names for the words I used?" she said. "What did the grand duchess say then, Signorina Chiara? Surely you remember that as well."

"She said an iron bridle to control your tongue would be a fine thing."

Donna Bianca nodded, as if she had been vindicated. She said nothing more.

"More hard things were said, on both sides. Then, Donna Bianca, you called little Prince Filippo a monster. You told her the grand duke as well used such words to describe his one legitimate son."

"It was a lie. I confess it. I wished to hurt her."

"She struck you across the mouth at that. I remember that I was shocked—it was unlike the grand duchess to allow herself to be provoked. I don't think she'd ever struck any other person deliberately, not once in her whole life. But you called her son a monster."

"And that is when she fell. She struck me, and lost her balance."

"You struck back. You'd had a lot more practice slapping people, hadn't you? I jumped to catch her and I would have, I would have saved her—but you struck her back and hit her shoulder and she fell."

Donna Bianca said nothing for a long time. At last, very quietly, she said, "I struck her back. I confess it. But I did not push her, and I did not mean for her to fall."

"You struck her," the cardinal said. "You confess it. And do you confess as well that you conspired with the grand duke to introduce a changeling son into his household? Do you confess that the woman Gianna Santi's deposition is truthful—that the two of you killed at least five women, and some unknown number of other children, in order to achieve your end?"

Donna Bianca looked down at her hands again. She knows, Chiara thought. She knows she's going to die tonight, and with the grand duke dead before her, she doesn't care. She doesn't want to live without him.

Steadily Donna Bianca said, "I confess it."

"Very well." The cardinal straightened. "Magister Ruanno, ask my secretary to step in, if you please. I will also require the priest and the executioner."

"Serenissimo," Chiara said. The words *priest* and *executioner* made her stomach lurch unpleasantly. "A moment, I beg you."

Ruan did not move. The cardinal turned and looked at her.

"I know the favor you wish to beg," he said. "Giovanna would have done the same—asked me to spare her life, to let her live out her years behind the walls of a convent, in solitude and penance."

"No," Chiara said. "I am not asking for her life. She knows what I want."

Vivi. Where is Vivi?

"I want no one to beg for my life," Bianca Cappello said, in a low voice. "Thank you, Signorina Chiara, for sparing me that. Your hound is with the kennel master at the Palazzo Pitti. She is perfectly well, and I am sorry I struck her."

"Enough," the cardinal said. "Magister Ruanno, I gave you an order."

Without a word Ruan bowed and went out. As he turned, his hand brushed against hers, for the tiniest fraction of a second. It might have been nothing but chance, but Chiara knew it wasn't. It was Ruan saying *Have courage*.

He came back in with two men. The priest was a Minorite in black and white, tonsured and sandaled. He had his hood up and his face was hidden as he murmured Latin prayers.

The executioner might have been an ordinary courtier, dressed in a dark red doublet of *moccaiaro* cloth and plain hose. Chiara had expected a hulking monster in leather, his chest bare and sweating, but this man—he was much of a height with Ruan, and had the same well-muscled shoulders. From swinging axes and pulling ropes, no doubt. He was masked and hooded and gloved, so no inch of his skin showed. In his right hand he carried a garrote, a simple loop of braided leather with a wooden handle securely knotted to each end.

He didn't speak. He bowed to the cardinal and stood in silence, awaiting his orders.

"Confess your sins," the cardinal said to Bianca Cappello. "Prepare yourself."

The priest stepped close to where Donna Bianca knelt, and put his head down to hers. They whispered together. Chiara wondered what she was confessing. The truth about her first husband's death? The truth about Don Antonio's birth? The truth about that night in the poison labyrinth? Or any truth at all?

She finished her confession. The priest straightened and held up his hand. *"Ego absolvo te a peccatis tuis,"* he said. *"In nomine Patris et Filii et Spiritus Sancti. Amen."* He traced the sign of the cross in the air, and stepped back. Donna Bianca lifted her head and looked at the executioner.

She saw the garrote—she swallowed, and then slowly and quite deliberately reached up and removed her veil. Her hair was braided and twisted, leaving her neck bare. She let the thin silk drift to the floor, and she put the diamond pin on the prie-dieu. Her jewels would be the executioner's due.

She stretched her neck, raising her chin, lowering her shoulders.

The swan, Chiara thought. Her device.

Then she closed her eyes and her lips moved. Was she praying, or was she whispering to the grand duke—*I will be with you soon, my Franco. Your Bia will be with you soon*. Her face seemed lit from within, as if she was expecting some enormous pleasure. But then, the things the grand duke had done to her, the ways he had taught her to take her delights, they were not so different, were they, from what she faced now?

The executioner stepped behind her. He drew out the garrote to its full length between his gloved hands, as if testing its strength. Chiara saw the muscles in his arms shift. She wanted to close her eyes but she couldn't look away.

The executioner waited. His eyes, behind the mask, shifted to the cardinal.

The priest prayed.

The cardinal lifted his hand.

The executioner crossed his arms, looped the garrote around Bianca Cappello's throat and jerked it tight with quick and terrible precision. Her eyes widened briefly and then went blank. Her body sagged against the loop of braided leather, stretching her neck all the further. He knew exactly where to place the loop, Chiara thought with horror, just like Ruan knew how to wrap his arm around my neck that first day in the grand duke's golden studiolo, and make me unconscious in an instant.

She managed to close her eyes at last. She clenched her fists, the crooked fingers aching. There was no sound but the breathing of the executioner, harsh with his effort, and the faint creaking of the garrote's braided leather. Let it be over, she thought. Let it be over quickly.

A soft sound, with the rustling of cloth. Chiara opened her eyes.

The executioner had let Bianca Cappello's body slump forward against the prie-dieu. She looked quite natural, as if she had put her head down to pray, and her face was hidden. He was looping the garrote into coils as if it was the most ordinary thing in the world, to strangle a woman and leave her body lying limp in her silks and laces like a wilted flower.

When he was finished, he bowed to the cardinal, still without a word. The cardinal nodded to him. He picked up the diamond pin and went out of the room, followed by the priest. Chiara realized she was holding her breath, and let it out in a great sigh. She wanted to cross herself, but her arms wouldn't move.

"She has died of the same tertian fever that carried off the grand duke," the cardinal said. "Unfortunate, but such fevers are common, and she insisted on nursing him herself."

"The mark on her throat?" Ruan said.

"I will have her face covered with a silk cloth when they open the bodies, for her modesty's sake. It will hide her throat as well. You may be sure the physicians will point out all the marks and symptoms of the fever when they draw up the death certificates."

Yes, Chiara thought. We may be sure. They will want to please the new grand duke. She stepped closer to Ruan. She was a little afraid to look at him, but even so she wanted to feel the warmth of his body close to hers. Life, in a room where death was so close—

"Serenissimo," Ruan said. "Shall we leave for Florence immediately? Signorina Chiara can lead us through the labyrinth to your brother's hiding-place, and then she and I will collect her little dog and be off to Cornwall."

Footsteps. Heavy ones. Metal and leather creaking. Chiara's knees turned to water with fear, and she looked around.

The six soldiers.

"We will indeed leave for Florence immediately," the new grand duke said. He smiled. "I will have my brother's mithridate for myself, and the two of you—well, lead me to the center of this labyrinth my brother spoke of, and perhaps I will allow you to live."

CHAPTER FIFTY-EIGHT

They rode south to Signa and crossed the ancient bridge to Lastra, then followed the Arno east to the city. A moon just past full had begun to rise in the darkening sky. The grand duke pressed the horses, and when one of them cast a shoe, he left the horse and the guardsman behind. With the remaining five guardsmen they arrived at the iron gate to the poison labyrinth as the moon reached its height.

The grand duke gave his brother's keys to one of the guardsmen, who tried each one in turn until he found the right one.

"Take the lantern, Signorina Chiara." The grand duke gestured to one of the guardsmen, who produced a lantern from his saddlebag and struck a spark with his flint to light it. "Now. Lead the way. You and you"—he gestured to two of the guards—"accompany me. Have your blades at the ready, if you please. The rest of you, remain here. Allow no one to enter, and no one but me to leave."

He's going to kill us, Chiara thought, no matter what he said. I wouldn't want to be one of those guards, either, because they're going to end up at the bottom of the Arno right along with us. He doesn't want anyone to know about the hiding-place or what's in it.

"Take care you walk in the center of the path," she said aloud. She lifted the lantern, and its wavering light made the intertwined tree limbs writhe like serpents. "The plants are poisoned, and the thorns will kill us all."

Ruan knew, of course. He'd helped create the *sonnodolce* from the beginning. He'd taken it himself for years. But in his prison—

You will not die or go mad without it. He gave me none after he imprisoned me, and although it was bad for a while, I survived.

Five years it had been for him without the drug. She herself was immune to the poison of the thorns, and that secret would be her weapon. Ruan, though, Ruan was as vulnerable as the grand duke and his guardsmen. A scratch, a single prick that drew blood, could kill him.

She looked at him. He looked back at her and nodded very slightly. *Lead us to the center, where there will be room to move safely. I will watch for my chance to take a blade from one of the guards. I will avoid the thorns—but if I cannot, at least I will give you a chance to escape.*

Was she reading his thoughts? Or did she simply know him so well she knew what he planned to do?

She drew one deep breath and walked into the labyrinth. Ruan walked behind her, then the two guardsmen with their swords drawn, and the grand duke behind them all. When they had made their way around the first double fold and back to the straight path, the grand duke said, "So this is the labyrinth where my brother concealed his hiding-place. I have walked in these gardens a hundred times, and never knew such a thing was behind the iron gate."

Chiara said nothing. They walked on. She thought of the night she had stumbled through the maze alone, without a lantern, burning with thorn-scratches and dizzy with the effects of the *sonnodolce*. So long ago, and in the summer, not October. She had been immune to the poison then, and she would be immune now. But Ruan, Ruan—

The path curved, then doubled back upon itself. The grand duke didn't speak again. Chiara held the lantern high. Most of the roses had finished blooming, but there were a few gallant blossoms left, enough to perfume the night air with their scent. The hornbeams had no scent, but the yew trees smelled green and medicinal, like the bags of rosemary and eucalyptus leaves the nuns at Le Murate had placed between their folded linens.

At last they came out into the clearing at the center of the maze. They clustered together, all of them keeping as far away from the thorns as they could get.

"There's a stone," Chiara said. "In the very center. When I found it, the night I was in the maze before, I didn't think it was anything but a marker, laid down to help the original workmen lay out the circles of the path. But it has carvings. Look."

She knelt by the stone—the grass wasn't lush and velvety now, but dry and crisp in the October chill—and placed the lantern beside it. One of the guardsmen pushed Ruan to his knees facing her. The grand duke came up and knelt down himself.

"It is a meteor," Ruan said. "A stone that falls from the sky, rich with iron. Look at the holes, like bubbles. It has been so hot the stone itself has boiled."

"I have heard of such things," the grand duke said. He touched the stone. "They are valuable."

Chiara ran her fingers over the carvings. The shield and balls of the Medici, the lily of Florence, and the weasel, symbol of boldness and resolution, Francesco de' Medici's personal device. A fourth design she couldn't identify.

"This is the place," she said. "I'm sure of it."

"We must dig under it to be certain," the grand duke said. He stood up and brushed his hands together fastidiously. "Signorina Chiara, you will do the work. Remember there are two swords at Magister Ruanno's throat, and at your own back as well."

He drew his dagger and tossed it to the grass beside her. Wordlessly she picked it up and began to cut away thick sods of grass from around the stone. It was sunk into the ground more deeply than it appeared, and it was very heavy, heavier than it should have been. Ruan had said—rich with iron. That was why it had such strange, rust-red patches and veins.

She stabbed the blade into the earth. Every thrust sent a shock of effort through her arms and shoulders, half-pain, half-pleasure. She scooped out the loosened earth and stabbed some more. She was driving the blade into Ferdinando de' Medici's treacherous heart. She was piercing Bianca Cappello's hand as it swung to strike the grand duchess's shoulder. As it doubled the leash and struck Vivi. She was stabbing Francesco de' Medici with his initiations and his secrets and his black, black shadows. Stabbing the men who had ridden her down so many years ago as she played in the street with her brother, then galloped on, leaving their lives in ruins. Stabbing Babbo, even, who had hated her for surviving when Gian was dead. Who had planned her own death in his mad quest to bring Gian back, and haunted her down through the years with his demons' voices.

You made a blast and a fire, she screamed in her head, *and you died. I made a blast and a fire, and I survived. I'll survive this, too, you'll see. I'll prove to you that I deserve to live—*

Abruptly the knife struck metal. The impact jarred her wrists. She lifted her head and realized she was sweating with effort. Her face was wet and her eyes were blurred and stinging.

"Chiara," Ruan said.

"Be silent," said the grand duke. "What have you found, Signorina Chiara?"

"It's a box of some kind."

She scooped the loose earth away from the box and dug a little deeper. She tried to lift the box out of the hole, but it was too heavy. It was the size of a footstool or a little larger, made of metal, too tarnished to identify. Around its sides there were more engravings, the same four figures that were incised into the stone.

"It's locked," she said. "A loop and latch. The earth has eaten away at it—I think I can break it."

"No. Put the dagger aside, Signorina Chiara, and stand up. Both of you, step back to the edge of the clearing, if you please."

The guardsmen swung their swords forward. Chiara put the dagger down on the grass—a dagger, dulled from digging, wouldn't be any use against blades in the hands of two skilled swordsmen anyway—and stood up. She looked at Ruan and looked away, so she wouldn't reveal what she knew he meant to do.

Together they stepped back to the hedgerow.

"Another step."

Ruan edged between her and the guardsmen's blades. The thorns were no more than a hand's breadth from his back, gleaming in the moonlight. Chiara felt his fingers close around hers briefly.

"Step back," the grand duke said again. "I am giving you a choice, both of you—the thorns, or a sword."

Chiara closed her eyes. She thought of all the drops of *sonnodolce* that had fallen on her wrist, for years and years, from that very first night in the bookshop's cellar—

Ruan moved before she could finish the thought, pushing her to one side and at the same time ducking under the first guardsman's blade to grasp the second man's forearm with both his hands. Was it the moonlight that made everything seem to happen so slowly, or the flicker of the lantern, or some magic effect of the ancient stone from the farthest heavens? She saw the grand duke's mouth open, shouting an order. The first guardsman began to turn.

If Ruan had been himself, with the hard heavy muscles he'd lost to his long imprisonment, he would have broken the guard's arm with a single jerk. As it was, he pulled the man to the grass and rolled over and over, grappling for his sword as they lurched perilously close to the thorns on the other side of the clearing. The first guardsman swung his blade, looking for an opening, unwilling to kill his brother-in-arms in order to kill Ruan. The grand duke jumped back, to the other side of the stone. He reached for Chiara.

—it didn't kill me, and now it's going to save our lives.

She turned and deliberately grasped a double handful of the rose canes. The thorns sank into her palm and fingers—saints and angels, it was pain like she'd never known before. Grimly she tore the rose canes away from the bush. Blood ran down her wrists, soaked into her sleeves, and dripped into the grass. The grand duke cried out and pulled his hands away. The second guardsman had Ruan pinned at last, so close to the hedgerow— blood on Ruan's face, from the fight or from a thorn? The first guardsman had his sword arched back over his head, preparing for a killing blow.

With a wordless shriek of fury and horror she swung the bunch of canes at the man with the sword. They lashed the air like whips, tearing his neck and back and shoulder, slicing through his padded woolen doublet as if it was the thinnest silk. He stiffened and shuddered, and although he managed to swing the sword down he had lost his aim and it thrust into the ground instead of into Ruan's heart. Chiara struck him again with the rose canes and he fell.

The second guardsman had stumbled to his feet. Ruan rolled away from the hedgerow, reaching for the pommel of the abandoned sword. Chiara slashed the second guardsman's face with the canes and he screamed like a woman, throwing up his arms to protect his eyes. Ruan dragged the sword out of the ground and came to his feet, gasping with exertion.

It was over. That quickly. Both guardsmen lay twitching, dying, dead. The grand duke faced them, weaponless. All around them, the poison thorns, the moonlight, and utter silence.

"Ruan," she gasped. "Your face. Did one of the thorns—"

"No, *meur ras dhe Duw*. Just the guardsman's fist."

"There are guards at the gate," the grand duke said. "If you kill me, they will never let you leave the maze."

"Perhaps," Ruan said. "Perhaps not. Chiara, are you all right? Your hands—"

She dropped the rose canes. Her hands felt numb.

"Let them bleed," she said. "Nonna always said it was good for wounds to bleed a while, because it cleans out the evil humors."

"You will never leave the maze," the grand duke said again. "Not without me."

She looked at him. She had never had such a large dose of the *sonnodolce*, all at once, and it made her dizzy. All her senses ran together, sight becoming sound, touch becoming taste, scent becoming sight again. The man standing before them, dressed in his rich scarlet and with a huge cabochon sapphire glowing on his finger—was it Ferdinando de' Medici or Francesco de' Medici, or some incomprehensible combination of the two? Whichever it was, it was the Grand Duke of Tuscany. She could taste the red lily crown on his head, hear the sharp, fleshy scent of lilies, feel the harshness of his breathing. She could smell his thoughts. *I have not killed my brother and his Venetian whore, only to die here in secret, at the hands of an English alchemist and a bookseller's daughter.*

"I will give you gold," he said. "More than you have ever dreamed of."

"Chiara?"

It was Ruan's voice. She turned slowly. From that first moment in the Piazza della Signoria when he had driven away the guardsmen with his whip, through terror and learning, love and hate, loneliness and pleasure beyond anything else she'd ever known, he had been there, behind her, beside her, holding her. He had thrown himself at the guardsmen knowing he couldn't prevail against them both, knowing that if he was pushed into the thorns he would die, all to give her a chance to fight for them both, and save both their lives.

"Ruan," she said. "I'm all right—a little dizzy from the *sonnodolce*."

"It is a miracle that you are alive at all," he said. "That either one of us is alive."

She said again, "I'm all right. The box, Ruan. We must open the box."

He stepped forward. The grand duke stepped backward one step and stopped, afraid. Ruan lifted the sword and said, "Turn around."

"I saved you," the grand duke said. His voice was high. "You would still be in that hole in the rock if I had not set you free."

"Turn around."

"A priest. You cannot kill me without a priest."

"Turn around."

The grand duke turned. Pale and weakened Ruan might have been, but he still had his height and his peculiar skills. He dropped the sword and got his forearm around the grand duke's throat, right up under his chin. With his other hand he pushed the back of the grand duke's head forward. The grand duke collapsed as if he'd been poleaxed.

Chiara threw herself down beside the half-uncovered box, picked up the dagger, and began to strike the rusted hasp of the lock. She seemed to have strength beyond anything she'd ever had before, although the strange sensations induced by the *sonnodolce* were already fading. After a few blows the hasp broke away. She brushed the pieces aside and put back the lid.

"Holy Saint Petroc," Ruan murmured. He picked up the lantern and turned it so the light shone fully on the contents of the box.

An enormous double rose cut diamond set in gold. A chunk of hematite, set in iron and copper. Between them, the moonstone set in silver, so perfectly polished that it might have been worn and re-set and worn again since the creation of the world.

This is a moonstone from the kingdom of Ruhuna, on an island far to the east, beyond Persia, beyond the Silk Road. . . .

"The amulets," Chiara said. "I wondered what had become of them."

"There's more. More jewels—Chiara, this will keep us in comfort all our lives."

Her hands throbbed. She said, "The formula. Is the formula there?"

He began to pull the jewels out of the box and pile them in the grass. There were a few odd instruments in the box as well, clearly with some scientific or alchemical function but not like anything Chiara had seen before. At the very bottom of the box there was another box made of polished cedar wood. It had been treated with some kind of wax to repel moisture. Ruan took it out and opened it.

Inside, packed in powdered gypsum to preserve it, was a single piece of parchment. Ruan took it out and brushed the chalky powder away, and Chiara recognized the writing from the great book that had been turned to ashes in the blast and the fire at the bookshop. Not Babbo's writing. The writing of the unknown original scribe, the even, heavy letters, faded by time. At the top of the page was written, *Venenum matri veterum effectus dulcedinem enim dico* sonnodolce. Some of the letters were smudged and hard to read. She puzzled it out. *The mother poison of the ancients, which I call* sonnodolce *for the sweetness of its effect.*

"That's it," she said. "It's all in Latin."

"More valuable than the jewels."

"We need to take the jewels too. Give me the dagger—I'll cut off the bottom of the grand duke's cloak and make a bundle."

"I'll do it. Have your hands stopped bleeding?"

"Mostly."

"How do you feel?"

She grinned at him in the moonlight. "A lot better than Ferdinando de' Medici expected me to feel. What are we going to do with him?"

Ruan slashed a piece of fine red wool from the grand duke's cloak and began to put the treasure in the center of it. "He will be unconscious for another few hours," he said. "I will bind his hands and feet with his shirt-lacings, and that will keep him immobilized until someone comes to find him. I have been part of enough death for one day, *awen lymm*, and he was right—he did set me free. But I will kill him if you wish him dead."

Wish him dead?

Grand Duke Francesco on the floor, sprawled in a horrifying welter of blood and vomit and feces, his night-cap fallen off and his head bare.

Bianca Cappello's body slumped forward against the prie-dieu, lying limp in her silks and laces like a wilted flower.

"No," she said. "I've had enough of death as well."

He ran his hand over his face. The cut over his eye had stopped bleeding. As if it was the most important thing in the world, he said, "*My a'th kar*, Chiara."

"You said that before. What does it mean?"

"I love you."

A final flicker of the *sonnodolce* made the words feel like an embrace. She said, "I love you too, Ruan."

"We will leave him, then. Once we arrive in Cornwall we must both write down everything we know, and send him letters to the effect that if either of us comes to harm, the information will be made public in all the courts of Europe. Jago Warne can be trusted to hold the papers secretly."

"And when he realizes we mean him no harm if he doesn't try to hurt us, he'll be clever enough—"

"And self-interested enough."

"—to know he has been checkmated." She smiled at him. "Will he be unconscious for a while? We have to go into the palace and find Vivi."

He smiled in return. "Remember how long you were unconscious, that first night."

"What about the guards at the gate?"

"I think a diamond or two apiece will persuade them to let us pass."

He had bound the grand duke and they had started out of the center of the labyrinth when the throbbing in her hands stopped her. She said, "Ruan, let's take some of the thorns. I need the *sonnodolce*, and we won't have the time or equipment to make it."

"Thank God one of us is practical."

He stripped the grand duke's fine gloves from his hands and put them on, then carefully began to break thorns from the rose canes. "Twenty-six," he said, "will give us half a year. Plenty of time to get to Cornwall and build a new laboratory."

"I will start the *magnum opus* again," she said. "I was so close, Ruan."

"We will talk about it when we are safe," he said. "Now let us go. We will leave the city by the Porta Romana—it is the closest. The grand duke will expect us to make for Livorno, so we will go farther south to Piombino instead."

"And find a priest to marry us?"

He laughed. She had never heard him laugh with so much pure happiness. "A priest," he said. "And then a ship as fast as the wind."

At the iron gate, the grand duke's guardsmen were happy to take a fortune in jewels and disappear.

The kennel master at the Palazzo Pitti welcomed them with relief.

"That poor little hound," he said. "She's been a-pining. Won't eat, won't play. I don't mind telling you, I don't have much use for that Grand Duchess Bianca."

The kennel boy Rudi brought Vivi in. She flung herself into Chiara's arms with a high cry, like a baby's. Torn hands and all, Chiara hugged her desperately.

Ruan said, "You will no longer have to deal with Donna Bianca."

The kennel master frowned for a moment. "That cardinal?" he said. "Yes."

"Don't want to know more," he said. "But I'll be keeping an eye out for little Princess Maria. The last of Donna Giovanna's girls. The boy's not bad, either, the one they call Prince Antonio. No get of the grand duke's, but that's not his fault."

"He won't be a prince any longer. Can you do something for Signorina Chiara's hands? Clean them and bandage them, and give her a pair of gloves?"

"That I can, that I can. Always treating the dogs' cuts and scrapes. *Mutter Jesu, fräulein*, what did you do to yourself?"

With the same gruff tenderness he would've used on a wounded spaniel, he sponged Chiara's torn palms with soap and water and strong liniment, then wrapped them in clean bandages and gave her some soft leather gloves.

"There you go," he said. "Change those bandages every two or three days. Take good care of your little hound, now. She has a faithful heart."

After that they made their way to the stables, where two star sapphires bought them two riding horses and a packhorse with double panniers. Ruan packed the red wool bundle into one pannier, and in the other made a warm nest with blankets. Chiara lifted Vivi inside, petting her and whispering to her.

"We have a long journey ahead," she said. "It's all right now. No one will ever hurt you or take you away from me again."

Vivi looked up and perked her ears forward. *You took long enough*, her expression said. *But I knew you would never leave me forever*. Her eyes were bright as ever, dark-rimmed, even though her face was white. She sighed contentedly and tucked her nose down between her paws.

Ruan checked the girths. "Up you go," he said to Chiara, helping her to mount her horse. He swung up on his own horse and pulled its head around.

The sky was just beginning to lighten when they reached the Porta Romana. The main barred gate in the center was closed, but there were four small portals, two on each side. Ruan guided his horse to the one farthest to the left. A man appeared from the shadows. Ruan put something into his hand, and after a moment he opened the portal.

"Come through," Ruan said.

They rode through.

"Wait," Chiara said. "I have to get down."

"Chiara, we have no time."

She was already scrambling down from her horse. The Via Romana was paved with stones of every shape and size, sunk in packed soil and worn by hundreds of years of horses and oxen, wagons and plain walking feet. She sank to her knees and awkwardly, with her gloved hands, dug one of the small stones free. It looked like a piece of Nonna's *schiacciata*, dimpled on its upper surface, light brown flecked with darker brown and white.

Oh, yes. Almond milk and schiacciata. We've come up in the world, mia nipotina, *since you've become a plaything of the Medici.*

"Chiara, what are you doing?"

"Good-bye, Nonna," she whispered. "I'll take this with me and I'll always have a little piece of home."

Travel safely, nipotina. *Don't forget me. Don't forget you have a sister. Don't forget your Babbo, who loved you once, before his mind was twisted.*

"I won't forget," Chiara said. "I'll forgive him some day, if I can."

He never meant it. Nonna's voice again. *He was mad with his grief. Let your new life be free from this poison,* nipotina. *Forgive him now, and go across the sea to the west with a light heart.*

Chiara pressed the piece of stone to her heart for a moment, then got to her feet, put the stone in her saddlebag and swung back into the saddle. She looked around at Ruan.

"You knew about the necromancy, didn't you? About Babbo meaning to sacrifice me to bring Gian back."

"I did not know. I guessed."

"I wanted to show him I was worthy to live. I wanted to be greater than Perenelle Flamel, all to show him."

He reached out his hand and touched her cheek. "You are worthy to live because you are you," he said. "Not Perenelle Flamel. You. Chiara Nerini."

She put her hand over his. Even through the glove and the bandages, she could feel his warmth.

"I love you, Ruan," she said. "I forgive him. And I will never look back."

CHAPTER FIFTY-NINE

Milhyntall House, Mount's Bay, Cornwall

17 APRIL 1589

Chiara kept the ingredients for the *sonnodolce* in a special locked cabinet—black, white, yellow, red. She knew exactly what they were, and exactly how to combine them—purified powdered charcoal made from oleander wood, crystallized sap from the root of the water hemlock, the crushed and sun-dried golden stamens of the nightshade flower, and the distilled and re-distilled essence of red lily petals. The page of parchment with the formula she kept rolled up in its cedarwood box, in the same cabinet. She had been giving herself less and less, from week to week. But this morning—this morning she was putting it all away. Closing and locking the cabinet for good.

The laboratory at Milhyntall House wasn't hidden away in a cellar. It was on the upper floor on the west side of the house, with windows facing west and south over the bay. Through the south window she could see the island of Saint Michael's Mount, with its ancient monastery. Ruan wouldn't go to the island—he said he could still feel the misery and terror of his father and mother and the other people who had taken refuge there during the rebellion, only to be driven out and imprisoned by the English. To her the island looked peaceful and remote. She could imagine the monks that would have lived there in past centuries.

"A rider has come from London."

She looked up. It was Ruan.

"Has he brought letters?" Ruan's riders from London always brought letters. He corresponded with the most astonishing people, from the English queen's occultist and advisor Dr. John Dee to a highly placed secretary in the emperor's household in Vienna, from a great doctor of canon law at the University in Ferrara to the French king himself, Henri III. All of them seemed to want Ruan to go and live in their cities and devote himself to their desires alone. No one would believe that Magister Roannes Pencarianus, the mysterious alchemist who was still whispered about in Vienna and Florence and up and down the length of Italy, would truly want to live on a windswept estate in Cornwall and do nothing but manage the workings of his own mine.

"A good-sized packet." Ruan shrugged the coiled whip from his shoulder, then bent his head and kissed the corner of her mouth. "What are you doing, *magistra*?"

"Putting the *sonnodolce* away."

"You do not have the components in suitable proportions. You require more of the red-lily distillate."

She looked at the glass jars. He was right. It didn't matter, but—well, maybe it was better to be safe. What if the voices came back after the baby was born? It would be the dead of winter, and there would be no lilies in the garden.

Ruan didn't know yet, about the baby.

"You're right," she said. "I'll collect some of the lilies today. I'm not going to take any more of it, though, Ruan. I've been taking less and less, half a drop now, every twenty-one days. I feel well—strong. I want to be free of it."

He put his arms around her. He was different. He'd always been a strange, uneasy combination of the workman and the gentleman, and you'd think that now, when he was lord of his own estate at Milhyntall at last, he'd have settled down and become a gentleman through and through. Just the opposite had happened. He was tanned by the sun and the sea wind from being outdoors at Wheal Loer. His hands had fresh calluses over the scars. There were threads of silver interwoven with the glints of copper in his dark hair, but when he smiled—oh, when he smiled, it was real, the good smile, not only his mouth but his eyes as well.

"Just so you have what you need to make more, if you need it," he said.

She put the cabinet aside. "I'll go down to the garden now," she said. "Come with me, and tell me about your letters."

They walked down the stairs. Vivi lay in the square patch of sunshine at the kitchen door. She did love the sunshine on her poor stiff joints. When she heard their steps she lifted her head.

"We're going out into the garden, Vivi," Chiara said. "Do you want to come?"

Vivi put her head down again and sighed with deep contentment. *No, thank you*, the sigh said, plain as plain. *I'll just stay here and bask in the nice warm sun.*

The puppies trotted in at the sound of her voice. They loved the garden. "Come on, then, Rudhloes. Owrlin."

It was the doctor of science in Ferrara who had arranged the matter of the puppies, whose names meant "Russet" and "Silk" in Cornish. The duke's hound master, it seemed, had continued to breed the little parti-colored hounds from the original pair that had been sent to Duchess Barbara of Austria as a wedding gift by the queen of England. With Duchess Barbara being Grand Duchess Giovanna's sister, and the two new puppies being—well, who knew exactly, but in some long and complicated way related by blood to Vivi—it made them special. Not that they needed anything but their own melting dark eyes and merry little white-flagged tails to be special.

Chiara picked up a basket and a small knife, and they went out into the garden, which was protected by the bulk of the house itself from the salt winds off the sea.

"One letter," Ruan said, "was from Dr. Dee himself. He is pressing me urgently to go to London—the queen has just sent her Counter-Armada to Spain, and imagines great victories on the sea. Dr. Dee is not so certain, and before she launches any further attacks he wants her ships better-supplied and better-armed. To that end, he has convinced her that I can make Greek Fire of particular purity."

"Can you?"

He laughed. "No," he said. "The formula for Greek Fire has been lost for centuries. Best that it stay lost, I think. Such weapons are often misused."

"Are you going to go to London?"

"Perhaps, in a month or two—Jago Warne can manage things here. Would you like to go? You have never been to London."

"No," she said. She knew she was dangerously old for a first childbirth—thirty years old by the time the babe was to be born, thirty, how could that be?—and wanted to stay home and be safe with the baby curled under her heart. "Not this time. Were there other letters?"

"One from the Ferrarese ambassador in Florence."

She walked on, to the bed of lilies. They were glorious in the April sunshine, masses of them, some white, some pink, some red as blood. The sweet pollen-y lily scent drifted in the sea air. In the center of the lily bed lay the piece of stone from the Via Romana. Already it had settled into the rich earth of Cornwall, and looked as if it belonged there.

She knelt down and began to cut the brightest and most perfect of the red lilies.

"I'm not sure I want to know the news from Florence," she said.

"Your sister Mattea has returned. She has a husband now, and a baby, and is living not far from the rooms we had on the Via di Mezzo."

"I can't imagine the Ferrarese ambassador being interested in my sister."

Ruan laughed. The puppies liked the sound and romped around his feet. "He is not. I particularly asked him to make inquiries. You know the Duke of Ferrara hates the Medici, and so he has directed his ambassadors to make every effort to entice me to Ferrara and the university there."

"Everyone wants you."

"And I want only you." He watched her cutting the lilies for a moment, and then he said, "Grand Duke Ferdinando has chosen a wife. Her name is Christine of Lorraine—she is a niece of the French king, so clearly the grand duke is aligning himself with France rather than Spain. They are to be married next month, with great celebrations."

She thought of her own hurried marriage ceremony in the shabby little church in Piombino. She had never even known the name of the church or its patron saint, and even so she wouldn't trade it, not for all the great celebrations in the world. She said, "I don't envy her."

"The ambassadors says Ferdinando is a good ruler. Better than his brother."

"It was always his nature to be a prince," Chiara said. She cut another lily.

"His nature, and Isabella's. They were the most like old Duke Cosimo. Francesco—well, he wanted other things."

"Yes," Chiara said. "Other things. I wonder how Ferdinando escaped from the labyrinth. I wonder what he said to people, to explain it."

"I am sure he created a fine tale—he is intelligent enough. And no one can dispute that he is a true Medici, as they would have done with little Don Antonio."

"If only Prince Filippo had lived. That would have been the best."

She continued to cut the lilies. Her basket was almost full. Some day—some day perhaps she would go back in secret, see the Duomo against the sky, and breathe the air of Florence again.

"Why have you chosen this moment to stop taking the *sonnodolce*, *awen lymm*?"

She tried out different words in her head but none of them sounded right. Finally she said the simplest thing.

"I'm with child. I'm afraid the *sonnodolce* might mark it."

Ruan crouched down beside her. "Chiara. My dearest love. Put down that basket and that knife, if you please, so I can embrace you properly."

For a long time they knelt there, their arms around one another. The puppies followed scents in the grass, twisting and curling like the paths of an invisible labyrinth. The presence of the red lilies was overpowering for a moment—the scent of so many memories. Would the grand duke place the red lily crown on this Christine of Lorraine's head? When he did it, would he remember Giovanna of Austria, how he had loved her once, how proudly she had borne the weight of the crown until the day she died?

It didn't matter. Not anymore. None of it mattered. Well, maybe only one thing mattered.

"Are you ever sorry?" she said at last. "That we never created the true *Lapis Philosophorum*?"

"No. It does not exist."

"It does exist. And you wouldn't be you, Roannes Pencarianus, if you didn't want to be remembered as a man who achieved alchemy's greatest glory."

He chuckled. "Perhaps one day we will try again, then. Just you and me—like Perenelle Flamel and her Nicolas."

"They found the secret of eternal life. They will live forever."

"So the story goes."

"Maybe we will be like them," Chiara said. She picked up the most beautiful of the red lilies, broke off the flower, and tucked it into her hair where the silver streak grew over her left ear. "Maybe we will live forever, too."

The Cast of Characters

Those marked with an asterisk are fictional.

THE NERINI, BOOKSELLERS OF FLORENCE, AND THEIR CONNECTIONS:

*Carlo Nerini, called Babbo, member of the Booksellers' Guild and some-time alchemist, killed in an explosion before the story begins.

*Agnesa Baldesi Nerini, called Nonna, his mother and the children's grandmother.

*Gian Nerini, his son and heir, killed in a street accident before the story begins.

*Chiara Nerini, his eldest daughter, who entertains ambitions of her own.

*Lucia and Mattea Nerini, his two younger daughters.

*Giacinto Garzi, a bookseller's son from Pistoia.

THE MEDICI AND THEIR DIRECT CONNECTIONS:

Cosimo de' Medici, Duke of Florence and later the first Grand Duke of Tuscany, creator of the red lily crown.

Eleonora of Toledo, his wife, long dead when the story begins.

Cammilla Martelli, Duke Cosimo's morganatic second wife.

Francesco de' Medici, Prince of Florence and dedicated alchemist, Duke Cosimo's eldest son and heir.

Giovanna of Austria, Imperial archduchess and wife of Francesco de' Medici.

The children of Francesco de' Medici and Giovanna of Austria who survived infancy:

> Eleonora de' Medici, later married to Vincenzo I Gonzaga and Duchess of Mantua.

> Anna de' Medici, died unmarried at the age of fourteen.

> Maria de' Medici, later the wife of Henri IV and Queen of France as Marie de Médicis.

Filippo de' Medici, the longed-for male heir.

Isabella de' Medici, Princess of Florence and Duchess of Bracciano, Duke Cosimo's daughter.

Paolo Giordano Orsini, Duke of Bracciano, husband of Isabella de' Medici.

Ferdinando de' Medici, a cardinal since the age of fourteen, Duke Cosimo's middle son.

Pietro de' Medici, Duke Cosimo's youngest son.

Eleonora di Garzia di Toledo, called Dianora, first cousin and wife of Pietro de' Medici.

AT THE MEDICI COURT:

*Donna Jimena Osorio, a distant cousin of Eleonora of Toledo, childhood nurse and companion of Isabella de' Medici.

Bianca Cappello, a noblewoman of Venice. Francesco de' Medici's longtime mistress.

Antonio de' Medici, a boy of uncertain parentage, claimed by Bianca Cappello and Francesco de' Medici as their son.

Pietro Buonaventuri, Bianca Cappello's first husband, murdered before the story begins.

Orazio Pucci, anti-Medici conspirator and one of Donna Dianora's supposed lovers.

Pierino Ridolfi, anti-Medici conspirator and another of Donna Dianora's supposed lovers.

Troilo Orsini, Donna Isabella's lover.

Various physicians, priests, courtiers, conspirators and guardsmen.

IN THE EMPLOY OF THE MEDICI:

*Tommaso Vasari, an alchemist in Grand Duke Cosimo's household, who disappeared mysteriously with all his books and alchemical equipment around the time of Carnival in 1566.

*Johan Ziegler, the Hungarian master of the Medici silver mine at Bottino.

*Caterina Donati, childhood nurse and later trusted serving-woman of Bianca Cappello.

*Gianna Santi, musician and serving-woman of Bianca Cappello.

SCIENTISTS AND ALCHEMISTS:

Nicolas Flamel, a Frenchman celebrated in various writings as an alchemist.

Perenelle Flamel, his wife and *soror mystica*, or sister in the art of alchemy.

Georg Pawer, called in Latin Georgius Agricola, a German scientist and metallurgist, author of *De Re Metallica*.

*Konrad Pawer, called in Latin Conradus Agricola, Georg Pawer's nephew, a charlatan who trades on his uncle's famous name.

Dr. John Dee, astrologer, alchemist, and courtier to Elizabeth I.

THE CORNISH AND ENGLISH:

*Ruan Pencarrow of Milhyntall, in Italy called Ruanno dell' Inghilterra, a metallurgist and alchemist.

*Mark Pencarrow of Milhyntall, his father, killed in the Prayer Book Uprising of 1549.

*Carenza Pencarrow of Milhyntall, his mother, dead of privation and a broken heart when Ruan was six.

*Jago Warne, Ruan's foster brother and later mine manager at Wheal Loer.

*Andrew Lovell, an Englishman who took possession of the Milhyntall estate when it was confiscated by the English after the Prayer Book Uprising.

THE PARTI-COLORED HOUNDS:

*Tristo and Isa, the foundation sire and dam of the famous Ferrara beagles, sent to Duchess Barbara of Ferrara as a wedding gift by Queen Elizabeth I.

*Rostig and Seiden, two puppies from a Tristo/Isa litter, sent to Duchess Giovanna as a Christmas gift by her sister Barbara, Duchess of Ferrara.

*Rina and Leia, two puppies from a Rostig/Seiden litter.

*Vivi, Chiara's own beloved companion, a daughter of Rina crossed back to her sire Rostig.

*Rudhloes and Owrlin, two puppies from the original line of Ferrara beagles, sent as a gift to Chiara in Cornwall.

Author's Note

The intertwined stories of Francesco de' Medici, Giovanna of Austria, and Bianca Cappello have fascinated historians for over four hundred years.

In letters and documents of the day, Francesco is universally described as melancholy, introverted, and obsessed with alchemy. He had laboratories in the Casino di San Marco, the Villa di Pratolino, and other palaces; he was the first European to successfully reproduce Chinese-style porcelain, and a few examples of this blue-and-white "Medici porcelain" still exist today. His golden studiolo in the Palazzo Vecchio, which was dismantled after his death, has been reconstructed at its original site, with its many paintings, hidden cubbyholes, and secret doors.

One of the paintings in the studiolo, *Il Laboratorio dell' Alchimista* by Giovanni Stradano, is the basis for my creation of Francesco's alter ego Franco. In the painting the master alchemist is seated, wearing his academic gown and cap (and spectacles!), surrounded by apprentices and workmen who are doing the actual work of alchemy. In the lower right corner, wearing a plain doublet and hose, his sleeves rolled up as he stirs a concoction under the alchemist's direction, is a workman clearly painted to represent Francesco de' Medici. Is this how Francesco saw himself, in his secret heart? It makes sense, given his actions throughout his life, and opens fascinating vistas of speculation.

One letter Duke Cosimo wrote to Francesco when Francesco was a young man expressed concern for Francesco's disrespect and ingratitude toward his mother. Other letters repeatedly show that Francesco believed himself to be less well-loved by his father and mother than his brothers and sisters. I have combined these pieces of information with the generally harsh child-rearing practices of the day to postulate some of Francesco's emotional issues.

As part of the scientific and anthropological Medici Project, many of the tombs of the Medici have recently been opened and their remains examined with modern biomedical imaging techniques. Francesco's strokes of apoplexy in his later years have been confirmed by evidence of facial droop, a clawlike contraction of his right hand, and an orthopedic shoe found in the coffin. The exact cause of his death remains uncertain. The official report of the day indicated that he died of tertian fever (malaria), although gossip raged from the very beginning that he had been poisoned. Tests run in the present day show in Francesco's bone tissue the presence of *plasmodium falciparum*, the parasite that causes malaria, as well as toxic concentrations of arsenic, which may or may not have been introduced as part of the embalming process or accumulated over Francesco's years of alchemical experiments. It seems to me that these two findings need not be exclusive of each other, and so I have given Francesco a severe case of malaria at the end of his life, and poisoned him as well.

Bianca Cappello's body was not entombed with the Medici, and her burial place is unknown. There is a document hinting that her viscera (and Francesco's) were buried in terra-cotta jars in the crypt of a church near the villa in Poggio a Caiano; at the time it wasn't unusual for internal organs to be buried separately from embalmed bodies. In the mid-2000s samples were collected from broken terra-cotta jars in the crypt indicated. The tissues were much degraded, but DNA testing showed that some of the tissue was reasonably consistent with Francesco's known DNA. The other tissues, although female, could not be conclusively identified as Bianca Cappello's. All the tissue showed toxic concentrations of arsenic, although again it's possible that the arsenic was the product of the embalming process. I've chosen to have Bianca murdered, but not by poison; at the time I write this there is simply no way to know for certain how she died. It is true, however, that she and Francesco died suddenly and mysteriously, within a few hours of each other, and that Ferdinando de' Medici was present in their villa at the time.

Bianca in life was romantic and impulsive; at the age of fifteen or sixteen she eloped from Venice with a banker's clerk named Pietro Buonaventuri, according to some versions of the story stealing a cache of her family's jewels as she went. In Florence she was much disappointed to find Pietro had lied to her about his grand connections. Many romantic tales are told about how she met Francesco, each more improbable than the last, but it appears that she did become Francesco's mistress not long after he married Giovanna of Austria. Somehow she held his affections as a mistress for twelve years, and historically he did marry her secretly only a few weeks after Giovanna's death.

I've always wondered how royal mistresses managed to hang on to their princes and kings and grand dukes—Diane de Poitiers, Anne Boleyn, Bianca Cappello—in the face of social pressure and courts full of other beautiful ladies. Given Bianca's ambition, determination and romantic heart, I think she would have gladly joined in Prince Francesco's play-acting, and in fact the Ferrarese ambassador commented that they played like children together. I suspect Bianca would have taken a great deal of pride in her secret power, and once caught up in it, been unable to extricate herself even when it took a dark turn.

No one knows with any certainty if the boy called Antonio de' Medici was actually Bianca's, Francesco's, both of theirs, or neither of theirs. What is known is that when Ferdinando de' Medici assumed the grand ducal title, he convinced the boy he was not the legitimate heir, gave him a large amount of property, and eventually arranged for him to join the Knights of Malta. All sorts of lurid tales have been told down through the centuries about Prince Antonio's birth, and the version I've chosen is one possibility.

Giovanna of Austria was the youngest daughter of the Holy Roman Emperor Ferdinand I, and thus the younger sister of Barbara of Austria, the Duchess of Ferrara, the heroine of my novel *The Second Duchess*. Her remains have been exhumed and analyzed along with those of her husband, and the pictures one can examine of her poor spine confirm the marked scoliosis she suffered. How on earth did she manage to carry seven—almost eight—pregnancies to term? The pain she must have suffered, and her courage in the face of it, are truly amazing.

As with Francesco and Bianca, the circumstances of her death are uncertain. It is known that she was heavily pregnant with her eighth child, which was stillborn; she most likely died of a ruptured uterus. Most sources tell some story of a fall, in varying circumstances. Since Francesco and Bianca married hastily and secretly just a few weeks after her death, of course there were whispers of poison. I've chosen my version of her death as one that incorporates the known facts, and might well have happened, given the circumstances and the personalities of those involved.

Only two of Francesco and Giovanna's children lived to adulthood, both daughters. Eleonora, their oldest, married the Duke of Mantua. Maria, the sixth child, married Henry IV of France and became queen of France as Marie de Médicis. Through her, Francesco and Giovanna's bloodlines were carried down into the royal houses of France and England. Louis XIV, the Sun King, was their great-grandson. Queen Henrietta Maria of England was their granddaughter, and thus Charles II, the Merry Monarch, was their great-grandson as well.

The murder of Isabella de' Medici, and the horrifying abuse of her body afterward, is taken from a letter sent in code to the Duke of Ferrara by his Florentine ambassador Ercole Cortile, who knew all the gossip and was in a good position to know any truths the Medici wished to hide. Details are corroborated in other letters and diaries. Sometimes the truth is more awful than any story a fiction writer can create.

There really was a red lily crown. In fact, there was a series of them. The first has been described as a circlet with open rays, with the red fleur-de-lis of Florence in the front, probably comprised of rubies or other red gems and/or enamelwork, and more red lilies on the tips of the jeweled rays. Cosimo de' Medici had it made for his coronation as Grand Duke of Tuscany, his previous crown as Duke of Florence apparently not being elaborate enough to satisfy him. Portraits exist showing Cosimo, Francesco, Ferdinando, and subsequent Medici grand dukes either wearing the crown, or with the crown resting symbolically on a table beside them.

Sadly none of these crowns survives today; possibly they were appropriated and melted down for their gold and jewels by Napoleon's troops at the end of the eighteenth century.

Tommaso Vasari (readers of *The Second Duchess* may recognize the name) and the mithridate/poison *sonnodolce* are fictional creations. Tales of mithridates go back to Mithridates VI of Pontus in the first century BCE, who supposedly made himself invulnerable to poison by taking a tiny daily dose of a combination of poisons. I remember reading A.E. Housman's *A Shrop-*

shire Lad in high school, and being particularly struck by the verse in "Terence, This Is Stupid Stuff" about Mithridates, ending:

> —*I tell the tale that I heard told.*
> *Mithridates, he died old.*

One of those memorized couplets that remain with one for a lifetime! I combined this semi-legendary story (semi- because through the centuries people really did try to concoct universal antidotes) with the stories told of cantarella, the poison of the Borgias.

In the sixteenth century, alchemy, like astrology, was still considered a science. Its division into magic on the one hand, and chemistry, metallurgy and other sciences on the other, was just beginning to take place. Some practitioners, like Chiara, continued to believe in the magical elements; others, like Ruan, were beginning to apply the scientific method and using alchemy to learn about the elements of the natural world.

Nicolas Flamel and his wife Perenelle were historical personages, although their reputations as alchemists were mostly a posthumous fictionalization.

The poison maze in the Boboli Gardens is, of course, fictional. At the time of Francesco I, the gardens were considerably smaller than they are today. In *La Descrizione dell'imperiale giardino di Boboli*, published in 1757, Gaetano Cambiagi describes a "fine labyrinth," now lost, in approximately the spot where I've placed Francesco's labyrinth.

The Prayer Book Rebellion in 1549 was a bloody uprising sparked by the boy king Edward VI's imposition of the new Protestant Book of Common Prayer on Catholic Cornwall and Devon. Thousands of Catholic rebels were massacred by an English army that incorporated mercenaries as well as English soldiers. During the fighting the working men turned on the gentry with the cry, "Kill all the gentlemen."

Many of the Cornish Catholic gentry and their families were besieged (some, like Ruan's family, in St. Michael's Mount) and later imprisoned, suspected of supporting the rebels. When the rebellion was crushed, the English Council issued a proclamation permitting the appropriation of the rebels' properties, which applied to the great nobles and those who supported them; for a while there was considerable looting and confiscation. It is in this setting that my fictional Pencarrows lost their estates and mine holdings to an equally fictional Englishman.

I consulted many books, papers, articles and documents in the course of writing *The Red Lily Crown*. I was also most kindly aided by historians, authors, librarians and other experts. Whatever errors and misinterpretations that have made their way into my fictionalized version of the story are entirely upon my own head.

Acknowledgments

As always, my family and my friends (including many writer friends) offered unfailing support as I worked on this book.

In particular I'd like to thank Lynne Smith and Sharon Ward, for pictures and anecdotes from their own visit to Florence.

Thanks also to Sam Rogerson of the Cornish Language Project.

Thanks to Danielle DeVor, for beta reading.

My amazing agent Diana Fox is always there with a reassuring and encouraging word when I need it most. I'd also like to thank her assistants, Brynn Arenz and Isabel Kaufman, for their thorough readings and critiques.

There's no one in the world like Betty Anne Crawford of Books Crossing Borders. Huge thanks to her for her kindness and support.

I've been fortunate to work with thoughtful and perceptive editors. Thanks go to Ellen Edwards and Gillian Holmes, and particularly to Rosie de Courcy.

And in the end as in the beginning, thanks to Jim and our own particolored hounds for putting up with me while I wander dazedly around the real world, my heart and mind lost in the sixteenth century.

The Flower Reader

Elizabeth Loupas

Secrets she must defend with her life.

With her dying breath, Mary of Guise entrusts a silver casket containing explosive secret papers to the young Scottish heiress, Rinette Leslie. Rinette must promise to hide the casket and give it only to Mary, Queen of Scots when she ascends the throne.

But Rinette makes one terrible mistake – before hiding it away, she shows it to her beloved young husband. Now, in a world of passion and violence, she becomes the target of the queen's most ruthless enemies. Can the ancient art of floramancy, through which Rinette can sometimes predict the future by reading the language of flowers, save her?

'Bursts with murder, intrigue and conspiracy theories'
Stylist

'This is a must read... A real bodice-ripping yarn with generous doses of love, honour, betrayal and tragedy, with Scotland's shimmering light as its backdrop'
No.1 Magazine

arrow books

AVAILABLE IN ARROW

The Second Duchess

Elizabeth Loupas

**Love, conspiracy and murder . . . *The Second Duchess* is a
dazzling novel set in Renaissance Italy.**

Barbara of Austria is plain, quick-witted and sensible. She also
desperately needs a husband because, at the age of twenty-six,
she is about to be packed off to a convent.

So she seizes what seems to be her last chance – a proposal of
marriage from Alfonso d'Este, Duke of Ferrara, Lucrezia Borgia's
grandson, clever, handsome, powerful – and widely believed to
have murdered his first wife, Lucrezia de' Medici.

Barbara goes into her marriage clear-eyed, fascinated by her
dangerous, enigmatic new husband and increasingly – recklessly
– driven to discover the truth about the death of his first duchess.

But the closer she gets to the truth, the more she realises her
own life is in danger

arrow books

THE POWER OF READING

Visit the Random House website and get connected with information on all our books and authors

EXTRACTS from our recently published books and selected backlist titles

COMPETITIONS AND PRIZE DRAWS Win signed books, audiobooks and more

AUTHOR EVENTS Find out which of our authors are on tour and where you can meet them

LATEST NEWS on bestsellers, awards and new publications

MINISITES with exclusive special features dedicated to our authors and their titles

READING GROUPS Reading guides, special features and all the information you need for your reading group

LISTEN to extracts from the latest audiobook publications

WATCH video clips of interviews and readings with our authors

RANDOM HOUSE INFORMATION including advice for writers, job vacancies and all your general queries answered

Come home to Random House

www.randomhouse.co.uk